PRAISE FOR
THE RAPE OF PERSEPHONE

"The author's command of the mythology is magisterial—she deftly weaves together a tale that revolves around the commerce between gods and humans as well as a brewing civil war among the immortals."
—*Kirkus Reviews*

"This is a brilliantly written work. The descriptions, the style, and the depth of the characterizations are nothing short of amazing."
—*Sublime Book Review*

"The author delights with a meaty, gritty, mostly aromatic, wanton and undeniably intoxicating portrayal of the times."
—*IndieReader*

"Brillhart's beautifully rendered prose and measured, meticulously detailed narrative keep the reader turning pages nonstop."
—*The Prairies Book Review*

"A fascinating synthesis of traditional and contemporary storytelling in this reimagined tale of lust, power, and grief—one that will resonate just as readily with modern readers as it did millennia past in the agora."
—*BookLife*

THE RAPE OF

PERSEPHONE

A Novel

MONICA BRILLHART

Quotations from the *Homeric Hymn to Demeter* (public domain) translated by Gregory Nagy. Full text available at https://uh.edu/~cldue/texts/demeter.html

Ferryman Press hardback edition ISBN: 9781737799122
Ferryman Press Amazon paperback edition ISBN: 9781737799108
Ferryman Press Ingram paperback edition ISBN: 9781737799139
Ferryman Press electronic edition ISBN: 9781737799115

Library of Congress Control Number: 2021925123

Book design and map by Eddie Diaz
Ratto di Proserpina sculpture in Rome, Italy by Gian Lorenzo Bernini
Cover photo © by Stefano Chiacchiarini

Ferryman Press, LLC

For Aaron,
who told me to write it, anyway.

CONTENTS

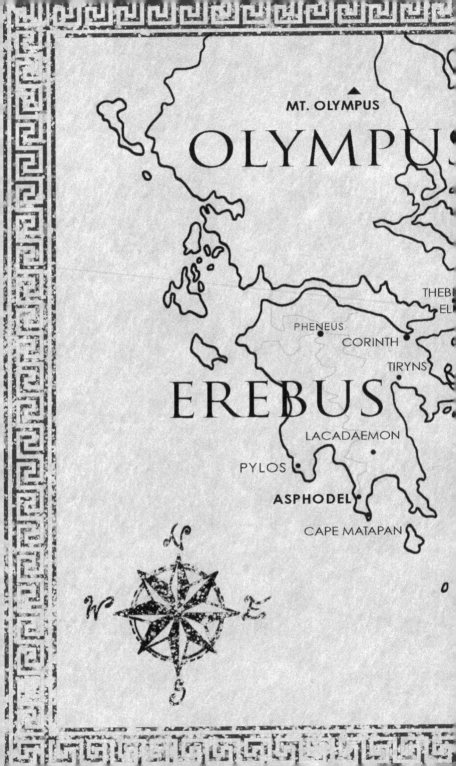

CYCLADES

CRETE

KNOSSOS　　▲ MT. DIKTE

Author's Note

Let's address the elephant in the room.

The first thing you probably noticed about this book was the *R* word.

When a draft of *The Rape of Persephone* was ready for review, I sent copies to a respectable number of beta readers. The title was among the first topics to arise. Some immediately encouraged me to remove the word *rape.*

"Soften the language, and you will sell more books."

"Nobody wants to read a book with *rape* in the title."

After many prayers and sleepless nights, I opted to move forward with it. Indeed, *rape* is a trigger word. The title acts as an indicator to proceed with caution; however, it has always been more than that.

In the original context, the word *rape* refers to the Latin word *raptus*. It means *seized* or *carried off* and does not necessarily imply sexual violence. In the seventeenth and eighteenth centuries, the word was commonly used in this context. The poet and satirist Alexander Pope wrote a mock epic poem entitled *The Rape of the Lock* about a maiden who had a lock of her hair cut off without her consent.

The cover photo for this novel comes from an exhibit in the Galleria Borghese museum in Rome, Italy. This statue by Gian Lorenzo Bernini is called *The Rape of Proserpina* (the Latin name for Persephone) and depicts Hades carrying her away. Peter Paul Rubens and Luca Giordano both also created paintings entitled *The Rape of Proserpine*.

All that is fine and dandy. But as I'm writing this, the year is 2021 and we've now experienced the #MeToo movement. You can't just throw that word around in the traditional Latin context and expect people to go along with it.

The truth is, I did it on purpose. The title has never been anything else. And it brought to light a question from my beta readers:

Was Persephone raped?

If not for the title, the concept of rape would never have come up. In other words, valuable discussions on what rape *is* and *isn't* would never have taken place. There are three variations of the word *rape*. You, the reader, are free to decide which definition fits the actions within the book.

The title promotes discussion. So, I left it.

*

At what point do gods become gods?

Mythology scholars like Joseph Campbell tell us myths aren't to be taken literally, but are representative of archetypes or archetypal patterns. In other words, common narratives exist within mythologies across the globe, from Zeus to Odin to Ra. These same commonalities play out in our modern world, too. If you've ever met a CEO, you've met a Zeus. If you've ever met a helicopter mom, you've met a Demeter. That moody recluse down the street? Hades.

These theories are both fascinating and true, but it was fun to consider another idea.

Ancient Egyptians believed their pharaohs were living gods who became eternal gods upon death. What if Bronze Age Greeks believed the same of their kings? What if, before the old gods and goddesses reigned over earth, sea, and sky, they ruled as men and women who were immortalized into godhood through oral history and art?

What sparked the imagination of Homer? The Muses, goddesses presiding over arts and sciences, were praised in Greek antiquity. Artists tend to have muses, and Homer was an unlikely exception. In researching the eras that predated him, I learned more about the three *M*'s (Minoans and Mycenaeans and mythology—oh my!) than I ever thought possible.

The Minoans were an athletic, nature-loving, peaceful people, their name derived from King Minos himself, mythological king and namesake of the Minotaur. His palace at Knossos is the largest archeological site on the island of Crete, initially damaged by an earthquake, circa 1700 BCE (three hundred years before the first mention of Zeus).

Perhaps the Minoan civilization, destroyed in a series of cataclysmic events, provides an origin for Persephone's story.

We glean most of what we know about the Bronze Age from paintings and carvings depicted on stone, or from ruins and relics. The first mention of Zeus came in the form of Mycenaean Greek, written in Linear B, the earliest discovered form of Greek. This was around the fourteenth or thirteenth century BCE—but the gods were revered before any mention of Zeus. For example: Potnia, the Minoan goddess, was found in statue form, worshipped as far back as 3000 BCE.

In July 2019, my husband and I flew to Athens and fanned out across Greece over a period of a month. Armed with an international driver's license and a thirst for answers, we endeavored to see it all. We drove from Athens to Eleusis to the fifty-two peaks of Mount Olympus and all the way down to Cape Matapan, at the southernmost point of the Peloponnese. Along the way, we experienced the spectacular landscape of Greece—a country roughly the size of Alabama. Finally, we boarded a plane to Crete and spent a week exploring the palace of Knossos. We even climbed Mount Dikte, the mythological birthplace of Zeus himself.

The most incredible location?

Located in the Mani Peninsula of the Peloponnese, the Caves of Diros are comprised of approximately 33,000 square meters of cave systems. Only a fraction of them have been explored. A massive cave-in around 3000 BCE resulted in the sudden deaths of those in an advanced civilization. Excavations in the 1970s revealed that the caves were used as burial sites during the Neolithic Period. Human remains were found, along with an ossuary and many other offerings.

Today, the Caves of Diros are underwater and tourable by ferry. While there is no conclusive evidence, archaeologists theorize that this may have been regarded as the entrance to the underworld in classical mythology.

*

The Rape of Persephone trilogy is a marriage of history and mythology.

Like a set of Russian nesting dolls, you will find myth within myth within myth in this tale. If you happen to be a mythophile, enjoy identifying them along the way. The overarching plot, however, is derived from the *Homeric Hymn to Demeter*.

The myth goes:

One day, the maiden Persephone is frolicking in the meadow when she spots the most beautiful flower she has ever seen. It is a narcissus, otherwise known as the daffodil. So enraptured, Persephone plucks it right out of the ground.

As soon as she yanks the flower from the dirt, the earth opens wide beneath her feet. A chariot bursts from inside the chasm, and Hades snatches Persephone in his clutches. Like a caveman with a club, he whisks her down to the underworld where she becomes his bride.

Meanwhile, Persephone's mother, Demeter, goddess of the harvest, scurries from neighbor to neighbor, asking: "Has anyone seen Persephone?" Not a soul has seen her. Terrified and distraught, Demeter encounters a savvy goddess named Hecate. Hecate tells Demeter that Hades stole Persephone away. Their only recourse is to appeal to Persephone's father, Zeus. He is the "god of gods," after all. Only Zeus pulls any weight with Hades, and getting Persephone back will take an awful lot of convincing.

The Rape of Persephone escorts you this far into the *Homeric Hymn to Demeter*, while exploring a much-neglected storyline within the myth itself:

What happened to Persephone in the underworld? How, if ever, did she come to love the man who seized her?

So wrote Homer: "And the earth, full of roads leading every which way, opened up under her."

When the historic earthquake struck Knossos in 1700 BCE, the earth opened there, too.

Might the heroes and villains of the Bronze Age have lived on through stories told over time, embellished as legends tend to be? It's not hard to imagine how myth and history might entwine.

Over time, a king becomes a god. A high priestess evolves into goddess. A ship called the *Narcissus* might become a simple flower.

Thus begins the story of a mother in search of an abducted child.

A child who would come to be known as Persephone, goddess of the underworld.

THE RAPE OF

PERSEPHONE

rape

noun

1: unlawful sexual activity and usually sexual intercourse carried out forcibly or under threat of injury against a person's will or with a person who is beneath a certain age or incapable of valid consent because of mental illness, mental deficiency, intoxication, unconsciousness, or deception
2: an outrageous violation
3: an act or instance of robbing or despoiling or carrying away a person by force

—Merriam-Webster's Collegiate Dictionary

PART ONE
THE ABDUCTION OF KORE

I begin to sing of Demeter, the holy goddess with the beautiful hair. And her daughter [Persephone] too. The one with the delicate ankles, whom Hādēs seized. She was given away by Zeus, the loud-thunderer, the one who sees far and wide.

—*Homeric Hymn to Demeter*

NARCISSUS

1

1694 BCE

The day the earth opens, a little ghost flies to the cargo ship.

With affection, Mother calls her this—*my little ghost*—but the endearment feels false this morning. Ghosts are invisible, mostly, and Kore is conspicuous, a pretty thing fluttering from sailor to sailor, asking in her feathery voice, "W-will you help me? Who commands this ship?"

She flattens a dove-gray hood atop her head so it will not blow away. One by one, the heads of the oarsmen turn. Their sea-weary eyes squint in refuge from the cutting wind. Grimy faces lower to smirk at her. They mutter in secret as if sharing the answer to a question only sailors know.

Her cloak flaps against air smelling of brine and dusting her lips with salt. It is early, before Helius rides his chariot above the horizon, before the slave awakes, the one who will first spot the barren heap of blankets upon the pallet where she sleeps.

She knows the slave girl will call throughout the house, an inquiry rousing her mother at once. And Mother will dash from vestibule to hearth, snaking through brightly painted corridors, calling for her in panic.

"Kore?"

Mother will know she has fled. She will cry out for Kore anyway. Stone walls will echo with:

"Little ghost? Kore?"

The thought sends Kore shouldering past men who heave wooden boxes into the belly of the ship for export. She hurries. She must find the captain. The ship departs at dawn, her chance to leave the island before the entire polis of Knossos is alerted.

After all, Mother is revered. Mother keeps friends in every home, on every farm, and in the palace itself, where King Lycastus rules and lauds Kore's mother as proudly as anyone.

Hours ago, Kore snatched her purse and ran away, veiled by night. The walk tired her legs and left her sore. As she searches the faces around the ship, her purse jostles. It is all she has, but it will be enough. Men will grant her anything for what rests inside.

Here at the port of Amnisos, away from the watchful eyes of the people who herald her mother, men prepare to sail at first light. They hoist laden cargo into a hull sealed black with pitch, and the sky blushes with the arrival of day.

One of the gritty, sweating sailors lifts a corner of his mouth and says, "Come over here, pretty. I have the help you need."

Another voice: "You! Girl."

The voice is lively despite the hour. A hand falls on her shoulder. He is a lean, ruddy-cheeked man, with a wiry beard thick enough to hide his lips. He smells awful.

"Y-yes, please, can you help me? Are you in charge of this ship?"

The man scowls. "Why are you running around alone?"

Kore glances at the stone path to the town. Mother will appear any moment. Not alone. She will bring a village of devotees to reinforce her message.

Selfish child. How could you do this to your mother?

"Out with it," the man insists. "What do you want?"

It pains Kore to shove the words out. Oh, but she is terrible at talking, unlike Mother. "Where d-do you sail?"

"Pylos."

"Is that in the territory of Olympus?"

"Nowhere close."

"Closer to Olympus than Crete?" She blushes. How silly! Everywhere is closer to Olympus than Crete. Another coastal gale catches her hood, unearthing long strands of hair that whip in the breeze. The first glimmer of dawn lights it bronze.

The man eyes the lines of her face, her hair, and overhead to scan the crowd—forty, fifty men, she imagines. These men, with their weathered arms, will soon propel them across the sea. As this man surveys the port, Kore looks, too. He must see her mother racing toward them with skirts gathered and temper ablaze!

But, no. There is no female in the area but Kore, only sixteen years old and lit with intention.

The man steps closer. "Who is with you?"

"No one."

"You are so weary of Crete, you would board the *Narcissus* with this dirty bunch of sea dogs?"

What a curious name for a ship. The nose of the vessel catches her eye—for that is what it looks like, a nose. A sleek, golden stem much like the beak of a hummingbird. Kore squints at the floral ornament topping it.

A narcissus, her favorite flower. The brilliant flower, tubed and joyously yellow—her favorite of all—so it must be destiny! Yes, fate! Destiny to find this ship, destiny to leave, to finally feel the secure embrace of a father.

"I would like p-passage."

He scrunches his brow. "Are you a sword?"

"A what?"

"Or a helmet?" he asks. "Are you a helmet?"

Hearing him tease her, the other men chuckle as they haul the last of their goods past the oar rudder on an upcurved stern. An ache creeps into her stomach, heart racing as she glances, again, toward the town.

"The *Narcissus* was used as a warship when the titans fell, but nowadays? She has a little belly of cargo. See it? Today we transport swords and helmets. If you are not one of those, you have no place on this ship. Find another."

It must be now. Now, she has the courage. Now, enough anger spurs her. By tomorrow, nostalgia will take hold, and her nerve will be lost to her mother's charms. This is how things have always been, the wounds of love as fierce as the love itself.

To flee her mother, Kore must put an ocean between them.

"Please. I can pay well."

"Yes, you would."

When he laughs, so does she. She amuses him. That's good! Men take to Kore—they always have—and she knows why. Because of her father, because all men are beholden to him, to treat his children as their own. Men often beckon to her, offering sweet figs to lure her in, crushing her tiny bones against their large man bodies. Most of the time, she laughs and wriggles, thrilled by how big and bulging they are, unlike Mother, who is fleshy and soft.

How jealous Mother becomes! Lioness eyes flashing a warning that could scare the gods, Mother wrenches Kore from their arms.

"Keep to me, Kore. I will not let them hurt you."

Kore rummages inside the purse hanging at the cinched waist of her girdle. She reveals two gold coins seared with the head of an eagle. She will need these coins again and again to fund her journey north. The purse jingles, but the sheer heft is enough to keep the pouch stable in jittery hands.

"Take it—" she says, thrusting two coins into his palm.

One eye squeezed shut, the captain plucks a coin and brings it far from his face to see it better. He smiles big enough to display small, gray teeth. A few at the bottom are missing, and naked pink gums show.

"How did you come by this?" Now he realizes she holds an entire bag. Yes, he respects her now for having riches like these.

"You c-can have both coins," she says, "if you take me with you."

The man grows serious. Studies her. With a snort, he takes her arm. "Yes, we can bring you along. You will be of plenty value to us today, I think."

THE MOTHER

2

The day the earth opens, the mother awakes to the lapping of firelight against her cheeks. One blue eye opens, squinting in the blaze that hovers above her face.

"Priestess," the slave girl, Asli, whispers. "Lyris has given birth to a son."

Demeter shields her face with one draping hand, blocking the glare of the torch. "All right," she croaks, clearing her throat as she waits for Asli to say more. The girl is twelve, Anatolian by blood, and faithfully terrified of her mistress, although Demeter has never given her reason for this. She cannot help but feel pity at how the girl cowers; therefore, she treats Asli with more patience than she feels, hoping the fear will run its course.

But Asli says nothing else.

"Good," Demeter says. "Blessings to her. Now put that thing out, and go back to bed."

Asli licks her lips. "She requests you. To consecrate the boy."

"Let Stavra do it." Grimacing, Demeter sits up, rubbing her arms as the blankets drop. She grabs one and pulls it above her shoulders. "I hold harvest ceremony this morning."

"Lyris insists on you. She says you are the High Priestess and her boy deserves no less."

Demeter gathers the blanket around her like a shawl. She slips her feet onto frigid stone and stands.

As a woman with an empty womb, Lyris was one of the more agreeable nobles. But once the seed embedded and her belly swelled, she turned into a demanding, irascible woman who would complain about the cold and balk about the coarseness of the blanket given to keep her warm. No one begrudged her foul mood. When a woman expands as painfully as she, others feel sympathy. It was not only her belly that burgeoned but her nose, hips, fingers, and ankles, plump as little piglets. Hers has been a miserable pregnancy from the beginning. It is easy for Demeter to forgive her belligerence.

Asli slides the torch into its vase. By the time Demeter boosts herself from the warmth of her pallet, Asli stands ready with the straight garment, robing her mistress with a quick precision born from habit. The rest is done within moments, flounced overskirt tied at the waist and open in the front to reveal the braided red and yellow robe beneath it. Demeter's tight curls shine like corn silk, swept high and back by Asli's steady hands.

Demeter loads a basket with ribbons, incense, and wine, and Asli extends a clay pot filled with fresh fruit—fruit reserved for today's ceremony and picked by Kore, her virginity purifying today's offering and keeping it holy. As Demeter closes her hand around the tough skin of a pomegranate, Asli bows her head. She is not allowed to touch these things. Girls initiated into priesthood exclusively handle any of the sacred implements, and Asli's social stature bars her from ever holding this coveted role.

Demeter watches Asli's reverence, how she studies each ritual as if storing it within a precious place in her mind. Asli would make a fine priestess. She appreciates it. Respects it.

Demeter frowns and glances to the hallway leading to where Kore sleeps.

Asli says, "Should I wake—"

"No. We will be back soon enough."

That is not the reason, and Asli knows it. Demeter informs Kore of each parting, making certain her daughter knows, despite her absence, that Kore remains foremost in her consideration. That child is her soul, the only love worth having in life.

And Kore, ungrateful and bitter these past few years!

If Kore knew the torment that accompanies motherhood, she would understand how each word of defiance poisons the blood bond between them.

Kore will not know this pain. Demeter devotes her life to sparing Kore the despair she has known in her own time.

Thus, alerting no one, she and the slave girl slip torchlit through the doorway of their home and wind their way through the polis.

KEEP TO ME
3

The captain, named Charon, lifts her over the cypress hull as if Kore weighs nothing, and oarsmen whistle with delight.

Morning sun blazes through the clouds, and the oars twist and wind into the ocean, propelling them away from the banks of Crete. Yes, fifty men, she counts—twenty-five on each side, their baked skin glossy with sweat. An odor rises from their bodies, like the smell of raw onions, and Charon walks among the stench, hollering commands that taunt, a man's challenge for them to do better. It works. They row hard, and the land shrinks. Disappearing now, the hills of golden dirt and verdant green brush.

I love you. I am sorry.

The tether between herself and her mother stretches, lacerates, and tears free.

Soon, land is gone. A vast ocean spans blue, vibrant all around. Endless. She is lost out here

where the sky and water unite in blue, lost to all who
know her, and most of all to her mother, who smells
sweet from the fruits of the earth. A smell stark in
contrast to the sharp stench of fifty men who row
hard while they stare at her.

What have I done?

Fear blossoms, the blood in her veins scorching
cold. Her body shivers with it, and she clutches
the cloak around her as the ship makes its rapid
transition into a world completely foreign to her.

Pylos? Where is this Pylos—and what will she
do once she gets there? She is stupid, so stupid! She
has never been anywhere alone, can scarcely speak
to people she has known her whole life!

She must remind herself of Father, for his
determination courses throughout her body, as much
as her mother's passion.

Nails digging half-moons into her palms, Kore
clamps her eyes shut and reminds herself of all the
pain she can pull from her mind. How her mother's
love turned sour as goat's milk, curdled in daylong
sun. Worse still, the praise and adoration in which
she basked as a little child—*Mother's little ghost!*—
mutated into criticism hurled at her like death-
bringing stones.

No, she will not acknowledge the good in her
mother. To keep herself from shattering, she cannot
regret a single choice.

Blood drains from her face. Dizzy, she finds a
bare spot among the boxes and sinks, knees to chest,

and hugs them tight.

Perhaps her mother does not love her, not for the truth of who she is. Mother loves what she dreams up, the sheer rapture of fantasy driving her to often say:

"You are like the vestals of Rome, like my sister Hestia of Attica. Dedicate yourself to the goddess, and love no other. Had I learned so much at your age, I would be twice the force I am now."

Twice? It cannot be, for she is force enough already.

She is Mother, not merely to Kore, but to all. She is *De-Meter*, Mother of Earth, High Priestess of Knossos, whose popularity bows in comparison to the king himself and few others.

The day passes at sea. Kore's mind turns over and over like the oar-ridden hands of these bare-chested men.

The woman known as Demeter had another name once, but Kore has no memory of such a time, a time when Demeter was not Mother but a girl like Kore.

As the fire of Helius burns higher and higher across the sky, she dozes, warmed by the rays, soothed by the wind.

"Your father might have better understood you. Let the world praise him, if it makes them feel loyal. Only a selfish, arrogant man would do as he did— and you, showing the same vanity!"

"Westward, Kythera!"

Kore jerks awake, eyelids fluttering wide and alert.

Two ripe-smelling men release their oars and lower the sail.

Blinking, Kore spots land fogged by distance. Greens and browns of earth stretch from the sea. Kore clutches the cloak and rises on uncertain legs.

She watches as Charon directs the men to veer the ship in a wide arc, the island of Kythera sliding by on her left. There is land also to the north—farther than the banks of Kythera but visible. Casting an eye to Helius, she judges the time. Late afternoon. Her stomach growls, confirming it.

By now, her mother must be wailing and tearing at her hair. Kore's eyes water, nose burning with the need to cry.

If the fear becomes intolerable, she can always go back. She can return, be home again in a day. It will be all right.

It will be all right.

My Kore

4

The city lies dormant, with a stray cat, its snout working inside a disemboweled rat, animating a cobbled walkway. The maze of workshops—potters, ivory carvers, metal workers—surround the temple with its bright red columns lit by the inception of daylight.

When Demeter reaches the steps of the home of Lyris, two slaves stand in the doorway. They bow their necks to Demeter, both green under the skin. One of them cries and wipes at her face to hide the tears.

Demeter freezes. "Why are you crying?"

"High Priestess," the taller one says. "We beg your forgiveness. Our mistress is suffering, cursing at us, at the goddess—and the blood—there is much blood—"

Elbowing past them, Demeter rushes inside. The acrid smell hits her at once. Blood. She can smell it from the common room beneath the high fumes of incense. Four men stand about. Lyris's father, Belen, clutches the hearth and steadies himself with one hand. Huddled near the window are Lyris's brothers and husband, whispering and inhaling fresh wind that wafts inside.

Belen spots her. His skin is ashen, and he drops his head to avoid displaying weakness.

"Where are they?" Demeter asks, basket growing heavy beneath a weakening arm.

Before he can answer, Lyris's mother, Mago, shuffles from the corridor, arms brimming with swaddled wool. Inside, a little pink arm escapes and strains upward with fingers as small as earthworms.

"Praise the goddess," Demeter says. A baby! The sagging skin beneath Mago's eyes, usually large and lively, steals any joy Demeter might feel. She reaches for the boy, but Mago clutches him tighter.

"Never mind him for now," Mago says, and before Demeter can ask, a scream, hoarse and ear-shattering, comes from the bedchamber.

Asli touches Demeter's sleeve, glancing sidelong into the hall.

"Damn it all!" a man shouts from the window. It is Nomiki, the husband of Lyris. "This is no place for us. She bore a grandchild, a male, as you demanded. After all your threats, Belen, you have what you wish. Why not celebrate instead of listen to this torture?"

Belen roars, "Your rotten spawn rips my

daughter in half. You will bear it! I will kill you before I let you run out of here like a—"

Inside the blanket, the baby cries with gusto. A strong, healthy child with good lungs. Down the hall, screams rise above the sounds of child and man.

"The boy came first. The midwife thought it was done, but there is a second child." Mago takes Demeter by the elbow, clutching the infant against a pendulous breast with one crooked arm. Pulling, urging her down the hall in the direction of the iron-sharp smell, toward the agony.

The baby cries, and from the common room the men fight. Wooden chairs groan against stone as they slide with the impact of the brawl.

Poor Lyris endured two years of misery at the hands of these men. Her father insisted on her marriage to Nomiki, which was his right, although Lyris, a girl one year older than Kore, had protested, finding him too roving from the start. But Nomiki had been born in the right family, with a large farm and enough boar to provide tusks for a third of the military helmets exported from Crete. After marriage, a year passed with no child. No amount of pomegranate seeds improved her fertility. Of course, the blame could not possibly lie with Nomiki, who spent more time with prostitutes and young boys than with Lyris.

They all knew it. Even Kore, who knew of these things mostly in theory.

Mouth agape, Kore had told her:

"T-the midwife made her put on a cloak and hold it tight all around her—wool, no air can pass through it, Mother. They put the myrrh between her feet and made her squat—squat wide like this—and poof, they set the incense on fire between her ankles!"

"Why do you still see her, Kore? She is married, with a life bearing no likeness to your own. I told you. Leave her alone."

"S-she said it b-burned so badly, her legs sizzled like a pig on the altar. But when she exhaled, they smelled the myrrh from her mouth, so her womb is clear. It is not her fault, is it, Mother?"

"You are not to bother her again; do you hear me?"

In her limited understanding, Kore was right. With no proof of blockage or wandering uterus in Lyris, Belen turned his suspicion to his daughter's husband. Adulterer. Demeter knows as much from Kore. Kore should stay away from Lyris and her stories! Demeter knows enough men like Nomiki. These men take and devour, enjoying the wickedness of it, spilling their seed into whores and boys and sheep until none remains to do his duty, as he vowed to his wife.

When Belen threatened to renege on the marriage agreement and place her with another husband, Nomiki at last succeeded in his duty.

Demeter passes beneath the doorway. At the foot of the bed, human blood pools, not that of a sacrificial goat whose blood is let in faith to the gods but of a girl the age of Kore.

Kore, who will never know this horror, never, not as long as Demeter has breath and voice and nails to claw.

The overturned birthing stool rolls on its side, and a slave catches it, needing something else to do beside watch this, and takes it to the corner. On the couch, Lyris goes limp, cheek turning from side to side on a vomit-crusted cushion.

"The baby can wait for your blessing, Priestess," Mago says. "He will still be with us in an hour."

From the bed, Lyris moans. "Our union is cursed."

"She goes swearing to her death one of Nomiki's whores placed her hatred on a curse stone and buried it. No one can convince her otherwise. That is why she wants you here to consecrate her son, to protect him from the spell of a whore." Bony finger clutched in the baby's fist, Mago turns her head to Lyris, a girl of raven hair and olive skin now washed of color, lips gray and broken with fissures bleeding from the sheer width of her screams.

Demeter crosses the room to a candlelit bed. Slaves throw cloth at her feet, soaking the blood, but the tacky stuff squishes beneath her sandals and between her toes. Two bull bladders, knocked aside by a flailing Lyris, leak hot oil onto the floor. Slaves fill them in hopes the warm compression may ease a suffering womb. Such nonsense is useless on the full-bodied pains of labor.

The midwife kneels between bent knees.

"She will die either way. I must use the blade. I am sorry."

Irises glinting through slits, Lyris cries, "Do it."

Dear goddess, save my child from this. She is yours; I will dedicate her to you again and again. I cannot watch this happen to my Kore.

Kneeling beside her head, Demeter takes Lyris's hand, cool and limp as dead fish. As radiance beams from her soft, shapeless cheeks, she conjures serenity. "Lyris of Knossos, set your intention for this child."

The peace in Demeter relaxes Lyris. "He is to be raised by my mother, Mago of Knossos, and my father, Belen of Knossos. He will grow to be as constant as the sky god Uranus above the clouds, and strong and bold as your Zeus, who one day will immortalize as god himself."

The words pinch the corners of Demeter's mouth into a forced smile. She turns, motioning for Mago to come with the child, and instructs her to remove the wool from around the baby and place him, chest to chest, against his mother.

"Do you feel his heart against yours?" Demeter whispers.

Tears roll down the girl's cheek. "It beats fast."

"May the love of your mother's heart flow into this child." Demeter raises her arms to the goddess Potnia, the comfort of divine presence thick as the scent of incense. "He will reap your compassion and kind spirit and will carry pure love with him always."

Demeter lifts her arms high and prays for the anguish inside Lyris to vanish. With fresh newborn skin against her breast, Lyris's brow no longer knits at the pain. She feels instead the life that grew within her thriving outside of her, squirming and robust against her breast, and Demeter praises the goddess for allowing Lyris a final glimpse of her life, fulfilling its purpose, and severed at seventeen. An outpouring of *storge,* the pure and unbreakable love of family, rushes from the crown of her head into the sky.

Lyris of Knossos, may you leave in love. Die with love.

Head veiled in blue, Mago presses her chin to her chest, unable to look. She weeps and nods at the midwife, who draws the blade from navel to pubic bone. Lyris passes out. Flaying the skin, the midwife fishes her hand inside muscle and sack, searching blindly for a leg, an arm. When the midwife fails to find hold, she grows bolder and plunges the other hand deep into the belly. The tendons in her arms tighten. She yanks and maneuvers, spilling blood onto stone.

Wound inside its own cord is the gray corpse of a girl child.

THE OPENING

5

"Girl! Come sit with Charon."

Charon sits inside a cabin made of four wooden poles wrapped and canopied in oxhide. There is not space enough to sit with him. She obeys, regardless.

As Kore navigates toward the captain's cabin, past the men with grimy faces, pumping their oars in unison, she hesitates. Slippery-toned, Charon says, "No time to be shy," and pats his lap.

Kore trembles from the chill of the ocean breeze. She has trembled all day, in fact. Already, the god of the sun retires his chariot toward the western horizon.

"Is that wh-where we are going?" She points to a flat-looking yellow stretch of land. Her stomach rolls again. If not for the empty stomach, she might have vomited by now.

Charon pulls her on his lap. "No."

The sailors stare, still smiling, as if there is

humor in watching. She forces a thin smile in return. She is ashamed at her lack of gratitude. There is no excuse for it!

"Are w-we nearly there?" The way he holds her makes her squirm. Men at home think twice before placing their hands on her in this way. They respect the consequences.

"We will stop to sleep in Matapan. The men will rest their arms, eat, piss—" He appraises her up and down, breath rotten as death. "What is your name?"

"Kore." She regrets it at once.

"Kore, eh?" Lifting his wooly brows, Charon must assume she is tricking him, trying to remain unknown by giving him a meaningless name like this. "Fair enough."

Kore, meaning: *young lady*. A child who is dedicated to the gods cannot have a mortal name, for a mortal name would turn her belligerent. Willful.

Mother made certain her child is merely a *kore*, a nameless gift unto the gods. Quick enough, the term caught on the tongues of every citizen in the polis. Young lady! How Kore loved it as a child. It was a promotion to be noted as a lady. But she is a child no longer, and when she hears the name, Kore cringes at how insulting and insincere it sounds.

In the fury of the wind, the cloak's hood dances. Her hair, wild and gnarled with salt and tangles, lashes at his face. He snatches at it and twists a lock around his finger, examining the bronze color that shines like the breastplates of soldiers. She pulls a length of it from her lips and holds it down against her cheeks.

The ocean rocks, no longer serene, turning her stomach and washing her face of color.

Charon clings to the swell in her hip and says, "I know who you are."

Her cheeks flush. Kore fidgets in his lap, but he holds fast. No. She will be calm. He is here to help her, to do as he is paid. Paid by *her*.

"Oh?"

"You belong to the priestess. What is her name? Seen her in ceremony at the palace once or twice. Seen *you* as a tiny child at the arena."

"N-no—"

Pulling at her lip, she glances around. The ship positions itself toward the cape of Matapan, aiming for the rocky banks. The ship bucks. A collective yawp rises from the men. All enjoy the thought of taming the ocean beast and are ready to conquer any rampant wave that challenges them.

"No what?" A calloused hand pinches the sensitive spot above her knee, and she jumps again. "No, you are not the same daughter? Or no, you are not a child? Hmm?"

"Keep to me, Kore. I will not let them hurt you."

The water beneath them no longer rests but stirs, wrestles the ship as her belly churns.

His hand cups her breast, squeezing it like testing fruit for maturity.

Her gut rings out in wild alarm, and Kore

squirms away, but he is not having this resistance, and she blurts, scarlet-faced, "D-Demeter is my mother, yes."

Perhaps she deserves whatever violence Charon imposes. She is horrible, selfish! For what she has done, the gods will make certain she pays.

Land is close. Driftwood and spools of seaweed lurch atop water. If she jumps overboard, she can swim for it. Probably they would catch her, sputtering and winded, and haul her back aboard. And they will hurt her worse for it, and she will deserve that, as well.

"Calm yourself. Your mother is not here now. Be a good girl for us tonight. You are old enough to have known what the journey will cost you."

The words tumble from her. "M-my f-father will be angry."

"You thought nothing about him when you took this ride."

That is not true! Her father is the reason for the journey! She almost says so, but the captain grabs her hand and presses it down into his lap. Despite all her mother's efforts, Kore knows what she feels, the thing hanging between a man's legs, hard as the limb of a tree.

"St—" The words stick on her tongue. The harder she tries to form them, the more she stammers. "St-stop. M-my f-fa—"

The ship bucks again. Her stomach turns, heart threatening to burst from her chest.

A few of the sailors observe, grinning and laughing. Those who do not laugh attend to turbulent water. They shade their eyes with cupped palms, looking out at the approaching land.

Kore tries to pull away. The captain clamps down on her knee.

"Be nice."

At last, the words spill from her as clear as she has ever spoken:

"My father is Zeus, the Liberator, King of Kings, and your master!"

Charon regards the purse. Yes, the purse! Proof! Gold, stamped with the crest of her father. No man holds treasure like this. Gold is reserved for kings.

"You lie—"

Frantic, Kore shakes her head. "I am on my way to him."

The captain considers, loosens his grip, and gives her a shove. Kore jumps up. The boat rocks underfoot.

Beneath them, Oceanus swells high. In one fluid motion, they plummet. Kore's stomach flips.

They say there are monsters in the deep, like the frightful creature with six slithering necks, each topped with a gruesome head full of shark's teeth. But that is nonsense, stories told to frighten children and to thrill adults.

The sky is cloudless. Charon tears his attention from her long enough to study it.

"Hold!"

The oarsmen stop, all at once. They drop the oars from blistered palms.

Charon jumps to his feet. The ship bucks like a bull in the arena, waves sloshing over the sides and foaming around her legs, soaking her skirt. Kore stumbles and sinks to the floor, scooting back as the men run and trample over each other.

Charon bellows, "Pull back!"

Arms row, each sinew and fiber of their muscles straining against the sea. Veins protrude from their foreheads, jaws set in the fight against Oceanus. Charon grabs at the sail. Four of his men assist, balancing the wind to push them farther out to sea, not to the jutting yellow land in the distance.

Waves knock at the hull, as solid as wood against wood. Water rises, this vengeful god bringing a white-foamed fist down along the hull. Men crumble beneath it, crying out. Their bodies float and collide. Saltwater pours over the side, and the men regain their footing, bracing their arms against the cargo boxes.

Kore yelps, unable to secure her feet. Does the god Oceanus seek to punish them? Punish *her*?

From the mast, Charon entwines the rope around his wrist and pulls, booming voice dwarfed by the roar of the ocean.

But the sky is clear! Even the wind is calm!

Water hits Kore square in the back, shoving her headfirst against the sharp edge of a pinewood crate. Blood bursts from her temple, and water engulfs her.

She screams. Salt burns inside her nostrils, down her throat, into her lungs. The water recedes long enough for her to gasp for air. Her hands claim hold of another box, and she lugs herself up, gagging and vomiting saltwater. Blood colors her vision.

Waves arc and crash with an explosion of water against cypress. The sail rips, and the mast splinters, collapsing. The rope around Charon's wrist jerks, and he shrieks.

With one grisly yank, the rope tears Charon's hand from his wrist, displaying nothing but a nub of wet bone and tendons. The blood spurts, turning to rivers down his arm. Charon gapes at it, his mouth a horrified *O*.

Bodies tangle and crash and claw for salvation. A knee, a foot, an elbow, all smashing into her as the ocean rages with a fury that must be invoked by the gods—and the sea rains down upon the *Narcissus*.

In the haze of water and blood, Kore watches the shadows of men rise from the bubbling white torrents collapsing from a sea of sheer fury. Their souls stretch from water to sky, shimmering with the radiance of death. Moans flood the cavities of her ears, louder than the roars of the ocean itself.

All of us, punished. All of us.

Groaning souls dart upward, as if inhaled by the fiery lungs of Helius, and vanish into a cloudless sky.

In the deafening roar of the waves, Kore surrenders. Arms go lax. Fingers uncurl.

Father, save me.

Unable to hear her screams, Father is lost to her now. Even Zeus holds no authority over death.

HADES'S LAW

6

There is a sudden heaviness all around. Demeter senses it where she usually cannot—not as Kore does.

"What can I do?" It is Asli, sweet cloudy-faced Asli, crouching with her hands hovering around Demeter's shoulders, not touching her but present.

"Tell Kore to lead the procession and prayers. Tell her—"

Her work has grown threefold. Two souls, she must usher into the afterworld. One, she must consecrate into this life. It could take half the day.

"Tell her nothing. Except a child is born and must be blessed."

No, Kore will not know of this, not any of it, not this morning. The harvest ceremony marks the initiation of holy rituals in which the land is sanctified and cleansed by the offerings, songs, and dances of virgin priestesses, the oldest and most prestigious of whom is Kore, who needs to keep her mind intact for such an occasion. Already, she will be terrified of conducting prayer on Demeter's behalf—her poor little ghost, whose nerves grip her so tightly by the throat, she often cannot get the words out.

Demeter's absence may be the shove she needs. Force the baby bird off her branch and into flight. But Kore has limits—and muscling through an entire ceremony, knowing her oldest friend has died today, along with the twin girl?

Perhaps Kore will know regardless. Lyris may visit her before word spreads. Demeter glances around.

Nothing. No spirits, no disembodied shades cast upon the walls.

Were she present, Kore would see them. She has for years; it is as though there was never a beginning to the phenomena, simply a burden that eternally was and will be.

It began with the leaping of the bulls at the palace arena, the day of the evisceration.

Her little Kore, she recalls, a beautiful child of five, gold of skin and hair. Golden slivers glinting in each scintilla of chestnut eyes. Kore—already proclaimed the most beautiful child on earth—such a seal of fate, at five!—and the women of the polis cooed and kissed little hands sticky from nectar, and the men scooped her into arms that slithered intimately around her innocent body, hands fondling in ways that made Demeter's pulse quicken. All of Knossos celebrated the gorgeous child, the magnificent result of a golden coupling between priestess and king.

In the arena, Kore snug in her lap, Demeter had pressed her nose and mouth to Kore's head, hair smelling of honey, as young Trapus quickened his stride toward the charging bull, a feat done at the games. The ultimate showman, Trapus had conquered the bull twice before, running headlong and thrusting his athlete's arms toward the horns, seizing them and vaulting over the beast with a flip that made the crowd jump and cheer at the skilled audacity of the performance.

"If you hide your face, you will miss it, little ghost."

Kore had peered on—how Demeter wishes she had not—and saw Trapus twist at the ankle, his gait altered in a slight but irrevocable way. His grip fumbled. The horn ripped into his gut, spilling tendrils of rope from an open midsection. The crowd screamed, cringed. The bull thrashed its neck and stamped to free the cadaver, unable to shake the impaled body. With each frenzied stomp, the bull crushed the ribs and legs of Trapus.

Fainting ran intermittent in the crowd. Beside them, a maiden vomited. Demeter threw her hands over Kore's head and crushed her face into her breast. Once the beast had been tamed and the body removed, Demeter grabbed Kore by her tearful face.

"Look at Mother—not there, not there, at me.

That man is dead."

Kore stared at the empty arena, dirt bloodied and littered with viscera, and raised a pointed finger:

"N-no, Mother. That man is not dead. He is c-coming to me."

But there was no one.

In Lyris's room, the midwife rubs and pounds the dead infant's back, hoping to force the life back into her. When she fails, she bites her lip between large, crooked teeth and places the baby in a wooden basket on the floor.

Mago sobs, and the living, male baby makes a raspy, bleating sound against his mother's breast, cheek searching for the nipple. Although Demeter cannot see the ghostly form of Lyris, her skin cools at an almost imperceptible gust of wind that happens when spirit departs flesh.

Both mother and child are gone. Demeter must stay and begin preparations. This is Hades's law. Since the end of the Titan War, when High Kings fell under the conspiracy of their own sons, the law of Hades was enacted across all the land, not exclusively in his own territory of Erebus. It is enforced by Zeus of Olympus and by Poseidon of the Cyclades. Gone are the simple funeral pyres of her own upbringing.

It is good business for a priestess, she supposes. But ushering the dead into the afterlife is now a three-day fuss that gives solace mainly to the living. How the husk is treated after death matters little compared to how the soul within it leaves the earth.

Wrapped in love for her child, Lyris left this world. Demeter fits her palms beneath the arms of the wailing infant and lifts him from a mother who grows cold beneath his live flesh.

A slave takes the child. Demeter yearns to hold him. Later. They must wash, anoint, and adorn the body in preparation for the funeral rites. And the same with the dead infant. Not complying with the burial laws is treated as a defilement of the land and punishable by law.

In compliance, Demeter sends the slaves to gather branches and flowers for the wreath. Others clean the area, mopping gore from the floor with arms that become stiff and heavy. A young male slave brings water and oils, and scoots the couch upon which Lyris lies so her feet are pointed toward the door.

Demeter takes the baby boy, asleep inside a fresh blanket, and strides through the corridor and into the common room, where the entire family gathers: aunts, nieces, sisters, and cousins, talking in hushed tones to Belen and Nomiki. Their tempers are extinguished and replaced with numb faces.

"Your son." Placing the boy into the arms of his dumbstruck father, Demeter orders all women to assist with the washing of their departed Lyris. To Belen, she says, "Ready the altar so we may consecrate the boy. There is much to be done."

As the women file into the corridor, the floor

rocks beneath her feet. Wooziness, surely, from the intensity of the morning, but no—it is not her own legs that waver.

The ground trembles.

A jagged seam breaks the stone floor in half. The crack in the floor travels into the walls. Stone falls from above and explodes at their feet. The women cry out while men stumble to protect them. The corridor to Lyris's room collapses.

The goddess Gaia rages below them, and Demeter crouches against the wall as a chunk of stone smashes beside her, covering her in dust. The sound of earth and stone and clay is deafening.

The earth opens from Knossos to the sandy banks and far into the sea, demolishing the city in a moment that seems to last an eternity.

When the shaking stops, Demeter slides her arms from around her head, finding the entire north wall of the common room gone and open to the sky. She spots the shaken young father huddled together with his family, still clutching the infant, all of them covered in dust and blinking their coated eyelids and coughing. Their safety registers in her mind for one blessed instant. One moment of relief. Thereafter, she thinks:

Kore.

UPROOTED
7

When the fringe of her lashes part, the world twirls.

Kore rests inside jagged stone. Entombed. Pulse quick and light, she moves her legs. Dampened fabric shifts against bare skin, and she sweats and shivers, body stiffening out of an innate need to steel itself.

She does not know where she is.

In the vault of her mind, there is nothing where her thoughts should be. She is fear incarnate, each fiber of muscle holding terror and pain. Kore struggles to focus on the stone around her. Scalding cheeks burn pink. The air cools, and a purple-red haze illuminates the cavern.

She does not know how she got here. Where she came from. She cries in her thoughts.

Stop spinning. Please stop spinning.

When her eyelids close, the stone walls vanish.

A new world appears. There spreads a wide expanse of green, stretching far enough to fall off the other side of the world.

She tumbles and floats onto emerald grass as round and fluffed as dandelions. Dogs with breath like feces lap her forehead in delight, paws digging into her shoulders. Pinning her down. They slobber, and she sinks her fingers into matted fur.

"Enough," someone speaks in a thin, cronelike voice. "Off the girl, you got it clean."

Kore sits up. Her body is heavy, as if she has grown root. In front of her is a young woman, not a crone at all but a girl with raven hair and olive skin.

A friend.

Her friend stands before her, hand extended.

"Lyris of Knossos, may you leave in love."

Lyris, yes! Eyes a frigid blue. But this is not right; they should be brown. Her body is wrong, too. Lyris should be bigger, rounder.

"H-her womb is clear."

Lyris bends to her, clasps an arm, and gives a strong pull. Little dogs bark and circle them.

Weird blue eyes alight, Lyris beckons and runs. She sprints away, feet crunching grass. Each time her foot hits the earth, Lyris bounces higher, buoyant. Meanwhile, Kore's own feet stick to earth that grips like tar.

She tries to say: *Wait!* The word hangs in her throat. Kore moans sickly as the dogs and Lyris fade into nothingness.

Her feet will not budge. In the sky, the god of the sun glares. Kore casts her gaze upward, and the flaming round face of Helius blazes merciless, uncaring. Burning her skin with the force of an unblinking stare. Despite the god's presence, she is alone. For as far as the meadow stretches, not a single person.

Helius bears a garish smile and looks at the space directly in front of her feet. Kore follows his gaze.

In front of naked toes, the most beautiful flower she has ever seen. White petals open to her, its cupped center bulbous and yellow and erect. A narcissus, the size of an open hand.

What a curious name for a ship.

Dread creeps into her chest. This is not right, as the frozen blue eyes of Lyris were not right. Kore stoops, drawn to it as if nudged from behind, and wraps her fingers around the stem.

She pulls. There comes a ripping inside the earth as roots pull free. The flower hardens in her hands and falls to ash.

Between her feet, the earth zags with a widening crevice. Her feet ease apart, one on each side of the rumbling earth, as the great divide rips the ground in two. Red cinders flare inside, and the ground burns her feet. Smoke billows upward, rolling between her legs and scorching her thighs.

"It b-burned so badly her legs sizzled like a pig on the altar."

Hot plumes enter the place between her legs, smoke billowing inside the womb, molten fumes rising into her gut and pouring into her throat and finally ejecting from her mouth like salted bile.

"When she exhaled, they smelled the myrrh from her mouth."

Gagging and heaving, she spits.

"Get it all out, girl," the crone voice says again. "You swallowed an ocean. All that salt will shrivel your insides. Get it out."

The earth widens, but her feet are no longer planted. Kore hovers above a bottomless chasm. Smoke expands. Her hair sparks with gold cinders, and her fingertips splay in the fiery rush of air.

From below, horses whinny. A chariot, encrusted in gold, bursts forth. Muscle and bone show beneath the decayed flesh of horses, dead but galloping. The chariot barrels toward her.

An arm extends and iron fingers bruise her waist. And inside the grip of godlike fingers, she watches her sunny flesh turn marble-white, blanching at his touch. There is a helpless, euphoric sensation of plummeting.

Kore jerks awake.

Again, she is surrounded by stone. The air is damp and cool. Kore spits saltwater and bile into a bucket near her head.

The voice of the crone comes again, clear and gruff, telling her, "When you arrive at the crossroads, tell death to go to the crows."

Telling her:

"It will not have you today, daughter of Zeus."

HECATE

8

After the flood, the port of Matapan lies in ruins. From where she stands, the old woman surveys all of it—the demolished ships, trees uprooted, clusters of men still searching rubble for bodies.

Today, they brought her four to nurse.

The old woman assumes there could be more in time. She has space now that one of them died, leaving her with a spare pallet on the floor next to the girl. Soon the rot will set in. The old woman stands at the cliff, waving rags above her head to signal someone to haul the dead man away. She cannot lug him out on her own, not with her back strained from day-long stooping over victims, cleaning urine and shit, mopping blood, and bandaging wounds licked clean by dogs.

She is Hecate, *klawiphoros,* key-bearer of Matapan. No one calls her this. They call her *hag. Crone. Witch.* Names flung with the intent to cut deep, but Hecate loves them, each name reflecting resentment. Revealing envy. Names like this are nothing but acknowledgment of her worth.

Klawiphoros. Fancy title. Zeus himself saw to it. No one argues with such a god among men, lest they face the electric wrath he harnesses from the sky. For her allegiance to the rebellion during the Titan War, she was appointed to the Council of Elders and holds the keys to each temple in Matapan.

Her gift is *pharmakia*, brewing concoctions to heal. If she pleases, she can inflict harm, but harm has never pleased her. In anger and despair, people bargain for curses. They plead for disease or death or someone to fall in love with them, which is always a curse for the one on the other end.

Though spat from the loins of nobles, Hecate never adopted their prissy ways. She was ill-suited for it. The gods must have had a laugh, as if they had granted these highborn folks a goat to raise instead of a girl. The child's play of girls never interested her—girls pretending to cook with mud and sticks and making themselves pretty for the elders. Piddle. Let the girls enjoy their fake cookery.

Hecate preferred the company of plants.

Like people, plants can help or harm. But unlike people, plants have no preference. Time with plants is never wasted, unlike time with people. Her enthusiasm for it paid off in time. Other girls married, but Hecate found she could stand on her own. After all, as long as there is man, there is a need to patch him up.

Over the last few years, blindness took her right eye, whitish blue with cataracts. No matter. She needs only one eye to see, and Hecate hunches beneath the yew tree, watching one of the landowners trudge his way up the dirt trail leading to her cave. Hecate cackles, shaking her head as he stomps up the hill.

Look at him hustle! The old bald-headed fool rushes to her. All the while stewing in his own sweat.

He thinks the corpse might be the girl.

His sandaled foot hooks onto a root. He trips and catches hold of a bush, legs scrambling to steady him. In its crescent state, the moon goddess appears to wink at her.

"Slow down, Phlaxis. The girl still lives. It is the fisherman drawing flies."

Faking solemn for her sake, the man nods as if the life of a fisherman bears as much worth as the child of a High King. Phlaxis cares more for his cattle than for the fisherman.

"Eighty-two dead today." Phlaxis huffs, scarlet-faced from the jaunt up.

"Mass burial."

The flood hit at the busiest time of the day. Midday, the port teemed with sailors, fishermen hauling nets from ships, sons eager to examine the bounty caught by their fathers. Safe on her crag, Hecate had watched the tide ripple far in the distance. She saw it coming moments before it crashed down, bringing with it the flotsam from a great ship. There was no time to warn anyone. From where she stood, it appeared as if Oceanus took in a big breath and exhaled a flood. It washed over the port and drowned bodies like ants in a pot.

"The largest burial procession Matapan has ever seen," he says with morbid excitement. Bearing witness to catastrophe enlivens dull men like this. Phlaxis revels in the spectacle of disaster.

Easily thirty years his senior, Hecate moves quicker, navigating stones and shrubs as nimbly as a squirrel. Milky eye be damned; the rest of her works fine. She leads Phlaxis under the doorway and into the firelit cave. The smell of sickness and spoiled flesh hits both of them. Phlaxis turns his head.

"In the morning, the curators are sending a runner to Asphodel." He tells her this to distract her, not wanting the iron-stomached old woman to witness him cringe at the odor. "The port is destroyed, and we need as much reparation as the High King can provide."

"Lies." Gooseflesh scatters atop her arms. "You do not ask Hades, High King of Erebus, for relief. You beg for mercy."

Few people gain an audience with Hades. No one strives to stand before his throne. They strive to run from it.

He is sometimes called Dark Zeus, but more often men whisper of him as the Unseen. Hades is infamous for judgment and atonement, exacting punishment upon criminals and the mentally deranged, training massive and skilled armies, like those in Lacedaemon or Pylos. With his quiet, severe nature, Hades the Unseen, ruler of the southern mainland, is the epitome of judicial authority.

Hecate shuffles past the first two bodies, both unconscious since this morning.

"We must see that Matapan is restored," Phlaxis insists. "And the Unseen needs to know about *her*."

"Finally, you say it. This is not about aid. Your half-truth cost me two minutes of my life, and I have none to spare." The thin buzzing of insects raises the hairs inside her ears. Although the runners of Matapan may not be the fastest in Erebus, if the sprint begins in the morning, news will reach Hades by the end of a day. "The runner aims to report on the girl."

"If a pile of Zeus's gold landed on our shores by error, would we keep it secret? Face the bolts of justice for our silence?"

She points at the clammy, graying flesh of the fisherman. "Grab the ankles."

Phlaxis bends. At first, he glances at the beardless young man in the first stages of bloat. His gaze shifts and catches the smooth, lively flesh of the girl, who lies flat on her back with one bare leg having kicked the blanket aside. The girdle is cut free by Hecate's blade. Dreadful as those Cretan costumes are, it is what saved the girl from inhaling too much water, her lungs constricted tight like a twisted sponge, unable to take in much of the sea. When Hecate freed her from it, she felt the girl's full, womanly shape under all those skirts.

Children of Zeus are notorious for their good looks. They are sealed with a crest of beauty, and this child is an exceptional sort, from the soft cleft in her chin to the plump lips ripe for suckling.

Dazed by this, Phlaxis turns his attention back to the dead man. He wraps his hands around cold, swollen ankles. "A child of Zeus is treasure to be reported."

"She has not been awake long enough to confirm it." Although she knows better, Hecate says, "It is rumor."

Phlaxis pulls the body, grunting from deadweight. "They say she declared it herself, hag. On the ship."

As the carcass slides across stone, easing from its position between the other ailing victims, Phlaxis ogles the girl again—he cannot stop himself—and hisses through his teeth.

She is awake.

Glassy eyes glimmer through an awning of thick lashes. She watches them drag the dead man away from the pallet beside her.

Phlaxis drops the ankles. The heels hit the floor with a hard thump.

"Girl," he demands, crouching next to her. He snaps his fingers in front of her face. "Can you hear me?"

The girl whimpers, a fat tear rolling from one eye. "Behind you are shades," she says, weak-tongued. "Two."

"Shades?" Phlaxis grimaces at the old woman. "She talks nonsense. It is the damned fever. Can you break it?"

Hecate turns to the third body among the four, a carpenter with his jaw slack and urine spreading out between his legs. Fingering the cold neck and finding no tick, Hecate says, "This one is dead, too."

"Behind you are shades. Two."

A peculiar claim. Lucky the girl is the daughter of a king, or she also might be branded a witch.

Phlaxis slowly stands, brow knitted tight. "Two dead in your care already, crone. Perhaps you are not capable of healing anymore. I have half a mind to take her into my care."

"Your brand of healing will have her waking up pregnant."

His face scrunches like an angry fist. Then, he erupts into belly laughs, which reverberate inside the shell of her cave.

Together, they drag the fisherman outside, where a waxing moon lends its smiling light. Beneath the yew tree, they cover the body with muslin and return to the cave for the second cadaver, gathering flies of his own.

The crown of her head bandaged and seeped through with a brown patch of blood, the girl stirs again. She struggles to leave the hazy territory between wakefulness and sleep. Phlaxis, ever enthralled, tries once more.

"Girl. What is your name?"

A few steps away, the last body rouses from the floor. Bloody stump eaten clean by maggots, the tall man with the fuzzy brown beard rouses. His hand was yanked clean from a wrist wrapped in bandages. He tells them, "Her name is Kore. Make sure Zeus knows that I helped her cross Oceanus. I only ever helped her."

"Who is that?" Phlaxis asks.

"The captain."

"His days of commanding ships are done." Seizing the legs of the carpenter, Phlaxis says with a snort, "Without a hand, he will be lucky to pass for a ferryman."

LITTLE GHOST
9

Amid the dust, no one can breathe. Demeter pulls the veil over her mouth as not to inhale rubble-born particles and squints. She steadies her sandals against crushed marble, climbing over the ruins of Knossos, and balances herself by extending one arm.

In the brown fog of the fallen palace, shapes solidify around her.

Someone helps another off the ground.

A short, bulky man flings rocks and digs for an upraised hand, disembodied fingers wriggling for help under stone.

A little girl totters, dazed among the ruins, emitting a shrill cry. An anxious woman scrambles up the side of a jutting column and clutches the child, both coughing and gagging as they embrace.

"Kore!" With the veil filtering the air, she manages to scream the name again.

And again.

As the air settles, stone dusting the ground like snow, Demeter gazes around. A team of men form three wide lines around a pile of debris. The first man in each line hauls portions of rubble from the ground, handing it over to the next man, who hands it over to the next. Working together.

Today, the harvest festival began at the palace of Knossos. Here, beneath mounds of jagged rock.

Kore was to lead it.

Knees quivering, the panic rises like fire. It blazes cold in her throat, her skin bright with shock, and Demeter is sure she will die. She screams for Kore again. Her voice rips through empty air, buildings fallen all around.

Calling will do no good. She must dig. She drops to her knees and claws at the rocks, throwing them aside. Newly broken stone cuts her fingers, but she lugs stone after stone. Surveying the area, Demeter struggles to orient herself.

Across the way, the men continue moving away the stones. One of them shouts, "Here! We have him. Careful."

Spitting out grit from the air, Demeter clamps the veil back over her mouth, knuckles bleeding. Her hand is caked with powder, beads of red congealing in the creases of her fingers. Tears make clean tracks down her face. She stands frozen, as if made of stone herself, a statue standing immobile among the rubble.

"Demeter!" one man calls. He waves her over. "High Priestess, come."

Scurrying on unstable ground, she lets the veil fall and uses her hands to steady her along. "Kore?"

By the time she reaches the men, she pants and coughs and rubs at the dust around her nose and mouth, smearing blood across her face. She recognizes them. Guards from the palace.

"Where is Kore?" she cries.

Two men pull a dust-covered body from the heap, each with an arm hooked beneath the armpits of a nearly unrecognizable figure. Under the clay powder, a purple robe as pale as twilight. Along with him, they drag a trail of blood across the stone.

"Prayers for the king," the guard says. The rest of them stand back, as if waiting for her to perform a miracle.

Dead King Lycastus, battered but recognizable by the royal finery he wears. In life, he was unremarkable, replacing a mad father exiled to Erebus for inhuman cruelty. The public prefers an unremarkable king to a deranged one; but Lycastus will have no legacy and, unlike the High Kings of the three major provinces—Olympus, Erebus, Cyclades—will not be deified in death. No one will worship him as they do Helius or Uranus.

Still, a king is a king.

"Of course." Her hands, those that often rise to invoke the gods, grasp at the strong, gritty arm of the guard. "Please. You have to keep digging. Kore!"

Demeter should have been here. She should have died along with the rest. As they dig, Demeter gushes thanks to the guards. She clutches the cold, stiff shape of the king. She sobs once, balling a length of his robe inside her fists and yearns to dig along with the guards, but they are capable. She has a duty here.

As the prayers tumble from her lips, she cannot stop watching them dig. Heaving stone from man to man. Pulling bodies from rubble.

She should be blessing the king's journey to the afterworld—and she does, she weeps the words—but in her voice is desperation for her child. Will they pull Kore from the ground, covered in dust like this? Her body, powdered ghost-white.

Where are you, little ghost?

As a little child of two or three, her daughter would patter through the house and hide. She was small and wispy, her hair a frosty white, and her white tunic would billow as she would disappear, always silent. And Demeter would tiptoe around in playful search of her, singing:

"Where can my little ghost be?"

Inevitably, Kore would leap out, laughing. "Boo!" She would run as her mother chased her.

Demeter longs for that now. For Kore to jump out. Surprise her.

Someone approaches from behind. She turns to Asli, who is clean and unhurt.

"Bow in the presence of the king," Demeter

whispers, pulling Asli down beside her. The girl glances at the body and cringes, not having recognized him.

"He is dead," Asli squeaks. Tears mount.

Demeter shushes her. "Stop crying." She stumbles into a crouch, pulling at chunks of debris. "There is no time for that. Dig. We will stay for a hundred years if we need. Kore could be alive."

"Priestess," Asli says, "what are you doing?"

"Dig!"

"I came to the palace as you told me to do," Asli says, "but Kore was not here."

Hands stinging, Demeter stops. "What?"

"They told me she never arrived."

Relief washes through her like a cool mountain spring. "She is home?"

For once, Kore's insolence is rewarded.

But Asli shakes her head. "I never found her." Scanning the demolished polis of Knossos, Asli does not finish her thought. Demeter understands why.

Kore could be under any of this.

MINOS, THE FALLEN

10

Once, he had been a king. Once, Judge Minos felt the weight of Knossos bear down upon his shoulders, and he held it aloft for seven years. His reign, countable on two hands.

Until the bull came along, Minos did well as king.

Within the palace of Hades, the *andron* is packed. On platforms of obsidian, cushioned couches press flush against walls painted gold and red. There are two men to a couch. Half of the room comes from Pylos. The man with whom he verbally spars is also from Pylos, a pockmarked nobleman with a nose like the pelvic fin of a sea bass. Minos should know his name but cannot recall it. Men cycle through the palace like beetles. Identities blur. Easiest to refer to the man as "my friend," although it is a lie.

Tonight, Minos acts as symposiarch. The burden

of presiding over symposium falls to him. His two companions never miss a party. Minos is surprised to find them absent. Rhadamanthus attends for the conversation. Aeacus, for the high-class hetaera, women similar to the regular kind of whore, yet cleaner and smarter.

The men are two kraters deep in wine, with slave-washed hands and feet. Bellies brimming. Cocks ready for later.

At this late hour, the nobles recline, myrtle garlands askew on the heads of those who plan to drink heavily, to stave off the wine headache in the morning. Two flautists, young and plain-faced, play their jingles and move in awkward dance, as if they have not been doing this long.

The purpose of symposium is philosophy, not debauchery, although the latter always follows the former. The subject of corruption often comes up in philosophical conversation. Minos does not initiate the topic, but men bring it up. The judge is well acquainted with it. Some might say he conquered it, though it cost him his throne.

To his fellow symposiast, Minos remarks, "For kings, madness is a sickness waiting to be caught."

Seated beside him, the nobleman snorts. "The best go mad, eh, Judge? Why do you suppose that is?"

Minos ignores the snide tone and explains with as much diplomacy as he can muster, "It is caused by *phobos*. Fear."

"Kings are ousted all the time," the noble says. "Of course, they are fearful."

"The fear of losing power," Minos says, "and fear that power itself is the pinnacle of life. After power, perhaps nothing better can be attained. All men seek hope. The promise of having something better waiting over the horizon."

The man tosses lentils into his mouth to pad a wine-soured stomach. "You would know."

Minos considers himself fortunate to be here today, no longer enslaved to his own soured mind, stripped clean of all he clung to before. Banishment had been a kindness. Once the title of king was stripped away, he found freedom in solitude, in nothingness, in having nothing else to grasp to his chest in protective terror. His mind is sound, and Minos remains thankful to the gods for the role he holds now. For dignity. Together, with Rhadamanthus and Aeacus, he provides council to Hades, High King of Erebus, advising on who lives, who dies, and who pays what price.

The Pylosian noble, who increasingly wears on Minos's good graces, continues with a tsk. "A kingdom lost over a damned bull." He shakes his head, mocking. "Had you killed the beast as you were told, you would still be the star of Knossos."

Philosophy has a way of escalating. Opinions and wine, a violent pairing.

Minos will not be lured to anger. This, he has conquered as well. "As I said. Kings and madness."

"Our King Neleus was not mad," says the Pylosian noble. "He was a good man."

"Indeed," he agrees. "King Neleus was not sick. But in time, it would have consumed him, too."

One of the hetaera senses the tension. The one coming to their rescue is named Minthe. Her hair is the color of blue-black sin, and she chews a sprig of mint. According to Minthe, she was named after the plant, but Minos suspects Minthe is not her real name, and she renamed herself. The mint became her crest, keeping her tongue as alluring as the rest of her.

Before the Pylosian can lose his temper, she sinks onto his lap. "Judge Minos is not the only expert on kings," she says with a lilt.

Whores are apt at diffusing.

"I have known many kings myself." She licks the crater-skinned face of the noble, to whom Minos mentally assigns the name Pock.

Pock allows a half-smile, unsure if he wants to set aside his righteousness. He has reason to be righteous. What happened to his king, what happened to the entire kingdom of Pylos, was atrocious.

Nearly two years later, it continues to plague them. Minos and his fellow judges hear of it ceaselessly. Hades will never let it go. Not until Pylos's attacker is brought to kneel before his ebony throne.

With a nuzzle and a wiggle, Minthe extinguishes the brunt of Pock's anger. The man grows red and wraps his arms around her fleshy waist and practically sings, "I suppose Judge Minos thinks we owe that bastard Alcides a debt for killing our king? Eh? Better to kill a king before he had the chance to go mad?"

"Of course not, my friend." When Minos forces a thin smile, his tired eyes disappear into the folds of his skin. "The criminal Alcides destroyed your home. He murdered your king. You lost thousands in battle and were left with a nine-year-old as a replacement king. For this, no leniency."

"Why," muses Pock, "has he gone unpunished?" He rests his hand high between the whore's thighs.

The challenge is meant to rile him. Ignorant of the complexities, Pock wants justice for his slain king and ravaged home. To him, the issue is simple; however, politics are riddled with complication. Rarely is anything simple.

Minthe, a good gossip if not philosopher, loud-whispers into the noble's ear:

"I bet Zeus protects him! Alcides is his bastard, after all."

"Wine," says Minos, raising his cup in the air. A slave fills the cup before he can lift it all the way. "And for my friend. His cup is empty."

Pock offers his cup but never takes his eyes off him. It is as if he knows Minos is the one who prevents justice.

The nobleman is not wrong about that, either.

Minos picks breadcrumbs from a silver and

bronze beard that trails to his chest. The slaves cut it exactly as he likes—tidy and hanging no longer than the clavicle. The crown of his head shines with naked flesh, but the hair along the nape of his neck is long and brushes his shoulders with silvery fluff. He mentally curses his brother and Aeacus for going to bed early. During Pylosian visits, it takes a great deal of effort to steer the conversation away from the bastard of Zeus, who destroyed their great polis.

Where the hell is his brother? Minos could use Rhad's levity.

"Maybe," Pock muses, "this is why Gaia mourns. Hysterical over the children who fail her."

"Ah!" Minthe smiles. "The earth shook, but I would not call the goddess hysterical. It was nothing but a grumble. My mother beat me worse."

"Your mother was right," Pock quips. Minthe's berry-red mouth opens in mock astonishment, and she swats him on the arm.

Yes, the earth trembled the day before. They were holding court when the floor quaked beneath their feet, cracks spreading like veins in a hand. Destruction at the palace of Asphodel was minimal, but Gaia opened her mouth and complained loud enough to drive slaves to mend the floor today.

Lately, Gaia revolts often. Does she cry for all the lost titans of the war? Rage at injustice? Is it not anger or grief at all, but a warning of worse to come? A way to get their attention?

"She was easy on us," Minos agrees.

"She was easy on *us*," Pock stresses. "We expected an import from Crete yesterday. It never arrived. Cost us three hundred bull tusk helmets. It may have cost Crete more than helmets."

Rhadamanthus appears in the doorway, a patchwork cat by the way his beard turns from orange to gray, speckled brown at the chin. He lingers, head down and forehead scrunched. Too serious for a party.

Minos has never been so glad to see his brother. "Brother," he beckons, "join us!"

Rhad gestures with his head, saying: *No. Come out here.*

His stomach turns. The phantom smell of honeyed bathwater plays inside his nostrils. Sober, unexpected arrivals like this never bode well. For instance, the day they caught up to him in Sicily and took him into custody for crimes of inhuman cruelty. They arrested him, naked, dozing off in the bath.

Minos makes an excuse for his brother and rolls himself from the couch, setting his cup on the mosaic floor. A slave retrieves it before his fingers leave the bronze. By the time he reaches the doorway, Rhad is already outside in the corridor, waiting. Candles flicker along the floor, casting wide yellow light onto stone walls.

Rhad is not alone. With him are two men in soldiers' tunics lined with decorative bands of red, yellow, and blue. The colors of Knossos. They bow in reverence to Minos, their former king.

"What has happened?" Minos asks.

"Knossos was destroyed." Rhad lays a hand on his shoulder. "All of it, under rubble."

"Gaia's work."

"Yes."

Minos's expression softens. "Knossos was lost to me years ago."

Rhadamanthus glances at the soldiers. "I know, brother."

"I ask again. What has happened?"

He looks to the soldiers, finding the answer in their bowed heads.

Rhad says, "Your son Lycastus has died."

One of the soldiers says, "He leaves an heir, your grandson who is also named Minos."

Minos has lost a son before. His first-born Androgeos was slain by jealous competitors after besting them at the javelin and at footrace. Murdered for excellence.

The bull takes blame for the downfall of the great King Minos. But it was not the bull that caused the madness. It was the loss of Andro. It drove him to vengeance, at any cost.

His form of vengeance cost him the throne. The bull was merely his chosen weapon.

Now, the news of Lycastus's death falls onto an exhausted heart—and Minos realizes that once experienced, a thing loses its power. The horror destroys you once. And when you recover, you understand you will always recover; the worst of it has happened and cannot happen in the same way twice. His wife, Pasiphae, accused him of loving Andro most. He did—of course, he did. But the truth is, his remaining family died the day of his exile. Minos has seen none of his family in four years.

"I see." The news of it leaves him tired, devoid of vigor, and yearning for bed. "Is there talk of godhood?"

"No," Rhad answers. Minos is not surprised. Lycastus was an average boy and surely made an average king. Godhood is hard-won. Once, Minos had hoped to achieve it. A goal that, in hindsight, seems laughable.

The urge to cry surfaces, an unwanted visitor. He clears his throat. "How many others?"

"Hundreds all over Crete, Judge," the soldier says.

"And a hundred more in Matapan." This new voice echoes from farther down the hall. Aeacus strides toward them, the bloated sag in his face suggesting a life with too much wine. He stretches his arms wide. "Suddenly, every polis needs help."

"You bore the burden of delivering difficult news," Aeacus tells the soldiers and plants a hand on the shoulder of each. "Join the others for symposium. Do not look so concerned. You may not be skilled in philosophy, but no one is interested in your mind at this hour. Drink, talk, fuck. Go."

With the soldiers out of the way, Judge Aeacus shoulders his way between the two of them, torso thick like a tree. "Tomorrow we petition Hades for relief in Matapan and Knossos."

Aeacus should not need reminding, but Minos does it anyway. "Poseidon commands all the islands. He will provide aid for Knossos."

"And Poseidon will remain grateful to the High King who helped him foot the expense," Aeacus says.

Rhad glances at Minos to assure him he means no offense when he says, "Knossos is not our concern. We must deal with Matapan, and there could be more who fell victim to Gaia's rage. We must conserve our resources."

Rhad assumes the best in people. It is his weakness. But Minos knows Aeacus and his cunning nature.

Numb, limbs heavy, Minos shuffles past his brother. When he reaches Aeacus, Minos stops. "On the night of my son's death, we will not discuss Alcides or war strategy."

"Absolutely not." Rhadamanthus furrows his wild, orange brow. "We are out of court."

"Tomorrow." Aeacus replies, unapologetic. "We will hash it out in front of the Unseen."

The Worst Terrors

11

On the third day of care, the girl remembers what happened. How she got here.

"Kore."

The old woman whispers it, and the word is like a key fitting into a lock. Kore does not know this place or this woman—but when the key turns, and the door opens, shame awaits. Her head feels full to the brim, ready to burst. The injury makes it this way, from where she banged it on the ship.

Kore watches the hag through slitted eyes. They have been alone for many hours. In the canopy of her lashes, her eyes are easily mistaken as closed.

The old woman talks to herself. Kore has been observing her, on and off, for hours. As plainly as if she speaks to someone right beside her, the woman announces each herb in her concoction.

"Licorice, elecampane root—no, too much. Better, better. And, oh, I suppose I could use horehound. Meh, I forgot the—oh, well. Hyssop will have to do for now."

When she grinds the herbs in the pot, she touches the powdery result from finger to tongue. She grunts, face flat and square like a man's. Kore has never seen hair cut short on a woman—sheared and poking up around her head in brambles. Her eyes are tiny holes, one of them clouded over, and a thin, birdlike nose separates the good eye from the bad.

As she holds an iron plate over the fire, the hag says, "Oh, gods' wounds, be careful. These stones will burn the skin right off the bone." She shakes fire-heated stones from the plate and next to Kore's pallet, pouring a pitcher of camphor water over them. Steam rises, and Kore inhales the moist fumes.

Kore supposes the crone could be talking to the dogs. Four of them circle her bony, veined ankles. Although she is old, the woman stands tall, unfamiliar with the hunched waddle of an elderly person. Tails wagging, the alopekis—squat creatures with long bodies and pointed ears—dance around the woman's step.

"All right." She grunts, making her way to the other side of the pallet. "Stop faking sleep. I need you to take the herbs."

Kore is hot, shaking.

"Open up. Your breathing is all wrong. Feel a tightness, do you? Here?" The old woman pats at her chest, concealed beneath a gray tunic. "For too long, you breathed sea instead of air. Now, there is illness in you. This will help."

Kore starts to speak, but her chest seizes. She coughs, barking worse than the dogs, unable to catch her wind and terrified by the burning in her lungs. The old woman tips a cup of fresh cold water to a hot mouth. Her face is scalding.

"You must suffer the fever. It exists to burn away the sick."

At times, Kore sees two of the old woman. Figures combine and part again in her vision. The room grays, normalizes. Arm heavy, Kore touches a trembling hand to her head. Cloth, with tacky wetness oozing through.

Kore shifts, swallowing to control any more coughing, and breathes the healing camphor.

"All right now?"

Kore nods.

"Open."

Hooking a cragged finger inside Kore's mouth, the old woman pulls and tucks the herbs between her teeth and cheek. "Let it sit for a while. It needs to soak up."

Her spit mingles with the earthen taste of herbs, pungent and bitter on the tongue.

"You are called Kore—do I have it right?"

Kore nods again. She hopes for no more questions.

"I am Hecate. The wave that ravaged your ship

killed almost everyone else on it and more down at the port. They have drowned or bled to death by now. But not you. You are strong."

"Strong-willed like your father."

Echoing inside her head, these phantom words pluck at a sensitive spot in her heart.

"Oh, I know you do not think so. In time, you will shake the fever. You will breathe normally again. There is a poultice of clay and herb binding the wound on that goose egg on your head. And once you are right again, I have questions, daughter of Zeus."

"My father is Zeus, the Liberator, King of Kings, and your master."

She chokes on an errant fleck of herb. Coughing, Kore buckles over. Hecate slips a bowl under her chin so she can spit. Herbs in rivulets string from her mouth, and she coughs hard, thick salty mucus springing from her lungs. With the pad of her hand, Hecate beats the soft hollows of her back. Kore spits again.

Sweating but cold, she clutches wool under her chin. She spins in place. Her body sits immobile, and yet the twirling continues.

"Lie down."

No.

She will not lie down. If she does, she will be lost to sleep again. With each shuddery breath, air whistles from her chest.

Sweat cool on her forehead, she braces her

hands at her sides, as if to steady the ground beneath.

"If I sleep," Kore mutters, "I-I will go back." Already, she envisions a green field stretching far and wide. The sky blazes the garish smile of Helius.

"Back where?"

"It happens over and over." Kore shuts her eyes. In front of naked toes, the most beautiful flower she has ever seen.

"Tell me."

"There is a narcissus. Beautiful—and I pick it. But when I do, the ground opens, and smoke pours out and floods inside of me—and from inside the chasm, a chariot races upward and—"

Inside the grip of godlike fingers, she watches her sunny flesh turn marble-white, blanching at his touch.

"I am taken."

Cold hand soothing Kore's face, Hecate tells her, "The worst terrors come in sleep."

THE UNSEEN
12

The soldier fights without seeing his opponent. Age twenty and visiting from Lacedaemon, the soldier towers, stout bones secured by layers of muscle, making him as immovable as granite. Breakfast digested, the soldier, Tychon, positions across from his opponent, shield fastened to a thick forearm, sword poised to strike.

The commander insists:

"This is battle, not a training exercise."

They are to pretend the fight is real.

Tychon's opponent has no trouble pretending. Ever since his return from Olympus, this scene plays out in a perpetual loop in his mind. It is the first thought assaulting him in the morning and the last to haunt him at night. He thinks of little else but the gnawing memory. Sometimes, it does not end with him shot by Alcides's arrow. Not today, for certain.

Face hidden inside a bronze helmet, the

opponent strides to the stalwart soldier. Like Tychon, he also holds a shield. His sword is holstered. At his side, a bow dangles from one fist. Over his shoulder swings a sack of arrows.

"A coward's weapon," Tychon says with a laugh. "Fight me sword to sword. A man kills his enemy up close."

The opponent drops the bow and sack of arrows onto the dirt between them.

"This is for you," he says in a voice so quiet, Tychon strains to hear the words.

From the sidelines, other soldiers observe. Early mornings, they train, taking turns.

"You heard him," the commander shouts at Tychon, "Pick up the bow."

They do not stand eye to eye. Tychon is a head taller. He is meatier than his opponent, who is built taut, muscled in the shoulders and lean in the hips. In a battle of brawn, Tychon would fare better.

"Keep the sword," he instructs Tychon. "Use whatever you can, whenever you can."

"I can rip you apart with two fingers," the young soldier replies through gritted teeth.

This Tychon is not a bad man. As a soldier, he is loyal, a hoplite who fights mainly with a spear, and has killed thirty-two men in battle.

Unlike Tychon, the opponent is not twenty. He is twice that and more, but under a rusted, battle-worn helmet, no one can tell. The helmet belongs to the army, a relic from wars already won, turning him anonymous. He could be anyone.

If Tychon knows who is under the helmet, he will pull his punches. Tychon will think twice before each arrow soars—off the mark by a calculated hair or two—and after a pitiful fight, he will submit and praise his opponent's skill and feign humility, claiming to be beaten naturally.

Pointless.

As he strides to the other end of the courtyard, the opponent calls out, "Tychon!" and turns to face him. "If you get the chance, kill me."

He takes his place and ignores Tychon when he hollers, "Hey—who are you?"

Through the eyeholes, the opponent glances up at palace walls of obsidian and red jasper. Three hunched figures watch from the second terrace. The judges, like crows on a ledge. Before hibernating inside the palace walls all day, holding court, they like to watch the soldiers train. Their morning amusement.

Under a dusty tunic that pulls tight across his chest, his right shoulder rotates in its socket. Each twist is like a knife ripping muscle to shreds. He welcomes the pain. Almost two years on the mend from the battle in Pylos, he still devotes agonizing hours to pushing the shoulder to the limits of pain. Abusing it is the way to heal and to harden. The arrow pierced him straight through, and he nearly died of infection, chasing that brat of Zeus's all the way to Olympus, where the boy hid behind his father's leg like a beaten pup.

The battle should never have ended that way. It should have ended in Pylos. But he had not been quick enough to recover his shield in time. The pointed tip of Alcides's arrow punched into him, puncturing clean through and sending shock waves coursing down his arm, through his chest, and up his neck.

Again and again, he relives it. A thousand times, plagued by how it should have gone. After the war with the titans, he lived five years of relative peace. Empty years, stagnant and without meaning. Nothing to drive him, until Alcides stirred up trouble.

Dozens of men, helmets and weapons set aside, watch from the perimeters. Some sit on the grass, leaning back against columns that blare with sunlight. Others stand, pretending to sharpen their blades, but all the while keeping watch over the men in the center.

From across the yard, Tychon raises the bow. The other soldiers whistle and holler in encouragement. Shields clang to amplify the lusty noise of competition.

The arrow flies.

The opponent watches it come, the arrowhead keen in his mind, its trajectory mapped out from beginning to end.

For a moment, the other soldiers believe he wants to die. He remains motionless. He does not duck or raise the shield or run from death's way. He simply observes the way Tychon angles the arrow, the way his right elbow juts downward, the angle of his chin, the placement of the pad of his hand against the bowstring.

The men stare in disbelief, watching the thing fly. The whistling arrow is upon him in an instant.

It will hit his throat.

He raises his sword and crosses the blade in front of his torso, diagonal from right hip to left earlobe.

The tip of the arrow clinks against the blade and falls to the stony ground.

The men roar and laugh. This spurs Tychon to fire arrows in rapid succession. The opponent walks into the line of fire, his shield catching every blow, arrows jutting in front of him as he charges forward. He finds no logic in dodging arrows. Spending the mind's energy that way impairs the ability to focus. With the shield, he catches the arrows one after another.

Belt. Shin. Shoulder.

Each blow sends a metallic *thunk* reverberating against his arm.

Hip. Chest. Chest. Head.

He storms closer. Tychon steps back, adjusting the alignment of his bow for the target, who charges as steadfast as a tightening vise. More arrows fire.

Knee. Belt. Shoulder.

Three paces from Tychon, the opponent raises his sword, shoulder singing in pain with the sudden movement, and slides it between arrow and bowstring. The blade slices the string, and the string hangs limp.

Tychon grabs for his sword.

His opponent takes one more step, hooking his ankle behind Tychon, and kicks his foot out from under him. Tychon falls flat on his ass. Shield flashing in the sun, the opponent swings his left arm. Tychon's helmet rings against it. His head jerks, sending the helmet sailing into the air and tumbling onto the ground.

A soldier of Lacedaemon is trained to show no fear, and he rolls onto the ground, grabbing for his sword.

The sword is kicked from Tychon's hand. A foot crashes against his cheekbone, and Tychon rolls onto his stomach. He starts to push himself up when his opponent steps on his wrist and stamps his other foot upon the young soldier's back. Tychon pants against dirt, blood pooling around his mouth and nose.

The opponent presses the sword against the base of Tychon's skull.

Beneath him, he pictures Alcides, son of Zeus, smug and spoiled, gasping on the ground.

He pushes the blade farther into the neck. The blade pierces flesh, blood trickling.

Tychon roars.

The word, still not spoken.

"Say it."

The cheers of the men fall silent.

"Yield," the soldier manages to grunt, crushed under the weight of his opponent.

Yield—the word he should have heard from Alcides.

The sword falls from his hand, plumes of dust wafting up as it thumps against the ground. Clamping down on the back of his neck, Tychon rolls and kneels, blood pooling between his fingers. Raw humility, true and untainted, downturns the corners of the boy's mouth.

The victor pulls the helmet from his head. The bronze feels like tin between his fingers. A second after it falls to the ground, the knees of soldiers fall as well. They remove their helmets to subjugate.

Sweat tickles his neck and soaks a tunic that hides the tendrils of a large scar. The scar from an arrow, bursting out of the central wound like the rays of the sun.

"You faltered when you switched to the sword," he tells Tychon. The boy glows with a tempting corona of colors. Normally, he would not pry into an innocent, but he likes to examine the character of his soldiers. He has no desire to hurt the boy further but wants to see the truth.

Tychon is virtuous overall. He kicked a dog when he was eleven, tricked his brother into drinking bull semen, and justifiably killed thirty-two men in battle.

The moment Tychon's eyes water, the victor

relents and walks away. "The physician will stitch your neck."

On his way out, he glances up at the terrace. Minos shuffles back into the shadows of the palace. Rhad shakes his head. Aeacus, the oldest of the three, chuckles.

At the squared opening of the palace, three black beasts emerge from the shadows. Their coats shine like oil. The mastiffs usher him inside. They answer to the collective name of Cerberus, trained to act as one entity instead of three. In truth, their master assigned a name to each—Proí, Mesméri, Nýchta. It seemed fair to permit them individuality, though he shares their names with no one. With them, he feels at peace.

Secretly, they delight in a good scratch under golden collars shaped like serpents, identifiers setting them apart from the other dogs. They delight in belly rubs and lean into him with bodies curled, their form of embrace. In public, however, master and beasts uphold the semblance of detachment and stoicism.

They are soldiers, after all.

For this reason, there is a mastiff for every guard in Asphodel. Soldiers need not always be men. He never worries about the character of a dog.

Later, as Cerberus accompanies him to the assembly room, the three judges are already waiting.

The herald calls, "His Majesty, Hades son of Cronus, High King of Erebus, the Unseen, Usurper of

Titans, Ruler of Souls, Master of Pylos of Messenia, Asphodel and Matapan of Laconia, Lacedaemon of Arcadia. Master of Elis, Achaea, Arcadia, Argolis. Omnipresent among mortals—"

There is more. Hades pays no attention. He breezes past the herald, past Minos and Rhad, and finally Aeacus. Black of hair and eyes and mood, Hades barges toward the throne room, ready to get on with the day. The hours he spends there comprise the majority of his life. There, he dissects the cruelest of men who come to him for sentencing, to plead their pitiful stories to a king who cannot be misled. He reads them as easily as etchings on stone. Excuses, lies—worthless when standing under the scrupulous attention of Hades the Unseen.

Those who kneel before him swear, "He knows the truth in you. He stands within your past, an observer but unobserved himself, viewing the core of your dirty soul."

At the squared doorway that opens into the throne room, Hades turns to the three judges.

"Why am I the only one going inside?"

Aeacus moves first. "We must talk before court—"

Minos adds, "There are matters—"

"Majesty," Rhad begins, simultaneously, "King Lycastus of Knossos has perished along with a hundred more in Crete—"

His head throbs above the ears. The knotted joints at his jaw ache from nights of gnashing his teeth, the muscles tense and tired.

"Hold it." He points at the former king of Knossos, whose face is serene, a placid lake with plenty of life under the surface. A calm man is easiest to stomach. The other two are worked up. "Minos."

"Word comes from the island of Crete," Minos says. "Gaia caused great disruption. Knossos bore the brunt of her anger."

Blue can be the color of sorrow. The deeper it shines, the greater the sadness. Hades sees it around Minos. "Condolences on the loss of your son."

"He was crushed under rubble, along with countless others," Minos says. "The entire city is destroyed and their ports inoperable."

Hades goes inside. They follow.

"Another port, too," Rhad says, "at Cape Matapan."

Inside the chamber, columns line the wall like soldiers standing at attention. Golden torches crisscross at the pinnacle of each one. Blue embers glow beneath a vented portal in the floor. The fragrance of myrrh arises from airy scrolls of smoking incense.

Crafted from ebony, the throne stretches tall and narrow with arms carved into the scaled skin of snakes. Behind it, on a pedestal lit by torches, rests his own battle helmet from the Titan War. The golden helmet is molded into a skull, teeth bared, chin pointed and jutting forward. The eyeholes and slashes of a skeletal nose allow air inside. So horrifying is the spectacle, any man who encountered him in battle would piss himself before Hades delivered a single blow.

"Send aid to Matapan," Hades instructs. When one of his territories suffers, he is quick to assist. The poleis of Erebus are his children.

"And Knossos?"

"What about it?" His shoulder pinches as he sits, and Hades twists it back and forth to loosen the muscle.

The three judges recline on the steps around him. Their chitons drape over a newly repaired floor.

"Though under the rule of Poseidon," Minos says, "Aeacus believes we should help in Knossos."

"I do. Send aid for repair," Aeacus insists. "True, Knossos is not your baby, but what father does not appreciate a caring gesture from his brother?"

Hades's old mentor never relents when his sight is set. Now, his sight is set on war. He considers. "Aeacus is right."

"Ha!" Aeacus scoffs. His face is flat and wrinkled as a hound's.

"It will be costly," Rhad warns.

"It will cost us lumber, stone, tools for masonry," Aeacus says, "but it will gain us an ally in Poseidon."

"The three of you are all brothers," Minos adds. "To whom is Poseidon more loyal?"

Hades contemplates. "Poseidon is loyal to Poseidon above all." They may share a father, but the three High Kings grew up apart. None were raised by the man who sired them. Cronus would sooner kill his young than tolerate the threat of them. As a result, they met as men, not as babes.

"We have tried to negotiate with Zeus for two years," Aeacus says. "Two years too many. You know where I stand."

"We know where you stand," Rhad says, as if consoling a bawling child who wants to be heard. Rhad's stance is the opposite of Aeacus's. It usually is. Appointing Rhad was intended to create balance and counteract Aeacus's severe nature, but after a while, the balance often deadlocked decisions. The vote of Minos swings the pendulum.

In this matter, Hades defers to Minos's casting vote. A war vote is the most crucial of all, and Minos finds himself torn by the cause.

Two years ago, a farmer accused Zeus's son, a man named Alcides, of stealing his cattle. Battles can launch over the pettiest things.

Arguments ensued. Alcides, with his impressive strength, overpowered the farmer during the brawl. The farmer fell backward over a wall that retained the cattle from the side of the cliff. Fell or pushed was the question. Accident or not, with the farmer dead on his Pylosian land, King Neleus refused to grant Alcides pardon.

Hades appreciates kings who do not bend in their convictions. A kindred mind, Neleus was committed to balance and integrity. When judging

Alcides, he did not judge the son of Zeus. He judged a murderer and insisted Alcides stand before Hades for sentencing.

In response, Alcides slaughtered King Neleus of Pylos and his entire family, with the exception of a son, Nestor—age nine—who escaped to Lacedaemon with his mentor.

Both Rhad and Aeacus look to Minos.

"If I cast my vote for war," Minos finally says, "we would be in a better position with Poseidon as an ally. Nevertheless, I have not cast my vote."

"Alcides should be brought to justice." Aeacus throws a conspiratorial glance to Hades. The old judge knows the right kindling to add to the fire. Hades is not blind to manipulation. "And there is no justice unless Zeus turns him over. His refusal is an act of war."

In Hades's gut, turning on a brother feels contrary to the laws of tribe and nature. Rhad feels the same way. Hades suspects Minos does as well. But brotherhood loyalty must be practiced by all parties involved. Zeus's arrogance has breached it.

"Erebusian kingdoms have the strongest armies," Aeacus points out. "Stronger than Olympus. King Lacedaemon holds the mightiest army under your rule. None can best them."

"There are no certainties in war," Rhad tells Hades. "You could be killed with no heir to succeed you."

"There is always someone to succeed you,"

Hades mumbles. Perhaps not an heir by blood. But always, someone lurks and plots to take the throne. This, the logic that drives kings mad. It drove his true father mad. Cronus of Olympus would snatch his newborn babies straight from the queen's womb, and he would cook them and eat their flesh, declaring no son would ever overthrow him. It took years, but the three secret-living sons of Cronus brought the titans to their doom. Together with Poseidon, he and Zeus reversed a reign of terror that had gone on for decades.

"We lost thousands in Pylos when Alcides sacked it," Aeacus argues. "If Zeus refuses to hand over his bastard, he forces your hand."

Zeus, his brother by blood. His brother-in-arms. Now an enemy.

Alcides wrought havoc on Pylos, burning down homes in a tantrum a child of Zeus would unleash.

When the army of Asphodel, led by Hades, marched into Pylos to regain control, Alcides managed to catch Hades in a moment when his shield had fallen to his side. The arrow burst through his shoulder. Shot, he chased Alcides all the way to Olympus, where the bastard claimed sanctuary under his father's land.

"Another thing," Aeacus mentions. "The runner from Matapan reports one of Zeus's daughters washed ashore with the wreckage of a ship. Another brat of Zeus, muddying up your land."

It is throwaway news. When the judge mentions

it, he has no agenda.

Hades's interest arouses. "Which daughter?"

"Zeus has two dozen bastards, easily." Rhad chuckles. "I do not know how he keeps track of them all."

Silence descends. The judges wait, expectant.

"Alcides is a bastard." Minos weighs after a moment. "That has no bearing on Zeus's favorites."

"What do you know about her?" Hades asks.

Aeacus smooths his beard. "She is near death."

Silence again.

"When I took an arrow to the shoulder, I was near death. Zeus did not turn his back on me in Olympus, and I intended to kill his son."

Rhad folds his hands in front of him. "Yes. You know Zeus and his fondness for *xenia*. Guests of Olympus are always treated hospitably."

"He patched me," Hades says, "and sent me home."

"Without justice," Aeacus stresses.

Hades tells them, "My brother made sure I had my health. We will do the same. Restore the health of his daughter. Once done, as a gesture of good faith, we offer to return her."

Aeacus smiles. "In exchange for Alcides."

The fact is, Hades is too old for war. That also applies to Zeus, the Liberator, not much younger than he. The philandering, gluttonous fool wears his beard gray now, still with the same thick, lustrous curls. War is an obsession for the young. It does not need to come to those extremes. The life of a bastard is not worth the life of entire armies.

Never fond of war, Rhad tells his brother, "If Zeus complies, we will not need your casting vote. Stay as neutral as you want."

Minos bends to his master, "In accordance with the law of *xenia*?"

And Hades, High King of Erebus, orders:

"Send a chariot to Matapan. And take her."

PART TWO
EREBUS

She [Persephone] was filled with a sense of wonder, and she reached out with both hands to take hold of the pretty plaything. And the earth, full of roads leading every which way, opened up under her . . . There it was that the Lord who receives many guests made his lunge. He was riding on a chariot drawn by immortal horses. The son of Kronos. The one known by many names.

—Homeric Hymn to Demeter

"Kore."

Hearing her name, she shifts upon the pallet. Mumbles.

"Wake up, girl."

She awakes to the urgent face of Hecate. The old woman crouches, placing a firm hand on her shoulder, saying:

"You need to speak to me now. There is no time."

"Time?"

Thoughts twirl, making her dizzy. Kore has no idea how many times the sun has set since she arrived. She may have slept through many. The last few days passed in a cycle of inhaling the moist heat of camphor, of sucking herbs against her teeth, of turning onto her stomach while Hecate beat the soft part of her back, knocking loose the stuff suffocating her.

The rest of the time, she spent in the meadow, picking the same flower, flinching at the same hand that grabbed and jarred her awake.

Kore rests under a pile of fur that tickles her chin when she exhales. Wet and weak, she bakes under the hides of animals, sweating out the fever.

"Tell me the truth," Hecate urges. "Is your father expecting you?"

"My father is Zeus," Kore remembers aloud.

"Why were you aboard a trade ship with those men? The child of a High King should have better escorts."

A brown-bearded man flashes in her mind.

"This is a cargo ship, girl."

"Swords and helmets. It carried swords and helmets."

"If your father had any inkling you were coming," Hecate says, "you would have washed up from the finest ship in the land."

"I-I can pay well."

With her father's coin, she had bought passage on the ship. Her hand slides to her waist.

"I had a p-purse."

Hecate picks up a pile of yellow cloth at her side—material from Kore's removed skirts—and displays the flap of the girdle with its laces cut. From one of the loops hangs a blue purse. "Was there something inside it before Oceanus swished you around?"

Her stomach sinks. Before, she had gold—a lot

of it—embossed with the head of an eagle.

The bag droops, empty.

Outside, the dogs bark, loud and sharp.

"Answer me," Hecate insists. "Are you the daughter of Hera, High Queen of Olympus?"

She shakes her head no.

"No." The crone purses her lips. Oh, but Kore should have answered differently—this disappoints the kindly old woman, and she has worked hard to make Kore well!

The old woman stands and scurries to the cave door. "You hail from Knossos?"

Kore nods, but Hecate does not notice because she keeps glancing at the cave opening.

The crone grimaces. "Yes? No?"

Kore begins to answer yes. She will say yes. The way she sizzles with fever, Kore's inclination is to admit everything. A sick child wants her mother.

"What is it?" the crone says, strangely impatient.

As the tears spring, her chest slices with burning pain, and she emits a hollow, unnatural cough. "M-my mother—"

The word *mother* ignites anguish. Crying floods the lungs with mucus. She coughs and gags.

"Yes?" Hecate prods.

The barking outside grows as frantic and quick as the blast of horns. Hecate pokes her head out the cave's opening and rushes back inside. The slate-gray robes brush against a smoothly worn ground of stone, dirtied with balls of dog hair and spilled herbs and stray, tumbling leaves. "Men are coming up the mountain."

"W-what?" Kore shrugs the furs off her body. Her arms are flimsy, and when she braces her hands against the pallet in an effort to sit up, her elbows buckle. The room grays and twirls again. Pain blares along her temple, and sparks of white float in her vision.

"Careful!" Hecate clicks her tongue and stoops over. Strong, gnarled hands, with their blue veins protruding on creped skin grasp at Kore's arms. Hecate lowers her back down. "These men are soldiers of Hades the Unseen. They are coming for you."

"B-but why?"

An orange dog darts inside the room. A speckled gray one follows close behind. Frenzied little heralds, they yap of an arrival.

"Listen to me," the crone hisses, voice thin. "Tell them to return you to Crete. Go back to where you came."

Kore wants to ask questions, and yet she is exhausted, muscles sore, and her eyes threaten to cross and close. In the past days, she has never been awake this long.

More ruckus from the dogs—both outside and inside—disturbs the usual quiet of Hecate's cave. When the hag crosses to the door, three hulking silhouettes block the sunlight at the entrance.

"Phlaxis," says Hecate, "who have you brought

here? More victims for me to cure?"

"These soldiers are from Asphodel."

In the far corner of the room, Kore peers at the shapes. They are nothing but silhouettes cut by the light of Helius. Two of them crane their heads to search around the room. Hecate's robed shape blocks their view.

"Ah. Welcome, guests. I am afraid this is a place for the infirm, and you are able-bodied. Especially you. My, my, your neck is as big around as my waist." The old woman swats the soldier on the rear.

The figure scrambles like an offended maiden. "Watch it, hag."

"Come outside, will you, where there is light?" she says, ushering them out. As if understanding an invisible command, the dogs bark and urge toward the legs of the men in an attempt to nudge them out. "Let an old woman see that handsome face of yours while we talk."

She manages to push the men outside the cave, and Kore's head rolls. She wants to stand, to run to the doorway and listen. She barely has the strength to remain conscious. Outside, masculine voices mingle with the ragged voice of Hecate. She disputes them. Kore can tell in the fluctuations of speech."

Kore's eyelids are bags of sand.

The insistence in Hecate's voice makes Kore's heart tick faster. She trusts the old woman. Being in her care prevents panic from rising, and panic could still triumph. Fear gallops inside her chest. Sweat trickles between her breasts and soaks the tunic she wears.

Beyond the cave, a male voice rises and lands hard, like a hammer chiseling marble.

The soldiers burst into the room, boots and armor jingling with each stomp. Behind them, dogs on her heels, Hecate yells, "She is not well enough. If you move her, she may not last."

The men charge at her, and she forces her arms to move, to shove the animal skins aside. Run. But she can hardly sit up.

As they rush toward her, mission-sent, the two men come into focus. Soldiers in tunics and bronze breastplates. Apart from their height, they could pass as the same man, identical with their full beards and large crooked noses and spindly eyebrows. They stop at the foot of her pallet.

The crone harps, "Send her back to Knossos—"

The tall one interrupts, "We follow orders from Hades, High King of Erebus—"

"Make sure she gets back to her mother—!"

Playing out in Kore's mind: the sunny face of a woman, cheeks long and soft, skin as golden as her hair. She smiles. A tiny finger—Kore's own finger—traces the few moles on her neck. She feels her mother's small breasts like cushions against her ear and relaxes upon the soft lap of a woman with wide birthing hips.

Mother.

As if in real time, memories flash. Her mother's

voice, stronger than the muscles of any man in Crete, invoking the goddess in prayer. Her chin points to the sky. Slender, outstretched arms lift slowly along her sides. A snake writhes from each hand, tongues flicking at the heavens as their bodies coil around her mother's arms. Fire blazes and sparks on the altar.

Hard arms slide under her legs and around her waist. Her head falls back. The room turns upside down and vanishes as her eyelids shut.

The barking multiplies and echoes off the cave walls. Her body shifts heavily inside capable arms, jostling with each step.

Hecate yells, "It is not safe to take her, you empty-headed brutes!"

Kore blacks out and revives when her body lands on wood. Her fingers touch smooth flooring, cheek cooled by its glossy surface. The surface jiggles roughly under her hips and ribs, and Kore lies facing the backs of men's knees, the brass of sandaled boots reaching high along knotted calf muscles. They stand before her with elbows bent, holding reigns that jangle with the flick of metal-cuffed wrists.

"Not safe."

A vision floods her mind—the flash of a gilded chariot rumbling out of a vent in the ground, fire-eyed horses pulling it out of the deep.

"Not safe."

She shakes violently.

She tries to say: *Who are you?*

She tries to force the words out: *Why are you taking me away?*

Throat and chest itching with the formation of these words, Kore breaks out in a fit of coughing. The wound on her head throbs in time with a frantic heart, the final thought of *"not safe"* dying in the quiet.

GIRLS WITH RIBBONS
2

For days, Demeter examines the dead.

The time for summer has passed. Soon comes harvest, where a constant nip hangs in the air while the sun burns bright. Wind blows crisp and continuous—a blessing. Any hotter, and the stench of sun-rotted flesh would be unbearable. Regardless, the citizens, the *damos*, burn incense to deter biting flies until the cart comes.

The front of the Knossos palace stands proud, supported by red columns and still displaying the mural of a charging bull. The east end of the building buckles into heaps of fallen timber and clay. Considering the majority of the polis fell under the rage of Gaia, the building seems spared by comparison.

Pulled from the rubble, unclaimed cadavers await the cart that comes to retrieve them for burial preparation. In front of the nearby temple, corpses line the steps in three rows. On the first row of steps, a dozen lay, covered, rigid and soaked through with blood. Demeter picks her way through them.

She lowers to one bent knee and lifts the corner of a woven blanket.

Short hair, matted with gore. A man whose face distorts from bloat. Blood-infused foam coats the lips and nostrils. Demeter drops the cloth and moves to the next.

"How much of this can you stomach?" says Ammon, playing the part of protective uncle. He is a respected priest, but today his role as her caretaker takes precedence. Though he raised her, Ammon never pretended to be a father. Instead, he trained her to be a strong model of piety for other priestesses.

"Come away from there." His hair reflects metallic silver, coarse and straight. While an increasing number of the *damos* search the city for Kore, her uncle Ammon accompanies her on this gruesome task. At the onset, the hub of the search centered around the house, Kore's most likely location on the day the polis collapsed. From there, the quest spread like a ripple from a stone's throw. By now, it widens beyond the polis and into farmland. Over forty search—and not one trace of her daughter.

Ammon cautions, "No one has been found alive in over a day."

Over the course of the last five days, Demeter has scoured countless bodies—twenty maidens, broken and bloodied. She distinguished them by their height, hair color, and body size. Freshly blossomed bodies, all dead and shriveled. They were daughters. Sisters. Many, as young as thirteen or fourteen, already wives. And she knows them, these faces from ceremonies and festivals—girls with ribbons in hair now streaked with gore and dirt.

The next heap emits a sharp, rotting smell from under the blanket. A young woman's hand pokes from one side, fingers stiff, white, and streaked with dried blood. Demeter kneels.

"On the morning Kore was born," she says absently, "I woke early to pains. I knew I should tell you it was time. I knew you would summon the midwife and the other priestesses, and I would give birth inside the temple, as comfortable as I could be."

Covering her nose with her shawl, she plucks the blanket and peels it aside with reluctant fingers. Flies swarm. "I wandered instead to the wheat field. I crouched down, with no one to tend to me, with no one to comfort me, and I bore down for an eternity."

Underneath the blanket, half of a woman's head is pulverized into a mess of crushed skull. Demeter has never seen what rests inside a person's head—clumped gray matter intermixed with bone; red cords connected to what appears to be the remnants of an eyeball, popped like a white grape.

Demeter notices the slave's tunic before turning her head and dry heaving onto the steps.

Not Kore. Praise to the gods.

Ammon winces, remembering the day of Kore's birth. Farmers alerted him that day. The niece he had helped raise was found cradling a squawking baby in the middle of the field.

Hers had been a family of farmers, abundant with crops of emmer wheat, barley, poppies, and corn. As farmers, they had prospered. As mortals, they failed when a fever swept through Knossos. Demeter and her elder sister, Hestia, bested the sickness. The difference in their ages called for different solutions. Hestia dedicated herself to the gods and joined a cult in Attica, where she remains to this day. But at seven, Demeter landed in the care of her uncle, a holy man of esteem. Thus, the land of wheat and barley became shared land of the Knossian priesthood. Wheat and barley from Demeter's fields are still used in ceremonial baskets, to stock the temples, and also to produce kykeon for religious ceremonies.

To these fields, she had returned to birth her child. When they had brought her back to the temple, Ammon slapped her clear across the face and hugged her tearfully before the sting of the blow dissipated.

Recalling it, Demeter murmurs, "I pulled her from my womb with my own two hands, and I nursed her in the field, both of us lying in the wide open, alone. Birth is an intimate thing. As intimate as coupling. As intimate as dying."

"You could have died on your own with no one to help you. You were foolish, Doso." Ammon frowns, using her birth name as a reminder of his wisdom over hers. She has not been called this in over a decade, when she had been named High Priestess and became *De-meter*, The Mother. The reference to her old self makes her fists clench.

"Let me search the bodies for you," her uncle prods. He squeezes her stooped shoulder. "Your Kore is not difficult to recognize."

The words are loaded with the things he does not say. Kore is easy to spot. He speaks first of hair like honey, sweeping her waist with streaks of sun-gold, like her mother's. He refers to her shape, plump in the places men desire and sleek around the ankles and waist and neck, the clear skin of a goddess, lips indecent. Many girls are beautiful, and yet this is not Kore's burden. Kore is desirable in a way that cuts to the quick.

"When I brought her into this world, it was only her and me," she says. "And when it comes time to usher her out, it should be her and me."

"I will not leave you to this massacre," he insists. "This is a man's job. You should be at home, awaiting news from those of us who can stomach this."

"Have you been listening?" Demeter hisses. "She is *my* child. This is no one's job but mine."

Where are you, little ghost?

A hiccup springs from her throat, bringing a

flood of tears. Surely, she has cried them all away by now. But no, there are more, pouring out of her like a steaming geyser. It is as though Kore vanished, taken up by the gods before she could be smashed by tumbling stone.

Where can my little ghost be?

"We fought," Demeter weeps, cheeks aching from the contortion of grief. "The night before."

In service to the gods, she and Ammon have spent over two decades together. For most of her life, she regarded Ammon as an ally, but lately, they quarrel often. About Kore. Now, he sounds like everyone else, offering unsolicited opinions whenever he feels like it.

"How many are there?" he asked her once. "I see young men tossing apples at her feet when she leaves the house. How many suitors have you turned away?"

Now, he reassures her. "Kore knows you love her. There is not a person on this island who does not."

She weeps, not certain anymore. All of Ammon's scoldings were warranted.

"Being a virgin priestess is a condemnation, Demeter. Every woman wants to be a mother. What do you punish her for?"

Demeter turns away her daughter's suitors all the time. And each year, the number grows. Men, approaching her after ceremonies. Men, bolder as her daughter blooms into riper age.

Men, coming from overseas to claim her.

Chastity holds little virtue for girls old enough to lose it. There is virtue in being fruitful, which prompts Ammon to tell her frequently:

"The purpose of leading a procession is to be presented as marriageable."

Demeter boils at the idea. How dare he treat the procession as a bride market! Theirs is a holy craft and a testament to the gods. When the gods are happy, the land will nourish and protect the people. Being a virgin priestess holds the highest honor among the gods. With this commitment, Kore sacrifices her future children, slaying them before they are born, a service to the immortal divine, who allow their people to thrive with bountiful health and harvests.

If more girls would make such an oath, Gaia might not rage so much.

What Ammon says is true. If "punished" to this fate of holiness, there was no point, in Kore's opinion, of leading a procession at all. And she simply did not attend, not that day.

Demeter bends over the next body. As time passes, the job becomes worse, the bodies in greater decay, the odor high enough to make her gag. She lifts part of the blanket and Ammon says, "Demeter—"

"Please, leave me to do as—"

"Demeter."

She spins on him. "Leave me, Ammon!"

Ammon regards the pathway, cleared amid the rubble. People trickle toward them. She recognizes them, two priests leading the way with a group of male slaves and one of the aged priestesses who presides over burial. Earlier, they were among the first to set out in search of Kore, torches raised as they pushed their way to the ports of Amnisos.

The priests whisper, heads bent toward each other and chins lowered.

Ammon turns his head to a different path. Another group of *damos* approaches.

"Why are all of you back?" Demeter demands. "There is still daylight."

Ammon steps forward to greet the other priests and asks the question to which the *damos* clearly have an answer.

"Where is she?"

CERBERUS

3

The night is lustrous with stars sprayed across a blue-black sky. Kore's shoulders and hips ache against the wooden chariot interior. Her head lolls to the side.

Underneath, wheels spin and jar her in place. The gallop of horses thunders in her ears.

Intermixed with the clomping of hooves, a gruff voice arises: "Can wrap those lips around my fat cock—"

The horses whinny and, through it, another voice: "Zapped by the bolts of Zeus—"

Awareness returns like an unwelcome guest.

"These men are soldiers of Hades the Unseen. They are coming for you."

A shock wave of panic courses through her. Kore shifts her weight. Her right arm is numb. When she stirs, the blood flows again, sending tingles of life through an otherwise dead limb. The air is damp with the faintest scent of ocean, and a river rushes nearby. White clouds stream from her mouth.

In her mind, she sees the sunny face of her mother and hears her warning:

"Keep to me, Kore. I will not let them hurt you."

The chariot hugs the face of a mountain wall. To their right, the river snakes through the canyon. The mountain range narrows and siphons the wind. Gusts funnel between trees and rock and blow without ceasing, pitching the chariot to and fro. Leafy branches gyrate overhead.

The canyon grows lighter. The moon is not full enough for such a glow. The glow comes from the road ahead. Arms shaking, Kore uses all her strength to push herself up. Animal skins fall from her shoulders, exposing them to the crisp night.

Before them, blocking farther entrance into the canyon, are three beastly heads, side by side.

Monsters. These heads are grander and taller than any palace. In their facades, hivelike crevices hold torches.

No. They are not monsters but monoliths, shaped like the heads of grisly dogs. Flaming craters illuminate each, as if fur and skin have rotted away, exposing bone and stretched tendon.

"Cerberus ahead," calls one of the soldiers.

One monolith appears to burst from the mountain on their left. It howls at the night sky with eye sockets ablaze.

The one in the center opens a shining yellow mouth that gulps a dwindling river.

The third monolith bares frightful teeth. A calcite tongue extends to form a bridge for the road on which they travel and swallows the chariot into its tunneled throat.

THE NEW NAME
4

The sun draws a clear boundary between time spent in court and time outside it. And the sun set long ago.

Regardless, on the other side of the door, Judge Aeacus says, "You need to hear this."

Hades pants, waiting for the pain to fade into a dull ache. Fire roars up his neck, down his shoulder, and to the tips of his fingers. To keep it from freezing, he stretches his shoulder to the limit until nothing exists except for the sensation of scar tissue ripped apart, a pulsing reminder of his failure in Pylos.

Cold sweat trickles down a bare chest, creating streams through a forest of hair. Tonight, he is crankier than usual and wants to be left alone. Once the day in court is over, everyone sees the last of him. While the judges indulge in their fun after night falls, dressing it up with a few words of philosophy as to disguise the boozing and fucking as an intellectual, aristocratic throng, Hades retreats to the solitude of his quarters.

He likes it that way.

Aeacus gestures for the High King to get dressed, and repeats, "You need to hear this."

The last time Aeacus spoke those words, Hades was twenty years younger. Aeacus had led Hades into the courtyard, surprising him with the unsolicited appearance of Poseidon, prince of the Cyclades, and a smirking, oddly-at-ease character with a wild tuft of curly brown hair and a rascality dancing in his eyes. Poseidon had hitched his thumb at the man.

"Meet Zeus. Our brother."

This man, this *Zeus*, whom Hades had never seen before in his life, clapped him on the back and slung an arm around Poseidon's neck, saying:

"Just wait. I am going to be the best friend you ever had."

Decades later, Aeacus appears stooped and diminished by time's passage. His eyes flash inside the swollen flaps of skin on his upper lids, as loose and weathered as the bags beneath them.

"Am I going to like whatever this is?"

With a little frown, Aeacus says, "It is not as good as the last surprise, if that is what you mean."

"The last one got us ten years of war."

"And it resulted in your ruling of all the south."

Hades shuts the door in Aeacus's face. A few minutes later, he emerges clothed to find Aeacus leaning against the wall opposite the door, arms folded patiently in front of him.

The old judge fixes his stare at Proí, the mastiff standing guard to the right of the door. This is a game they play while Aeacus waits. Who will divert his gaze first? The great creature stares back at the old man. A fleck of pink mars his snout. This subtle marker differentiates Proí from his brothers.

Aeacus breaks his gaze. "This way." He tosses a bit of raw lamb to each of the three dogs. Large tongues retrieve the offerings from an otherwise pristine floor.

The upper northeast corridor travels from the royal apartment into other wings of the palace, putting an acceptable distance between Hades and the judges who sleep in the upper northwest quarter, as relatives might dwell in the house of kin.

At this time of night, the enormous bull mastiffs remain to guard the corridors. They are silent guards. To intruders, they give no warning. Their attack catches victims unaware. Unlike humans, these animals do not march or jangle their armor while keeping watch. And unlike with human guards, the enemy does not realize he is being attacked until he hits the floor.

"Before you *do what you do*," Aeacus cautions, "keep in mind this man comes to you seeking restitution."

"What for?"

"A terrible crime," Aeacus assures.

There are rules about this. Judicial matters require all three judges, and yet Aeacus violates the rule intentionally. When it comes to Aeacus, Hades forgives much. It is hard not to forgive a man who taught him how to be a man himself. During his younger days, Hades had revered him as all-knowing and wise. To an extent, a man is blind to the faults of a mentor. The cure for such blindness is time and exposure. Time reveals the fallibility of men, including those once worshipped as heroes.

"This is a matter for court."

Aeacus continues, "All men have sinned. Whatever offenses he may have committed, they are not at issue. He is not here to stand in judgment."

"Is that so?"

"When you hear what he has to say, you will understand."

Within the corridor, one torch lends enough fire to light the way to the next.

This is how kings die. They follow trusted advisers and find an ambush waiting.

Aeacus is more than a trusted adviser. Had his father never appointed Aeacus as his mentor, ten-year-old Hades would have grown to be a different man. The cuckold king who raised him kept up the fatherly charade, clapping his boy on the back in public and bludgeoning him with his fists in private.

But there was no denying Hades bore an odd resemblance to Cronus of Olympus, who had visited the polis of Asphodel once and whose visit correlated with the queen's pregnancy.

Raising another man's son produces resentment that breeds brutality. Of this, Hades is aware. It was Aeacus who saved him from the same fate as his mother.

Following the wizened judge, Hades observes the light around Aeacus. This glow radiates from all beings. It is that prickly current existing between two blankets pulled apart in winter. It is the fuzzy sensation between nearly touching palms. This indefinable charge is invisible to men—often felt, not seen.

In order to perceive the faint luster of red radiating from around the man's shoulders and head, Hades needs to do nothing. He spends no energy there, reads it as part of the language of the body. Without focusing, he takes it in as most people take for granted the shadows on the ground, accepting them as an extension of the body itself. His sight registers:

Sharp red, redder, faint yellow.

The colors slip through a filter in his mind, and a word bubbles up:

Excited.

This field emanates from people, from objects, from elements. When Hades blurs his eyes for a moment, colors swell where they are most highly charged. Mixed with the right palette, the emanations offer malice. Guilt. Shame. And when he pushes, he can home in on the root of them.

This is what Aeacus refers to when he stops at the entrance to the megaron, "Go easy on him. He has a story to tell."

They enter the rectangular hall, surrounded by four columns carved into figures of skeletal soldiers holding spears next to their marble-boned, armored bodies. In the center, a round hearth smolders with red-orange cinders. Smoke twirls upward. The south wall is not a wall but open to a sky with a thousand stars and to the sounds of night—of trilling cicadas and waves exploding against the cliffs. The sharp autumn breeze sweeps through the open two-columned porch, fanning hearth-born smoke into reckless spirals of whitish gray.

The man in front of the hearth gazes into the embers.

Flat, lifeless yellow orange.

Dishonor.

The man turns, face long and narrow without being gaunt. A large, porous nose hooks over a white mustache, ears poking out on each side of his head like handles on a jug. His burgundy himation is lined with gold thread, draped elegantly over his shoulders to keep him warm in the cold, open breeze.

Creon.

For a moment, Creon stands frozen, as if grabbed by the throat. He bends down, wincing as he presses a brittle knee to the floor.

"Creon, regent of Thebes," Hades acknowledges.

Creon gawks at him. "My God," he whispers.

"Not yet."

"It is you. The Unseen . . ."

The old judge slaps the side of his leg twice and clicks his tongue at Cerberus near the door. The mastiffs sit upright, severe and menacing until Aeacus calls for them. Once summoned, they patter to him. Aeacus sits next to the hearth and feeds them bits of meat.

Creon murmurs, "I never imagined I would stand before your throne."

"You are not standing before my throne. If you were, you would be charged with refusing burial rites for two hundred seventeen men, including your own nephew."

Creon struggles to stand. He braces his hands on his thighs and pulls himself off the floor with his shoulders turned in on themselves, as if shrinking back without taking a step. "They were the enemy."

Aeacus groans at Creon's ignorance.

"Does the law indicate all men warrant a lawful burial unless they are the enemy?"

"No—"

"All men."

"Please allow—"

"You left them to rot on the battlefield. That is defilement. You poisoned the land."

Creon throws a helpless expression to Aeacus, who no longer tries to feign obscurity. He opens his mouth as if to ameliorate. Instead, he tells Creon, "You might as well take your beating. You were never going to get out of it."

This information, Hades gleans from pressing into the glow. He peers at Creon from the corner of his eye, flipping through the colors like leaves disturbed from their pile. This visceral process is hard to shut off. Aeacus should know better.

Hades pushes into the dimming, sickly shade of yellow that turns a decayed green.

Dead.

The story of Creon, written in the field around him. Creon, brother of the famed Jocasta, the woman married to her own son—Oedipus. Together, mother and son produced two boys. When Oedipus abdicated the throne over charges of patricide, regicide, and incest, his boys fought each other for it.

Hades recalls reports of two boy kings trying to share a rule like they might share a blanket. It was doomed to fail. Inevitably, one of them no longer wanted to share, and they went to battle.

Maybe all brothers eventually do.

They killed each other that way, in battle over the same sorry piece of land that would become tainted by the unrested spirits of two hundred seventeen slain soldiers. Thebes was planted high in northeastern soil ruled by Zeus, but the law of Hades abides across the terrain of all three territories. As Hades adopted Zeus's law of *xenia*, so, too, did his brothers adopt the law of sacred burial. Thus, it must be upheld by all.

Creon's eyes pool with pink tears, unable to

move from the sidelong scrutiny of the Unseen.

"The nephew you favored in battle was blessed and buried, as per the law. And the other? The one you disliked? What came of him?"

Creon recoils at the newfound pain in his temple and wipes his eyes. Blood streaks his flaccid cheeks like war paint. The regent of Thebes gasps when he finds it on his hands. Around him, all emanations turn yellow in various, muddy shades.

Aeacus smirks. The meaty treats are gone. The mastiffs no longer care to sit beside him. Instead, they circle the legs of Creon in a single turn, as sharks might circle prey. Creon freezes, his irises the only parts of him brave enough to move.

"You thought you could get away with letting him rot alongside the Argive soldiers on the battlefield."

"I was angry he betrayed his people by bringing in the Argives to fight on his behalf," Creon implores. "He fought as if his own countrymen were the enemy. He teamed up with outsiders, killed soldiers he grew up alongside. Slew them over lust for power!"

"What Polynices did," Hades says, "is irrelevant. He is not here. You are."

Feverish, sniffling, Creon says, "I was wrong. I admit it. I relinquished the bodies to the families who begged for them. Every last one of those two hundred men were sent back."

"Two hundred seventeen," Hades corrects.

"I complied with your wise law. Please, I beg you. I repent."

Hades says, "Judge of Erebus, tell the regent of Thebes what lies under the ground."

Aeacus gives a look of shrewd understanding. "Tombs."

Creon wipes bloody hands on the elegant himation he wears.

"A thousand years ago," Aeacus continues, "elaborate underground caves were used as burial tombs by the natives."

Creon squints at the floor. "Under this palace?"

"There was no palace a thousand years ago," Aeacus says. "They say Gaia is in an uproar these days. They say she has chosen now to revolt. But the earth goes through periods of unrest. A thousand years ago, the earth shook as violently as ever before, and the caves collapsed."

Creon's brow furrows. "How can you be sure?"

"Back then," Hades says through gritted teeth, "people respected the dead."

"They paid homage, honored them with gifts and prayers." Aeacus adds, "They slept beside their deceased. Every night."

Creon searches the face of Aeacus. "Why do you tell me this?"

"When the caves collapsed, the mourners were crushed," Aeacus explains. "Smothered. Others died after many days without food or water. Imagine that. Trapped underground without a trace of light, with the dead, knowing you are soon to join them in the afterworld."

"Terrifying," Creon agrees.

"How many bodies do you think are beneath us?" Hades mutters.

Creon glances to Aeacus. He fears answering incorrectly and hopes for a hint in Aeacus's face. Creon shakes his head and hesitates. "How many?"

The smile that creeps upon Aeacus's face reminds Hades that the old judge still finds pleasure in watching people squirm. While loyal, he is by no means magnanimous.

"A few hundred," Aeacus answers. "Roughly the same number you let rot on that field."

Embers crackle. The man is waiting for the relevance. But part of his punishment is not knowing. Ambiguity.

"Tell me," the High King asks, "why do you come to me now?"

At those words, the hues radiating from Creon turn to blue with red flares. The regent's eyes are already shot with blood—Hades does not care. When he presses into the colorful field surrounding him, he pays no attention to the vessels firing inside Creon's eyes.

Hades pries into the blue.

Sorrow.

He follows the shade of red.

Vengeance.

He sees large, muscular hands squeezing the

neck of a woman. Those same hands crush the
windpipes of children, and their small, bewildered
faces issue betrayal. The strangling hands are
attached to veined forearms the size of melons.
They flow into thickly muscled arms and hulking
shoulders. When Hades glimpses the face of the
murderer—this monster who strangled his wife and
sons—his body bursts with a sudden sweat.

"Surely, you will not help me. Not after
what I did." Creon, the old regent, babbles. "My
daughter, Megara, and my four grandsons have been
brutally murdered. The man who killed them goes
unpunished."

Hades looks to Aeacus. Aeacus looks back, as
if to say, *You see?*

"My sweet Meg." He weeps. "Killed by her
own husband. The father of her children. A man I
trusted with all my soul."

To his suffering, the High King holds no pity.
Hades understands the balance involved in the
regent's lament. Nature specializes in polarity.
Creon's treatment of his unfavored nephew
inadvertently caused the suicide of his niece,
Antigone. Not long after, Creon's own daughter
was murdered, with the heads of his four grandsons
acting as a sort of taxation on what his past actions
had caused. Sowing and reaping is not lost on Hades.
He spends his life making certain it happens in one
way or another.

"Who was this man?" Hades knows but yearns

to hear the name spoken aloud.

Creon answers, "As a boy, he was my pupil, and I, his mentor. We spent years together, and I trained him well. Naturally, when my daughter was old enough to marry, who better to marry her than this man whom I already treated as a son? He came from the highest possible lineage. He was strong, a valiant warrior."

"This weasel should stand before the throne of Hades," Aeacus goads.

"Yes!" Creon chokes on snot and bloody tears. "It is law for such offenses!"

"Where is this man now?" Hades asks.

Creon still crouches on the ground, broken and cowering. He rolls onto his hip and sits, arms hugging his knees, head hanging from exhaustion. The front of his tunic is stained a faint red. "Zeus sent him to Tiryns, to be sentenced by King Eurystheus."

Aeacus croaks an amphibious laugh. He finds humor in the absurdity of the whole thing. King Eury of Tiryns is known for what they call "spectacle sentencing." With Zeus and his own tendencies for showmanship, Hades is not surprised his brother selected this particular king to carry out "justice." To please the citizens with elaborate, morally founded entertainment, King Eury doles out the most asinine punishments around.

Proving this, Creon explains, "He is being given feats of strength. If he succeeds at them, he is absolved. This punishment is an insult to the lives of my daughter and grandsons."

"You did the right thing," Aeacus assures. "The High King takes special interest in matters of unrequited justice. He can demand restitution for your family."

The old regent presses his forehead to the floor. "Thank you."

"It is a long journey back to Thebes. Judge Aeacus will find a place for you to settle."

Aeacus nods once.

Creon picks himself off the floor. His head hangs low, chin to chest. Aeacus places one hand on the man's back as he ushers him out of the megaron.

At the door, Creon says, "Wait." He turns to Hades. "His name. I never told you."

Hades says it for him. "Alcides."

Creon falters. "Yes. You know him as Alcides. But these feats will grant him a new name, a fresh identity with which to build a more honorable life. Zeus already refers to him by it."

Aeacus asks, "What name is this?"

And Creon tells him:

"Heracles."

UNDERWORLD

5

The regent descends lower than he expects. This makes him nervous.

When Aeacus tells him, "You will stay in the lowest southwest quarter," Creon does not anticipate this many stairs, spiraling into an oblivion even torches fail to light.

Exhausted, Creon follows. "I am indebted to His Majesty." Bloodshot eyes squint in a futile attempt to see better. Although Creon has no idea, they will never again work as sharply. The world, blurrier for the rest of his days.

For decades, Aeacus has observed the aftermath of Hades's "insight." The first time occurred before they were formally acquainted. In those days, Aeacus had been king of the island Oenone. As a matter of fact, all of the judges had been kings, though people tend to think Minos was the only one. He snorts when men accidentally refer to the judge as "King Minos."

Aeacus chalks it up to time. Separating the rule of Minos and the rule of Aeacus? Years. The more years elapse, the more your old identity wears out like old sandals. For Minos, four years have passed since being stripped of the throne. For Aeacus, decades.

Adopting Hades as his ward was never his heart's desire. Aeacus did it as a favor. Nonius, the cuckold king of Asphodel, hated the boy and wanted Hades out of his sight. The man who took him off his hands would be rewarded. Believing Nonius would help him reclaim his throne, Aeacus begrudgingly agreed.

He could have selected from a hundred boys to train under his hand. As a boy, Hades was an odd little brooder. Scarcely speaking. Often absent.

Their first encounter—an evening meal among nobles and kings. Earlier that day, the queen of Asphodel had been burned on a funeral pyre, and the dinner that followed had a solemn air to it. Hades glowered at his plate while his father explained to a table of aristocracy his poor wife died of illness, leaving him without a queen.

Aeacus found himself glancing to the corner where Hades sat, fuming, glaring at an imposter father with total hatred.

No, the queen of Asphodel did not die of pox, as Nonius insisted. Her skull had been crushed by a husband's violent hand.

As Nonius peppered the air with lies, his eyes began to water. They grew red. He attempted to blink the sting away. Instead, a bead of crimson formed in the innermost corner of his eye.

Plunk went the bead. Splat went the blood against the table. Nonius excused himself, leaving the table of nobles agog.

And in the corner, Hades returned his gaze to his plate and resumed eating, the hatred in his face replaced with distress.

While others regarded him as strange and resigned, Aeacus suspected potential. Any mentor can work wonders with anger. It is perfect fuel.

With the right nudge, a silent boy of ten evolved into a vengeful boy of eleven.

And now—every interrogation and sentence, powered by the righteous anger of Hades. This includes the judgment of Creon, although the regent does not yet understand he is being punished.

Despite the presence of the mastiff at their sides.

Despite the sheer depths to which they are traversing.

The air grows cold and damp, flames brightening cragged walls that seem to glisten a sickly green. Leading the pack, a single guard lights the way with an upraised torch.

For Creon, two things provide solace as they commence this undeniable lowering into the earth.

First, the slave girls. With them, they carry olives, cheese, lentils, onion, salted fish, and loaves of bread. They carry grapes and apples. In this procession, there is enough food for half a dozen men, and Creon almost weeps from the generosity. Men are always shaky and drained and deliriously grateful after they crawl out from under the inspection of Hades.

Getting away from him is the biggest relief of their lives. Even when they are condemned.

Aeacus recalls his departed wife, Psamathe, and how she looked the day after one of their arguments. One night, he might have torn her apart with insults, belted her in the stomach until she could not draw a single breath. Then, the next day would come, and Aeacus would have gotten over his fury, whatever it had been about—and Psamathe would tremble with relief when she realized his mood had abated and the punishment concluded. For the next day, she would be depleted but giddy that the storm was over for a while.

Aeacus sees this in Creon. This time Aeacus is not the punisher. Simply the escort. With a pleasant and uncharacteristic, eye-twinkling smile, he accompanies the regent of Thebes, glad to show their guest to the finest quarters around.

Far beneath the palace, the walls reflect torchlight as a glassy ocean reflects moonlight. Their procession is lengthy:

Guard.

Mastiff.

Regent.

Judge.

Slave.

Slave.

In time, they reach the bottom. Creon glances around. The slave girls huddle close together. Already, the dog growls with keen animal perception, a perception both akin and inferior to that of the High King himself.

Without Aeacus, the dogs would not exist. Without Aeacus, the High King would never have been.

"What is his name?" These were the first words Hades ever spoke to Aeacus. Back then, Aeacus brought with him a hound. He needed to lure the reclusive boy.

"Cerberus."

Easy to seduce a child with a dog. To earn his trust.

Aeacus shudders with sinister delight. His spine prickles. On his arms and legs, silver hairs rise.

They arrive at a wide, circular dead end.

"I do not understand." Creon's voice is tinged with worry.

The guard steers them forward, toward a vertical depth in the wall. As they approach, Creon's face lights with realization. An unlit corridor.

"Understand," Aeacus says, placing a hand on the regent's shoulder, "we want you to be comfortable. This is by no means intended to torture you physically. You are regent of Thebes—

acting king of Thebes—and you will have the most comfortable living arrangements during your stay."

Guard and slave enter the corridor. The guard's torch lends visibility. Overhead, stalactites hang like spikes.

"Where have you taken me?" On instinct, as might any man walking into a trap, Creon turns as if to flee.

The guard needs do nothing but provide light. The dog takes care of Creon, blocking his escape with teeth bared.

"This?" Aeacus opens his arms, palms up. The narrow walls of the corridor reflect coldness on his outstretched fingers. "It does seem dismal, but on behalf of the caves of Tartarus, I guarantee your safety." He adds, "For self-inflicted harm, we are not accountable."

Lit by fire, the corridor glistens with mossy patches. Creon spots squatty, impenetrably thick doors spanning ahead on both sides. Ten doors total. Eight are occupied.

From behind one comes a muffled cry.

Creon turns to Aeacus. "Did you hear that?"

"No."

He did, of course. They all did. In answer, the mastiff lets out a single bark that echoes down the hall.

Then comes the banging. Men, suddenly alert to their presence, pounding on the insides of the wooden doors. Screaming:

"Help me!"

Screaming:

"I will comply!"

Creon blanches.

"I apologize for the noise," Aeacus says. "I hope they do not keep you awake."

"You promised me sanctuary if I came forward," Creon sputters.

"I did."

"You swore you would not tell him of my crimes!"

"I did not."

Behind the walls, men scream. Creon grows red in the face. "He knew everything!"

Aeacus grins. "He did."

The guard unlatches the door nearest them. He stoops to go inside and stops short after passing through, sliding the torch into a sconce on the wall.

Aeacus motions to the door. "Please. After you."

"Tell the regent of Thebes what lies under the ground."

The dog growls a warning at Creon's side.

They enter. Creon's face registers the certainty of the horror awaiting him. His eyes burn red and cheeks droop, and Aeacus can see the fuzz of his beard quivering. Creon expects a dungeon. Expects chains.

"Elaborate underground caves were used as burial tombs."

Inside, a beautiful red couch, piled high with cushions and fur and blankets to keep the most thin-skinned person warm. A wool rug covers the water-smoothed stone beneath their feet. In the back, there is a marble slab fashioned into a bench with a hole for pissing and shitting. A basin. The slaves unload goods onto the long table next to the door. Among the goods, several four-wick lamps are crafted of alabaster.

Other than the mossy, serrated cave walls, this could pass for any room in the palace.

Creon blinks rapidly. He wipes at the cold sweat on his face. "Why are those men screaming?"

"The High King believes in equity," Aeacus says. "You have done nothing for which to be beaten or starved or tortured. You have committed a crime against the land, and there is no better punishment than experiencing the aftermath of this crime."

"When the caves collapsed, the mourners were crushed."

He continues. "This is the best method of getting through to you, I am afraid. The torch will not burn long. Make good timing with the lamps."

A disembodied shadow passes along the wall and disappears as quickly as it came. The dog whines, thin and airy, in the back of his throat. Task complete, the slaves scurry from the room, tittering concern as they go. From behind the other doors, frazzled cries for help carry on and on, calling after the pattering feet of slaves in flight.

"Fear not. The cave will not collapse. It is secure. Rest. In time, I will come for you."

When Aeacus marches out into the corridor, the dog hurries after. The guard slams and bolts the heavy door with an iron bar. Behind him, fists beat in mad percussion, frantic as the clashing shields of the dancing Kouretes. And though this is the most satisfying part of his work, Aeacus cannot leave the lower northeast quarter fast enough.

No man comes this close to the underworld without a bit of his own soul sucked dry.

UNHOLY

6

Mother, I am lost.

No one ever tells her where she is. Why she is here. What will happen to her.

Of one thing Kore is certain: this is Not Olympus.

In Not Olympus, Kore finds herself alone for the first time. She has never been alone. Not like this, abandoned inside a vast, virtually empty room. There is the bed on which she convalesces. There is a table for a two-handled jug of water and a basin. A hearth. And there is a rectangular hole in the floor beneath an arched cove at the other side of the room.

Fever renders her prone to death. Her first night in Not Olympus, it soars high, and Kore wakes in a strange bed, cold and shivery and steeped in sweat.

Waking, Kore spots the dying blaze in the hearth.

A noise.

Grating and gritty, like the moving of a stone away from a tomb. Constant, unending. The hair inside her ears prickles—the noise is *close*! So close, Kore might believe the noise does not come from anywhere external at all; both the origin and destination rest inside her very ears.

Her heart cries out in terror. It is a sort of desperation her shaken, five-year-old self experienced when lost in the crowds at a ceremony. As people congregated after her mother completed prayers for harvest, Kore often discovered herself lost inside a forest of legs. How quickly the people of Knossos would crowd around her mother, thanking her and bestowing gifts. Kore would weave among the legs like tree trunks, people's willow-branch arms hanging at their sides.

Face flushed and tearful, Kore would push through the limbs, crying.

"Mother, where are you? I am lost!"

Of course, it was not so. She was not lost, simply drowned out by voices of praising men and women, turned invisible behind their shuffling legs and dangling arms. Her little heart beat like the wings of a caged bird.

"Here I am, little ghost."

Mother's hand would find her arm and scoop her up into a fleshy embrace. She would perch Kore onto a cocked hip that seemed the perfect place to sit with her knees clamped to her mother's waist and her arms wrapped around her shoulders so she could smell the pretty fragrance in the locks of Mother's hair. Curled around the one who nurtured her. Safe.

Even when afraid, she was safe with her mother.

As a child, she was scared all the time. The things she saw! The things she heard! They scared her because no one else could see or hear them, and it made Kore feel wrong, as if she were born with a faulty set of eyes and ears that were extra-sensitive like a dog's.

Yet Mother consoled her. "You have such an imagination, little ghost."

At first, Mother was sweet, ruffling the fine near-white baby hair that practically floated around her head. "The gods blessed you with a creative spirit!"

As Kore grew, the good humor in her mother's voice began to fade. Like the day the bull tore the man in half. Organs inside his body were suddenly outside of his body, on the dirt, being stamped by hooves. From their seats, Kore saw the sharp point of the bull's horn growing from the man's naked back, strings of red hanging from the horned tip like a flag.

The bronze of his skin peeled away from him like a shadow. What pulled away, this *color shadow,* formed a second man whose movements were fluid and light. The thing that remained attached to the bull, Kore did not understand. It was the man, but it was not the man. It was his *outside part.* Like a snake, his spirit had molted and left the remains of the man's outsides impaled by the bull.

But Mother told her, "That man is dead."

He was not! Kore told her so. After that, humor no longer sweetened her mother's voice when Kore pointed out the color shadows she spied during burials or at deathbeds or accidents.

"You have such an imagination."

This, her mother never said again. Instead, she said, "Shh, stop telling stories, Kore. The gods punish liars."

And now Kore is here, in this place without a name. Waiting for daytime to come and take away the fear that intensifies with night. She is scared and wants her mother—not the one who exists now, but the one who would ruffle her near-white baby hair and say, "The gods blessed you with a creative spirit!"

Mother of Then and Mother of Now, contrasted sharply against each other. How could they be the same woman?

When the sun rises, the slaves centipede into the room with pots on their heads. They pour water into the hole in the floor. Kore watches through half-closed lashes, stinking of sickness and sweat.

Sleep pulls her under, like a hand folding around the ankle of a swimmer. Kore resurfaces with a jerk of the legs. Two slaves remain in the room. They appear to be her mother's age in drab tunics belted at the waist.

She manages to say, "Where—?"

The taller slave draws near, opening her arms to help Kore up. "*Beni bekle.*" She speaks in hushed insistence, but Kore does not understand the tongue.

These strangers plan to bathe her. She protests but finds herself too tired to let out more than a whine. With arms made strong by years of servitude, the slaves hoist her from the bed and into shock-cold water. Her chest heaves. The water hurts her very bones. They bathe her, shivering, in perfumed oils of violet and lily.

Throughout the torture of bathing, they change the bandage on her head. Afterward, they deposit her onto fresh-lain blankets and leave her alone again.

Her teeth rattle, and the fever remains.

Mother, I am lost—help me!

She thinks it, but Kore does not say it. There is no one to say it to. That mother is gone, replaced by one who will strangle her if she gets a chance. Especially now that Kore has run away.

"Your father might have better understood you."

He might. Kore clings to this. It is all she has—the promise of a father who will see her stubbornness for bravery and her peculiarity as distinction. So, she rests and waits and longs for a mother who can no longer hear her crying that she is lost.

Night two, a grating noise shocks her awake. Louder tonight than the previous one. Stone scrapes the ground, rumbling and crackling. Kore sits upright, forgetting the sickness until the muscles in her arms and legs remind her. The wound on her head itches and stings. Rain patters against closed shutters, and Kore peers at them.

Delicate ankles slip from under the covers. The floor is cold underfoot. Kore stands and takes five quick steps to the window. She presses it open. Flecks of rain kiss her scalding face. Kore expects to see men pushing rock against the gravel path.

Obsidian walls stretch from side to side and below. Torches flicker and hiss at the gentle touch of rain. Far below, the stone path is empty save for two enormous dogs. Kore leans against the side of the window and lifts her face to the cool drizzle.

Behind her, a man says, *"Deliver me."*

Kore turns. The dead man stands close, like a friend might stand close when telling a secret. He is two heads taller than Kore with a flat face and flat nose and tidy beard. His eyes are white pinpoints.

"She threw my body in the square!"

The room grays in and out. Shaking violently, Kore rushes to the bed, collapses, and rolls over to stars dancing in her vision. She fumbles for the blankets.

The shade warns, *"He is coming. No—He is here."*

Looming over her bedside, an inhumanly tall shape. Its arms are twice the size and length of a regular man's. The shape is pure black, featureless.

"Unholy," Kore whispers. A hot tear streams from one eye. She will faint and the demon will gobble her up.

The arm reaches for her. Kore blanches. Wheezing burns her chest. She cannot muster a scream.

The hand touches the center of her chest. She thinks of a stream's cold, flooding water as it rushes over hot legs. The same coldness washes through her chest and floods her limbs and extinguishes the fire that keeps her sick.

In the morning, Kore wakes in a puddle of her own sweat.

The fever is gone.

BRAVE ENOUGH

7

"A few men say she boarded a trade ship to Pylos."

Her cheeks flush. Demeter glances at the citizens who gather around her in a circle.

They all judge her. It is in the faces of men and women and children, weary from days of laborious searching. Their backs and legs and feet ache. They are hungry. Many still mourn their own losses and put their grief aside to help their High Priestess. Now the search is over, and the time they spent no doubt feels wasted on someone who cannot be found. Behind their downcast faces and crinkled brows, the crowd studies her, as if to say:

Why did Kore get on that ship?

What would cause your own daughter to cross an ocean to get away from you?

With the sun slipping behind the horizon and the sky bruised with pink and purple, Demeter's eyes

dance along the faces of the people. Heat rushes up
her body in a tidal wave of embarrassment. It never
occurred to her Kore could muster the will and
stupidity to do such a thing. How could she imagine
the child who hid behind her skirts could be brave
enough? And a *trade* ship, no less! Demeter's nails
dig crescents into her palms from squeezing tight.
She presses her fists into her stomach as if she were
kicked. Kore makes her seem like a tyrant and a fool
in front of these people. Her uncle Ammon's cheeks
are flushed. He is embarrassed *for* her.

As the noises of the city fade under a light
buzzing in her ears, a sudden giddiness arises.

"She is safe?"

"Perhaps," the priest, Theoklés, hesitates. "Men
at the port say they saw the captain pulling a girl
onto the ship at dawn that day."

That word. *Pulling*. Demeter will never admit
to being relieved he used it. It implies force. And
that would be terrible, just terrible. All the same, it
soothes her it is not judgment in their faces, after all.
No. They are frightened for her daughter, and they
should be!

"She was *taken*?"

"Well—" says Theoklés.

"Someone took my child?"

"They say she looked eager to board."

Vehement, she shakes her head. "Nonsense!
My Kore would *never*!"

But Demeter knows what he is thinking. What

all of them think.

Why would she be in Amnisos at such an hour?
Why would she be in Amnisos at all?

At the back of the crowd, people disperse. They take the time to squeeze her arm with encouragement; however, the collective decision appears to be the same.

The matter is closed. Kore does not lie dead beneath a fallen city. The *damos* disappear from the square in front of the temple. As they slip away, it is like watching a life rope slip away.

Have they not heard what Theoklés said? A man absconded with her child! Perhaps she was taken from her own bed. Kore must have been terrified, screaming all the way! But if this were so, why did Demeter hear nothing? Nor Asli. At the most silent part of the night, they surely would have. In the guilty recesses of her mind, the question repeats:

Why would she be in Amnisos?

The timing of it mounts like a sickening puzzle. It takes hours to get there on foot. If Kore sailed at dawn, she would have needed to leave home earlier than Demeter that morning. By the time Asli summoned her to bless the baby of Lyris, Kore was already floating away.

Demeter shivers and clutches the cloak around her. Her ears ring. She blinks around at Ammon, at the donkey-drawn cart that comes to carry the dead. From the constant clearing and shuffling of rubble, dust still floats in the air. The muscles in her legs shake.

"I left," she explains, "and never tried to wake her. I never saw her."

Ammon takes her by the arm and tells her to come. It is late, and he will take her home. Feet shuffling, she allows him to steer her.

Home. It mocks her. The entire city is demolished, and yet her own home stands untouched. She and Kore dwell outside the temple with eight other priestly homes built close enough together to practically adjoin.

Of the eight homes, seven collapsed as if crushed under the foot of a giant. Roofs caved in. Rooms exposed. Uninhabitable.

In comparison, her own home appears obscene. It is small and simple with white stone and a clay-tiled roof impervious to shaking. The frames around the windows hold strong. The gods chose to spare the home of the High Priestess. Spare in the vainest of ways.

Inside the courtyard, the well is whole and brings forth clear water. The loom stands undisturbed next to the wall by the door, and a few errant threads dance in the light breeze.

Arm around her shoulders, Ammon escorts her into the kitchen where Asli heats water over a flaming hearth. Wiping her hands on her tunic, she startles to see Demeter like this. Stricken and pale and clutching her stomach.

Asli freezes. Waits. Fearing they found Kore

among those bodies. Demeter shakes her head. Asli relaxes.

"I have drawn you a bath. The dust is awful in the polis." She reaches for the pot of heated water on the ground. It takes several of those to fill a tub, lugged by the arms of a young girl as solid and strong as the house itself.

A dry lump collects at the base of her throat.

Ammon takes the pot from Asli. "Let me."

Together, priest and slave leave the room. Their muffled, secretive voices intermingle in the courtyard. Talking about her. Talking about what became of Kore.

Where are you, little ghost?

She is alive. It is all right. Kore is alive, and this is what matters.

Her hands splay across her belly. She hates the flatness of it. Empty like this room, this house, this life. After Kore was born, she would gaze at the beautiful infant asleep in her basket, and Demeter could not stand it. How strange to *miss* pregnancy. The slow rolling of an elbow across the inside of her womb. The straightening of a leg and the lump of a foot through stretched skin. Without the life inside of her, she felt devoid of part of herself. Part of herself had split and formed this independent being all of her own.

During those postchildbirth longings, Demeter had to scoop Kore up and feel the warmth of the tiny bundle against her breast, smelling the newness of her soft downy scalp and warming her lips with the heat of baby skin. The emptiness, otherwise, might kill her.

But it was never as empty as now.

She was never as alone as she is now.

Demeter glances around. The perfection of unbroken pots. Bronze cups polished high. Baskets full of fruit and eggs and wheat.

Possessions are intact. The gods spared their High Priestess these *things*. To the outside eye, it appears she lost nothing. The first sob erupts and another and another.

Demeter snatches a bronze pan by its tubed handle and hurls it against the wall, smashing a hole into the fresco of running bulls. In the center of the head of a bull, a crater of crumbling stone. The destruction drives her. Weeping, she sends a jug flying. It explodes next to the door. She grabs anything in reach: a pot, a plate, wooden utensils. Demolishing and feeling relief. Destroying everything in sight while screaming inside the emptiness. Apples tumble and roll across the floor. Hands like claws, ripping wheat from its basket and tearing at it, tearing as she wants to tear her own hair, and she does—she sobs and moans, ripping at her hair in raw pain. Clumps of yellow hang from her fingers, mixing with the wheat.

Demeter scratches at the skin on her arms, the chaos a mirror of what her world has become.

Hands grasp her arms. "Priestess!"

Heaving, Demeter surveys the kitchen, a mess that should have been caused the day the earth opened. She wails, and the shame sinks in.

"Priestess, be still. Please, please be still . . ."

Demeter clutches the girl by the arms, pulls her in, and squeezes the slave girl in a death grip. Together they weep, and Asli's hair is slick against Demeter's hands. She rests her nose on top of Asli's head, smelling her like she smelled the scalp of a newborn long ago. Asli is afraid to embrace her in return—not like Kore, who is loving and full of affection.

"She went to Pylos," Demeter mutters into the part of the girl's hair, "so I will go to Pylos."

"But there has not been a boat at port since the waves destroyed it."

It is true. Most of the naval fleet Minos built in his formative years, the impressive rows of ships lining the port of Knossos, were destroyed, if not damaged and inoperable. Ocean travel ceased the day Kore left.

There must be a way. She will swim, ride the back of a whale—fly, if she must!

Kore has sailed an ocean with a group of men who spend days, weeks, months at sea without their wives and the release that comes along with the company of a wife. Now, they have a bashfully enticing girl to do with what they want.

Demeter feels sick. She banishes the thought and lifts her face to an intact ceiling as tears dry cold against her cheeks, and she prays to the gods it has not come to that.

As if in answer, Demeter swears she hears the distant voice of her daughter:

"Mother, I am lost—help me!"

SISYPHUS
8

The day arrives when Hades finally mentions the girl. Asking in a snide tone:

"Is the child of Zeus healed yet?"

The High King needs say nothing more. Minos interprets a command in the words.

Minos receives reports, on and off, of the girl's health. It is true the girl is up and walking around on legs as weak as a newborn calf. Apparently, the malady gave way and fever broke, giving her the stamina to make progress. But healed? Minos cannot say. Regardless, the question Hades poses is not the question he wishes answered.

The Unseen wants to know how much leverage he has with the girl.

It is after breakfast when Minos seeks her out. On the ground floor of the palace, he makes his way to the east staircase when he spots two guards standing at the double doors leading to the courtyard.

The doors stand wide-open. The guards mutter to each other in confidential tones. One laughs, and the roguishness in the laugh stops Minos in his tracks. He retracts his foot from the first step and turns to them.

"The word *guard* implies a certain level of attentiveness," Minos says, "and yet it seems I have caught you both *off guard*."

Abashed, the guards bark a militant apology and resume forward-staring positions.

Minos goes to the open doors between the men. At this hour, fog hangs low to the ground. It will not burn off until midday. A long rectangular pool splits the yard down the middle. Scattered leaves of yellow and rust float on top. Stone walkways zigzag through fauna and brilliant purple oleander.

The damp sea-salt air wets his cheeks. It is cool but not windy enough to be uncomfortable. Minos squints. At the farthest end of the courtyard, the grass is littered with black mounds. In the middle of those shapes sits a lean figure, cloaked in blush-colored wool. She stares directly ahead, toward the vined arch leading to a monument on its marble pedestal.

The grass moistens his sandaled toes. "Hello."

The figure does not turn. The black mounds on the ground shift lazily. Not mounds but dogs. Eight or ten surround the girl, lying there almost as if they were drunk. He gets closer. Trained to recognize him, the mastiffs do not growl, and when they bare their teeth, it is because they are yawning.

As he gets closer, they right themselves and sit with rigid composure, heads lowered and eyes glinting through fog. When the dogs move, the girl rotates at the waist and spots him.

Minos slows and throws a quizzical glance at the dogs before returning to the girl on the grass.

Strange. She looks familiar. It must be Zeus's blood that makes it so. All children of Zeus are remarkable in some way, and this one exceeds the standard. And she is no child—not to any man, anyway. Heavy lids give her an almost mournful appearance. Her golden skin lacks the flush of vitality. Succulent lips part, and Minos cocks his head, bewildered by her appeal but feeling very old at the same time.

"The dogs like you, I see," he remarks.

"Oh." She sighs, mouth curling into a faint smile. "I s-started with two. The rest joined along the way, I s-suppose."

"How could they not follow such a pretty girl?"

He hopes to earn a smile, but she studies him with an intensity that makes him shift his weight from foot to foot. Minos glances at the mastiffs again, alert and ready to maul him if he gets closer. It is good they guard her well. Curious but good. Of the three judges, Aeacus is the only one who has rapport with them, and he bribes them with meat.

"What may I call you?" He forces himself to stop ogling her. He ogles the giant statue instead, pretending to admire the aesthetics, the protruding veins in the neck and definition of muscle in a straining chest and arms.

She gives a demure bow of the neck. "Whatever you like, *kyrios*."

It is the term for *master*. She intuits his authority, though he has not stated it. Minos expects her to ask who *he* is. Instead, she balls the plain white material of her skirt into her fists. She says nothing at all, and when Minos turns, her eyes are dewy. Anxious, she pulls on her lip.

Minos holds out his hand. The dogs stiffen. When the girl puts a death-cold hand in his, they relax.

She steadies herself by bearing her weight against his palm. He notices the dainty bones in her wrist and fingers and how she moves with a lightness that could be blown away by a simple breeze. The whole of her, borne away like a feather. Cheeks high with color, she struggles to stand. Thin, wheezing air labors from her lungs.

With a crinkle of the brow, he asks, "Do you know who I am?"

Chin to chest, she gazes up at him and shakes her head no.

"My name is Minos. I am one of three judges for Hades, High King of Erebus."

At first, nothing. Finally, she gives a light and simple:

"Oh."

"I have come to check on you. You have been ill for some time."

"I th-think perhaps I died. Many times over, I died." She swallows, lashes fluttering, and twists a tress of bronze hair around her finger. "Do I sound mad?"

"Well, you are not dead, are you? You stand in front of me, as fresh and lovely as the oleander."

"Th-thank you."

"It is the truth."

Jittery, her words seem to catch on an invisible hook until she finally tears them loose and spits them out. "I mean—thank you for taking care of me. F-for making me well." She squeezes his arm with such candor and appreciation, it warms his heart.

"A child of Zeus," he says, "is a child of ours."

Her cheeks glisten with mist, and she twirls her hair around and around a tapered forefinger.

"You must be eager to see your father after such an ordeal," Minos says.

"Yes, please, I am!"

"Tell me your name, and we will make certain he knows you are safe."

To this, the girl hesitates and flushes again, "O-oh, but I would not want to worry him. If you tell him about me, I mean, I suppose he may w-worry too much. Will you send me there? To be with him?"

"Why were you far from him, silly child?" he chides. "Was your mother with you?"

Her face falls. "M-mother?"

"The queen," he says. "Hera."

Nothing.

"Was your mother aboard the ship with you?"

Doe-eyes cast downward, the girl opens her mouth to answer and bursts into tears. Her hand touches her chest, as if it hurts to cry. The wheezing grows quicker, more insistent. The way her lips curl into a grimace strikes a sensual chord, and yet Minos also sees a child here, assumes it may be the child inside a woman's body that galvanizes him in the first place.

"What is it?" Minos urges.

"You seem k-kind," she mews, wiping at her cheeks. As though she did not expect him to be kind.

Minos shrinks at the memory of the atrocity he committed in his lifetime—the offense that landed him before the throne of Hades. In reverie, he shivers.

"For kings, madness is a sickness waiting to be caught."

Madness may be the wrong word for it. How many hide their sins under the guise of madness? Rage can drive a man to it, he supposes. And Minos had been enraged. The death of a firstborn son could produce nothing less. By the time word reached him that his child had been murdered by a bunch of jealous Attican nobles, Andro's body was two weeks cold. The former King Minos had gone to the docks, expecting a homecoming celebration. Instead, he was given a plain box of pine with a rotting corpse inside.

Minos considered war over it. The genteel polis of Knossos would never have stood a chance. The *damos* would have formed a militia with little to no skill in battle. Violent action was not part of their culture. In fact, the palace has no fortification wall to protect it from invaders.

Perhaps that is what made King Aegeus of Attica cocky. Minos could practically hear his logic:

Minos will not retaliate.

Minos is a peace-loving ruler. We need not worry about him.

Still, sending a dead prince home to his father was bound to stir up trouble. As a type of compensation for a life taken unjustly, King Aegeus sent him fourteen youths of noble blood. Wards intended to serve the polis of Knossos, creating bonds of friendship and marriage as to maintain the peace and form long-lasting alliances between houses.

The usually calm King Minos did not accept such a peace offering. These fourteen lives would never replace the son who died.

Minos is lost in these thoughts when the girl tells him:

"I w-wish I could answer you."

He frowns. "What does that mean?"

"I want my father. If I could be with him—"

Gentle, as not to break her, Minos clasps her by the arms and lowers his chin so they are eye to eye. "A daughter of Zeus, especially one your age, should have been with him all along. From where did you set sail?"

A furious shake of the head.

"Forgive me if I am a dense old man and do not understand you."

She says, "I am the daughter of Zeus—I am! —I had his coin to prove it. B-but please, I am sorry, I do not remember more."

Dumbfounded, he blinks. "You cannot remember your name? Your own mother?"

The words prompt a hysterical reply from the girl. "Please, are you angry with me?"

On her temple, above her brow, is a jagged, pink scar, upraised like a worm against flesh. Occasionally, during battle, a man is stricken on the head and, upon awakening, finds himself confused or unable to recall certain things. The phenomenon is not uncommon, but the child has been recovering for weeks, and he cannot imagine her mind being blank after such a long time.

"O-oh, you cannot be angry with me, not when I finally found someone to talk to."

"All right, all right," he consoles. "Calm yourself. Do I look angry?"

She sucks back tears. "No, I suppose n-not."

"No." As he backs away, the dogs mill about. He swears there are more of them. At least twelve. "Your job is to recover. Think of nothing beyond this."

She glances at the statue twice her height beneath the arch of vines. Minos gestures to the statue of a man with palms pressed against a large boulder and knees bent to help him bear the weight.

"You like the monument of Sisyphus?" he says, eager to distract her from crying.

"I hear him. At night."

"You hear who?"

With her head, she gestures to the monument. "Him. Pushing th-that."

Minos tips his head, glancing at her curiously. "What do you know of Sisyphus?"

She shakes her head and nibbles her pretty lip.

"Do you know where Corinth is?"

Again, she shakes her head.

"Well," he says, studying the chiseled marble, "before the new ruler named it Corinth, it was called Ephyra. King Sisyphus ruled Ephyra during the reign of the titans. Your father did not like him."

"No? Why not?"

"Sisyphus was as iron-fisted as the other titans, for one thing. Zeus despises tyranny, and Sisyphus committed one of the worst offenses, according to your father. When anyone tried to cross from Olympus to Erebus by way of Ephyra, Sisyphus slaughtered them on sight."

Her face is lit with girlish fascination. "How t-terrible."

"It became a real problem for Zeus. Refugees attempting to flee Olympus were met with certain death. It was clear King Sisyphus was not on the right side of the war. You have heard of *xenia*, Zeus's law of hospitable travel?"

She nods.

"It was the outrageous actions of Sisyphus that caused your father to create this law. Thereafter, Zeus resolved to dethrone him and replace him with an Olympian ruler. So, he sent his brother to take care of it."

"Brother?"

"Yes, dear," Minos says, palms up to imply the walls around them and the ruler whom she will likely never meet. "His brother, Hades the Unseen, High King of Erebus."

The girl's chest rises and falls at a faster rate. She gazes off into space at the mention of the name.

"The Unseen d-did capture Sisyphus," she thinks aloud. "S-Sisyphus died here."

For such a lovely innocent, she is a morbid girl. "Do you know how he died?"

"He was crushed." She studies the monument. Morning sun flashes against marble. "And his body was thrown in the public s-square."

Minos eyes her. "Who told you that?"

To which she replies, "He did. S-Sisyphus."

The vines surrounding the monument rustle and stir in the breeze. The girl shivers, eyelids sagging. Vigor drains from her face.

"I cannot imagine the cold air good for you," Minos says. "Shall I help you back upstairs?"

Afterward, with the girl winded and flushed from climbing stairs, Minos returns her to her room. The mastiffs adhere to her right and left, dual shadows.

Before he walks away, she touches his arm. "Judge—"

"Yes, my dear?"

"Might the slaves bring sage and rue?"

"Sage and . . . ?"

"Rue," she says. "They will help me s-sleep."

To this, Minos agrees. It pleases him to indulge such a sweet thing. The girl thanks him, and Minos watches her slink back into the room, trailed by dogs.

He rubs his beard. Early morning subsides to midmorning. By now, the other judges should be gathering in the assembly room, awaiting the appearance of their king.

Minos lingers at the mouth of the corridor which leads to Hades's bedchamber. Soon, a familiar *click-click-click* echoes in the distance, mastiff paws against stone. At once, the austere ruler of Erebus rounds the corner. Over one shoulder— the one punctured by Alcides's arrow—a chlamys made of imported Egyptian silk flowing into a bell-like sleeve. His face is freshly shaved by slaves. The High King refuses to keep a beard, claiming it "hot and itchy." When the day grows late, the beard insists on coming regardless and peppers an arrow-sharp jaw with black hair speckled with silver.

Hades does not stop walking. His brows cast a shadow over black-lashed eyes with black irises that appear as tunnels into a void.

As Minos falls in beside him, Hades says in his nearly inaudible voice, "Well?"

"She is glorious," he admits, "and charming and mostly healthy. I believe she is the child of a future god."

"Then, why are you colored with regret?"

"Because," he hesitates, "she is withholding. She claims to remember nothing."

At this, Hades huffs a humorless laugh.

"And yet, she knows me. I am sure of it."

"You seem k-kind."

This, she said, as if anticipating a monster. Something about this agitates his memory. He cannot shake the familiarity.

"Bring her to me," Hades snaps.

Bowels churning, Minos conjures the sweet image of the girl's face. "It may behoove you to be careful with her. She is not fully well, and the act of meeting with you can have a damaging aftermath."

"Do it."

"Now?"

"No, not now," the king answers. "We are in court, and she is not a prisoner." And when Hades speaks again, the words land heavy. "She is a guest."

Nevertheless, Minos does not feel assured.

No Memory
9

Sage burns day-long, hanging thick in the air. The scent reminds Kore more of wood than of flowers. Slaves maintain a flow of it and replenish it before the odor can fade. At her bedside, rue decorates the table with its gray-green leaves covered with soft hairs.

In Knossos, her mother considered sage and rue essentials, in their house, especially.

"These items send prayers to the gods for a peaceful home."

At a young age, she learned the purpose of sage and rue.

To test their power, she summons enough bravery to call out: "S-Sisyphus. Come forward."

The mastiffs sit beside her, ready to protect her from unwanted visitors.

The shade does not respond.

Kore sighs with tearful relief. Oh, she must

thank the judge when next she sees him. Kore places a hand on her throat, choking with shame. He was kind to her, and she repaid him by telling him nonsense. She repaid him with deceit.

The late afternoon radiance of Helius comes through the open window and spreads a long block of light against a floor polished high by slaves. Kore paces inside the light, absorbing the warmth.

But it was not a lie—not really!

Most of what Kore spoke was truth, and the rest of it, omission.

As soon as it registered the man standing before her was King Minos—or rather, *Judge* Minos— color drained from her face. Tale told, Minos went mad and killed many children.

And yet he is compassionate! Reformed, surely!

Rumors, too, of his wife, Queen Pasiphae, copulating with the bull and producing a monstrous offspring whom they kept locked away: a deformity part bull, part man. Mother said it was absurd, for bestiality would produce no such creature.

As a child, she spied King Minos often in the arena. He sat not far above them in his privileged royal box. Mother would point him out, proud of their king, and when the madness took him, no one was more crestfallen than Mother.

"It is like watching a star fall and vanish forever! To think he once held you as a babe in his lap, even for a brief moment."

With tears, her mother said this, making Kore

cry too. She hated to see Mother sad.

Kore struggles to recall what she told Judge Minos. If she thinks about it too much, the ugly feeling will fall over her chest and shame will eat her alive.

She has denied her own mother. Forsaken her. The woman whose happiness is dependent upon her own. The most intimate relationship Kore has ever known.

Forgive me.

No! Kore cannot think this way. Already, she sailed an ocean and survived the devastation at sea and the sickness in her body. She has come this far. If she admits her name, he might remember her. If he knows her mother is Demeter, High Priestess of Knossos, Judge Minos might ship her home, and all of this will have been for nothing.

However tight Demeter's grip in the past, it will tighten threefold now that Kore has displayed an outwardly defiant will. If they send her back, she will never again escape.

So thinking, Kore resolves to repeat:

I have no memory of any of it.

Even when Minos visits again, this time at the behest of the High King.

THEÍOS
10

This will be quick. What Minos could not accomplish, Hades will do in an instant.

The dogs laze in front of a cavernous hearth that blazes high and brightens an otherwise dim room. This is a small space for convening with the judges before or after court to discuss any outstanding concerns. Hades will not scrutinize the daughter of Zeus inside the throne room, where he meets with transgressors under examination for violent or dishonorable acts. They meet on neutral ground, in the assembly room.

In court, they lack a third judge. Several days before, Rhadamanthus set sail for Knossos on a diplomatic mission, along with two other trade ships filled with lumber and materials for port reconstruction. In his absence, Minos and Aeacus remain to advise. Even so, Rhad's position on war with Olympus is no mystery. Peace, at all costs.

Lately, Hades is less and less inclined to agree.

Court is over. His face itches with new beard growth, already thick enough to make him anxious. The pressure against his skin annoys him.

A table crafted thick with ebony shines in the corner to the right of the fire. Around it, chairs. Near the hearth, there are two more chairs, one cocked to each side, and a table in the center with a krater of wine.

Aeacus pours two kylixes and passes one to the High King.

"To justice," Aeacus toasts.

The day needs to end. Where is Minos with the girl? A little too hard, Hades sets his glass on the table. Wine sloshes over the side, and he shakes the spillage from his fingers. He grimaces at the stiffness in his shoulder. Some men gain life from being around people. Others are diminished by the leeching act of socialization.

Day's end, his temple always aches from the strain. His jaw throbs from gritted teeth in court, and his eyes are ringed with purple.

The sky grumbles, rattling the windows. Outside, it rains hard. It pelts the shutters along the westernmost wall. Clouds conceal the setting sun. Lightning veins the sky, reminding him of Zeus and the show he conducts in Olympus. It is the King of Kings' signature, the thing lending mystical severity to his legacy—and it is a good trick.

The pandering shit.

"When you release Creon from Tartarus," Hades says, "send him with a message. If King Eury has Alcides, he is to bind and send him to me."

"You believe he will?"

"No, but my point is clear. I know of Alcides's crimes and will not relent on—"

Minos appears at the doorway. He treads slow and keeps a fixed watch behind him, as though escorting someone more sluggish than he. In the hall, paws tick against marble—a familiar sound Hades does not hear anymore, and yet he hears the distinct difference between the sound following him daily and the one filling the corridor. It is the difference between a sprinkling of rain and a deluge.

At once, his attention splinters in three directions. An otherwise keen focus spins out of control and leaves him frozen with eyes darting from place to place, unsure where to look.

First, the daughter of Zeus. Sun-bronzed hair, twisted into a coil and draped over one sleek shoulder. Skin the same shade of bronze. The white silk of her chiton pulls taught across large, round breasts and tighter at hips that swell from a gold-roped waist as small around as his thigh. His eyes roam to the cleft in her chin and tiny freckle on the outside corner of one eye. Wet, swollen lips immediately bring to mind the fleshy part between a woman's legs, and he bristles, skin ablaze.

His focus stalls here first, and it occurs to Hades the field around her body appears colorless in his peripheral vision. While it should be the first point of focus, Hades finds himself looking there secondarily, an abrupt afterthought. He forces his attention to the light—not the girl herself, who is a distraction from the light. When he does, he is staggered to find no color at all but a blameless, white glow wavering in density. Patches of light, solid as a flame. Other patches, opaque as water in cupped hands.

At last, the dogs.

One by one, they flood the room, prompting Minos to wave his hands and call, "Tch-tch! Shoo!"

Two are appointed to guard her. Two.

Paws continue to tap, and thick-muscled canines crowd half of the room. Minos tries to rally them with his body as a sheepdog might rally a flock. The dogs remain, droopy-eyed and tongues wagging. There must be fifteen.

Beside him, Aeacus nettles. "What is this?"

"Damned if I know." Minos opens his arms wide, herding them.

With a curt snap of the fingers, Hades draws the mastiffs' attention and points to the door. "Get out."

The dogs whine and yawn and stretch their necks, tormented by the admonishment. They mope from the room until none remain, Cerberus included.

"Majesty, this—"

"You, too." He swaps attention from Minos to Aeacus, ordering, "Out."

The judges shuffle out, abashed as the dogs. Then they are gone, and it is him and the girl.

Arms hanging limp at her sides, she gawks at him. Her brows are upraised and eyes widened to display the whites around richly brown irises. Soon, the whites will turn murky and pink and eventually stricken with red—if Hades chooses—and he admires them for a moment before pushing in.

Hades takes two steps toward the girl standing on the opposite side of the room.

The girl sinks to her knees. He contemplates her wet mouth, and perversion burns down to the groin. The roaring *thu-thump* of his heart pulsates in his ears.

Without color, he has no idea where to prod. He concentrates on a dense patch of white where the light is most charged, but the charge fails to hold and fades to translucence. Simultaneously, other areas flare—in the center of her forehead, near the divot of her clavicle. The field fluctuates before he can grab hold of the light he targets.

"Get up," he monotones.

She stands, cheeks flushed.

"Take a seat." He motions to the chair to the left of the hearth.

She scurries and sits on the edge, hands braced against her knees and the tips of bare toes burrowing into the rug.

Around her, the field swirls. Frazzled, Hades takes a wild shot, nerves high, and pushes into a spot at random with more force than intended. Pain sears at the temple. It is sundown, and he has spent all day surveying men. By now, his head aches but the pain is tolerable. But pressing into the light of the girl is excruciating.

Inside the light, a woman raises her arms to the sky. Her head flings back in ecstatic prayer. In each hand, the neck of a writhing snake. An altar smokes. At the base of the altar, a wooden basket full of ceremonial snakes. A congregation of worshippers gasp and point at the basket, horrified. Among the snakes, sitting with her baby-bird neck craning to the priestess, is a little girl barely able to walk. She has managed to crawl over the side of the basket and sits amid the pile, and the serpents slither around her little legs and waist.

The girl is not afraid.

Temple throbbing, he stares at the girl herself rather than the field around her. He feels mildly nauseated. Hades sits in the chair across from her, elbow propped on the armrest, chin in hand with fingers draped across his mouth.

"Do you know why you are here?"

"I-is it because of my father?" she asks in a near-whisper.

"That is why you are in Asphodel," he murmurs. "Do you know why you are *here*?"

Meaning, with *him*, here, in this room alone.

She shakes her head. The coil of hair tumbles apart, sliding down her back and falling in her eye. She gazes up at him and says timidly, "Are you hurting?"

"What?" Unconsciously, he has been massaging his jaw. He folds his hands in his lap.

"Y-your eyes are red."

He flushes. Restrains himself from rubbing his temples. "What is your name?"

"Kore."

"That is not a name," and it is not—*kore* is as meaningless as *girl*, *maiden*, or *daughter*.

"It is the one I kn-know."

Hades searches the light. Presses in. Pain shoots through his skull. The brightness is like the blinding reflection of the sun upon the sea.

"Where are you, little ghost?"

He lets go, shuts his eyes, and squeezes the bridge of his nose. When he pulls his hand away, small flecks of red dot his thumb and forefinger.

His chest pounds. *What is this?* After years of service, his own body is turning against him.

Before he can compose himself, the girl sails toward him like a windblown leaf. She falls at his feet. "Are you i-ill?" Long, willowy arms press upon his lap. He jumps at the touch.

Her fingers cup both sides of a scalding jaw. Touching him again, more intimately. His chest pounds hard enough to rock the fabric of his clothing. Stroking the side of his face, Kore fawns with thick lashes aflutter. He watches her plump lips form the words, "Y-you are bleeding."

This time, when he looks at her, he allows the light to slip into the background before it can lash out at him further.

She wipes at a shadowy beard, looking from his jaw to mouth and directly in his eyes. Irreverent. No surprise from the brat of Zeus and sister to Alcides.

He closes his fingers around each of her wrists, capturing them. They stare at each other.

"D-do you know my father well?" she coos.

"We fought as brothers in the war."

"B-brothers, yes." She is oddly unperturbed by the stronghold on her wrists. With a coy half-smile, she lilts, "May I call you *Theíos*?"

Uncle. His lower belly flips.

"Cute," he deadpans, fully hard, and pushes her away by the arms. "Sit in the chair."

"O-oh, but I am comfortable here."

"Sit in the chair."

Kore shrinks back, obeys him. Once she is seated, he waits for the heat under his collar to dissipate. When Hades clears his throat, his temple blares with residual pain. "You told Judge Minos you have no memory."

"That is why I am here?"

"On the day the earth opened, your ship crashed into the cape of Matapan. Survivors reported you are the daughter of Zeus. Does this sound familiar?"

Kore nods.

A child of High Queen Hera holds the greatest bargaining potential. The more powerful the mother, the more powerful the negotiation. Nobody likes a distraught queen, particularly a king. They like their queens placated and willing to spread their legs at night. Keeping a mistress happy is seldom a priority. More mistresses wait to take the place of the last.

"Now you," he says.

"Now me wh-what?"

"Tell me what I am missing."

She shrugs.

"Tell me about the priestess."

Her face pales. A little pink tongue slides over her bottom lip, making his mind wander. "P-priestess?"

"She who invokes the goddess Potnia."

Clean tears spill down her cheeks. Those eyes shine bright and clear.

"I believe," Hades says, voice flat, "the priestess is your mother."

Kore shakes her head and dotes at him with a too-precious upturn of the brows. "P-please believe me, *Theíos*. I have not been well, but p-perhaps I will remember more in time. If I saw my father again, I would remember everything!"

The white halo swirls, tempting him to peek one more time. He could. He wants to. But if he starts bleeding again, she will rush to help, and he does not want her hands on him. She is too trusting, and he, too full of violence. In letting the light recede, he relaxes and discovers wicked gratification in observing the girl at the core of the light. Listening to her wheeze through tears.

"A mother will stop at nothing to assure

her child is safe," he tells her. "A mother is your strongest ally."

"B-but not a father?"

"Not always."

"If you were my father," she says, searching his face in earnest, "would you not want me?"

This, she does not stutter.

"Would you not want me?"

The day needs to end. End. His head aches, and Hades thinks about dogs and colorless light and, moreover, the bleeding. He flounders, disoriented. The nagging ache in his skull makes it hard to concentrate. And he needs to get away from the girl. He will enjoy her more in his head.

"Do you have any questions for me?"

"M-my father. When can I go to him?"

"When you are better."

"Oh, b-but am I not?"

"No, 'Kore.' Not yet."

"Because I cannot remember?"

"You will."

"S-soon?"

"Soon."

"Theíos," she whimpers, sap-sweet, and he winces, liking the way she says it. "I will try. Honest I will."

Damn her. Hades leans forward, elbows on knees. "Anything else?"

Kore surveys the room, and with the utmost simplicity, asks, "What is wrong with this place?"

He blinks.

"W-what I mean to say is—" She struggles, playing with her hair. "Oh, I suppose I am not sure what I mean."

Hades stands. Walks to her. Sensing he is done with her, she stands.

"As long as you are here," he says, "you will be taken care of." Catching his eye for the first time: a shining pink tendril on her forehead, under a mass of hair that swoops over her brow. "And you *will* remember."

He reaches up and pushes the hair aside with one finger. She is lying. Even with a blow to the head, she is lying.

And he sees his hand fall to her cheek, sees his thumb tracing along the side of her face where her ear and jaw convene, watches as his hand trails lower, over the dimpled chin. He has not touched anyone in a long time.

"You better not be lying to me," Hades mumbles, menacing and tender, and leaves with nothing more.

PART THREE
DISTURBANCES

She [Persephone] cried with a piercing voice, calling upon her father [Zeus], the son of Kronos, the highest and the best. But not one of the immortal ones, or of human mortals, heard her voice.

—*Homeric Hymn to Demeter*

THE APPLE

1

At sunrise, Demeter stands behind the altar with hands snug under the armpits of an infant boy. She props him upright for the room to see.

The baby is alert, neck rolling until claiming the strength to hold his head aloft. He drools and clutches her finger. It has been weeks since Kore vanished, and the family of Lyris has not named the child.

"Agori," Demeter calls him. *Boy*. Until they name him, she will call him what she wishes.

Agori gurgles. He squeals for the sheer delight of squealing.

He is not strong enough to sit on his own, and the consecration is overdue. It is hard to hold him. Hard because she longs to squeeze him and revel in his helpless weight in her arms and smell the newness of infancy on his skin. Hard because showing love to another child feels like a betrayal to Kore.

A shaking earth halted the ceremony when she visited before, on the day they lost Lyris and Mago and the second infant. At this ritual, the remaining family. Belen and Nomiki have not been in the same room since the death of the baby's mother. Aunts and cousins and uncles and neighbors convene in solidarity to benefit the soul of a child.

Unto the gods, she declares, "I speak for the parents and guiding friends, this day pledging the polis of Knossos to raise Agori with love and steadfastness. We bestow blessings upon his childhood."

She anoints Agori with water and says, "Oceanus, god of the great earth-encircling river, wash over this child, bringing your powers of daring and acceptance into his life." With salt, she sprinkles his naked belly, full of milk from the wet nurse. "Gaia, goddess of earth, ground this child with your powers of resonance."

Inside the common room, the altar smokes with incense, fumes symbolizing *eros* between man and the gods. The sweet smoke of styrax and myrtle leaves floats like webs around the fat-ringed knees of the child. Dimpled elbows flap—he is a little peacock enjoying the appreciative noises of those inside the room. Demeter passes the baby to his father. Proud Nomiki, new to paternity, cups the baby's head in one hand and naked buttocks in the other. Agori flicks his legs back and forth, flails his arms. Flinging wine upon the fire, Demeter sends the hiss of sacrifice to the gods.

From the basket on the floor, she retrieves two snakes, neck in each hand, and spreads both arms to the sky.

"We call upon the goddess Potnia to nurture and protect Agori, son of Nomiki, as he grows in physical size and in divine understanding. We honor the life-giving cord that connected child and mother."

Serpent tails hug each forearm. From his father's hands, Agori gawks, chubby face, contorted and uncertain. Demeter is fascinated by the ingrained tendency of babies to trust snakes.

Man is taught to fear. Taught by life and its tragedy. Fear of snakes is a learned fear.

Even as she grew, Kore never flinched at snakes. This magical girl, the priesthood once declared Demeter would not love like a "real" daughter. Kore remained invalidated until Zeus poisoned a father he had not met until that very day and declared himself inheritor as the son of Cronus.

After, when Zeus was no longer a wild, bare-chested scamp raised by goat-herders, when he lived in a palace at Mount Olympus rather than a cave at Mount Dikte, suddenly, Kore became exceptional to more people than Demeter.

Suddenly, Kore was the child of a future god. A girl who sat with snakes and did not recoil.

Demeter returns the snakes to the basket. When Agori wails, the men beam at the health of his lungs. Belen and Nomiki, both widowed, smile as brightly as if their women were alive, as if half the north wall was not open to the elements from where the stone buckled.

When the ceremony concludes, the family greets her with gifts of food and linen, which they need far more than she. She feels guilty to accept them. They will be offended if she does not. She smiles wanly and thanks them.

They call her *High Priestess*, but today their praise strikes her as disingenuous. Yes, now they revere her. But before, they chastised her for surrendering to a man who was not her husband and destroying any chance of acquiring a good match later.

People no longer regard Demeter as ruined, but chosen. If Zeus the Liberator deemed her worthy of his seed, she must be blessed.

Such high praise for the man who first spotted her at a fruit cart outside the temple. A tall, mischievously grinning young man with unruly burned brown curls down to his shoulders. She felt him before she saw him—felt the motion against her back and realized someone had lifted her hair and was *sniffing* it. She spun on him, and there he was—barrel-chested and wearing a torn and dirty tunic drooping from one strong shoulder.

"Stop it!" she had whined, a lanky and childish girl of fourteen snatching the end of her hair from his palm.

"Not possible! I smelled the jasmine in your

hair from across the road."

He was twice older, the right age, and this made her blush at the understanding that men approaching thirty usually took brides around her age. That is when girls began bleeding, and bleeding meant men could put babies in them. But Demeter was newly fourteen and hardly thinking about those things in any serious way, not until the burly, thick-bearded man at the fruit cart snatched her hair.

"Who are you? I have not seen you here."

"No," he said, chomping at an apple. "I am from Dikte. But I am nobody. Just an escort for the goat." Behind him, a pretty brown and white spotted goat with a perfect pink nose and perfect little horns.

"You are stupid." She snickered.

"Stupid? What a terrible thing to say to a potential suitor. And one who owns a goat!"

"Stop." Her cheeks had flushed as she giggled. And he had continued to flirt with her in the bustling trade quarter in front of the temple, carried on with her as she warmed to his wit. From across the square, two women called to him from the doorway of the wool merchant. Small, brunette women, tanned from the outdoors. Their faces were worn by time and hardship, but in their youth, they might have been beautiful.

Zeus left with them, and Demeter had been glad. Her friends had caught her eye from a few carts away, and they whispered and stared at her excitedly. She would return to them, tell them all about the man she met.

As Zeus turned to walk away, he grabbed another apple from the cart.

He tossed it in the air.

Out of reflex, her hand flashed in front of her, and she stooped and caught the thick-skinned fruit before it hit the ground.

As he receded into the crowd, smiling big, he pointed at her and cried, "You caught it! See, everyone? She caught my apple!"

"It was an accident!" She cackled, hand over mouth. "I did not mean to!"

"Too late! No taking it back." He winked at her before disappearing, and she knew what that meant.

She had caught the apple.

She had accepted a proposal to be his bride.

Once, Demeter had been as naive as Kore leaving on a trade ship. Every bit as unaware of what might happen to her.

The common room overflows with the family and friends of the infant, Agori. Although autumn arrives with crisp winds, the room swelters from the burning of the altar and the collected bodies of men and women and their children. New smells come from the kitchen, of herbs and onion and meat cooked strong and gamy.

Her hair clings to her forehead in damp ringlets. She peers over shoulders for the brightened doorway of an exit, any exit. Anything to free her from this room where people celebrate as if nothing happened weeks ago.

The merriment makes her want to weep.

She pushes her way to the back of the room until she stumbles into the cool, clean air outside Nomiki's home. The sky is gray, clouds speeding across a faded sun. Wind rustles leaves, sending hay and brush tumbling across the grass. In the distance, across the horizon of a rolling hill, a group of men march toward a clay-bricked shed at the far end of Nomiki's land.

A hefty stick is propped on the shoulders of men, one man on each end. Between them, a carcass hangs with legs tied to the wood. The body sways with each step the men take. They return from the woods, carrying death with them. She squints, hoping for a better look.

From behind her, a man says, "Boar."

It is Nomiki. His hair is bone straight and thick as a horse's mane. He is no taller than she, with a sturdy, compact frame reminding her of Asli.

"They have been hunting boar," he tells her. "We need the tusks for helmets. And the meat provided for today's feast."

As the men grow closer to the shed, she spies the ugly, spindly-haired creatures hanging upside-down, tusks curling from the jaw like talons. Demeter shudders, queasy.

"Eat. You look pitiful these days."

True, Demeter has not eaten much since that day. She has not slept much since that day, either.

At dawn and sunset, she walks the port, hoping for signs a ship might sail again. So far, nothing. Their port remains leveled by the flood, the ships crippled.

Nomiki strides away with bumbling steps as he navigates down the hill toward the shed where hunters take the boars. His duty, to survey the collection before they pry the tusks from their sockets and send them to the metal merchant for helmets.

"Wait. Nomiki!"

At the bottom of the hill, Nomiki turns.

"You are making helmets. Why? There are no ships to transport them."

"Three ships from Asphodel came to port. Told us our last shipment did not make it to Pylos."

"Came to port when?"

"Late this morning."

Ships from Asphodel.

When he says this, she rejoices that she is no longer paralyzed by the sea. If ships arrived from Asphodel, ships will return to Asphodel—and Asphodel and Pylos are sister *poleis*. Asphodel, located at the top of the middle finger of Erebus, where a ring might be worn past the knuckle. And Pylos, at the finger to the west of it.

The word *Asphodel* lands hard on the ear, as unpleasant as the words for which it is synonymous: *judgment, punishment, death.* What business could their ships have here? Regardless, cold relief rockets through her veins. Better a ship from the land of

Hades than a ship from Poseidon.

Demeter has feared Poseidon's return for nearly as long as Kore has been alive.

She cannot admit, not for an instant, she had hoped for Zeus to roll into the horizon with a dozen golden ships, masts raised and a gold-threaded eagle on white flags. She wonders what he looks like now. Old? Fat? Bald? She relishes the idea of him losing his appeal.

He came around twice before the day he took her. First, at the market. Later, to the temple where he lifted her by the waist and planted a wet, hairy kiss on her cheek as she was about to walk down the aisle at procession. Last, under her favorite tree, which she called the rain tree because dew collected in cupped leaves overnight and left cold droplets falling from under it, no matter what time of day. *Plunk. Plunk. Plunk.* The perfect place for shade during the hottest days.

She was under it, dozing, when she heard him.

"This is when I carry you off and make you mine."

A cold splat of dew on her cheek. "Carry me where?"

"You are right. This is more comfortable." He sighed and plopped down beside her under the rain tree. Sprawled out beside her, propped up on his elbow. Squinting upward and laughing at the dew. "This is great."

The tree beside them was a skinny cypress with

the goat tied to the trunk. Chewing straw from the ground.

"Do you take her everywhere?"

"She likes to walk. Besides, the woman who raised me died, and this was the goat whose milk made me the strong, magnificent creature I am today. She is practically my mother now."

"Goats do not live that long."

"Shh, call her Amalthea. She does not know she is a goat, so she can live as long as any human."

"You like to tease me." She considered it and said, "I am sorry you lost your mother."

"She was not my real mother. My real mother is in Olympus with my father."

"That is far."

"It is far." He took her hand from the grass and turned it over inside a big palm. "Soon I will be, too."

"You will be what?"

"Far away. At war."

"What war? There is no war. Stop teasing me. I do not like it."

"There is no war yet. But you will hear of it soon, and you will think of the man whose apple you caught."

"And do your real parents approve of you being in this war?"

She had no idea how to interpret the grimness of his smile—until months later when she heard of the murder of Cronus of Olympus by his youngest living child: Zeus.

"It was my mother's idea. And my father will definitely not approve. What about your father? Where is he now?"

"Oh, he has been dead for years. I live with my uncle in the priesthood."

"I like that," he said and rolled almost on top of her. "That means the child I put inside of you will be holy."

"No!" She tittered, but in her head, she had already given up. "You will do nothing of the kind!"

In an instant, he was kissing her hard and insistent, her head resting inside his palms. With the beard and curls, the hair on his chest and belly and back, it was like being taken by a bear and crushed beneath his weight. The thing between his legs ground into her lower belly, and he was inside of her. It hurt, but she knew it would, had been told by other girls it hurt, but only at first. She would marry him and bear his children, as many as he wanted— an entire house full of them, giggling and clinging to their legs. She tried to relax and let him do what he wanted, and then it was finished, and he seemed happy.

The apple, still ripe, sat by her bedside, every day a reminder since the day they met.

After, no trace of him. The goat, Amalthea, he left tied outside her home the next morning. It was not until her pregnancy was halfway over that the world learned of the assassination of Cronus and the liberator, Zeus, who freed Olympus from a king whose cruelty knew no bounds. And when she learned of this, she also learned Zeus the Liberator had taken a bride, Hera, as his queen.

Demeter let that apple mold and shrivel, watched it grow furry and white and green at the bottom. After a long time, the base of it melted into sludge, and Uncle Ammon followed the stench and held his nose and cursed at her for stinking up the house.

Now, she darts for the side of Nomiki's home. Demeter can make her way around the farm until she finds the main road. She must get passage on an Asphodelian ship. This, she vows, hurrying until her legs freeze in midstep.

"Told us our last shipment did not make it to Pylos."

Dread, sap-thick, courses down her spine. She runs back to where she saw Nomiki, and he fades into the valley and arches back up toward the path to the shed. Demeter flies down the hill, stumbling over knotted grass. As she rushes toward him, Nomiki turns.

"Priestess?"

"Your shipment to Pylos," she says. "When did it sail?"

"The day of the shaking."

She clutches at her chest, twisting her head to conceal the ugliness of her tears.

"Demeter, please go back to the house. Get

something to eat. You are not well."

"At dawn?" She sobs.

"Yes, at dawn," he stresses, not understanding why it matters. "Bits of the ship washed up in Matapan with . . . can you guess? Helmets. Our helmets. All of them ruined. Thus, I need to make more, and you need to go back into the house with the family."

"Who told you this?"

"One of the judges of Erebus."

Demeter pales. "Not Minos?"

"You know he is not permitted here," Nomiki says. "His brother, Rhadamanthus."

NOT IN DANGER

2

"*You* *better not be lying to me.*"

No sleep, not tonight.

Kore laces her fingers over her chest and stares, wide-eyed, at a ceiling inlaid with gilded tile. Legs suffused with blood, they ache as if she had run the length of Crete. Long-neglected muscles, alive again and groaning.

Tonight, the dogs do not comfort her. They have been a gift so far. During the day, guards shoo the mastiffs back to their official posts and maintain a semblance of order. But at night! At night, there are few guards and many dogs, and no one to keep them from spilling into the room until their smell overpowers the smell of sage. If not for the comfort and safety, Kore would consider them an infestation.

It is late, and the sage burns low. The servants will not return to replenish it until morning. The more dogs amass, the more intimidated the slaves.

Kore rolls onto her side and counts the mastiffs to divert herself from the words circulating in her mind.

"You better not be lying to me."

At twenty, she stops counting. More gather outside the door and spill into the corridor. Kore senses it.

The mastiffs do not touch her. She does not touch them. They are colossal. As tall as her chest! But she feels safe with them, especially when she hears the grinding noise—through which the dogs sleep, for they seem not to notice it.

Sisyphus, Judge Minos called the statue outside.

The dogs snore. Their hulking shapes fill the room, the heat of their bodies palpable enough to snuff out the chill in the air.

Tonight, she had sat in the company of the High King, the one whom they call by strange names like the Unseen.

Uneasy, Kore flips onto her back again, caught in a whir of the mind.

Not long ago, Mother took her west to Chania, and they spent the day picking through the mountains until they climbed high and came to a cliff overlooking a valley. Stricken, Kore beheld great majestic peaks that spanned wide, blanketed in every shade of green imaginable. She could not take it in because of the magnitude, like trying to wrap her arms all the way around the earth. They towered long before her and will tower long after she is gone.

She felt dwarfed, insignificant, and humbled by the glory of the mountains.

When Kore stood before the High King, it was like stepping into Chania and trying to take in the grandeur of those mountains all over again.

She hates the thought of being out of his favor. Hades is her father's brother—and yet he is full of questions and terribly grumpy and serious, making her long to please him more, to be the one who might make him smile or touch her again as he did, which made her breath catch in her throat until he said those awful words that made her skin run cold.

"You better not be lying to me."

But why should it matter who her mother is?

It is simple. She belongs with her father, in Olympus. Why does he insist that she answer a question she cannot answer (not ever!) forcing her to be deceitful? This is not who she wants to be! Not a liar to the one who ensures she is fed and clothed and made well, as an uncle would.

Kore rests with eyes half-closed. Her thoughts— monkeys on a vine, swinging from one to the next to the next.

She told the High King her name. By accident, it slipped out.

The dogs snore like little bears.

How does *Theíos* know Mother is a priestess? How did he know, when she cleverly withheld her name from Judge Minos so he would not remember her?

Her eyelids droop.

Mother must be livid.

"Not be lying to me."

Chances are, she will not see Mother again for a long time. Years will pass before her mother's boiling anger will cool to a simmer. Then Kore will try to mend things.

Kore floats alongside the longing, as though her body drifts away without something to anchor it. No mother's arms to keep her close. To hold her in place.

Mother, blaming Father for any trait in Kore she finds despicable. Blaming his blood.

"A mother is your strongest ally."

Theíos says this, but of course, Father will be an ally, too! He will love her and recognize himself in her—and she, in him.

Inside the shell of her body, the sense of falling, plummeting. Near sleep. Beneath the covers, she shivers. The night grows cold, and Kore nestles into the blankets.

She is nearly asleep when hands seize her ankles.

Kore gasps and flings herself upright, wildly alert. Hair tumbles around her shoulders.

No one is there. The floor gleams clear and naked. A two-wick oil lamp burns beside her bed. The sage, extinguished into ash. Her ankles buzz from the memory of touch.

"S-Sisyphus?"

In the distance: howling. First, a lone dog, then another and another, collecting into a dirge of mastiffs braying together in mournful chorus. As she eases onto her back, pulling the blankets up to her chin, she realizes for the first time:

Empty.

The dogs are no longer in her room.

This time, she is not asleep when she feels it. Unmistakable, there is a distinctive *plop* on the bed as if someone sits hard next to her shoulders.

Kore yelps. She leaps to her feet, legs working quick. As though in bed with a thousand spiders, she scampers away, brushing the badness from the silk of an eggshell white gown. Tiptoeing backward, she watches the bed, expecting something to immortalize.

In the perimeter of her vision, a shadow. Kore spins. Nothing. She rotates to the bed, to the wall, and to the open doorway that shows a squared entrance into the corridor.

Fingers land on her shoulder.

No-no-no. Do not look.

Unholy.

Her neck rotates toward the west wall, cut by her own shadow.

Cast behind her, a grotesquely elongated shadow with hand outstretched. The man-shaped creature slides a lock of her hair between thumb and forefinger.

Kore runs. Into the corridor, she flies as her legs

struggle not to tangle up.

Where are the dogs? Where did they go?

Right and left, on the floor, candles light the corridor. Flames flicker as she darts by, gown forming a trail of wind.

She runs fast. Her lungs ache and whistle. She breathes through an imaginary reed. Kore reaches out and plants a moist hand onto a pillar for support.

At the end of a dimly lit hallway, she spots a shadow slipping from around the corner.

Footsteps.

Kore attempts a step, dizziness enveloping her. She will not make it farther than two steps before hitting the floor.

Shaking, she presses her shoulder into the pillar and slips behind it. She hides between wall and column, hoping to go undetected. Surely, this unholy thing does not seek her out. Surely, it is a shade lost inside the void, wandering.

Steps, louder.

She cannot get enough air. She sinks to the floor.

A flat, low voice orders, "Get up off the floor."

Her body is freezing and light and floating away. Breath, spinning out of control. Heart fluttering like a trapped moth.

Someone grips her by the fleshy part of her arms, and Kore is hoisted. Her feet land flat and firm against the floor, and she is propped upright, back against wall.

Theíos.

Her hands fall on a rigid, muscled chest. Kore laughs with relief and weeps in terror. She chokes on salty tears and scans the corridor in both directions.

"I-is it gone?" she blubbers. "Where is it? Where is it?!"

He hits her. Her ears ring. She has never been stricken by a man, and although her mother lands a solid blow at times, there is no equal to the teeth-clashing impact of a virile hand.

"Look at me."

On both sides, the hall narrows into darkness.

"No," Hades scolds and seizes her jaw. "*Look* at me."

He is caustic and grim, and heat stirs inside of Kore. She flushes deep into the belly. Close-set eyes tether her. Connection made.

He holds her head in place. "Breathe."

Hades counts to a steady five, and she draws in a single torturous breath. Her lungs struggle for air. At the count of five, he tells her, "Hold."

She stops breathing. With him, it is easy to stop breathing.

He commands the exhale: "Two . . . three . . . four . . ."

In this vein, they stand in the corridor, facing each other.

Count. Breathe. Hold. Sigh.

The in-breath, like drawing close. The out-breath, like pressing in.

This new rhythm takes hold of her lungs, and

she exhales slow and steady. The pattern of breath, trained at his instruction. Everything below the waist throbs in time with her pulse: feet, knees, thighs, and the taunting place between the legs.

He takes two steps back and scans the corridor with a scowl. "What is wrong with you?"

"Th-the-there's s-something in my r-room." Fat, hot tears stream down her cheeks. His face shimmers in them.

"Something?"

"Th-the man from the statue. Sisyphus."

Theíos is the second person to ask, "What do you know about Sisyphus?"

She shakes her head. She knows nothing. She is a stupid girl, imagining things.

"You have such an imagination."

"You are not in danger. You are afraid, and fear cannot harm you." Out of the corner of his eye, Hades scans her up and down. "Now, get back to your room."

"Please," she cries, rising on her tiptoes, "not alone." Kore takes his hand into two of hers and tugs. "I will feel safer with you. P-please, *Theíos*?"

At this, Hades grimaces, more irritable than before. "Stop that."

"Stop wh—"

"That."

Kore flinches. What does he mean? This is the first time she hears him raise his voice—and it is raised at *her*. She will die if *Theíos* does not like her.

Biting her lip, Kore fights the urge to cry and stares at the floor.

"Get out of here."

"I-I—"

"What? Spit it out."

She hiccups a cry. "I do not know the w-way."

He snatches her under the arm. It hurts. "Come on." Fingers digging, he drags her along at a pace faster than she can comfortably walk. To loosen his grip, Kore puts her hand over his. He clenches tighter. She submits to the pain of force, moving as quickly as he does, surprised she ran this far from her quarters. She is like a punished child caught by the ear.

After several turns through identical corridors, her surroundings assimilate.

"Which one of these is yours?" he snaps.

She points, lip quivering. "That one."

"Now you know the way." He releases her arm with a poorly stifled shove.

Kore stumbles and secures her footing. Her face runs scarlet, and she drops her gaze to the floor before the shame floods in. Everything about her annoys him. She is too sensitive and childish for someone of his stature. He is king first and uncle second. Pursing her lips, Kore scurries away. Why must she speak? No one cares what she has to say. She has nothing of value to offer. Words trip from her tongue and make her sound witless.

She hurries through the doorway to her quarters,

abashed. The room is freezing. One wick of the lamp has extinguished; the other flickers dimly. The rest of the room, black as death. As gooseflesh breaks, the fine hairs on her arms rise.

She searches corners. Nothing emerges.

Where is it?

Kore rushes to the bed and tumbles onto a mattress stuffed with soft leaves, rustling under blankets while wrestling them up over her shoulders.

Far across from her, movement in shadow.

Kore breathes in.

One.

Two.

Three.

The darkness spits forth a square-shouldered silhouette. Upright beneath the covers, Kore propels herself back with both legs, slamming into the wall and hardly feeling it.

The figure is not a shade. She sees short hair, high forehead, cheeks sculpted by bone and hollows.

A terrible yearning takes hold, and for a moment Kore nearly exclaims and leaps from the bed and throws her arms around the High King's neck. But something ominous flashes in his eyes, and she clutches the blankets over her mouth to keep from betraying his severity with a smile, for he cringes at childlike enthusiasm as much as he cringes at tears.

He takes two steps. Stops. Looks at her.

Kore says nothing.

He takes two more steps. "Where are your

dogs?"

Blankets clutched to her mouth, Kore shrugs.

He turns and walks out of the room. Nothing for several minutes. Kore lowers the blankets to her lap and sits motionless, staring at the doorway.

From the hall, a tapping.

Dog on each side, Hades reappears. He holds a dry, green stalk and walks to the table at her bedside. He uses the single wick to light the plant, and the heavy smell of sage infiltrates the space.

"You talk too fast," he says. "Take a breath. Slow down. Say less."

His mood, a passing storm.

"*Theíos*?"

One last time he looks at her, and Kore admits to herself he is handsome.

Breathe.

"Do you . . . like me?"

He turns away. "No."

Her heart goes mad. *Breathe. Two. Three.*

Kore sinks into the blankets, watching him go. When he is gone, she wipes her cheeks and kisses the air to summon the dogs closer. They come. They curl beside her, happy to keep her warm, pacified by the soft sweet-smelling body of a woman.

THE JUDGE'S SHIP

3

At the coastline, Demeter looks to the west. In the hazy afternoon sun, three enormous black ships lined with gold are banked there. She cannot see the crest marking the center of their red flags, but she assumes it to be the heads of three dogs. From where she stands, the vessels appear long and thin as bones.

By the time Demeter navigates the narrow walkways and returns to the palace of Knossos, she is winded and staggering. These weeks subsisting on scraps of food and naps driven by sheer exhaustion have caught up with her.

Much of the palace still stands. For several days, people have come in and out. Outside, slaves salvage rubble to use in the reconstruction. They use pulleys crafted from wood and rope to hoist stone. Their skin is caked with chalky powder, muddy tracks of sweat rolling down their backs.

High at the steps to the palace, she spots a group of little girls in yellow tunics with garlands in their hair. They spin and watch their skirts bell, swinging their arms and enjoying the slap of fabric against their hands. Little novitiates, waiting outside for a ceremony to begin.

On wobbly legs, Demeter ascends the stairs.

"Nani," she calls to a small girl.

Nani turns and waves, jumping up and down. "Priestess Demeter! Did you come to see me in possession today?"

She means *procession*. Demeter smiles thinly. "Are there guests inside at the ceremony? Men from across the sea?"

The child says yes with ringlets bobbing. As Demeter walks off, Nani says, "High Priestess? Did Kore die?"

Demeter stops. "Not at all, little one."

"Did she run away?"

"Of course not! She was taken."

"Who took her?"

"Bad men. Listen to me. Be cautious with those you meet. You can never know who might want to hurt you."

Nani stares up at her, swaying in place. Oblivious.

Demeter squats next to the child and takes her shoulders. "You are going to keep close to me when your mother is not around, yes? You do not want bad men to take you?"

Brows high, Nani shakes her head quickly.

Nani's mother should tell her these things for her own safety. Demeter gives her head a shake. "Never mind. I am going to bring Kore back. Will this make you happy?"

"Yes!"

"Show me the guests who arrived in big boats."

Nani points and grabs Demeter's hand and pulls her along, the pads of naked feet thumping against the dirt and pebbles on Royal Road. She leads Demeter past the theater, around the corridor, and into West Court, where the altar base is prepared and slaves place kindling inside three circular pits in the ground for an animal sacrifice.

When Ammon presides, he will stand behind the altar. A grand, royal box is positioned directly behind the priestly position, and the future king sits, already differentiated from his grandfather by calling him "Good Minos." He is a young man with his wife and children and guards. In the courtyard, worshippers kneel. With royalty in place, the procession will begin any moment.

"Thank you, Nani. Hurry back to the processional corridor. Quickly, before they begin."

Guards from Asphodel stand behind the king, along with an official-looking man wearing a long chiton of pale blue and green, pinned at the shoulder by a gold serpent. He is balding with tufts of hair sticking up around the crown, wild and wispy around his ears. His beard is multicolored. A shiver runs along her spine. He resembles his brother. To this day, Demeter cannot think of the former king without the old disappointment of watching an idol fall.

As High Priestess, there is nothing strange about her approaching the royal box. Nothing strange, either, about standing next to it, for often priests and priestesses of higher rank will position beside the royals, if they are not presiding over the ceremony. She sidles up to the canopied seats, hands laced in front of her and head high with a dignity she does not feel in the slightest. She feels desperate, impatient. Demeter smears a benevolent smile across her face.

"High Priestess," the guard next to her greets. Savas is his name. She helped him the day they found King Lycastus under the rubble. A bronze nosepiece hangs from the center of his helmet, making him recognizable by the sheer enormity of his size.

She tilts her head to the guests from abroad. "Who are they?"

"Take a gander at the one in robes. Does he remind you of anyone?"

Demeter shakes her head. Men like Savas love to relay information if they can brag about how much of it they have.

"That," he says, "is one of the judges of the Unseen." He fakes a maudlin shiver. "All the way from Asphodel."

"Why?"

"To help with reconstruction, they say."

"Yes, but why?"

He says, "According to the judge, 'it is an act of brotherhood for Crete and the Cyclades.'"

"Brotherhood?" She watches the maidens stroll up the aisle with baskets of fruit and wheat. Behind them, the smaller girls with ribbons dangling from wreaths in their hair.

The guard smirks. "That ought to make Zeus feel like an ass. Hades sends three ships to aid with Poseidon's territory, and Zeus does nothing?" Demeter ruffles at the name, used twice too many. He mutters, "Apologies."

She pretends hearing the name of her child's father is privilege and focuses on the procession. Ammon appears last, leading a goat for slaughter.

She whispers, "You heard of the wreckage at Matapan?"

"*Narcissus.*"

"What?"

"The name of the ship. *Narcissus.* It destroyed half the port. What it did not destroy, Oceanus did." As an afterthought, the guard says, "I thought you were detained with a consecration today." He realizes that she, Demeter, should be walking alongside Ammon. It is a harvest festival where blood will be spilled in sacrifice for a plentiful reaping. Her favor with the gods blesses them with bounty each year.

She whispers—or tries to whisper—but anxiety makes her louder than intended. "Nomiki says his shipment washed ashore in pieces. Did anyone survive it?"

"Did anyone sur—? Wait. Your Kore left on a ship. The same one?"

"She did not leave!" she hisses. "She *was taken!*"

All heads in the royal box turn. She flushes. Gods help her. Everyone knows by now.

Savas keeps his outward attention on Ammon, who lifts the blade. Out the side of his mouth, he whispers, "All I know is they found a few alive."

"Kore?"

"I cannot say."

In front of the center pit, Ammon drags the knife across the goat's neck. Blood collects inside a bronze bowl.

"After the ceremony," she says, "introduce me around. I want to talk my way onto the judge's ship."

He shakes his head. "Rhadamanthus will stay awhile."

"What for?"

The young son of Good King Minos shushes them.

The guard pauses long enough for the attention to refocus on the sizzling of blood against hot stones. "Poseidon arrives soon, with more aid. We have been asked to stand guard while they meet."

She pales. Mind reeling, Demeter tries to remain cool. "I need to leave *now.*"

"Judge Rhadamanthus came on a passenger ship. The other two are trade."

"Leaving when?"

"Patience." Savas puts a firm hand on her arm. His eyes convey a warning, reminding her that Kore put herself in serious trouble when she fled with a bunch of sailors. "It will not be long before you can sail."

He is not wrong. No need to argue. The gods blessed Savas to be a skilled gossip, and she has been disruptive enough.

"Stay afterward, and speak with the judge. Rhadamanthus is bound by honor to assist in matters of Zeus's children. We all are."

When Ammon calls for silence and prayer among the worshippers, the crowd takes to their knees. The king and queen kneel, as they must heed the authority of the gods if they are ever to become gods themselves. With them, the guard subjugates and raises his head to the sky, along with a hundred other craning necks. Demeter slips away and rushes alongside the palace until she is out of sight.

Minthe in the Dark
4

He needs it dark. Whomever the slaves deliver, Hades has no interest in seeing. She is a means of relief, dependent upon illusion: an illusion that will break with enough light to discern physical features. To see the colors.

Hades waits by open shutters, letting in cold air. Rain pummels stone and dusts his face. Far below, the river divides canyon walls, gulped by the open mouth of Cerberus. In the downpour, the monoliths glow faintly. Other kings can have their walls, their fortresses. The polis of Asphodel perches high on a cliff, guarded by monstrous canine heads with soldiers for brains.

Back to the open door, Hades perceives a flicker against the wall. The slave comes with one of Aeacus's prized hetaera. A woman designed to relieve the pain begging for release.

What he wants, he denies himself. While he

may not devour what he craves, neither will he starve. Rotten fruit of Zeus's loins: shiny on the outside, spoiled beneath the skin.

A daughter is most profitable when unplucked. Kingdoms multiply through marriage arrangements with other kingdoms. For the arrangement to be taken seriously, Zeus will demand assurance she remains intact. Hades cannot touch the girl named Kore, lest she lose her value.

Otherwise.

He had examined the swells of her nubile body, draped in thin, pointless cloth. Kore, hysterical and fragile, with visible nipples tenting silk and the shadow of her navel hinting of more mysterious places below.

Touching her. Breathing her. Striking her.

As she retreated to her room, he watched. Her cinched waist sloped into round buttocks. Unable to rid the image of swaying hips, he followed Kore to her quarters. He started toward her in that bed, roused by the way she hid behind the blanket, afraid of upsetting him again. He stopped himself. Advanced toward her again. She trusted him. She gazed at him with adoration, and some internal device snapped him out of the spell. He hates her whining naivete, yearns to destroy it, but stays his desire all the same, too manipulated by innocence to force her legs open and ruin the simpleminded child there.

Now, to the slave, he says, "Leave the woman."

He balls his fists. Jaw muscles flex from gritted

teeth.

Once the slave's torch disappears, Hades turns toward the outline of a female form. Lightning shows him more than he wants—a woman with a long, upturned nose with wide nostrils and hair pinned high. Her face is whitened with lead powder, lips an unnatural red. She gives off yellows of fear. Flares of orange intrigue.

Minthe.

He rejects her name as soon as it slips to mind, but—too late. The illusion bursts. The game is ruined.

He slams the shutter doors, barring the light. If she is smart, the whore will not say a word.

She is not smart. "Should I—"

He grabs her face, her scream wet and vibrating against his palm. The pungent floral oil on her skin is unlike the memory of Kore's softer smell. His body drives him forward while his mind scrambles to concoct fantasy.

"May I call you Theíos*?"*

Flinging her around and grabbing her by the hair.

"Do you . . . like me?"

Throwing her over the table.

To fool himself she is pure, he presses her legs together and enters from behind. He keeps his hand over her mouth, refusing to let her ruin it with the reality of voice.

"P-please, Theíos*."*

Wedged behind the column, Kore had cried in a state of panic. It felt good to hit her. Hades recalls a gut-driven flash of the arm and the sharp impact of flesh against his hand.

He rams into the bent frame suffocating behind a covered mouth. The fury bursts. An instant of delirium, the release of pressure.

It felt good to hit her, and then it did not. Afterward, sympathy blanketed him like a curse.

Hades releases the whore, and the tainted energy covers his hands and forearms and pelvis. The field radiating from her contaminates him.

Other men seem to enjoy this. They *get* to enjoy this.

With darkness, he may avoid the colors, but he cannot avoid the sum of her essence sticking to him like tar. She pushes away from the table and stands, a feminine outline hunched and trembling in the scant light from the doorway. He wrings his arms as if ridding himself of the corruption Minthe absorbs throughout debauched days and nights. He feels her shame and self-loathing and desperation for attention.

Get it off me, he thinks, but says, "Are you all right," with no true concern.

She gasps for air, adjusting her clothes and hair. Her voice crushes the illusion further with its pinched, nasal inflection. "Yes, Majesty."

"Leave."

Minthe practically trips as she backs away and

rushes into a semilit corridor. He flicks remnants of the experience from his wrists and arms.

She is gone. Disgust tightens around him as he paces, stretching his arms and neck. This is why he hates to touch. Touch, a perpetual bath in the sins of others. The sensation turns his stomach.

When he ran his fingers along Kore's face, he felt no such contamination. He opens the terrace doors, noticing the silence, and finds the rain has ceased. Clouds parted. The moon, a sliver.

For a long time, he listens to a distant ocean. It exists as a mirror for a moon creeping its way across the sky. He tries to picture Kore, grasping at the memory like one grasps to recall a dream. The harder he fights to conjure the memory, the more irritable he becomes.

Hades leaves the room. At the doorway, Cerberus falls in behind him, but he snaps his fingers and instructs them to stay. The dogs make a wide loop back to the entrance of his doorway.

He walks because he cannot stand still. He slips through corridors because memory falls short of reality.

Hades finds his way to Kore's room.

Stretched on either side of her, two mastiffs. Dogs, as long as she. One willowy arm is thrown around the bulk of a dog, pert nose smashed into a canine shoulder blade.

Their ears prick. Both dogs sit tall as Hades walks inside.

They relax. Rise. They slide off the bed like mammoth slugs.

To Hades, they surrender the girl.

If she wakes, she wakes. He lets it be.

Kore rolls onto her back with chin slumped to the side and body open like a starfish. Perhaps what attracts the dogs also attracts him. Perhaps it has been too long since he saw the light of an innocent.

Hades observes the ebb and flow of white. He presses in.

The silver-blue hand of the ocean sweeps over a trade ship. Men are crushed by water and bludgeoned by their own oars. A mast swings in the chaos, and rope plucks the hand of a captain straight from the joint as blood spurts.

From the ocean, shades arise from the bodies of dead men. Shades, as visible as mortal men, ascending from sea into sky.

"What is w-wrong with this place?"

Phantoms rarely register to the human eye. Yet the girl who calls herself Kore sees them.

"Th-the-there's s-something in my r-room."

He flips through the sequence of her life in short, agonizing leaps. Plucking little pieces from an untainted past:

Priestess.

Mother.

This golden waif, at five, at eight, at twelve. Always sheltered by the prestige of being Daughter of Zeus.

The Mother.

De-meter.

She whispered hotly into a gullible ear: "*Keep to me, Kore. I will not let them hurt you.*"

This confused the little girl, never observing these bad men Mother told her about because of the one phrase echoing throughout her sixteen very-young years of life. One phrase shielded her from the hardships known by other girls:

Daughter of Zeus.

He squints at the brilliance of the light and backs away, dizzy. His pulse roars in his ears.

At the agony in his head, Hades recoils. The visions fade.

A pregnant drop of blood falls from his eye and stains the white silk of Kore's gown.

THE BLUE PURSE
5

To everyone but the slave girl, Demeter keeps her mouth shut. Anyone else would talk her out of this. Asli is a safe ear.

The slave girl is preoccupied with folding Demeter's priestly robes. While she readies her mistress for sleep, Asli spies the satchel beside the bedside table. In it, fruit, bread, and water in an otter-skin jug.

Asli fidgets with the latch on a maple chest, unquestioning.

"In the morning," Demeter instructs, "go to the home of Priest Ammon. You will serve him until I return."

She states it matter-of-factly, as if they have discussed it all along, but this is the first Asli hears of this plot. Kneeling before the open chest, she folds a flounced skirt and nods into her lap.

Demeter relaxes when Asli accepts the news

without protest. "Good."

"I knew when I saw the ships today." Asli closes the chest and latches it.

"Knew what?"

"That you would go back with them." Asli looks at her hands, holding back whatever she wants to say. Asli has not been around long enough to witness the closeness between mother and child; she joined their household when the fighting escalated, when a sullen child rebelled through silence—a punishment Demeter hated and returned with the constant barking of orders, of dreaming up new ways to protect her daughter that, no doubt, resulted in more resistance. Their nights, once spent weaving or singing together, turned to picking and jabbing and twisting the knife. This is the Demeter and Kore that Asli has come to know. Them at their worst.

It must confuse her to see the love now. To see Demeter, hair yanked thin from hysteria, scratches up and down her arms from her own nails, thinner than she has ever been, and eyes cavernous from lack of sleep. Perhaps she emotes in a way that causes Asli to shy from her, this God-invoking priestess raving like a banshee at the loss of her estranged daughter.

The slave glances at the satchel. "I will pack a blanket, too."

"Thank you."

"The gods will show favor to you."

"If I am worthy."

Asli tips her chin. "If a High Priestess is not

worthy, there is hope for no one."

Beyond this, no words of farewell. No indication of attachment. Demeter supposes Asli will miss her. Supposes she will miss Asli. After the slave departs, Demeter walks to her bedside.

The floor is cobblestone, covered by a wool rug made from her own loom. Beneath the rug, a loose stone. Demeter used to stub her toe on it. The rug prevents that. She lowers to her knees. She pulls the rug back.

One stone is a shade lighter than the rest. Demeter nudges it back and forth until the stone budges. She curls her fingers around the edges and removes it. It weighs nothing, but today, it is as heavy as the world.

Demeter has not moved the stone since she got the purse. Fifteen years ago? It must have been. She was nursing then.

She lugs the thing away and sets it aside with a clack. Hand shaking, she reaches into the floor.

She does not want to feel it. Demeter swore she would never use what she hid in here. Vowed she wanted nothing from him. *Wants* nothing from him.

She feels knotted roots underhand. Pebbles and powdery dirt and cobwebs. Demeter frowns. She rolls onto her knees and hooks a finger into an oil lamp atop the table near her bed, burning with a single flame. Lowers it to the hole.

Nothing but dirt and darkness.

Kore.

How did she know? Demeter touches her chest, strangely glad to be thwarted before she could stoop to using Zeus's gold.

Kore took it. She took it when she ran off. Perhaps it will be the thing that saves her, the stamp of an eagle on coins of gold, backing her story about being the daughter of the King of Kings. No one wishes to offend the man who is rumored to summon lightning from the sky and fry whoever personally offends him. They say Zeus can hurl bolts directly into the crown of a man's head.

As proud as she tries to be, Demeter takes advantage of his fame. Uses it in ways far more effective than coin. Common men have no need for money. Common men, the *damos*, survive by trade, through goods and services shuffled from man to man until all are fed and sheltered. These years with Kore, Demeter has needed Zeus's reputation, not his gold. Despite her pride, she uses what Zeus gave her—his blood—in order to protect Kore from life without a present father.

Demeter pushes herself up. At night, Asli leaves bread, cheese, and water. Lately, Demeter has not eaten. She pinches a large chunk of bread and shoves it into her mouth, a pasty wad rolling against her cheek like cud. She drinks from the cup. Breaks a piece of cheese. The taste of food reminds her of how long she has gone without.

Eat. Get stronger. Sleep (can she?) for a little while.

Demeter swallows. She eats as much as she can and rests in a semiconscious state. Twilight sleep, like floating on her back in a current.

The wings of cicadas buzz outside the window.

"Poseidon arrives soon."

The night races by and, with it, her pulse. As time passes, anxious blood inhibits sleep. Finally, at the point in time where it is closer to day than night, Demeter rises and pulls a rust-colored chiton over her head, then drapes a green himation over one shoulder for warmth.

Demeter throws on her cloak. She has never left the island before. Never, in fact, been aboard a ship or wandered the earth on her own, with no support except what the gods bestow.

Her stomach sours. Before she can rethink it, Demeter slings the bag across her chest and slips from her room into the courtyard.

AT PLAY WITH MASTIFFS
6

Sometimes when Kore wakes, there is blood on the blanket. Not a lot, but enough to catch her attention. Spying it, she touches the soft line of flesh on her head where the wound used to be. She stands up, turning her arms over and twisting to investigate the backs of her legs. She wipes at her nose and inspects her fingers. Finding nothing, Kore checks between her legs, for blood can come from the cut there, too.

Usually, there are one or two droplets, never two nights in a row. Once near the knees of her gown. Another time, at the ankles.

This morning she sees it again. Kore stands on bare feet, stretches, and stops.

A dried red circle upon the stone floor.

There is a strangeness in this place that goes beyond grating noises at night and shadows slipping around corners. Asphodel is swamp water to the spirit, stagnant and dingy and weighted. In Knossos, she would spend the days outdoors in full sun, surrounded by friends who would laugh and braid her hair and a mother who never left her in peace— and Kore took all of it for granted! Friends. Mother. Levity. None of it appreciated as she appreciates it now. As a child, she pitied herself for having only her mother and uncle as familial companions while other children swung from the arms of fathers, held the hands of siblings and cousins. She would watch them, feeling sorry for herself.

Without the dogs, Kore might die of loneliness.

At the doorway, a dog stands on each side. Their ears arc into points, much like the ears of a pig, and their lips droop from imposing, flat-muzzled heads. Their coats shine from morning light filtering through cracked shutters. Smiling, she watches their short, stubby tails wag against the floor.

They struck her as fearsome before. No longer. How lucky she is to have the loyalty of beasts like these! Even when they pounce on her lap, forgetting their size, and dig their nails into her thigh. Or when they become overexcited and jump up, knocking her to the floor and nudging her with their smashed-in noses. They do not mean to hurt her. They love her!

Because mastiffs flock to her during the day, none of the slaves comes around anymore. The dogs frighten them. Kore pats her lap, and they trot to her with tongues flapping. One stops to sniff and lap the speck of blood on the floor. The other places heavy paws on her lap and wets her neck with a tongue the size of her face.

No use in searching the dogs for wounds. Kore has combed her fingers through every inch of fur to no enlightening end.

The giant dog licking her ear, she calls Skylos, which means *dog*—not clever at all. The other one she calls Allo, which means *other*. Like Mother, she is not good at naming things.

In the middle of the night when she wakes up, gripped by anxiety, loss gnawing at her gut, Kore assures herself she will see Mother again. The more days pass, the sicker the heart. No one has come to see her in days. At first, she gave a word of thanks for it. No one asks further questions. No one says things like:

"You better not be lying to me."

Oh, but seeing *him* would not be bad, would it? By day, Kore plays with the dogs outside and, along the way, throws inquisitive glances down corridors and into neighboring rooms. Since that night in her room, Kore has not encountered her *theíos* once. In the palace, she sees the same slaves, the old judges—Minos and the other one whose face is scrunched up like one of the dogs. She sees soldiers and guards, and once she saw a prisoner in chains being led through a room where he would stand in judgment before Hades.

Yet she never sees the High King himself and finds herself scanning the area, hoping to run into him, if only to say hello. It would not be so bad if he were irritable or mean because the more Kore thinks of it, the more she thinks he could one day like her a little, if he does not already.

Besides, he is just grumpy. He does not mean what he says, and if he does, she will try extra hard to gain favor. She must! What will Father think if she cannot gain the approval of his brother? She will win him over . . . if she ever sees him again. She vows to earn a smile. A touch, perhaps.

She recalls the way his beard scratched the palm of her hand, soft and prickly at the same time. What might it feel like to run her lips over it?

A slave peers inside the doorway with fabric folded neatly in her arms. She is tall, gaunt, and a little older than Mother. The woman dresses her daily and yet never says a word. Never looks Kore in the eye.

"Good morning." Kore manages to smile. She has tried many times to talk to the slaves like she talks to Asli at home. They do not speak her tongue.

The slave inches closer to Kore. The dogs growl.

Kore bops Allo on the nose. "Tch! B-bad!"

Allo whines and, following his example, Skylos stops growling and whines along with him before both fall silent, heads lowered to the cautious slave.

"Come on, y-you are safe. They will—" Kore pauses before she says the next word because it catches on her tongue. Ever since that night, she hears *Theios* reminding her:

"Take a breath. Slow down. Say less."

She breathes and says slower, "They will behave." To prove it, she shoots a stern look to Skylos and Allo.

Eyeballing the mastiffs, the slave comes forward.

Kore pats their heads as the slave removes her bedclothes and replaces them with a pale yellow chiton, belted by a golden rope. The clothing here is far more comfortable than in Crete, where corsets cut into the waist and dig beneath the breasts to prop them up high, and where the flounced skirts are rigid and coarse between the fingers. In Asphodel, women drape fabric over their bodies and are done with it. Her breasts feel loose and tickled by the soft linen. She is more aware of her body here.

As the slave dresses her, Kore studies the woman's bare arms and fingers. No wounds.

Once they trust the slave is harmless, the dogs make a lazy path to the door and resume their positions on either side.

"I talk to them all the time," she says as the slave weaves the golden belt around her waist. "Dogs listen well, and they never tell you that you are s-stupid or selfish. I was scared of them at first, but I had to s-surrender and love them, and now they are mine, I think."

The slave winds gold with deft fingers, looping it around and around her middle.

"Do you think wh-when I go, the High King

might let me take them?"

It is pointless to chatter. The slaves are as obedient as the dogs and twice as trained.

"I do not suppose you have any cuts?" She points to the skin on her head, trying to get the slave to understand. "Bleeding?"

The slave thinks Kore is complaining her head hurts. She motions to the scar on Kore's head and asks in a hoarse voice: "*Aci*?"

"N-never mind." Kore forces another smile. "Thank you."

Before she leaves, the slave replenishes the sage and rue. The rue is fresh, sharp with the smell of morning. The heaviness in the air lifts, but Kore likes it better outside where the bad feelings are muted.

"Ready?" she encourages the dogs. Tails wag. Every morning, the same routine. Dress. Eat. Play with the dogs. Nap. Wash. Think. Pray. Cry. Dream.

Along the way, mastiffs wait along corridors, conditioned to expect the girl with a cascade of bronze hair. Each dog joins the pack, and they all go to the courtyard. Kore winds through the palace with an army of dogs.

Perhaps this is the day when she finally runs into Hades again.

Does he stay secluded all day?

Already, she grows braver, far braver than at home. For practice, Kore challenges herself to say hello to anyone she meets, and it works—though the slaves do nothing but bow and the guards leer and never say anything back. Their responses do not matter. What matters is, she does it regardless and forces herself to speak to complete strangers with no one behind her to finish her sentences when she stammers too much. As long as she had Mother to fall back on, Kore fell back.

Winded from the journey across the palace, Kore pulls open the ebony doors. She gasps.

The courtyard teems with hulking black shapes—more than she has ever seen!

Every dog in the palace must gather here. Their necks are bare. No, this is not all of the dogs. Hades's dogs wear golden collars of a serpent biting its tail.

Kore stands at the open doors, scanning the courtyard. There is nowhere to play when the grass is crowded by dogs.

Beside her, Skylos bumps her hand with his snout. Allo nudges the small of her back.

"A-all right. I know."

A few of the dogs nearest the door close in. Whimpering, begging her with their weary, golden eyes:

Play with us.

She takes an uncertain step forward. Canine shapes cut through fog, whining. When she considers their life of sitting still or moving in violence, it saddens her. Kore walks toward the center of the courtyard, this one unlike the courtyard with the monument of Sisyphus. Here, a wide yard of green, unadorned by flowers or pools. Along the sides of the courtyard stand gnarled trunks and branches of pomegranate trees. Red fruit speckles grass as the dogs loom closer.

Kore clears her throat. "All of y-you, listen!"

The dogs sit.

Kore blinks. She licks her lips and fiddles with a strand of hair. "Th-this will o-only work if—"

"Slow down. Say less."

Arms raised at her sides as if parting them, she cuts a line down the center of the dogs. She sweeps her arm around the crowd of dogs on the right. "You!"

Dogs herd sheep. She can herd the dogs. With her body and widened arms, she sways them to the wall to her right. "Here. Stay."

With the other group of dogs, she does the same, herding them to the wall on the left. "Stay."

Within minutes, she positions two lines of dogs on each side of the courtyard. Tails wag. Watching them, making certain they do not move, Kore grins at the orderliness. Mother might be impressed if she were here. The shapes of men linger inside the shadows of the east and west entrances. Guards. They must have come for their dogs—and yet none of them move in.

Kore trots to one of the trees. She plucks a fallen limb from the grass. Making her way to the northernmost part of the courtyard, she pulls off the leaves and stems and breaks the stick at a length the size of her forearm—a size easy to hold inside canine jaws.

Standing between the two lines, Kore raises the stick and kisses the air to get their attention. All heads point her way, and tails gyrate faster.

"You—" she says to the first dog in line on her left, and motions for him to step forward.

Kore gestures at the first dog in line on her right. "—And you. Come."

They do.

Kore hurls the stick as far as she can. The dogs dart for it. Their tongues flap from happy, open mouths. On the way to the stick, the dogs smash into each other in an attempt to derail the opponent. Kore jumps and claps and laughs. The smile fits genuinely on her lips.

Jaws snap at the stick. Both seize it and growl and wrestle, and one jerks the stick away from the other. The other dog bears down harder, and they race toward her, joined by their hold on the stick, no longer competing but simply running in the bliss of play.

In this vein, the game continues. The first dog in each line competes for the stick. About fourteen dogs into the game, a hunched figure hobbles toward her.

The dogs remain alert but do not budge. They recognize him as they recognized old Judge Minos that day.

"Beware the mongrels," a gravelly voice warns.

"They are defense, not pets."

"Oh." Kore winks at the dogs. "D-do *they* know that?"

The man coming out of the fog is a judge of Erebus—the one with the haggard face and long steel-gray hair. Kore saw him the night she met Hades.

"My, my. Look at you. Healthy and whole, if you ask me."

"Wh-what do you mean?"

"You are supposed to be sick, are you not? Too sick to remember a thing?"

Kore hugs herself with one arm, not liking the weird twinkle in his eye or the half-smile or bitter words. At night, she relies on dogs to protect her from shades. Now, she finds herself glancing at the dogs because of a human.

"Calm yourself," the old man says. He smells of sour milk. "I suppose the light will do you good. You look pale."

"I am tired, I guess," she says, not knowing what else to say.

"Tired? How can you be tired? You sleep all day, when you are not commandeering our watchdogs and putting the High King at security risk."

"O-oh!" Kore flushes, backing away from the old man. "I am sorry. P-please believe—"

"I do not believe a damn thing you say, girl. But I see no reason to let you go until you start telling the truth. It is simple, understand? Tell us your tale, and we will send you on your way."

"T-to my father, you mean. To Zeus."

The old man smiles a wide grin that stretches his jowls. He surveys the yard. "You must be bored senseless. This is how you spend the day?"

"Wh-what else might I do?" she nearly pleads. The truth is, she *is* bored and would love to do something other than cry and sleep and throw sticks.

"Come with Aeacus," he says, stepping closer. "I will show you things. I might let you play a game with me, too."

It happens in an instant. Aeacus reaches out one ragged hand and plants it on her shoulder. Beside her, Skylos reacts as quick as a sneeze. The mastiff rears up and lunges. Giant paws knock against his chest. His feeble body flies backward. Snarling, Skylos pins Aeacus to the ground, and Allo joins in and towers over the crumpled figure of a man who made the terrible mistake of putting his hands on her.

All other dogs growl and let out deep, emergent barks that ricochet off stone walls.

Guards fly to the scene. Armor clanking, they run to the aid of the judge. The dogs remain intent on defending Kore, who stands with her hands over her mouth.

Spears upraised, a guard cries, "Down!" and "Settle!"

The dogs snap at the air. They stand on hind legs, drool flying. A pack of mastiffs growl and circle any guard who stands in the way of protecting their newfound treasure.

From above, a needle-sharp whistle. The dogs halt.

At the top of the palace in the center terrace, Hades stands with hands braced against an obsidian railing. Joy leaps from Kore's gut to her chest.

No one makes a sound.

Without raising his voice, Hades commands, "To your posts."

The dogs slink away. One massive paw slips from Aeacus's chest, and the beast lets out a yawp of complaint. A few guards hustle to the fallen man and help him to creaky knees.

At last! Kore beams and, with a little spring, rolls onto tiptoes and thrusts an arm into the air. She wiggles her fingers in an enthusiastic hello.

"Do you . . . like me?"

Hades's face remains placid, eyes like pits from the distance.

"Sorry about your judge!" she sings, brighter than she has felt in weeks.

From the terrace, Hades turns his head. She follows his line of sight. In the far-right corridor gathers a group of guards, watching the show. They scatter and disappear.

Judge Aeacus shuffles to his feet and dusts the himation with agitated hands.

In the yard, there are more people than dogs. Kore hopes she has not caused so much disruption they view her as a troublemaker. Of the dogs, Skylos and Allo remain. Guards make a fuss over the judge, although no real harm was done.

By the tilt and direction of his head, Hades is staring at her. A pleasant buzz charges her arms and breasts and legs, heartbeat hard and slow. A lump hangs in her throat.

"Do you . . . like me?"

He had told her no. Yet Kore knows he watches over her. She has suspected for days, and now she is sure. At night, *Theíos* visits to make sure the unholy shades of Asphodel do not harm her. And although she stands too far away to be certain, Kore bets her uncle's eyes are shot with blood.

Hades leaves.

"What did I tell you? They are not pets! They are dangerous creatures who are not to be domesticated for your amusement!" Rubbing his hip, Aeacus limps to her. "Your childishness could have gotten me killed!"

Before the old man can continue his tirade, Skylos and Allo rumble in their throats.

"You see?" He spins to the guards and commands, "Take the dogs. They require rebreaking."

"P-please let me keep them with me . . ."

"Do you think we keep the dogs at bay because we are callous monsters? No! We do it because they serve a purpose, and deviating from that purpose puts us at risk. Understand?"

Chains wrap around the necks of Skylos and

Allo. They toss their heads like horses.

"I-I am sorry," she says, more to the dogs than to Aeacus.

With apathy, they retreat. As the guards lead them away, they regard her with gratitude for the joy she gave them up until now. They have experienced a glimmer of love, but accept the old ways with complacency. They are used to being alone. They accept the fate of "rebreaking," whatever that means.

The courtyard is empty. She stands in the center of the grass. A cold breeze whips her hair. The translucent husk of a cicada blows across grass and stops at her toes. This ghostly but tangible shadow of its former self, Kore picks up between two fingers and lets it roll, hollow, inside her palm.

Stupid, selfish girl.

The husk crackles inside her fist. She opens her fingers, and fragments of the cicada skin fly away with the breeze.

Strange how it can be so, but Kore senses the invisible pressure of a person staring. Eyes have this sort of power.

Optimism pulls her attention to the terrace. She would not mind Hades staring, but the terrace remains empty.

An uncanny magnetism pulls her line of sight to the left.

At the double-doored entrance to the palace, a sallow figure. His fine clothes appear colorless. His skin also appears colorless. As soon as she spots the shade, he disappears inside.

Kore scurries out of the yard and back inside. Candlelight creates a path along the floor, like a trail of peanut shells leading her to the correct staircase, to the correct wing, pointing all the way to the quarters where she sleeps.

She peers around.

Without the dogs, without her plants and herbs, Kore feels like a coward. Better she run back to her room where she can at least pretend to be safe. She begins to do it—and she sees him.

From the doorway, the shade of Sisyphus appears, saying:

"Tartarus."

Her body runs cold. The hairs on her arms rise.

Sisyphus beckons with a tilt of the head. She should not follow.

Or perhaps she is merely a coward. Perhaps the shades are as lost and lonely as she.

Kore follows, shirking the light lain for her on the ground, leading to a room cleansed by sage and rue.

THE WHITE BULL
7

Standing in judgment, a man will bleed from the eyes.

Upon seeing Hades for the first time that day, Minos struggles not to react. The eyes of Hades are webbed with veins, which turn the whites to red. Looking at them makes his burn and water in sympathy.

Minos understands the pain. The long-term consequences.

Five years after kneeling before the throne of Hades, Minos still has difficulty viewing things from afar. Faces are peach blurs until he draws close enough to discern features.

"Majesty," he says with tiptoeing concern, "are you well?"

Hades's eyes blaze like those of his victims. "Well enough."

Judge Aeacus takes cautious steps toward his

former pupil. The tortoise-like folds in his neck stretch as he cranes for a better look. "By the gods, what happened to you?"

Once, Aeacus had asked Minos the same question—when Minos himself stood in judgment.

"Ah, the revered King Minos, bereft of title and dignity. What happened to you?"

It was as useless as asking a child to confess to breaking a pot when you saw him do it; for the Unseen dug into his guilt and knew the truth within an instant.

At first, a prickling sensation—no cause for alarm. Soon commenced a blistering discomfort of an unwanted particle in the eye. Discomfort evolved into painful burning. He blinked tears that rolled into his mustache and trickled to his lip. Tears tasted of iron. Eyesight went from crisp to murky red.

Minos had knelt flayed before the infamous Unseen and his two judges.

Aeacus. And Rhadamanthus, who gaped at him as if he were an imitation of his brother and not his brother at all.

Hades had spoken softly. "There is remorse in you. For what are you remorseful? For your allegiance to me and my brothers during the war? For turning against the titan kings?"

"No, Majesty. I do not regret this allegiance."

During years spent in service to Hades, Minos has witnessed strange things. In his lifetime, among the presence of nobles and kings, he has never encountered a king who deserves posthumous deification more. It took time to grow accustomed to what they call "insight." In mortal form, Hades wields more godlike powers than Minos can fathom.

Somehow, Hades knew Minos regretted more than getting caught.

"Your remorse spans the course of years."

"Yes, Majesty."

"Poseidon rewarded you for the use of your fleet in the war. Start there."

How had he known? Head pounding, blinking in rapid succession, Minos struggled to think. There was no way to strategize for words that might spare him. No way to pad to the truth.

"Poseidon sent me a gift."

"He sent you a white bull."

Knees aching against marble, Minos shuddered.

"Yes, Majesty. A rare albino a year old. He commanded that I sacrifice it to the gods as a gesture of gratitude for granting us victory over the titans."

"Did you?"

"Majesty. I regret I did not."

"Why?"

"It was rare. A striking creature. I sacrificed a bull, but not the one given to me by Poseidon, High King of the Cyclades."

"This is your first repentance."

"Yes. I hid it away with a sense of pride in ownership. It was never mine to own. I know this now."

"Tell me about the bullpen."

The puttering of torchlight cut the silence of the throne room. Minos barely had the strength to keep his head aloft.

"Indeed, I commissioned the stonemason to craft a grand bullpen for the beast. It was . . . elaborate."

That was when Aeacus piped up, saying, "What is that you say? Elaborate or labyrinth? My ears are not good."

How humiliating to be laid bare in front of his own brother, Rhadamanthus, who had admired Minos until now.

"By design, the pen was not unlike a labyrinth. It was crafted adjacent to the arena. The bull was reared to be part of the games at Knossos. Being housed inside a maze tended to rile him. When riled, a bull is more exciting to watch. I regret the labyrinth and for provoking aggression in this sacred creature."

Though his head and eyes ached, the burning subsided. No longer had Hades needed to pry. Minos purged freely.

"My son was a skilled athlete in the arena. What an affinity he developed for the creature. At bull leapings, he vaulted over the horns as if they were engaged in a dance. All of Knossos celebrated the skill of Androgeos. When he begged to take part in the Panathenaic Games of Attica, I allowed it. I wanted to show him off. Pride and indulgence. Both, my sins."

To which Hades said, "And you paid for those sins."

When Minos cried, real tears flowed with blood.

"I paid with his life. Of course, he bested the Atticans at their games—and they murdered him for it. No doubt, King Aegeus was horrified to learn what happened. He thought he could pay me off with the sons and daughters of Attican nobles. He thought it would create peace. Nothing could repay my loss. Those children meant nothing to me."

Afterward, Minos felt his surroundings fall away. No longer did he kneel at the foot of a throne hugged by narrow walls and pillars. Something shoved him into another time, when sorrow over the death of Andro had begun to consume him during the night. He would numb himself with wine, and while the palace slept, Minos would stumble out of his quarters, beyond the palace, and to the neighboring arena where the white creature resided in its pen. Drunken delusions had intermixed with sorrow. At times, he would swear the bull spoke to him with Andro's voice. Under a moonlit sky, with irises flaming red, the bull had snorted pure rage and called, "Father, avenge me."

Attica had sent him fourteen children.

Caged inside the labyrinth, the bull would thrash and gallop in search of an exit. The exit always led to the same place. The arena, barred by a massive wooden door.

Faithful to their king, guards had done as directed. They had pried sleeping children from their beds at night and led them to slaughter.

Reeking of wine, Minos had yanked the lever to open the door.

Within the arena, the children had screamed with fear as the bull flew from imprisonment, maddened by the endless maze from which there seemed no true escape.

Morning had come and, with it, horror. The bull had been covered in the gore of children. Their broken bodies had littered the arena floor.

As quickly as Minos had been thrust into the scene, he returned and found himself back at the foot of Hades's throne. His knees were numb from kneeling, face caked with crimson tears. The fluff of his hair was drenched and plastered against his neck with sweat.

At last, Judge Rhadamanthus spoke. "Majesty, perhaps my brother succumbed to the madness of kings. It is a timeless infection that will exist as long as there is hierarchy among men. Power is a god demanding sacrifice."

Hades had known better, muttering, "As is grief. King Minos of Knossos, you have committed crimes of inhuman cruelty. For this, you are banished from the island of Crete. You are stripped of your throne, family, and respect. I release you into the care of your brother, Judge Rhadamanthus. Until I call upon you again, take time to heal. This is my command."

It took days to heal. The pain subsided. The whites in his eyes returned. His vision cleared.

Thereafter came the offer.

Instead of crawling away from the caves of Tartarus, broken and without home or esteem, Minos was given an opportunity to redeem a tainted legacy. In the end, a man can be reduced to his crime, with nothing to correct his reputation.

"Why would you want a man like me? Surely Rhadamanthus has played a part in your leniency."

"Judge Rhadamanthus is a good contrast to the darkness in Aeacus. You are acquainted with the dark as well as the light. I rely upon you for balance. My offer is self-serving, not lenient."

Now, as Hades passes the hearth, he squints and turns his head from the light. He does not answer Aeacus's question.

"What happened to you?"

Something has happened, but Minos knows not to press him. The physical pain is enough. Hades does not need his judges needling him.

"Might you want to," Minos hesitates, glancing at Aeacus, "take a day to rest?"

"Today, you are my insight," Hades grumbles. "You are here to advise. So, advise."

Poseidon!

8

When she reaches a moonlit coast, Demeter finds ships banked on sand, having been pulled ashore to avoid waterlogging overnight. Up close, the ships intimidate and make her head spin with a loss of equilibrium.

Demeter searches the body of the first ship, inspecting the frame for the lowest point. Wind cuts through her ears. The stern arcs high, curved like a tail. Sand crunches underfoot. Damp from the tide, it clumps between her toes. Her leg smashes against an oar propped diagonally, and she rubs her shin.

The call of a seagull echoes between the hulls. Waves hiss and spray freezing mist on her toes.

Overhead, Demeter discerns the flap of masts in the wind, two of them as large as her house and the foremast about half that size.

At the opposite end of the ship, Demeter spots the lowest point of the vessel. Below an upcurved prow stretches the flat oak surface of the rostrum. She places both hands on it. Wet. She uses the sleeve of her cloak to dry it and avoid slipping. This time, she uses all of her strength to hoist herself up and plant her knees onto the rostrum.

Keeping hold, she pulls herself to the hull. Gathering all of the strength in her arms, Demeter drags her upper body over the side of the deck as her legs flail with an impetus to drive her body over the hull and aboard the ship. The ledge digs into her ribcage, cuts into her waist. In a sudden shift of balance, she falls over and crumbles onto the deck. Water sloshes inside the otter-skin jug planted against her belly, secure inside the satchel.

Standing on unsteady legs, she pushes her hair away from her face. Her vision adjusts to new surroundings.

On each side, there are rows upon rows of benches for oarsmen, split by a narrow aisle. They are shaded by an upper deck, where Demeter supposes the captain will sit.

In her lifetime, she has never found reason to board a ship. She does not know the first thing about ships. There is no place to hide. Every spot on the ship is open and visible to fifty oarsmen.

How long had Kore planned to leave? She had managed to study the anatomy of the ships and had known you cannot hide aboard. She had known the purse full of Zeus's gold would validate her claim of being his child. She had planned it, all of it. The argument they'd had the night before Kore fled had not been the tipping point into a spontaneous runaway attempt.

Ears aching in the wind, Demeter sniffs back tears, wiping a salty, chapped face with the back of her hand.

She sits hard on the bench, head in hands. This is not the way. At the palace today, the guard, Savas, told her:

"Wait. It will not be long before you can sail."

In a few days, she can charm her way on Rhadamanthus's ship. It is safer. Even if the old judge is a lecherous worm, he is elderly and soft, and she has little to fear from him, other than the unfortunate notoriety of hailing from Asphodel. But Savas told her more than this.

"Poseidon arrives soon."

Knuckles aching from the cold, she rubs her hands together and squints. Large wooden boxes stack at the front and back of the ship. If she can pry one open, she can empty the contents and hide. But what would she do with the contents? She would need to haul them out of sight; otherwise, the captain will be mighty confused when he arrives in the morning to find dozens of bull tusk helmets— or whatnot—tossed overboard. She laughs at the foolishness of it.

She laughs at where she is.

She laughs at how crazy she is to sail from Crete now, not three days from now, when a visit to the palace to speak with Rhadamanthus would doubtlessly put her at risk of encountering the person she least wants to encounter.

Demeter last saw Poseidon when she last saw the purse. The soft blue pouch full of gold. She buried it under the stone the day Poseidon sailed off and went back to his own palace in his own land, far east of Knossos with its luxurious white sand and crystal blue sea. It was Poseidon who gave her the purse.

"Zeus wants you to have this."

She hates it. Inasmuch as she wants nothing from Zeus, she knows, regardless of her pride, the benefit of giving birth to his child follows her to this day. Favored. *Ha.*

"Poseidon arrives soon."

She cannot be here for that.

When she met Poseidon, Kore was an infant. Demeter recalls the heaviness of her otherwise small, muscular breasts. They ached with milk. When Kore cried, they leaked and soaked her dress with circular patches.

By then, her popularity among the priesthood had grown, as the newly claimed maternal role edged her into a different category of priestess: no longer maiden but mother. Demeter devoted her utmost focus on mothering her child. She devoted equal focus to mothering the earth through a lifetime of servitude to the gods. Her ceremonies filled their baskets with wheat, barley, and oats. They produced grapes sweet on the vine; they filled the fishermen's nets with tuna, mullet, and cuttlefish.

It happened the citizens of Knossos began to recognize her favor among the gods. She had come from the right family. She had borne the right child. By the time Kore could crawl, Demeter had advanced far enough to conduct a procession at the palace of Knossos itself.

Word came: Poseidon, High King of the Cyclades, would visit Knossos.

She heard it whispered time and time again:

Poseidon!

Poseidon . . .

How excited she had been! Poseidon, a High King who would no doubt one day live among the gods. All her life, she had lived on the island and seen the same faces day-to-day. A royal visitor from afar was enough to have the entire polis in a state of frenzy.

Demeter ogled him at the welcome ceremony. He had a blazing orange-red beard and hair falling past the shoulders, shock-blue eyes, and an incredible upper body full of mountains and ridges she had never seen before nor since. She danced alongside the beating drums as the ceremony began, this sunny priestess made lush and round by motherhood. She danced herself into a sweat, realizing the ritual seemed more like a show for the High King, studying her during the procession. Winking. Making her blush again, as she did that day at the fruit cart with Zeus.

Later, she would think that what happened that day was a punishment from the goddess Potnia for using the ceremony to flaunt herself in front of a king who had a queen waiting for him at home.

Later, Demeter would think a lot of things.

A high gust beats against the masts, snapping loud enough to make her jump. She gets up. She gazes around. At the end of the boat, near the stern, she spots a ladder.

Demeter passes through the center aisle and finds the ladder propped against an upper deck. Hitching her skirt, she climbs it. The ladder wobbles. She ascends slowly.

On the top deck, she finds the captain's box, his view singular and critical, therefore, at the highest point of the ship. Beneath a cypress overhang, the box contains a seat propped high on a wooden pedestal. Demeter considers it.

She crouches. The pedestal is long and flat. She knocks on it. The wood is sturdy. She uses the pad of her hand to bang harder.

Hollow.

If she can pry the outer panel of the pedestal away, she could hide inside. Right under the feet of the captain. In a tiny enclosed space. For many hours.

Demeter laughs again. Strange, choked laughter. What she would not do to get away from one man!

The entire ceremony came and went. Poseidon

had ogled her but never approached her. She wanted to feel desired again after many moons of growing fat, her nipples widening and toughening. Meanwhile friends would tell her:

"No man wants to be measured against Zeus."

But Poseidon was no man. He was a deity in the making.

The memory of Zeus ruined the rain tree for Demeter—her favorite place now a reminder of deception and abandonment. She began to frequent the palace stables, where the finest horses dwelled, and she would comb their manes and stroke their long snouts. The horses came to know her, enjoy her apple-laden visits.

After the ceremony on the day of Poseidon's visit, Demeter went there. Kore was fast asleep inside the palace under the watch of a dozen little novitiates dying to imitate the coveted role of motherhood. Still buzzing from an afternoon of dance and praise and prayer, she offered apples to the white mare she called Forada. Dull light hid behind plumes of slate-gray clouds rolling in. In the distance, a flicker in the clouds. A growl from above the clouds. It would rain, but the horses were safe inside the palatial stables where the most beautiful resided.

From outside the stable doors, voices of men carried, and a group of guards walked inside with Poseidon leading the way. Laughing, they walked to the royal horses. Poseidon saw her. Fine white linen covered his groin and thighs; a wide gold belt covered a rippled belly. His bare chest was made peach-bronze by small curls of hair. He turned to his men and whispered commands.

Demeter pretended not to notice.

When she looked up, the men were gone. Poseidon came forward with a purposeful stride that made her flinch. She was not safe; this was not an innocent way of feeling desired again, for such games were lost on kings. They had nothing to restrain them.

Next to her, the horse whinnied.

"Take off your dress."

Poseidon issued this command while pulling off the belt and letting it fall to the dirt floor.

She could not believe it. Her skin burned pink, sweat bursting with the knowledge that she could do nothing.

Except.

Suddenly, her arms flew around the neck of the horse, and she pulled herself up and kicked the flanks of Forada hard. The horse neighed, front legs rearing up, and bolted. Demeter's head whipped at the force. She clung to the wide, muscled neck, the coarse hair of a white mane whipping around her face, into her line of sight.

She smelled the animal scent of horse in flared nostrils. Hooves thumped against dirt and grass— they sped fast, but Demeter could not see! She felt rain, cold little teeth biting down. She tried to crane her head around and saw nothing but wild strands of horse hair blocking the view. More hooves from behind. Mud flew.

Forada's leg tangled against a fallen branch, and Demeter snapped forward, smashing her nose on the top of the horse's skull. She sailed over Forada's head, thrown far, and hit the grass hard enough to knock the wind from her. The ache in her lungs and back, unbearable. Her shoulder hurt. Her wrist throbbed. She tasted blood. Tried to move.

Could not.

Hooves again, drawing near. She rolled over onto her stomach and blinked and squinted against blinding rain.

"Where are you running to?"

Standing over her, Poseidon. Ominous clouds rolled behind him. Large dollops fell from the sky.

"You made me chase you out here. I will have what I came for."

Now, standing in the captain's box of this ship, Demeter considers shoving herself inside a cranny beneath the captain's feet in order to run from Poseidon again. It seems perfectly reasonable, being trapped inside as in a tomb, trying for hours to keep quiet and hold her bladder.

Demeter crouches. She runs her fingers along the pedestal. She might pry the board open. The tip of her forefinger traces along the thin crack of a board nailed to another board. But how can she pry it off?

Demeter stands. Far below, a single yellow dot bobs along the shore.

A torch.

Demeter throws herself to the floor. Keeps quiet. Who combs the beach at this hour? Did he see her? Chewing the inside of her lip, she remains otherwise motionless. She waits.

From below, a *thump*. Clomping footsteps. A man's voice calls, "Hey! Who is there?"

Demeter presses her cheek to the floor and clamps her hand over her mouth.

A burly figure with torch uplifted emerges, upper body surveying the deck.

"Hey! You there!"

She is frozen.

In the downpour that day outside the stables, she had been frozen, too. Poseidon had pushed her cheek into the mud and taken her like an animal in the fields. She tasted blood down her throat and in her mouth, and to her horror, warmth had spread out over both nipples as her own cries triggered an unburdening of milk. There was no reason to fight. There was nothing she could do.

Now, there is nothing she can do. The man does not budge from the ladder. He stands half above deck, half below, torch raised.

"What are you doing?" the man bellows. "Are you drunk?"

Demeter sits upright. "How dare you? No, I am not *drunk*."

Everyone drinks their watered-down wine, but drunkenness implies weakness and dishonor. Lit by popping fire, the man peers at her, head and face completely devoid of hair. Neither beard nor brows. His skin shines bald. A smooshed nose and cleft lip harden his face.

"Look, lady, I find you slobbering on the floor of my deck in the wee hours—what should I think?"

"My name is Demeter, High Priestess of Knossos." Truth is all she can muster. Rubbing her temple, she mumbles, "I am here because I hoped to sneak aboard."

He looks around. "Sneak inside what, exactly?"

"Inside what?" She snorts a laugh. "Indeed."

"Why do you want aboard my ship?"

"You are the captain?"

"Iasion."

"Iasion," she says. "I need to find my daughter across the sea."

"How did she get over there?" he spouts. "Somebody take her from you?"

Demeter pauses. "She ran away."

"And she is worth the trouble?"

"She is beyond worth."

The captain sighs and cocks his head. "You need a ship."

"I do."

"I need something, too. Make a trade?"

Inside, she cringes and shrinks. Demeter waits for whatever comes next.

Iasion stays where he is. "Too many ships have been lost to Gaia's temperament nowadays. My men and I need protection from the gods. Can you make it so?"

She blinks. "You . . . need me to bless your ship?"

"Well," he barks, "*can* you? High Priestess, you said."

Quickly, she answers, "I can."

"We leave at dawn. Join our camp and rest, if you want."

"I prefer to be alone." She squints off-deck. "Did I walk right past your camp?"

"You did. The watchman pointed you out."

Demeter breathes a laugh. Some stowaway.

"Do you need a blanket? I can find you one."

"Do not trouble yourself," she says, dizzy with fatigue. She could sleep through the world's end. "I am grateful for your help."

Iasion blows air through flapping lips and waves dismissively. "Gratitude is for beggars. Do your magic, Priestess, and I will get you across the sea."

The top of his egg-shaped body descends and, with him, the light of the torch. She watches the light fade beneath the deck as Iasion makes his way back to camp.

When she curls up inside the captain's box, she pulls a blanket from inside her satchel—packed by Asli, whom Demeter misses with a sudden pang—

and draws it around her, knees bent for warmth. She falls asleep, haunted by the High King of the Cyclades, and how his ruddy hair clung to his scalp, neck, and shoulders in the downpour. It dried in the sun as he talked to her afterward. Poseidon, brother to Zeus, chattered as if their coupling had been normal. As if nothing prevented her from carrying on with the day. And yet, she did carry on.

She does, even still.

EURY OF TIRYNS
9

The herald announces: "Eurystheus, King of Tiryns."

Judge Aeacus tilts to the throne and mumbles a sarcastic, "*This* is a surprise."

By his tone, it is not a surprise at all.

Hades sits tense on a high-backed throne. At his command, the two lamps behind him remain unlit. The glare would be too much. Thus, Hades sits in shadow while Aeacus and Minos stand distinguished by firelight cast from nearby pillars.

King Eury of Tiryns lowers himself to both knees. "Humble gratitude to the Unseen for receiving me." He removes a modest bronze-leafed crown and places it on the ground in front of him.

The aisle is long and narrow. Above the throne, a round window casts a circle of light upon King Eury. The figure of Eurystheus is also round, from belly to head. He is bald save for a patch of thin hair above the ears, but his beard grows long and thick.

"Why do you quail before Hades, High King of Erebus?" Minos begins. "Have you a confession?"

Plump as a fed tick and sweating beads, King Eury clears his throat. "I came to beg for clemency."

He has done something wrong, and the Unseen already knows what it is. Aeacus knows, too. The bond between those two is as ironclad as father and son.

Minos resents how Aeacus wrangles private meetings with the High King, always in his ear and whispering antagonizing words to sway Hades to his own agenda. Granted, Aeacus played an essential part in the war. He orchestrated the brotherhood between Hades, Zeus, and Poseidon long ago. Three brothers, separated by distance and different mothers. If not for Aeacus, the titans might reign still. For that, he is to be respected. As for the rest of it, Minos looks upon Aeacus as a mangy old dog that a boy has had his entire life and cannot bear to put down. The boy will always be loyal to his dog. And so it is between Hades and Aeacus.

"Clemency for what offense?" Minos probes.

"You protect the son of Zeus," Aeacus blurts. "His name is Alcides, no matter what slick name he hides behind."

King Eury says to the floor, "I have heard reports that Creon, regent of Thebes, has come to you demanding justice for his daughter and grandsons."

Minos tries to place the names and the references

without claiming the truth—he has no idea what they are talking about. He refuses to show ignorance and grows red in the face when Aeacus lifts an arrogant chin and snaps, "One does not demand anything of the Unseen."

Eury glances to the shadow on the ebony throne, unnerved he cannot see the silent High King to whom he asks, "Has His Majesty ruled on this matter?"

Hades remains silent.

"Creon is on his way back to convey the order," Aeacus says. "You might have crossed paths with him as you entered the monoliths of Cerberus."

So. Aeacus managed to finagle a meeting between Creon and the High King. A meeting from which Minos—by design—had been excluded. Early on, the three judges collectively agreed no judicial matter would be discussed unless all three judges were present—or, as in the current situation, if one of the judges were absent. In this case, the full council must accede that business of court proceed as usual.

Minos bristles. Hades must see him flash with colors of annoyance. Still, Minos controls his response. His memory assimilates things muttered during symposium by guests, of war stories told. "Ah yes. Creon, interim ruler of Thebes."

"Alcides murdered his own wife and children!" Aeacus says. "The crime is punishable by death. Creon acted righteously when he brought this grievance to our attention."

Minos remains stone-faced. He will not show his ignorance in this matter. Any man standing before the throne should believe all judges are aligned and in agreement.

King Eury bows his head. "Alcides blamed the crime on madness, caused by poisoning."

"Poisoning by whom?" Aeacus practically spits.

"Queen Hera."

"And what does Queen Hera say about this?" asks Minos.

"That she meant to kill him, not drive him mad."

Aeacus laughs. "Hades is not the only one who wants Alcides dead."

"Please understand," King Eury says. "When Zeus sent his son to me for punishment, I believed he deserved proper sentencing from Asphodel. I do still. Zeus would hear nothing of it. He demanded I create a situation in which Alcides could redeem himself."

"Was Zeus equally permissive with the queen for poisoning his precious son?" Aeacus says.

"He punished Queen Hera in a way that would most wound her."

"How is that?"

"Zeus branded Alcides with her name, bonding them as mother and son. The bastard will forever be known as her namesake. Heracles."

"He is to be brought before the Unseen,"

Aeacus orders. "There will be no redemption for this 'Heracles.'"

"Mercy, I beg of you. But if I comply, I will be stricken for it. Zeus will have me killed."

"Do you think your fate will be better if you do not comply?"

"Yes."

Aeacus scowls and clenches his fists. The silent Hades straightens in his seat. Heat rolls from the both of them, and Minos wishes his brother, the peacemaker, were here to cast light.

To the High King, King Eury explains, "I come to you for grace because I cannot surrender Heracles without dying for it, and I believe you find honor in those who are forthcoming. I come with hope you recognize honor in me."

"The High King discovers little honor in Asphodel," Aeacus says.

"Tell me," Minos interjects. "What form of redemption have you crafted for Heracles?"

"I thought to devise ten labors in total," King Eury says. "I hoped good might come of these labors. He might, for example, slay or capture notorious beasts."

"Such as?"

"You may have heard of the lion terrorizing the hills of Nemea. Farmers would often find their flocks and their cattle eviscerated. It began with animals. Over time, the lion advanced upon small children. Nemeans claim the lion was invincible to arrows."

Aeacus throws a knowing look to Hades. "Alcides prefers to fight with arrows. Coward."

King Eury's cheeks blaze scarlet. "This was my strategy to bring Alcides to justice. Arrows would do him no good. He discovered this himself, and yet he did not relent."

"He succeeded in the labor?"

Eury gulps. "The son of Zeus killed the lion with his bare hands."

With a snort, Aeacus says, "Impossible."

"It is impossible," marvels Eury, "to a normal man. Forgive me, but the blood of Zeus runs strong in his veins. They say Alcides possesses the strength of a god. I fear him. Rarely do I witness change in a man's heart. If Alcides is capable of murdering his own wife and children, what might he do to the fat old king from Tiryns? Since his victory over the lion, I have sent his feats by herald. I have no wish to provoke his anger."

"These feats," Minos prods, "are to slay or capture deadly beasts, you say?"

"Mostly," Eury replies, glancing at the Unseen, who lives up to his name in the most literal sense. "The stables of King Augeas are the largest in Erebus, with thousands of livestock. They produce a mountain of shit. I ordered him to clean the stables in a single day. The labor was meant to humiliate him."

Before Aeacus can butt in, Minos speaks. He is tired of Aeacus running this court. Minos is ready now. Ready to prove to the High King he can get what he wants without declaring an indefinite war on Zeus. No one has to die in this standoff between kings. No one, except perhaps Heracles.

"What if," Minos asks, "there is a way for you to meet the requirements of Zeus, appease the Unseen, and still live another day?"

"I would surely do it."

Aeacus quips, "Never volunteer for the unknown."

"If I can pacify both High Kings, I swear it will be done."

Minos projects his voice. "The Ten Labors of Heracles. How many has he completed?"

"Five."

"Five?" Aeacus growls with a lift of spindly brows. "How hard could they be?"

"He had no assistance with them?" Minos asks.

"I suppose he had help with one."

"There," Aeacus snaps. "This nonsense can end. He fails the labors by accepting help. We demand he—"

"My fellow arbiter," Minos interrupts, "if Zeus is not reasonable enough to surrender his son to Hades, do you believe he will care about your technicality?" He tsks. "Come now. We are men of wisdom. There is another way."

"What do you propose?" Aeacus looks to where Hades sits observing—always observing.

"Heracles will maneuver through your feats

one way or another," Minos instructs Eury. "If he cheats in any way, you will simply penalize him by adding another feat. This will show Zeus you wish his son nothing but success."

"Of course," Eury says uncertainly. "I suppose he cheated twice. He had help with the serpent of Lerna. And he accepted payment for cleaning those stables."

"Then," says Minos, "give him two feats of penalty. Twelve in total."

Eury considers. "Perhaps I could command that he steal the—"

"Do whatever you like," Minos says, "with all labors except for one. The final labor will be decided by order of His Majesty, Hades, High King of Erebus."

"It will be, per his order."

"Wonderful." Minos smiles. "For the final labor, Heracles must capture Cerberus, the mastiffs that guard the Unseen."

For the first time, Hades makes himself known.

He laughs softly and seals the order by agreeing.

"Eurystheus of Tiryns, this is your command. See that it is done."

DAUGHTER OF ZEUS
10

Then, there is the matter of Kore.

His head still blares from nights spent in the girl's room. After each encounter, Hades had lain in the cold darkness of his apartment and observed the pain like a bystander witnessing the torture of another. It hurt to do anything. Stand. Cough. Endure light. The whites of his eyes bloomed full red, and the top of his skull ached with a rising pressure.

Is it her light that poisons him? The innocence? The presence of godlike blood?

From the ocean, shades arise from the bodies of dead men.

Or is it because she sees the dead?

"Un-holy."

If this is so, the palace of Asphodel must be the worst possible place for the girl to land.

The daughter of Zeus is cursed with a gift. Throughout his life, Hades has carried his own curse of sorts, has learned to integrate it and hold it close like a sacred wound justifying an occasional wallow in self-pity and the continual need for solitude. He is a man burdened by a numen that simultaneously saps and empowers him. But the burden is *his*. His misery is exclusive and peculiar, and sharing it diminishes the thing, especially when considering the one with whom he shares it. Nothing in Zeus is within him: not boastfulness, charisma, or indulgence. And no divinity in Hades dwells in any brat of Zeus.

Part of him hates her. She plays dumb but knows what she is doing. Every flutter of the lash and intimate touch. She thinks she can control him this way. Use the influence of an absent father to hide behind, like her half brother.

But when Heracles arrives to complete the twelfth labor, Hades will be waiting. No more hiding behind the skirts of Zeus. Not for Heracles, nor for Kore—who can claim him as father by bloodline alone.

He must decide what to do with her. After a week of examining the girl, Hades has assimilated enough hard-won information about her past. It is worth the burst vessels and blurred vision and agony in his head.

"She has never met Zeus," he informs the judges midday. They gather in the assembly room where bread and wine are served.

"What are you saying?" Aeacus asks. "She is not the child of Zeus?"

Ignoring the food, Minos nurses a krater of wine and reclines in front of a dim fire. "He is saying she is not the child of Hera."

"She is of no use to us anyway." Aeacus grunts. He chews the bread and reconsiders. "Not unless you do what I suggest."

"What is that?" Minos asks.

"Make her a slave of a different kind."

Hades's vision works better than yesterday, but a gray haze distorts everything he perceives. In a blur, colors of menace and lust shimmer around Aeacus.

A perverse chill scampers up his spine. Though he grimaces, Hades's imagination stretches to Kore in her transparent gown . . . shackled inside his room. At his disposal.

Minos leans forward. "Are we not executioners of law?"

"What of it?" Aeacus says.

"Law declares: you may not defile a girl without permission from her father," Minos says, "any more than you may defile a slave without permission from her owner."

"When we ambush Heracles, Zeus will be raging mad. This alone may earn us a war. A raped daughter will not make a difference."

"You are shortsighted," Minos argues. "Once we have Heracles, we release Kore to her father as an offering of peace. Regardless of who her mother is, she holds value through blood alone. She is a commodity of Zeus, who will arrange alliances by selling her into marriage for political gain. Anything you do with her will ultimately affect Zeus. I do not care if she is a complete stranger to him. She is his property. Discovering a lost daughter is discovering new wealth. Think for once. Or are you too busy conniving to drum up a war?"

"Your plan will drum up war quick enough!" Aeacus scowls. "Capturing Alcides—"

"Heracles," Minos corrects for no other reason than to annoy.

"Nothing," Hades interrupts, "has changed." His temple throbs in time with the healed wound on his shoulder. His rapid pulse magnifies the pain. "Our opportunity is in the twelfth labor. We will not act beforehand."

The words of Aeacus hang in his mind, like matured fruit Hades dares not snatch.

"A slave of a different kind."

He will not, no matter the temptation.

THE GUARD
11

Twice, Kore has followed the shade of Sisyphus. Twice, he has led her to a corridor yawning into a wide doorframe to somewhere mysterious. A single guard, spear held erect, stands post. At his side, a mastiff sits tall enough to reach the guard's bronze-plated chest.

She often marvels at the size of these animals. Dogs practically as big as horses!

Torchlit eyes of horses in decay.

Kore blinks. How strange for the old dream to spring up now, buried and resurrected in those once-empty vaults of her mind. The dream stopped when they brought her here. It has not crossed her mind in weeks. She recalls the smell of cinders underfoot and the grip of a godlike arm snatching her around the waist.

A chariot barrels toward her.

"I told you to go away," says the man in the

bronze helmet. A weak chin and bloated cheeks fade into a thick neck. By the twinkle in his eye, Kore gleans he does not really want her to go away.

His dog faces her dogs. In theory, she supposes the dogs should be at odds with one another, since she wants to pass through the doorway and the guard refuses to let her.

"What do you want down here?" he grumbles.

She has gone away twice, but the shade will not leave her alone. If she does not do what it wants, it will keep pestering her—snatching at her legs at night and playing with her hair and tickling the bottoms of her feet while she sleeps.

"What is in there?"

"You asked me that yesterday," the guard says in a clipped, wooden voice.

"You did not answer me yesterday."

"Same goes for today," he says. "Skip away, girl, and let it be."

Kore pulls on her bottom lip and sways from side to side like she does when she is trying to figure out what to do. Her new dogs (she will not name them, not love them too much, or it may end in punishment for them) look up at her, expectant.

Oh, but they love her, even if they should not! And she, them.

She reaches down and pets the one with the white patch on his neck. His fur is short and silky.

The guard shifts where he stands. The way he looks at her, she has seen it before. Men get hungry, her mother warns, as if there is danger in it. On the day she sailed aboard the *Narcissus,* Kore discovered her mother was right. On the ship, the captain—Charon—had groped her before the waves came and demolished the ship.

"Be a good girl for us tonight."

But she has nothing to fear. Not here.

As if hearing her thoughts, the guard adjusts himself *down there* and laughs in a way that embarrasses Kore.

"Best be glad you are who you are, daughter of Zeus. Without those dogs protecting you, I would teach you to mind me."

"And my *theíos.*"

"What?"

"I have protection from the dogs," she tries to speak slowly, "and the High King. H-he would not allow you t-to teach me anything."

In her periphery, the dogs posture themselves toward him. Their ears lie back and heads lower.

He angles his spear. "Settle down," he cautions the dogs.

The mastiffs grumble in their throats.

Kore feels bold, strangely petulant. It is dreary and melancholic here. Skylos and Allo have been taken away. It is unfair to the dogs to grow close, and so the mornings spent playing with them stopped, and she is bored! Bored beyond compare! The specter, while spooking the fine hairs on her arms, is the only interaction she gets beyond the slaves. The shade of Sisyphus insists on showing her something, and she will see it!

Cocking her chin the way her mother does when she is particularly bossy, Kore plants her hands on her hips and blows at a strand of hair from her eye. "My *theíos* says I can go anywhere I want, and y-you have to do what I say or . . ."

Her skin buzzes with empowerment and nothing much to lose. "Or the dogs will eat you!"

In rapport, the dogs ignite—all three of them. The fur on their necks stands straight up. They growl and bare their teeth. Smile flashing, Kore folds her arms.

"Now, you listen—"

The guard steps toward her.

The dogs snarl. Massive jaws snap in strange succession, foam flying from loose jowls. The dog nearest the guard—not one of Kore's but *his own*—lashes out with teeth sharpened by gnawing on the bones of goats and cows.

The mastiff clamps down on the plump, stubby elbow of the guard. Blood squirts onto the skirt of Kore's gown. The guard howls and drops the spear. On instinct, he jerks his arm away. As soon as he does, the mastiff clamps down harder, and the skin tears with a wet rip. The bone pulls apart. The guard shrieks and beats the top of the mastiff's head.

Her body runs cold. At first, she cannot move.

"N-N-N-no!" she manages, gasping. "Bad! B-bad!"

The mastiff releases the arm. It dangles weirdly from the elbow, hanging from the threads of thick muscle and splintered bone. The guard clutches it like an infant against a mother's breast. His face is greenish white. He falls against the wall, sliding down it before losing consciousness. His helmet clanks against stone. Blood and urine pool around him.

Crying, Kore clamps her hands over her mouth. "W-what did you d-do?"

The dogs whimper and lap at the blood and urine. The other—the one previously guarding the entrance to the corridor—nudges her closer to the doorway that opens wide.

Tiny white eyes cut through the darkness.

"Come with me to Tartarus."

Wiping at wet cheeks, she sniffs and follows the shade. Tacky warmth squishes between her toes, and Kore disappears into the corridor, bloody footprints glistening in her wake.

TARTARUS

12

Days since the incident in the yard—and now, another disturbance.

Summoned by Aeacus, Hades marches to the lower southwest quarter and stops cold. At the end of the corridor leading to the caves of Tartarus, there should be one guard standing post with one mastiff. But there are at least *twelve* mastiffs, all with a stance threatening to attack if anyone attempts to pass.

Against the squared entrance slumps a half-conscious guard. He sits in a widening pool of blood, legs splayed and cradling a mangled arm. His face is deathly white, lips colorless. His helmet is off, hair clumped with sweat. Yellowed teeth chatter.

From behind Hades, guards fan out and poise their spears. A vibration of *phobos* comes from them. Guards radiating fear—a grave offense in this job. The tendons in his neck constrict. Hades stretches it from side to side.

Aeacus says, "He is going to bleed to death."

"Majesty, forgive me," the wounded guard utters. "I failed you."

"*She* is down there," Aeacus snarls. "This is her doing."

Dainty red tracks glisten on the floor. Five perfect little toes and a slender foot with imprinted swirls. Stamped in congealed blood. Hades can scarcely believe such a weak-willed creature could have the insolence to do this. Heat courses from foot to crown.

"The dogs turned on me," the guard mutters, eyelids sagging.

Aeacus begins, "The girl needs to be beaten—"

Hades stares at the golden-eyed mastiff in front. "Move."

The dog yawns. A few others fidget. But they do not move.

"She has intoxicated them, fed them fermented fruit." Aeacus dares not step closer after what happened in the yard. "They were obedient before she arrived. There is no other explanation fo—"

"Move *aside*."

This time, the dogs obey, reluctant. Hades lights with a red-hot anger that makes the dogs move faster and snaps his fingers. His own three dogs lead the pack away from the scene.

Armor clangs as guards rush to the man on the floor. They stoop to him. When they accidentally disturb his partly severed arm, he yelps and turns whiter.

"Once she sees her first specter," Aeacus assures him, "the brat will come flying up the stairs."

"No."

"No? You want to yank her out by the hair? You spent enough time there as a boy. No need to relive it. Let her run out on her own."

Before the judge can protest further, Hades passes through the doorway. He takes a sharp corner, and the hall comes to a dead end. Onward, there is only descent. The circle in the floor is surrounded by iron poles linked together by chains. Wooden steps bring him down steeply, and he uses one of the ebony rails so he can take them two at a time. The cave takes shape around him, baring fangs of stalagmite. Torch flames crackle along walls green from slick moss.

Hades does not linger. He descends fast. The staircase reverberates with hollow footfalls.

The last time he took these steps, it was by choice. That was twelve years ago, the day he brought Sisyphus to the caves of Tartarus and intended to leave him there. He shakes his head to clear it. There is no escaping memory. Where he represses the one of Sisyphus, another awaits to pounce and conquer his nerves.

"You spent enough time there as a boy."

Although he revisits Tartarus of his own free will, it was not always this way.

As a boy, he was often dragged here. By the

one who called himself his father but was not of his blood. Nonios of Asphodel was simply a man with a roving wife. How could a tortured little boy understand the difference? How could he know his father was punishing him for his mother's sins?

"No need to relive it."

To his far right, he spies an out-of-reach crater in the wall. An iron chisel glints inside, next to a leather sack covered by webs. Discarded mining tools from before he was born.

The creation of Tartarus began with a vertical shaft. As a king, Nonios accumulated wealth through mining. Slaves dug horizontal tunnels, searching for ore. Discovering traces of gold and silver, the slaves were ordered to tunnel deeper. Because of their size, young boys could traverse the cross sections of galleries. They alone enlarged them into chamber rooms and hoisted pillars of rock to support the roof.

Indeed, beneath the earth, they found gold and silver and ore.

They also found collected bones from a long-collapsed burial site.

Thereafter, with lungs caked in soot, sweating slaves began to see specters. They heard the smothered moans of men and women. Howling. Shrieks of pain, alive for one thousand years and clamoring.

Distractions like these caused the slaves to toil faster. Chambers were secured haphazardly, and caves collapsed as they worked to appease a king who had no interest in their well-being.

All the same, Nonios of Asphodel was industrious and made use of the failed project. Beneath the palace rested caves snaking on each side of a single tunnel. It was the perfect place to chastise a child who was not his own. Within Hades, there was no raucous boyhood charm. He was invisible even then—shy, serious, withdrawn. He did not speak until he was nearly five, and his father called him dimwitted and peculiar.

"Something is wrong with him."

Tall and skeletal with muscles like rope wound over bones, Nonios could nonetheless overpower a boy. As his father pulled him down by the collar, each step bruised the backs of his heels. His mother, attempting to defend him, was beaten into stillness so Nonios could subdue his son without a hysterical woman clinging to his leg.

At times, Hades spent mere hours barred from light and human contact. Other times, days. He never knew what to expect. Not knowing was part of the punishment.

Before those days in the caves, Hades would notice lights shining from the bodies of people. He saw their spectrums of color shift and assumed all people saw this, but his father had mocked him, and his mother had worried. He realized this set him apart from others—and it was shameful if he spoke of it.

He spoke little.

After the caves, Hades could observe stories within those flashes of color. Stories told in pictures and murmurs of things once said. In their histories, he read their sins, leaving him tired and aching in the head.

He saw more than he wanted to see. When he touched, he felt more than he wanted to feel.

Holding the hand of his own mother might result in his arm throbbing and infecting him with her hopelessness and terror. In her past, he saw the truth of her tryst with Cronus, and he came to understand the cuckold's resentment and knew there would never be fondness between them. When his mother died, she left him alone with a man who despised him.

Her absence meant more time in the caves. Hades deadened his mind to it. He grew immune to the howls of the dead, hardened to their weeping, and impervious to any voices or touches he felt in the dark. What Hades suffered earned him the iron-thick exterior he uses each day of his life.

His "father" had been right about one thing. It was an ideal venue for punishment.

Thus, in his reign, Hades transformed the caves into a dungeon. Still, compassion is not lost on him. He gives the prisoners food. He gives them light. They have a place to shit and sleep and bathe.

Hades rushes down the steps, growing uneasy and heavy at once. He hears nothing but crackling flames and the faint drip of water. Suddenly, Hades stands at the base of a rounded pit.

He spots Kore immediately. This is a place where light does not enter. Yet there is light around her. A beam of white radiance, originating from nowhere. Back to him, Kore faces the mouth of the tunnel leading to prison cells. Her hair streams down to the waist. The bottom of her gown is soaked crimson, and naked underparts of her feet are red-pink with dried blood.

She levitates. Her toes hover less than a finger's length above the stone floor.

His face drains of color. Anger diffused, he unclenches his fists. The atmosphere of Tartarus weighs on him as if pressing down on his shoulders, and his legs are like marble slabs secured in place. Yet Kore hangs as if weighing nothing at all.

"Kore."

No reply.

Hades advances.

He says to no one in particular, "Put the girl down."

Nothing.

He reaches out and slips his hand over her wrist. Fingers envelop death-cold skin. His palm accepts a euphoric hum. There is no sin rubbing off and dirtying him.

On each side of the tunnel, a torch flickers. Though he gazes at the girl dangling like a pluck-ready fruit, from the corner of his eye, he catches the figure of a man in the archway.

Hand falling to his side, Hades peers around her slender arm.

There—a man, dim and gray and standing tall. Eye sockets blaze with pinpricks of white, and the bearded jaw stretches wide. Inhumanly wide. This abomination will speak, and Hades cringes, dreading the voice of the dead one called Sisyphus.

"Of this, you can be certain. She will throw my body in the square. Damn your law. Damn you."

Before he walked the road to death, the condemned man once flung these words like a curse. In a final act of defiance, Sisyphus ordered his wife to throw his corpse in the public square, violating the law of Hades as he violated the law of Zeus.

No more. Hades will not bear one more moment of this. He turns and throws one arm against the soft middle of Kore's stomach. At once, she crumbles over his shoulder. He focuses on departure, on getting himself and the girl out of the belly of Tartarus. In his haste, he forgets the effect of touching her. A thrum of pleasure bleeds from shoulder to stomach to groin. He nearly drops her.

Grabbing the rail, Hades climbs. Kore stirs awake. He slides her down his torso and plants her feet flat against the step. As much as the stair will allow, he backs away. The vibrations of bliss subside.

Kore licks plump, bluish lips. Her pupils are tiny, and she struggles to keep her head upright. It rolls back, exposing a long slender neck.

She murmurs, "He bade, and I followed."

"Kore." Hades grabs her jaw, shakes it.

Blood rushes into her lips. The pupils expand. Brown irises, transparent like muddy water, cast to the bottom of the soiled gown. With two fingers, she lifts the skirt and examines the stuff caking the bottom.

"*Theíos*?" Kore looks up, guilty. "I m-may have hurt someone."

"We are leaving."

"I-is the guard hurt badly? Are you mad at me, *Theíos*?" Weak in the legs, she reaches out and takes his arm for support. "I am sorry. I was wrong—"

He shudders, fists balled tight at his sides. Paradoxically frozen with an urgency to move.

She springs to her tiptoes and flings willowy arms around his neck, flooding him with the clean vibration of her. She mashes against him, molding woman body to man body, from shoulder to ankle. Soft, round breasts conform to the rise of his own chest, and he stands immobile, sick with a desire that fuels his anger in a vicious cycle of lust and rage, lust and rage.

He keeps his fists to his side. Wet lashes tickle his neck, and one frigid hand slinks around the hot, mad pulse in his throat.

"*Theíos*," she whimpers. "Hold m-me. Please."

He swears that her lips brush his jaw. When she urges her pelvis against him, he hungers for the friction. His hands climb over the swell of hips.

Delirium closes around him, and a high bell of alarm sounds from every pore.

The slope of a lower back.

The cries wetting his neck.

She has him. He stormed into the deep, intent on dragging her out, and now he explores the sinuous-snaky curve of her lower back and buttocks. He can think only of fucking the child of Zeus—one who was floating in midair after she assaulted and mangled a palace guard and broke into Tartarus for sport.

"She has intoxicated them."

He and the dogs. She has them all.

"Listen to me," he says, gripping the plump part of her arm. He pries her away. "Stop crying. You need comfort for nothing. Upstairs, a man was torn apart. Do you know what losing a limb does to a soldier?"

Kore's gaze is abashed, and she wipes away tears. Patches of pink brighten her cheeks.

"It makes him *useless,*" he spits. "That alone will kill him in the end. Who will comfort *him*? Hmm?" He squeezes her arm harder, making her yelp. "You?"

She clutches her arm, helpless and vulnerable. In her breathless, wavering voice, she huffs, "P-ple—"

"Shut up. You consider no one but *you*. You are a whining, arrogant pest—"

She shakes her head fast. "I s-s-swear I will

n—"

This time when she reaches for his arm, he pulls away. "Get your hands off me. I am a god among slaves. On my land, in my house, you are *nothing*."

Hades takes one purposeful stride, and she steps back, pinned against the metal rail.

"Do you want to find out what will happen if I catch you down here again?"

"N-no." She shakes her head, chin to chest.

A fat tear hits the dusty step. As he leans into her ear, her breasts rise and fall under a cascade of gold-bronze hair.

He smells the lavender in each strand. "Who are you to me?"

Kore folds her eyes into his like fingers linking, intimate, and says with a sweet, obedient child's lilt, "In your house, I am nothing?"

Yet underneath the act of submission, she controls him with his own need to dominate her. Victory quickly sinks back into festering anger, ever-present and cyclical.

He finds himself staring lewdly at her mouth. With his head, he gestures upward.

"Get upstairs."

Back in the southwest quarter, slaves mop blood from the floor with large strips of linen. To find Aeacus there after all this time does not surprise him. Hades is glad to offload the menace of Zeus so he can think.

Scowling, he asks, "Have they taken the arm

off?"

"Presently." Aeacus smirks at the girl, whose hands are folded humbly in front of her.

"In Erebus," Hades says to Kore without looking at her, "punishment is just. You cost him an arm. Today, you help amputate, heal, and comfort someone in need of it. This is your penance."

He says to Aeacus as he barges away, "If she passes out, throw water and help her back up."

The little ghost does as she is told.

PART FOUR
RITUAL

The peaks of mountains resounded, as did the
depths of the sea, with her immortal voice. And
the Lady Mother [Demeter] heard her. And a sharp
akhos seized her heart. The headband on her hair
she tore off with her own immortal hands and
threw a dark cloak over her shoulders. She sped off
like a bird, soaring over land and sea, looking and
looking. But no one was willing to tell her the truth

. . .

—*Homeric Hymn to Demeter*

IASION'S LAMENT

1

Demeter sleeps, and in the morning, the oarsmen bring forth a goat for sacrifice.

When the pyre lights, it lights upon the shore where the sand is licked smooth by night tides. Gathered around are well over fifty men dressed according to crisp weather, with tunics instead of bare chests, all of whom regard her as piously as any citizen in Knossos.

Beforehand, the captain, Iasion, fed the goat herbs that rendered the creature weak and drowsy, until it finally collapsed into a heap on the sand. In case it stirs awake, oarsmen tie the legs.

Standing before the masses, fire blazing thin and fierce in front of her, Demeter drags a blade across the neck of the goat and catches blood inside a bronze bowl. In a palace ceremony, the High Priest conducts a blood sacrifice, with the High Priestess flinging blood against flame-heated stone so it sizzles and smokes to catch the attention of the gods. But there is no priest here. Demeter must do the job appointed to the holy, regardless of sex.

"We call upon Gaia, in all of your steadfast nurturing, rage not as these men pass upon your beloved son Oceanus, great god of the earth-encircling river. Unto you we lift our prayers and humble sacrifice. Allow us to cross your waters in grace."

Gods and goddesses of land and sea, Demeter summons at first light. Iasion strips meat and viscera from the goat, and they place the succulent portions onto metal plates, cooking the offering for consumption. Into the fire, he offers the bones, the essence of the goat's earthly form.

The sky beams orange at the horizon. As the chariot of Helius dawns, Demeter calls upon the god of the sun to smile upon them and clear the skies for serene travel.

Gods and goddesses are needy of praise in the same way mortals are needy of praise. Immortality does not erase pride.

As she pours the libation onto the fire, sealing the prayer with an uprising of steam, she finds it implausible that one day, generations from now, future priestesses will be sending praise unto men she knows in her lifetime. Men and women will spill blood to satisfy the thirst of Zeus and Poseidon, these kings who cannot be satiated in life, so how could they possibly experience fulfillment in death?

And what noble acts outweigh the depravity in them so they might become gods instead of fallen kings such as King Minos, whose crimes earned him banishment?

As the oarsmen tear cooked meat with their teeth, Demeter recalls the snide words of Poseidon as he examined her wrist and wiped blood from her nose that day in the field. Poseidon, thinking he did her a kindness by tending to wounds he had caused.

"Why do women behave like this is the worst thing to happen to them? I have seen men mauled, mutilated, near-death, and they snivel less than a raped woman. You are safe and will go back to your home with the privilege of my seed in your belly. From this, you could benefit."

There had been nothing to say. Poseidon motioned to the wet circles spreading out over her nipples.

"Does my brother know about the child?"

"What?"

"The girl you bore belongs to him."

"How do you—"

"Zeus told me to seek you out if I came to Knossos. Said you would welcome his brother, out of respect to him. And the way you danced for me today, I believed him."

"I dance for the gods."

"As I said."

He had smiled, straight-toothed and gleaming white, cocking his chin high and readjusting the saddle on his horse.

Now, robe whipping in the early morning wind, Demeter scans the faces of the oarsmen. She searches for signs of malice. She searches for depravity. But as they come to her and take her hand and kneel, thanking her for the priestly blessings, she sees men made vulnerable by the gods and goddesses they worship.

Iasion brings her meat from the goat. Demeter nibbles on it, not hungry, yet she must partake in order for the gods to bless her, too. His bald head reflects the sunlight.

"Do you have children?" she asks.

Iasion's men scatter toward the ship and examine the sky and sea. Both are tranquil. Iasion observes as the men ascend to deck and assume seats and steady the oars.

"Sit up top, under the shade," he says, spitting into the foam lapping at their ankles. "You can have my box. I move around a lot. No point in wasting a good seat."

Demeter follows the line of oarsmen to take her seat on the ship. Wooden ramps allow quick ascent, and Demeter hitches her skirt as she keeps pace. Once aboard, Iasion waits for her to climb onto the captain's overlook. Her knuckles grow stiff and cold as she grasps each rung and pulls herself up the ladder. Clumsy, compared to these men. They are at home here. They are sure-footed and graceful in their quick maneuvering to set sail, despite the late start due to the ceremony.

Half-stumbling onto the upper deck, Demeter finds a cushion stuffed with goose feathers and a rough, woven blanket on the seat Iasion instructed her to take. These things had not been here when she tried to stowaway last night. Demeter watches the round-shouldered captain adjust the sail, and she sits without speaking. The wind cuts into her ears, and she pulls the hood of her cloak tight under her chin to keep them from aching.

Beneath her feet, the earth shifts. The prayers did not work. The gods have finally forsaken her. The earth will open again, as it did that day.

Gaia, be still, she prays. Demeter clutches the wooden bench to steady herself. She stumbles and finds herself looking to Iasion in a guilt-ridden frenzy.

Unperturbed, Iasion hangs on to the mast for balance and shouts orders below. No, it is not the earth that moves. The *ship* moves. Demeter clutches her chest.

They forge against the tide and drift to sea by force of brawny arms. Crooked at her sides, her elbows shake and muscles tense. Her shoulders, tight toward her ears. Thighs and buttocks, clenched. Jaw set. Rubbing her arms, Demeter wills the muscles to loosen, pulling her shoulders down and wiggling to ease them.

The sea barely rocks. The arms of the oarsmen guide them safely into calm waters, and the gods accept them with mercy.

Do the gods have mercy?

From the cycles of the earth and sky, she judges them as temperamental as mankind. Holy tantrums on land and in the heavens and waters. Yet with destruction comes rebirth. So it is with man, and so it is with the gods.

"When I see him, I will tell Zeus about his child," Poseidon had told her. "He will be pleased, and you will be rewarded. It is a gift to bear the child of a god."

"There is nothing I need—"

"Shut up. Would you reject a blessing from Gaia? From Uranus? Humble yourself for what my brother gives you—and what I may give you, if you are worthy, and I am not sure you are."

Demeter touched her belly and cringed. Her cheeks ran hot.

Poseidon approached her fallen mare, Forada. Front leg askew, the horse emitted a shrill whinny, the song to their consummation, raking at her nerves and making his cavalier attitude intolerable. With his sword, he stabbed the beast through the skull, and the cries ceased. Demeter's ears rang with them.

"I will take you back. Why do women cry so much? I will call upon you again before I leave. Next time, lie down for me, and you will not walk away with a bloody nose and a dead horse."

He gave her the soft blue purse, the bulk surprising her.

"My brother wants you to have this."

Inside, riches she could not fathom.

"You act surprised. Zeus speaks fondly of you. When you hold value to a god, you are remembered. Use it or not. The choice is yours."

A voice interrupts the reverie.

"I had seven."

Demeter jumps in her seat. Had she nodded off? Iasion braces both arms on the rail and admires a tranquil, blue-green sea. He turns, head growing pink from the sun, beaded with sweat despite the chill in the air.

"Seven children," he clarifies.

Demeter clears her throat. "Had?"

"I lost them in the massacre at Pylos."

"What massacre robbed you of your children?" she says, voice nurturing as udder-warm milk.

He sighs a great sigh, as though the burden stoops his shoulders and neck. "The weak suffer unfairly in war. Women and children, I mean. When the son of Zeus rampaged against King Neleus of Pylos, his soldiers ravaged the city."

Her face falls. "Son of Zeus?"

"Alcides was his name," he says. "His men burned half the citadel. Half the citadel, and all of my children."

She rubs at the tension in her neck.

How many bastards have been sired by Zeus? The shame swallows her, fresh as the day he abandoned her with the seed of Kore nesting in her womb. The captain lost his family to a child of Zeus. Demeter will not upset him by admitting to have given the world another one.

Iasion coughs to mask the sadness in his throat. "The more I speak of them, the more real they seem. It haunts me. When they died, I had been at sea nearly a year. I had not yet held the youngest in my arms. Discussing them makes them die all over again." Iasion turns his head back to the water.

She swallows with a dry click. How long since she saw her own child? And what if Kore's death were real—how might she learn to tolerate life again? Shivering, she wrenches the hood beneath her chin. When her tongue passes over her bottom lip, she tastes salt.

"Do you know where your daughter is headed?"

As they sail, they look in faith to the ocean. They do not look at each other, afraid shared misery will magnify and make their losses unbearable.

Demeter says, "I do not know if she is even alive."

"Was she alone?"

"I . . ." she begins and stops. Demeter pulls herself up, disoriented from the sensation of being on the water. No stable earth beneath her feet. Once she steps out of the shade, the warmth of the sun seeps into her muscles and bones. "I believe she acted independently."

"A girl sails across Oceanus on her own? She is either terribly courageous or terribly stupid."

Leaning against the rail, Demeter stabilizes and watches the foam rush against the hull below. "Once when Kore was this high, I found her pinching her finger and wincing. In it: a little stick with a venom sack. She had been stung, picking flowers. And this is what she told me—she told me she had *offered* her finger because she thought the bee might need to sting her. '*Need* to sting you?' I said. 'No, little ghost, the bee stings when threatened, and after it spends the sting, it will die.' And do you know she cried and cried after that? Not before it, mind you, not at the pain of the sting itself. She cried and said, 'Oh, Mother, I killed the bee.'"

"May the gods help the well-intentioned."

The question he wants to ask lingers on his tongue. *What happened to make her run?*

If he asks, she will pepper the truth with offerings of poison; she will tell him of Kore's strong-willed temperament and deny doing a thing to earn it. What she accused Kore of—the truth—was proven when she ran away.

"Only a selfish, arrogant man would do as he did—and you, showing the same vanity!"

Kore did not have to run. Demeter never meant the things she said. By now, Kore should trust Demeter's heart, not her words! When Iasion turns to her, she is armed with self-righteous denial. But the captain asks nothing. He merely squints through the blinding sun and says, "I hope you find your *kore*."

He says it the way most say it at first, as if the name is silly and invalidating. In time, people adapt to the habits in place around them, and soon Iasion will say Kore's name without judgment.

It is peculiar never to have named your child properly. But she cannot stomach the idea of using any name dreamed up by a man who called upon her as he might a whore. When Poseidon kept his promise and sought her out again, she complied and lay very still while he took his time with her, not needing to hurry through the biting rain and the cries of a crippled horse. After, she asked him why. Why return to her when hetaeras are paid to fulfill this urge in kings?

Poseidon explained, "If your hands are dirty, and you need to wipe them, do you wipe them on a soiled cloth or a clean one?"

She turned her head. Demeter hoped this would be the end of it, but years later—a handful of years—he found her at the palace on another one of his journeys. Again, he came to her seeking pleasure, and she did not fight. Kore, nearly seven, was chasing chickens in the yard while he got dressed and watched out the window.

"Your child needs a name."

"She has a name."

"She is Persephone, decreed by her uncle Poseidon! Zeus will agree."

"She is Kore of Demeter, and none of your concern."

This time, when he left a gift, he made sure she used it, unlike the bag of gold collecting dust beneath a stone in the floor. Within days, she was anointed High Priestess, the cruelest gift of all because she wanted it, and there was no option to refuse.

Again, she hoped this would be the end of her encounters with High Kings. May the memories die without a fuss.

Then, in recent days, a ship arrived with white masts and the crest of an eagle woven in the center. Nine years after her last encounter with Poseidon, a young man had approached while she threaded the loom outside. His hair, a mix of bronze and brown. His chin dimpled. She glanced up from her loom and gaped at this clean-shaven young replica of Zeus, years younger than Zeus was when she had met him.

As the young man introduced himself, her face fell. He and Kore had the same cleft chin and eyes the color and shape of chestnuts. He wore a gilded breastplate. Embossed into each side of a polished helmet were wings of gold. He removed it as he stood over her and took a knee to show respect.

"My father sent me," he said. "I am Hermes, son of Zeus the Liberator, Loud Thunderer, King of Kings—"

She cut him off, brow creased.

"What message do you bring from Zeus?"

"I am here to discuss your child, the offspring of His Majesty—and my sister. Persephone."

"Come inside. Quickly, before my Kore comes

home."

Aboard the ship, as they now speed toward Matapan in a day-long journey, Demeter takes her seat in the captain's box and squints toward Iasion, busy shouting below deck through the hole in the floor where the ladder connects. She is blessed he does not ask more. Demeter hopes he does not ask the question going through his mind:

"Why did the child run?"

She cannot tell anyone about what happened when—not long ago—the messenger came and stated his business with Kore.

AMPUTATION

2

They cut off the arm just above the elbow. Kore wrenches a fat strip of linen around the guard's upper arm where muscle blooms fullest, and she does as the physician tells her: twist the rope until her forearms cramp from strain. The physician likens her efforts to damming a stream and, impervious to the chaos, hums a tune while he positions the wooden block.

The axe is swift and exact. Blade hits bone, issuing the wet crack of meat cleaved on a stump.

"Done it a thousand and one times," the physician says with a grunt. His hair is white-silver and shagged at the ears.

Kore rends, tugs, and winds the makeshift rope together, cutting off the blood—for how can river gush with a dam in place?—and yet hot, tacky sap splatters on her feet. Waist-down, her gown is soiled with the aftermath of a dog attack.

The guard lost consciousness before the blade

descended. With the arm out of the way, the cheerful physician brings a red-hot metal rod from a nearby fire.

"Cautery," he says, "is a good trick. When you sizzle raw meat, does the blood not stop?"

When he presses scorching metal to bloody stump, she remembers the sight of the captain's hand being yanked from bone and another ugly image of that day in the arena when the bull impaled a young athlete. Flesh cooks, hisses like animal flesh against a sacrificial fire. The guard screams awake and thrashes. With the flailing of a man twice her size, it is impossible to keep the linen taught around his arm.

Kore clamps her eyes shut. She refuses sight because the other senses assault her regardless. The smell of burning skin. The piercing screams of a man losing his arm because she insisted on having her way. In the back of her nose and throat, Kore can taste the metallic particles of blood, her own lungs constricting from the sizzling flesh.

"You cost him an arm. This is your penance."

Yes. She does it with blind acceptance and will do more, if need be.

Inside the agony of the room, Kore floats beyond her physical body. She sways in place. Her body laments with an invisible sensation of torment. The guard's pain is *her* pain, and her heart breaks in union with his suffering.

She welcomes suffering because she deserves

it.

"In the morning, we will banish this darkness within you."

There is no escaping the darkness. No new beginning, not for her, not when the sheer nature of her being gives her away. People see this impious behavior erupting no matter where she goes. If Mother saw her as a "willful child" in Knossos, and Hades sees a "whining, arrogant pest" all the way in Erebus, it stands to reason that Kore takes herself wherever she travels. When she finally meets her father, he will notice the ugliness, too—for though she runs from land to land, she cannot run from herself.

When the guard passes out again, the physician dunks the charred stump into a bucket that Kore lifts with arms weak from twisting the cloth. Water ripples and sloshes over the side. Once clean, the severed arm shines blackly.

As told, Kore applies the salve.

As told, she wraps the arm.

"How did you charm the dogs?" the physician mutters. With a clean rag, he wipes blood from his hands. "They say you had a part in this mess."

The waxen guard snores oddly, gray lips open and parched. The room stinks of blood and burned skin.

Arms spent, she says, "M-may I please go?"

He gestures to the door. Kore goes.

Numb, she trudges into the corridor, caked from

the forearms down, pale yellow skirt soiled red. She picks at the clots caught under her nails. The bottom of her hair clumps together with blood. From around the corner, two shapes emerge from shadow.

Dogs. Not the same ones she had earlier. They have been switched out again.

With a palace constructed with obsidian walls, it could be any time of day and appear the same. It could be sunset. Perhaps later. Earlier. Paws tap alongside her as she winds through the corridors and up a series of narrow staircases to her quarters.

Inside the room, two slave women await. They spy the golden figure slinking inside the doorway with her skirt marred with gore, and they cannot move for a moment. They stare with mouths agape. In the center of the room, the inlaid pool steams with freshly perfumed water.

At once, the slaves rush to her, peeling the sticky, crimson silk from her body like molted skin.

"Do you want to find out what will happen if I catch you down here again?"

Sometimes she suspects the High King is playing a game with her, a game she does not know how to play. Sometimes, she suspects the sternness is a test to determine if the daughter of Zeus is strong or weak, if she is worth the trouble of having around, or if she needs to go away altogether. Perhaps *Theíos* thinks she causes mischief on purpose so he will do it, which would be terrible because Kore needs him to see her as more than a little girl. He tests her, and this is part of the game. But there never has come a time when she has set out to please someone and failed. Now will not be the first. She will shift and shine, like a jewel cut into many dimensions, and when he turns her around under intense scrutiny, she will reflect back whatever he desires.

Near-scalding water licks at her naked belly. She eases down into it, watching creamy skin blush pink. Teardrop breasts submerge and sting. As the whole of her body and hair surrender to the water, crimson threads cut through and turn clear liquid to rouge.

The slaves rake her clean with coarse, dripping rags sweet with lavender. Her skin burns as they rub the blood away.

"Do you want to find out what will happen if I catch you down here again?"

Stewing beneath water, Kore's heart pumps faster, and she feels a strange swelling between her legs that reminds her of petals opening to spring light. The slaves wash blood from her hair, and hugging her legs to her chest, Kore lays her cheek on the wet surface of her knees.

She recalls how this same throbbing sensation came over her down in the caves, among the dead, when she threw her arms around her *theíos*'s neck and pushed against him, how all she wanted was his hands on her body. If he touched her, she would find safety. And for a moment—one thrilling moment that made her lower belly flip—he pulled her close and ran his hands up her back until he grew angry and shoved her away.

The slaves finish. Kore stands, restless and wringing water from her hair. When one slave attempts to dry her, Kore takes the cloth from the woman's pruned hands and wraps it around her shoulders.

"Thank you." She motions to the pallet of blankets and cushions where she sleeps. "I will sleep now."

The slave bows and leaves the room. The other retrieves a tunic from an ebony chest carved with snakes. Before the slave can clothe her, Kore takes it from her grasp. She motions to the doorway.

"Thank you," she repeats kindly. "I will dress myself. G-good night."

The slave departs. Kore watches the doorway, wondering if the High King's anger has abated. Wondering if he might grow protective tonight and come check on her.

For a long time, Kore stands still, bare flesh open to the cold air, considering. It occurs to her that what stands between them is the child in her, the part of her she hates and gets her into trouble. The child grates on him and grates on her, too. A child has no place here. Lately, playing this role feels inauthentic, like wearing an outgrown tunic. Anyway, the mind of a little girl does not think about the hot chill she felt in the caves when he whispered dismally in her ear and got so close that they breathed into each other's mouths.

"Who are you to me?"

Kore shudders. She considers the tunic in her hands.

"Do you want to find out what will happen if . . ."

She lets it slip from hand to floor. Reluctant, Kore pulls on her bottom lip and crawls, naked, into bed. It takes an eternity for her heart to stop racing. Only then can she sleep.

HADES RESOLVES

3

There is no reason for him to return to the northwest quarter where the girl sleeps.

Hades now knows what he needs to appraise her political worth. Since King Eurystheus's plea for mercy and the subsequent arrangement for the twelfth labor of Heracles, the girl called Kore is not truly needed for an exchange. He will have Heracles regardless. The daughter is nothing but a peace offering once the son is dealt with.

In the lamplit comfort of the girl's room, a red, rectangular glimmer catches his eye. Hades moves past the dogs, their ears barely twitching as he enters. The bath in the center of the bedchamber glistens, undrained. A fly lands, causing a small ripple on the bloody water. The smells of lavender and iron and sage collide.

Hades will not pry into the light any longer. Searching Kore further would hurt and weaken him.

And there is no reason for him to be here.

None at all.

Next to the bed, smoke twirls from sage. From the wick of an oil lamp, a flame reflects wheat-gold against a damp mane of hair. The girl lies on her back with one hand curled beneath her chin. Save for the small freckle in the corner of her eye, her face is opaque and shines with a flawless golden tone. He studies the closed lids and smooth brow and puzzles at the sight.

The scar is gone.

Where the thickly healed wound once ran from hairline to forehead, unblemished skin takes its place. He follows the tousled hair over sleek shoulders and the hollow in the center of her clavicle.

Her shoulders are bare. The blankets are tucked under her arms. Asleep, Kore turns her head, stretching the long tendon of her neck, and her hair shifts and falls away from her shoulders. Suddenly, Hades understands there is nothing between his hand and her naked flesh except a blanket.

"Hold m-me."

He spies the tunic in a heap on the floor. His pulse roars in his ears. Inside him exists the war between lust and rage, always at odds, although he feels they are the same base desire and unable to be parted.

He wants her to wake up. If she does, he will take her. The thought of catching her unaware holds him back. He wants her to see it coming. He wants the understanding to register fully so humility can wash over her, and she will vibrate with energies of anticipation and surrender and an innate desire to be claimed.

"Make her a slave of a different kind."

She rolls onto her stomach. Her hips rock as she settles, comfortable with her arms bent between her chest and the pallet. The blanket shifts, draping low to the waist, and shows the dramatic slopes and indentions of her back.

Every flutter of the lash and intimate touch.

Every tear and whisper and parting of the lips.

She thinks she can control him this way.

And in a moment of clarity, Hades understands that when the twelfth labor of Heracles is complete and the son of Zeus is in custody, he will not be satisfied. This scenario he has lived a thousand times—of finally clutching the man by the neck and prying into the sins of Heracles until blood pours from his eyes, and he begs for death as an end to the suffering.

Hades plucks the blanket and slides it off the swells of her body. The movement will wake her. She will feel the light tickle of fabric against buttocks dimpled above each luscious hemisphere.

"Are we not executioners of law?"

The backs of her thighs converge into the soft underside of her ass, plump and sweetly curved. He imagines the smoothness of her buttocks against his hands, consumed by sheer fantasy of parting her, of slipping fingers into the crevice and finding it slick and ready for him.

The arousal pains him. Moisture blooms at the tip of his sex. His mind blazes clear and resolutely lucid. He has adapted to the fantasy of capturing the son of Zeus, and—true to the fickle nature of a god—grows increasingly harder to satisfy.

Nevertheless, what Minos said is true.

"You may not defile a girl without permission from her father."

Of course. They are executioners of law and no less beholden to it.

But it is decided. Hades will have both children of Zeus, completely and righteously.

And, for the last time, he leaves the girl untouched.

WORDS OF PROPHECY

4

The journey ends at a makeshift port at Cape Matapan. There must be a hundred men hauling lumber and hammering on broken ships that can be salvaged from the disaster. If Demeter did not know better, she might say every man in the city volunteers to help rebuild their port. Trade is as valuable as the harvest.

When Iasion helps her onto the sand, Demeter careens. Her legs sway, and she grows disoriented at the solidity of earth beneath sandaled feet.

"Steady there," Iasion warns.

She braces herself on his arm. "I feel like I am still on water."

"Wait until you try to sleep. You will swear you are still aboard the ship." He helps her navigate through the crowd. "It will wear off."

She strains to hear him. Hammers pound, steel driving into wood. Work crews yell orders. One crew shouts louder to overpower the orders of another crew. It escalates in a cacophony of men competing to be heard. The noise is deafening. Beneath all of it, the crash of waves and cries of seagulls.

As he leads her out of the chaos, Iasion heads toward a dirt road winding into the agora within the city. Men listen to poets and philosophers in the square and meander toward the perimeters where the marketplace will soon shut down for the night.

The destruction here is milder than that of Knossos, with homes and buildings closest to the sea suffering the worst fate. The gathering place in the center of Matapan teems with merchants packing up their stalls after a day of selling goods near the colonnades.

Iasion moves quickly. His bulky shoulders maneuver back and forth, adept in veering through the streets without bumping into a single person. Demeter knocks shoulders with at least three disgruntled people. With each collision, she mutters apologies.

The sky grows hazy with orange hues stretched along the horizon. Tonight, she will sleep at the temple in Matapan. Iasion takes her there, at her request.

Once they pass through the agora and back onto the dirt road, the chaos ceases.

"We sail for Pylos in two days," Iasion tells her as they shuffle toward temple steps separated by a stone ramp. In Matapan, the temple is rectangular and compact, with a trace of gold and blue embellishment at the height of each pillar. "I will ask around about survivors from the wreckage you mentioned. Find me in the agora. Late morning."

Demeter thanks him. He disappears between a small group of young men scurrying home for the day. In the short time she has known him, she has never asked Iasion for a thing; yet, freely, he provided her with what she required, expecting nothing but a single blessing—a blessing that kept her as safe as it kept the rest of them.

A salty film cakes her hair, brittle and grimy to the touch. Her wet nose numbs from the cold. She walks into the peristyle surrounding the temple, a porch swept neatly and lined by sturdy columns with minimal damage from the quaking earth.

A beggar snores. He nuzzles one of the columns and drools. His face is burned red from the sun, lips blistered. A large tunic hangs from his shoulders, and he has the sunken skin of a man who has shed weight quickly. Demeter sees this happen to the sick and infirm. Flies circle around the bandaged stump of a wrist.

Nearing him, she smells the rancid odor of old wine and soiled flesh.

The bandage is bled through and crusted a brownish red. She stoops down and touches his cheek above the line of his beard. No lice in the beard. No fever. His wound must be clean, but the bandage needs changing. While he is not clean, neither is he filthy.

He is no beggar but a drunkard.

Sighing, she rips a clean piece of fabric from her skirt and sets it aside. She unwinds the soiled bandage with two fingers. The drunkard's wrist is covered in a thick scab and new skin growth. The scab oozes blood from a few fissures. Otherwise, it heals.

From her satchel, she pulls out the otter-skin jug and rinses the wound. The drunkard jerks awake.

"What are you doing?" he barks.

"Hold still while I dress your wound."

"Why is it bleeding again?" His words slur, and he burps noxious gas.

As she winds the clean strip of material, she says, "You must have hit it when you passed out."

"Where is my wine?"

"Drink this."

He tips the jug into his mouth and spews water like poison.

"You need water and food."

The drunkard slaps the jug from her hand. It hits the dusty stone and leaks a trail of water.

"You," the drunkard growls. "I know you. I need no help from you. Unless you are a whore, leave me be. Are you? Will you be my whore?"

Demeter stumbles to her feet. She snatches the jug from the ground and kicks the man in the knee. It hurts her toes. The man cackles as she storms away.

"Have I offended you? Come back, whore. I

want your healing."

She quickens her pace. Exhaustion covers her mind with a fog. As she passes through a doorway into the center of the temple, her legs and hands tremble.

Within the cella, a rectangular hall of worship, a giant statue of Potnia, mother goddess, raises her arms with snakes in hand. The stone portrays stiff, circular breasts with erect nipples and a flounced Cretan skirt. The strict posture and stately headdress create an austerity that humbles Demeter. Inside the presence of the goddess, she finds strength.

To her right, Demeter observes the plinth of offerings. On this square slab are arrowheads and semiprecious stones. A rusted sword. A hairpin of bronze leaves. She fishes inside her satchel and leaves the empty otter-skin jug. She has no other, but the sacrifice shows faith the gods will bless her twice over.

The day is nearly done. Offerings will be collected soon and stored inside the treasury.

The cella is simple, without windows. Two colonnades divide the nave flanked by two aisles. For a moment, she fears the temple of Matapan is not built like the temples in Crete. Finally, Demeter spots the door at the far end of the room.

The adyton.

It is a place restricted from the public and reserved for those belonging to the priesthood. Oracles may enter as well. Never the common man.

Demeter goes to the door. Knocks.

Before she pulls her hand away, the door creaks open. Standing before her, the oldest man she has ever seen. His beard is stark white and hangs thinly to his navel. He stands, bare chest concave in the center. The skin around his nipples hangs loose. The bones in his shoulders protrude. A long wrap hangs to the floor, covering him from the waist down. Leathery skin shines with sweat.

"Well?"

Heat rolls from inside. She hesitates to disturb him during his practice. His pupils are enormous circles overtaking the brown of his eyes. Behind him, she spots an amphora with handles sprouting from the long neck. Without looking, Demeter knows the pitcher contains kykeon.

Questioning him is pointless. The kykeon flows in his veins, and his spirit intermingles with gods.

"Forgive me," she says. "You are in discourse with the gods."

"No," he says, "right now I am in discourse with you."

"I am Demeter of Crete, High Priestess of Knossos. I come seeking sanctuary."

A slow grimace creeps onto his face. He tips his head as if to get a better view from under bushy white eyebrows.

"High Priestess." He sighs and waves her inside. "Welcome."

Her muscles relax as soon as she steps into the

heat. Coals blaze and steam hangs in the air. In a moment, sweat will break out over her skin, but for now, Demeter relishes the warmth after spending a cold day at sea. A shrine sits along the wall to her left.

The old man asks, "Have you eaten?"

Inside the satchel, the bread and fruit remain untouched. Earlier, a rocking sea made her queasy.

"No."

"Good. You have fasted." The wizened priest grabs the amphora by both handles and sloshes it at her. "Drink and join me, High Priestess of Knossos. You may have sanctuary."

So far, her status has earned her transport and shelter. The old mix of guilt and resentment tries to surface. Demeter squashes it. She has no time to resent the title bestowed upon her by Poseidon and his conspirator, Zeus. Her association with them may have gained her the position of High Priestess, but she alone maintains the respect needed to keep it.

Demeter drinks the bitter potion. The amphora is light with less than half the brew remaining. The old priest has drunk his weight in kykeon.

"There comes forth a prophecy." He widens bony arms covered in a thin sheet of muscle and skin. Knobby hands outstretch to the shrine, and the priest's eyes roll back beneath white brows that grow long and spindly. "Tell me, High Priestess, if you see."

Like the drunkard, he seems to recognize her. She imagines it, surely. In priesthood, they are kindred. His divinity recognizes her own; that is all.

But the way the priest peers at her with familiarity, how he welcomes her inside with little question—

He hums, "I begin to sing of Demeter, the holy goddess with the beautiful hair . . ."

In the steaming, flame-yellowed room, Demeter shudders despite the heat. Sweat peppers her skin.

"And her daughter, Persephone, too . . ."

"What did you say?" Steam billows from the coals. The air pulsates, and the floor oscillates like the deck of the ship.

No, he did not say the name known by few. Even Kore remains ignorant of the name given to her. The priest carries on with mutterings, hushed and fading in Demeter's ear.

Demeter slurs, "What name did you say?" Wet beneath clothing, she pulls off the cloak. She weighs the kykeon in her hands, surprised to find it empty. She drank more than she thought.

The old man circles, whispering, "She sped off like a bird, soaring over land and sea, looking and looking. But no one was willing to tell her the truth, not one of the gods, not one of the mortal humans . . ."

"What truth?" She reaches for him and staggers. Demeter peers at the smoking altar.

Through steam, she focuses on the shrine.

The idol is the shape and size of two large melons balanced on top of each other. She is Gaia, goddess of earth. Pregnant with the world, Gaia drapes serpentine arms over her belly. Pendulous breasts rest on a stomach as round as the earth itself.

Stone arms pull from the body of Gaia. They turn to vined branches and writhe upward. Demeter blinks back sweat.

The rotund body grows as thick and twisted as the trunk of an olive tree. Mother Gaia blossoms silver green leaves.

Demeter swears the old man sighs a name she last heard from the messenger, Hermes, not long before the earth opened.

Persephone—

The one with the delicate ankles, whom Hades seized . . .

Demeter hears these word hissed from tree leaves. The divine brew is quick and potent. Her bowels churn and stomach roils.

"What did you say?" The room blurs and clears. Demeter pulls off the himation, finding her earthy green chiton soaked with perspiration. Sweat pools under her breasts.

"Where the girl was Demeter knew not," says the priest, "but she reproached the whole wide world . . ."

No longer does the tree of Gaia grow. The trunk thins. It shrivels as a person might shrivel. Gaia, with her tree body, is stricken with a pestilence that turns the leaves brown and brittle. The body of mother earth, skeletal and reaching toward the heavens in plea. The leaves, dry and whooshing. In the watery blur of her vision, she peers upward at dead leaves. They flutter . . . brown, small—not leaves at all, but locusts shrieking together in a battle cry.

Their dead-leaf wings burst outward, swarming wide and obscuring the figure of the old priest whose voice permeates her head.

I begin to sing of Demeter, the holy goddess with the beautiful hair . . .

With a cry, Demeter throws her hands over her head and drops to the ground. The wings of locusts flick at her skin and catch inside her hair.

"Stop," she pleads. To the goddess. To the priest. To all of it, she begs an end. The long, sleepless, and hungry days weaken her as she has never been before. She is not strong as she usually is for a ceremony. In her frail state, these visions are bulls in an arena, set on trampling her.

The priest looms over her. In a void, he stands alone. Tree, idol, and room vanish. She cannot see her own body. The withered, bearded face of the priest hovers.

Silence now. His whispers cut the quiet.

"There with angry hands, she broke the ploughs and sent to death alike the farmer and his laboring ox . . ."

Demeter cries, "I cannot understand you."

The old man sinks to his knees in front of her.

How can his hands be cold in this heat? They are dry, death-cold hands, folding around her own. Squeezing.

He says again, "I begin to sing of Demeter, the holy goddess with the beautiful hair."

She knows what he will say next. Her mind adjoins to his, mesmerized by the singsong words.

And her daughter, Persephone, too.

He smiles with a soft wisdom.

"Come now, my child," he croons. "Do not be too stubborn in your anger."

And with prophecy hanging from his lips, the old priest falls dead to the ground.

TWICE THE FORCE
5

In the morning, the slaves drain and clean the bath.

In the morning: fresh sage and rue.

Her hair, still damp and sweet-smelling.

The faint crescent of dried blood under otherwise clean fingernails.

Sage fumes hang in the air. Kore is clean and the room is clean, and yet something is *wrong*. Finally, Kore knows what it is.

She knows exactly what it is.

During the night, the dreaming mind runs rampant. Do dreams happen in the mind? Perhaps dreams are real, happenings in another time, another realm, one inaccessible during waking moments. Dreams serve a purpose. Her mother calls them "whisperings of the gods."

What dreams swept her away while she slept, Kore does not remember. But in the morning, her first thought is of Sisyphus. Of what happened to him.

Yesterday, Kore followed the shade of Sisyphus into the cold and damp underbelly of the palace. All the way down, her skin burned cold with fear, and after a long descent, she found herself at the bottom of a pit. A bone-rattling vibration filled her body: ecstasy, like her mother experiences in a ceremony when she summons the goddess to fill her until she goes rigid and entranced. Her teeth thrummed as the pulsations resonated from an invisible gong in the center of her forehead.

Her feet left the ground.

And her mind transported to another time. A time when a former king stood with wrists chained together. Ankles loosely chained together. The one named Sisyphus stood at the base of a steep incline. Guards escorted him up, and their sandals crunched upon a rocky path. Sisyphus wore no sandals, as he was a prisoner and earned no right to comfort. The bottoms of his feet bled, and the dirt clumped crimson-brown with each step.

She heard the orders that led him to this place. They came from Hades's own voice, devoid of emotion:

"A man prone to violence finds it easier to kill than show mercy. A thief finds more ease in stealing than in giving. It is a burden to reject your nature. To starve it into submission and to be, instead, a man of honor."

Every person in the polis of Asphodel gathered

to watch the spectacle. Children climbed trees for a better view. On each side of the uphill path, people negotiated their way between fallen tree trunks and bushes. They strained to get a glimpse of the punished ruler who trudged between guards, his steps short because of the chains.

"King Sisyphus of Ephyra, in this life, you submitted to your nature. You chose not to bear the burden of honor. There is no avoiding this work. Now you will bear it."

Walking the path to his own execution reduced Sisyphus to tears. Cheeks splotched red, nose dripping and snot glistening in his moustache. The *damos* pelted him with rotten fruit and spat upon him with the merriment of watching another suffer while knowing they were safe.

A golden shaft of afternoon light beamed down upon the path and the object blocking it. The boulder was the breadth of three oxen. Wedged between the boulder and the path were stones chiseled into triangles, keeping the thing in place.

Two guards braced each side of the boulder as a third removed the triangular wedges with swiftly cautious hands. A fourth guard unchained the doomed king. No mortal could bear the weight of the boulder. Everyone knew it.

Sisyphus braced both arms against sandstone and dug his bleeding heels into the ground. The ground popped against grating stone. Sisyphus's hands remained planted, but as the thing crunched its way down the rocky path, his feet scrambled backward, stumbling to secure hold and failing. Tangled legs lost purchase and were the first parts of Sisyphus crushed beneath the boulder. Toes and ankles and shins, cracking like shells as Sisyphus shrieked in agony.

The boulder rolled as far as the hips before his body mimicked the effect of stone wedges. The crushing ended at his hips, where bladder and bowels ruptured and leaked foul poison into his bloodstream. The shrieking drove away the crowds. Even the most calloused Asphodelian citizen could not tolerate it.

In time, the sun descended. His body drew flies, although the king still lived, coming in and out of consciousness until finally submitting to death in the early hours of the following morning.

"May the burden you avoid in this lifetime be heaped upon you for eternity."

Inside the depths of Tartarus, the tale unfolded for her. She saw it and came to understand why Sisyphus chose *her*, Kore, child of a High Priestess.

Safe in her room, Kore opens the window. She raises her chin to the sky. Queasy, she inhales autumn air. Her lips mouth words to the goddess Potnia, who nourishes and protects with lion and spear and snakes, with doves and double axes. How mighty she is without showing a sign of fear! Not like Kore, who is always afraid.

Winds circulate, scattering her arms with

gooseflesh. Amid billowing clouds, a single white formation cuts the sky.

She could swear she hears her mother's voice, magnified and all-encompassing. At her core, she trembles. Her bones shake like breaking earth.

"Dedicate yourself to the goddess and love no other."

Potnia manifests in the clouds with plumes of ethereal hair streaming around the crown of her head. She stretches majestic along the skyline, looming in robes crafted by swirls of cloud and mist.

Kore's face lights. Although she falls to her knees in supplication, Kore respects her mother's wisdom: never drop your face to the ground when in the presence of gods. Doing so implies shame and unworthiness. In order to be filled with divinity, she must keep her chin high and be willing to receive. Wide-stretched, open arms become an extension of an open heart.

Tears of gratitude stream down her face. She giggles at how silly and faithless she has been since leaving home. The important thing is she knows better now.

She knows exactly what to do.

Gods and goddesses come before parentage or land. They are the essence of all things. In Knossos, Kore devoted all day either in worship, sacrifice, or in preparation for the two. Her days were spent in glorification or sublimation to the holy.

In a place like this, how could she not yearn for

those practices?

A place like this needs the blessings of the goddess more than anywhere. More and more, Kore finds Mother is wiser than she thought. After all, it was Mother who said, "Had I learned so much at your age, I would be twice the force I am now."

CARAVAN AT FIRST LIGHT

6

"No court today. Enjoy the spread."

The assembly room smells of bread and fish. Not long out of bed, Aeacus hobbles, stiff from sleep. A pinch in his lower back shoots down the centers of his legs. Today, the air bites sharper than the day before, making it harder for his joints to set in motion, reminding him of rust on the hinges of a door. Walking loosens him up, but it takes a while.

From the table, Minos smirks. He tosses a grape into the center of his beard where his mouth gapes open. The old fool has not stopped gloating since King Eury left. Aeacus loathes to admit the plan to ambush Heracles is a good one. He should have thought of it himself.

Aeacus inspects the opulent spread—a feast, really—at a time when nobody's stomach is awake enough to digest it. Nobody but Minos, who shoves honeyed bread into his mouth and washes it down with goat's milk.

If Hades is sick, Minos shows no concern.

Wincing, Aeacus passes a blazing hearth. "Gluttony early in the day."

"And a beautiful day it is."

Tall windows divide the north wall into threes. The shutters on the right and left windows are closed. The center window, wider and taller than the others, opens to a brutal wind, cold and piercing. Ugly gray clouds roll in from the north.

"What are you grinning about?" Aeacus stomps to the shutters. "Close the window before we freeze."

From here, the view of Asphodel is complete. The palace is carved into the side of the mountain and perches on the uppermost point of a seaside cliff. To the rear of the palace, the bluff plummets far down into the ocean where waves explode against rock. From where he stands, the view spans the length of a river-divided valley. To the north and south of the palace are plush mountain ranges of verdant green. Fog clears around the monoliths of Cerberus. Though obscured, a dirt road scales down the mountain, hidden by trees, until finally coming to an end at Cerberus. From this vista point, a traveler can be spotted hours before arrival. At Cerberus, guards and mastiffs make certain no man comes in or out without due inspection.

This morning, slipping into the fog at the foothill of the range—a long caravan of horses. They trail like a centipede, bronze helmets of men glinting in the occasional slip of sunlight. Leading the caravan is a solitary rider.

"What is all this?"

The caravan slips into the valley. They must have left at first light.

"As a matter of fact," Minos says from behind, "court is halted for the foreseeable future."

"Where is Hades?"

"He is gone." Minos pops another grape into his mouth and munches.

Aeacus fights the urge to grab a loaf and hurl it at him. "Gone?"

Minos laughs a full-bellied laugh.

"What are you keeping to yourself? I have a right!"

"A right?" Minos says. "Oh, I suppose you do. And I had a right to know about the arrival of Creon of Thebes and any dealings made as a result."

"Petty," spews Aeacus.

"The caravan will escort Hades to the closest port at Kambos. From there, he insists on traveling alone."

"Traveling where?"

"Olympus."

For once, Aeacus does not know what to say. Hades tells him everything. Does he not? Their bond formed the moment he gave the boy his first dog. Bereft of mother and attention, Hades had jumped at the chance to forge a lasting bond with an adult male who did not beat him senseless. Aeacus taught him how to hunt, to tend to wounds earned in battle, and to kill a man with an actual sword—an undertaking Hades had bemoaned because it was harder than what he could do naturally, without weapon. Oh, how he had whined!

"Why do I need to learn this? I can kill my enemy without touching him."

"Pick that sword back up, boy. You will learn to fight as mortals fight. Think. What happens to you when you make a man bleed from the eyes?"

"To me?"

"Yes. When you traipse through a man's past, unseen."

What the boy said next had raised the hairs on the back of Aeacus's neck.

"There is no past."

"Nonsense."

With a faraway glower, Hades insisted, "Everything is now. There is only ever now."

"Listen to me, boy. When you are in battle, ten men will try to kill you at once. What are you going to do? Hmm? Your power will serve you well when things are simple. But the sword is quick—and you must be skilled at it. Pick it up."

Aeacus blinks away the reverie. As a boy, Hades kept no secrets from his mentor. Aeacus believed it would always be so.

Minos says, "Hades has reached a decision about the girl."

"When did this happen?" His haunches rise.

When Aeacus pushed for a decision, he was accused of being shortsighted. "'Nothing has changed,' remember? The king told us not two days ago, right in this room!"

"I suppose it was something I said." Minos smiles.

Aeacus scrambles to remember what Minos refers to. The harder he tries, the thinner his patience.

"Your face is mighty red, friend. Have a bite to eat."

"What is he doing?" Aeacus huffs. "And why did he tell *you*?"

"He thought I might be impartial."

"Tell me he took the girl with him." Aeacus shifts from foot to foot to keep his lower back from seizing up. Suddenly, it feels tighter than ever. "We should be rid of her after the incident at the caves."

"We are keeping her." Minos oozes something similar to joy but more vindictive.

"What?"

"The daughter of Zeus," he says, "will soon be High Queen of Erebus, wife to the Unseen. Between households, contracts of marriage are as binding as blood."

The idea hits him like an arrow to the back. His mouth opens, but words fail him. This will end as terribly as the first time. Almost twenty years ago, Hades had married a month before the Titan War. He hardly knew the girl: Leuce, Aeacus believes her name was. She did not last long and ended up a bloody splatter when she went over the cliff's edge. She was a mousy thing promised to Hades at birth, and they both hit marriageable age right before Zeus poisoned his father and incited the uprising. Aeacus steadies himself against the table. He sits.

"Ah," Minos says with a wink. "I see you are overcome with joy."

"She is a nuisance!" Aeacus explodes and wags a gnarled finger. "She endangers us all with her recklessness. You and your sanctimonious garbage about law and equity! If Hades had listened to me, he would have sent her back to wherever she came from after he fucked her bloody *without* aligning his house with that conceited prick in Olympus!"

"You speak like a man who wants war."

"I want what is just!"

"You want Hades to rule above all," Minos lulls, waving at a single fly circling a tray of fresh-cut fruit. "You want Zeus, King of Kings, to be cast out by an all-seeing ruler who will keep you by his side as he rises higher and higher to godhood. You want him to murder his own brother and anyone who gets in his way, all so you can elevate your status among men."

The fly circles.

With a swift flash of the wrist, Aeacus snatches the fly in midair and crushes it. For an old man, he is still as fast as he was when he trained Hades to fight by sword, spear, arrow, and brawn. "Are you not the clever one? You think this marriage will keep the kingdoms at peace after we snag Heracles?"

"It provides a barrier, you see, to breaking peace." Minos drops the smug facade. "Both brother and son-by-marriage will he be. What greater bond can form between men? Other than the one you forged yourself, of course."

Minos chuckles and makes his way to the corridor. "The day is early. Enjoy it. Myself, I have the pleasure of strolling the grounds with our future queen."

"I hope it rains, and you both catch your death."

At the door, Minos stops. "I will mention nothing to her until Zeus accepts the arrangement. Go ahead, treat her as poorly as you wish. One day soon you will answer to the girl, and she will remember every cruel word you have ever uttered. They always do."

KORE'S REQUEST

7

Dogs by her side, Kore scours the corridors until she spots two guards entering from the courtyard. When they realize she intends to address them, the men stop.

"I am Kore," she says, careful not to stutter.

"We know who you are," one responds.

Despite herself, Kore is nervous. She hopes the guards do not notice. Hidden by helmets, their expressions are indiscernible. It must be terribly hot and uncomfortable to wear a helmet all the time. She feels sorry for them, and yet they will push her around if she lets them.

"I w-wish to see the High King."

They chuckle and glance at each other through tiny slits in bronze. "Do you?"

"Please."

"He is busy. What do you want?"

"I want," she starts, pausing to inhale, "to see

the High King."

"We cannot give you the High King," the other guard chimes in with shoulders relaxed and stance at ease. "The best we can do is a judge."

Her stomach drops. They claim Hades is busy, and of course, he is—he is ruler of all of Erebus.

But she knows better.

"Shut up. You consider no one but you. You are a whining, arrogant pest—"

No, they do not withhold his presence because he is busy. They withhold it because he does not wish to see her anymore.

She fights back the tears. Trespassing into those caves was an unforgivable offense, and now *Theíos* hates her. Her newfound strength evaporates, leaving her with a sudden desire for death.

She nearly begs the guards to appeal to him, but yesterday, she had been stubborn with the man guarding the caves of Tartarus. He could die because of her childishness. No doubt the mastiffs at her side sense her current desperation and will not hesitate to respond to it with violence. Being pushy might cost these men their lives.

Kore swallows the sorrow. "Judge Minos, I suppose."

"Certainly, young Kore of Zeus." The guard bows in mockery. "Anything else? We would not want you to sic your dogs on us."

"Thank you. The j-judge can find me in the yard." Before they say anything else, Kore squeezes between both men. The dogs fall in beside her, and the guards eyeball her massive protectors.

She speeds through the doors and into the hazy morning light. Once out of sight, Kore leans against the pillar and sobs.

"We would not want you to sic your dogs on us."

"You cost him an arm."

She buries her face in the palms of her hands. Fingers trail into the smooth line of her hair. The pad of her middle finger searches for the protrusion of scar. Usually, when she pokes at it, the pain distracts her. Searching, she feels nothing.

She walks farther into the courtyard where the long, rectangular pool stretches from the palace to the monument of Sisyphus. At the water's edge, she kneels and observes the wavering image reflected in water. She pushes a lock from her head.

No scar.

In her reflection, the sun catches the crown of her hair. It reminds her of her mother's in this light—an illusion, for the hair of Demeter is sunnier than Kore's. Hers always reflects an undertone of darkness despite strands of yellow. Today, pale fingers twirl around the length of her hair, and the locks appear golden as fire.

"Where can my little ghost be?"

Kore lifts her hands to let the sun god bronze sallow skin. She should spend less time indoors. She needs more color to look healthy. She must look healthy in order to meet her father. Perhaps the goddess healed the scar, rewarding her for answering a divine calling. For being more like her mother instead of a mischievous brat.

In the distance, clouds cast an ominous shadow over the mountains. The air cools. She waits a long while before the arrival of Judge Minos. By the time he appears, nine mastiffs lounge in the yard, and rain clouds are minutes away.

She bows.

Minos squints as if trying to focus clearly. A crinkle forms between silver brows. "Good morning."

"Good morning," she manages. Rumors of his crimes baffle her to this day. How sad such infamy corrupts an otherwise genteel figure in history. Otherwise he, too, might have become a god.

He says, "You look different."

"D-different from what?"

Minos laughs soundlessly. With open hands, he gestures to her and tips his head with a humility that strikes her as queer. "I am told you wanted to see me."

Skeptical as she should be, Kore trusts him. "Yes."

"The pleasure of my company?" Minos asks, glancing at the sky.

"I have a question." She catches herself. "Oh, b-but of course, I am honored by your company."

"A question? I am intrigued. Let us walk for

as long as the sky allows." He offers an elbow. She takes it.

Behind them, the dogs fall in line. For a moment, Kore fears they will attack the old judge, but they decide to trust him. What better judge of character than a dog?

"Tell me, my Kore." He pats her cold hand. "Do you know who I once was?"

"You told me," she answers carefully. "You are Judge Minos."

"Yes. Now, I am *Judge* Minos. And you are from Knossos, I have been told."

Together, they stroll toward the arched vines before the monument of Sisyphus. She purses her lips. Did she tell him she is from Knossos? So many days have passed, she scarcely remembers the lies anymore.

"Um," she stalls.

"Therefore, I was king for a large part of your young life." To her horror, he stops beneath the archway and says, "Would it surprise you to learn I remember you?"

The hairs on her arms stand up. "Me?"

"Prettiest girl in all the land," Minos says. "Child of a liberator and a High Priestess. This is not commonplace heritage. Eventually, I would recall such details, even an addled old judge like me." With one finger, he taps his head and makes a funny face Kore should laugh at but cannot because she is frozen from being caught in a lie.

"And this is how the High K-king knows things about me?" She studies the monument, faking interest, trying to seem unperturbed. "You told him?"

"Are you not curious about your own past?" Minos cocks his head. "Having forgotten it, as you say."

Uneasy, Kore digs her big toe into the grass. "But what more do you know?"

"I know when you saw me just now, you bowed as one would bow to a king."

She says nothing.

The former king of Knossos keeps his head tilted to one side and gazes at her with soft blue eyes like her mother's. "My dear Kore, tell me the truth. Why keep up this charade?"

She buries her face in her hands, blinking away tears. She must not cry like a child. Her voice is soft, muffled by cold palms. "I am ashamed."

"What is it?"

Her face crumbles. Oh, but she *is* a child! "If you know nothing about my mother, you cannot return me to her. You could send me back, a-a-and I can never go back—"

Minos lifts his arms a fraction. He plans to take her shoulders because he is caring and wishes to comfort. Suddenly, the dogs growl, and he drops his hands.

Kore snaps out of the tears. She will not be the reason he is hurt. "Tch! No!"

The mastiffs whine and sit back.

Eying the dogs, he says, "Is it so terrible in Crete?"

"It is not where I belong."

"No doubt your mother misses you."

Kore hopes not. That would make the betrayal much more shameful. She insists, "I love my mother. I do."

"Of course, you do." Voice calm and warm, he says, "Allow me to reassure you. A father holds dominion over you from birth. He holds dominion over you until the day your husband assumes dominion. With these laws, there is no room for the clutches of a mother."

"You will not send me back?"

"We will not send you back."

"Thank you . . . truly." It is what she has wanted to hear, and yet there is no comfort in it.

"Here I am, rambling on," he says, "and you have something on your mind." Dollop after dollop of cold rain plunks against her shoulders and head. Minos casts his interest on the clouds. "And we have no time left for strolling. Back inside, I am afraid."

Arm in arm, they walk the length of the pool.

"Well," she considers, "I am the child of a High Priestess, as you said . . ."

"Go on."

"Why are there no priests or priestesses at the palace of Asphodel? I have seen no sacred ceremonies at all."

"Asphodel is a place where men come to answer for their crimes," he says. "Indeed, there are no ceremonies inside the palace like there are in Knossos."

"Why not? Is Hades not a pious king?"

"The *damos* prefer to worship on their own. Priests and priestesses come by invitation."

Kore can tell Judge Minos minces his words. "Your priests fear the unholy."

He studies her. "Unholy?"

The rain picks up, and they take refuge under the terrace of the second floor. Thunder rumbles.

"Those who remain trapped here. They are unsettled."

"Dear Kore. They *should* be trapped and unsettled. They are prisoners."

"Not the prisoners. The dead."

"Few men enter these walls by choice. This includes our holy men and women."

"Those who truly invoke the gods should not fear," Kore protests brightly. "Not all priests and priestesses are holy, did you know, Judge? Some hold position because of prestige."

"Prestige? Yes, child, I suppose they do."

Kore loves to impress him with keen observations, which is what he appreciates most, or at least, it works so far.

"I can do it!" She practically leaps. "Oh, please let me. In Knossos, I hoped to work w-with f-funereal rites, b-but Mother says that is a job f-for a c-crone—"

"Calm down," Minos urges. "What exactly are you asking me?"

With a freezing hand, she cools her hot cheeks, touching one and the other. "To conduct ceremony and hold rites. Here."

Minos stares, incredulous. "Rites for?"

"Well," she says and points to the monument of Sisyphus at the end of the courtyard, "for *him*. And any others. This place needs to be purged of those who are trapped. There is no other way but by invocation and sacrament and—"

"You do have a peculiar fascination with Sisyphus," Minos interjects.

"He wants me to help. I know it."

The way Minos looks at her is not unlike the way her mother came to look at her. "Because you hear him at night," he clarifies.

"He is trapped, and I know why."

"Why?"

Corners of her mouth downturned, she admits, "Because his death was cruel."

Minos glances up at the sky.

Kore stammers, "I-I do not mean to say *Theíos* is cruel—"

"You can say it," Minos tells her. "It was true then."

At the mention of him, her heart flutters. "Then?"

"The condemnation of Sisyphus was Hades's

first significant ruling as High King. Young kings often want to set a tone for their reign. They want to be revered and believe fear is the path to reverence. Compassion is rarely part of the plan." He considers and says, "Particularly when your sole counselor has an iron fist. In the aftermath of Sisyphus's death, Hades had a big decision to make. You see, Sisyphus himself was a tyrant, as the titans had been. This is what the new generation sought to correct."

"*Theíos* did not want to become a tyrant," Kore says, wistful.

"It is a good sign when your conscience catches up to you. It proves you have one. And if you listen to it, do as it says, even better. That is when Hades called upon my brother, Rhadamanthus, to be his second counselor. My brother offsets the severity of Judge Aeacus."

"If my *theíos* wants to do what is right and good, he will be happy for me to purge these grounds." One of the dogs nudges her hand, wanting to be petted. She gives him a distracted ruffle between the ears.

"That is a question for another day," Minos says. "The Unseen must determine if it is appropriate."

It is exactly the response she hoped for because now she can say, "May I please see him? O-only for a little, I promise." The more she talks about him, the hotter her cheeks grow. "I understand he is busy."

"You might say that." Judge Minos yanks the heavy golden handle and opens the door to the palace. "I am afraid he is away on political matters."

"Oh . . ." A moan escapes her throat involuntarily. "Are you sure?"

Minos frowns. "Am I sure?"

Impatient, he holds the door for her. Kore walks inside, and the dogs follow. She thinks about last night. The guard. The arm. The pit in the ground where Hades discovered her. And she thinks of later, too, when she crawled into bed naked out of, well, the need to be seen differently, she supposes.

Stupid girl.

"I fear perhaps . . ." She swallows. "He dislikes me. I understand, I do! If he would give me one last chance—"

"He is away on political matters," Minos insists. "You must be patient. He may not return for another moon. These things can be complicated."

When the judge totters away, Kore for the first time finds herself studying *him* instead of the reverse. She understands how her own lies must have shone clear across her face.

Brother, Welcome

8

By land, the journey to Olympus is arduous, at best. Hades knows this from ten years of war waged from north to south and back again. The terrain from Erebus to Olympus is divided by the ranges of Mount Taygetos. It is cut by the chasms of Kaiádas, where traitors and criminals are punished by the mightiest soldiers in Erebus. The journey is slowed by the river of Queen Styx of Pheneus. Stalled by narrow passage through Corinth, where Sisyphus once ruled and called it Ephyra.

Beyond Corinth, the land is no kinder. Gaia is a curvaceous goddess. The regions of her body, uphill and downhill.

Hades is not a patient man. With Kore, he has practiced a restraint that requires too much of a thing he lacks. When he travels to Olympus, he travels by sea to cut the time and effort. Water queasiness is the worst of it. Otherwise, he heals in total. It has been a long time since Hades ended a day feeling well. Since the extracurricular visits to Kore at night, he has never been so sick.

Eyes stinging and watering pink throughout the days.

Head throbbing as pressure mounts.

Roiling nausea.

Loss of consciousness more than once.

Toward the end of those night visits, Hades thought it might kill him. At times, he finds the promise of permanent sleep appealing. But most of the time, he knows what happens in death is unlike sleep. It is only the body that sleeps. A man's essence remains. Thus, the suffering remains.

Nine days, he spends at sea. It does not suit him, but he reminds himself Poseidon does this all the time. Those years at war, Hades saw his seafaring brother once or twice. Poseidon led the islands during the uprising with the use of the Knossian naval fleet, courtesy of Minos himself. While Poseidon conquered by way of sea, Hades had slipped beneath the ground of Erebus as a mole might, using underground tunnels and cave systems to infiltrate the enemy from below.

Over the course of nine days, Hades has plenty of time to ponder his brothers. His coconspirators. The conspiratorial type of man is scarcely loyal to anyone. They will turn on each other when stakes are high.

On the tenth day, the tedium of ocean travel

ends, and he finds himself at shore, staring at the fifty-two peaks of Mount Olympus. An oarsman runs to the nearest polis and returns with the fastest horse he can find. The black-maned stallion is gray and ordinary. Hades prefers fast rather than fine. He prefers the comfort of a simple tunic and robe, without ornamental embellishments to draw attention along the path to Olympus. For the same reason, he abandoned his crown, a golden wreath of entwined serpents and briar thorns, inside the palace of Asphodel.

Soldiers accompanying him on the journey equip themselves with horses, and when Hades instructs them to stay where they are, they flash colors of dismay.

He is faster alone. The pomp of a full cavalry will slow him down, and already, he grows impatient that the journey to Olympus and back could mean a complete lunar cycle. He will not drag out the encounter with his brother any longer than necessary.

Along the way, deciduous trees give way to black pine and fir. Higher up the range, conifer forests stretch farther than the eye can see. The world of Zeus is lush and decorous with eagles soaring overhead in dignified welcoming.

Here, wildlife communes with man, not in a state of fear but in a state of cohabitation. Harmony, it seems, is the specialty of Zeus. Fox and man, both unflinching. Predator and prey can meet at the watering hole, calling a truce until later.

There is no mystery behind his brother's reputation of glory and his own reputation of severity. Olympus gleams from a natural outpouring of beauty from the gods. Erebus holds the oppressive lands of mining, military, and prisons.

The sun shines brighter in Olympus. The air, more fragrant. Wine, sweeter. The birds sing a prettier song. Shit smells like the narcissus.

When Hades enters the citadel of Olympus, the citizens continue to go about their day. He looks straight ahead to avoid the emanations of many people at once. The colors of man, when emitted by a crowd, can become irritatingly distracting, as a dog might be distracted by twenty rabbits simultaneously. It is overwhelming, each of their fields trying to pull him in. The colors tug, wanting attention, and offer worlds of information a mind nudge away.

In time, faces regard him curiously. He is a stranger. But he has visited Olympus in the recent past, and some recall the fearsome brother of Zeus from before—when he galloped into the citadel with his shoulder swollen and oozing pus and demanded, with his face pale and fever raging, that Zeus surrender his brat so Pylos might know justice.

Yes, some remember him. From the corner of his eye, two men shine with the light of recognition.

He keeps his focus ahead and climbs to the palace nestled into the foothills of Mount Olympus. He does not regard the whispering voices as he passes through the agora and closer to the palace itself. Several of the *damos* have taken off in a sprint.

Quick informants.

The palace at Olympus, hoisted by mountains, sits high above three towering levels of stairs, each adorned by purple carpets spilling down steps like rich wine. The walls gleam white, trimmed with gold and purple, colonnades stretching three times the height of any other palatial structure. Golden foliage blazes from treetops, flashing autumn colors like kingly jewels.

By the time he reaches the bottom of the steps and slides off his horse, a young man descends the staircase. He is accompanied by two Olympian guards. The young man, golden brown curls catching sun, wears the white and purple robes of a prince. He is beardless, dimple-chinned.

At the bottom of the second tier of stairs, the prince, Hermes, stops. Fixing his gaze on Hades, Hermes absently shakes something inside a closed fist. A faint impression of Kore rests in the prettiness of Hermes's face.

Hermes and the guards wait, blank-faced, for the High King of Erebus to ascend the first flight. They flash the orange-green of impatience.

With a little bow of the head, Zeus's son says, "Greetings, High King of Erebus. My father never told me you were spontaneous. Twice have I seen you outside your realm, and both times a surprise!"

Hades says, "Are your visits to Erebus

announced?"

"I transport prisoners." Hermes laughs, good-humored, fiddling with the thing in his fist. "Crime is hard to predict. Otherwise, there would be none."

"What is in your hand?"

As if genuinely surprised to find it there, Hermes glances down and gives a half-cocked smile. "This?"

He tosses the toy to Hades. Turning the object over between two fingers, Hades inspects it. Each side of the cube is painted with small dots. "A cube of bone?"

"Something I made. There are two." Hermes grins. "They are called dice."

Hades gives it back to him. "What do they do?"

"They are for games," he says, and when Hades does not respond, he clarifies, "For *fun*."

Hades blinks.

This son of Zeus lives a privileged life in which there is room for *fun*. The word strikes Hades as foreign. He stares at the young man, letting his eyes roam the colors around him.

Bronzed curiosity.

Green-yellow.

Red.

The hues equate to fear. They hint of aggression.

Hermes prattles about fun, as if he can loosen the anxiety with chatter. But the way the men stand in front of him, shoulder to shoulder, tells Hades what he needs to know.

If the gods were to judge the armies in the realms of the three High Kings, they would discover the fiercest in the land of Erebus, ruled by Hades. Lacedaemon, the hub of military genius, falls within the territories of Erebus. This alone is the reason Zeus has always needed his allegiance. Without Lacedaemonian armies, his brother would have been up against a terrible force during the Titan War. Discovering Hades of Erebus at your doorstep, with the mightiest armies amassed outside the polis, would be a terrifying thing to behold.

Zeus may be well-liked, but Hades is well-armed.

"Be at ease," Hades murmurs. "There is nothing to fear from me."

Hermes's fear softens. He blushes. "Of course not." He pretends to laugh. "We are kindred. Allies."

Hades squints up at the proud-beaming palace fit for a god.

"You ride alone?" Hermes surveys the area. He searches the road for Asphodelian guards atop horses and finds nothing but the curious faces of gathered crowds. Children peer around the legs of parents, vying for a better view. They see the Unseen!—and can scarcely trust their own eyes.

Hades ignores the question. "I want to talk to your father. Take my horse."

Hermes gestures to the bottom of the staircase, and a guard immediately attends to the fatigued animal. "Well," he says. "Welcome, Hades, High

King of Erebus."

Inside the entryway, guards stand in a long line. Muscled breastplates shine with gold. They stand motionless as he passes—all of them shielded, helmeted, and carrying sheathed swords.

"Allow me to clear the throne room before you enter," Hermes says. "My father sees many people throughout the day."

"When I enter," mutters Hades, "the room will clear itself." He walks fast, jaw set, chin lowered. Hermes intends to keep up the pace, so they walk side by side. Guards fall in behind them and along the sides.

In the assembly room, men and women cluster in small groups. They await the attention of Zeus, and each wears the finery of nobles from Olympian territories.

They are surrounded by gold-trimmed colonnades of marble and lush blue-curtained walls. Hades keeps his focus ahead, toward the entrance of a throne room protected by four helmeted guards. He strides forward, and their bodies flash defensively. They stiffen and poise their spears.

"Stand down." Hermes lifts a gold-cuffed hand to placate them. They relax their spears, alight with caution. To Hades, he says, "I suppose an announcement by the herald is out of the question."

"Open the door."

Massive doors part, carved and gilded and slow due to the sheer immensity of them.

Inside, a ridiculously enormous throne room. Wide-open space. The throne sits high up on a ludicrously tall set of stairs. The back of the white-marbled throne bears the outstretched wings of an eagle. The arms are carved into the zigs and zags of thunderbolts.

It has been two years since Hades last saw his brother. The beard of Zeus shines a chilly gray. The silver has not completely overtaken his mustache or the burnished brown hair on his head, but his beard—a source of much vanity—mocks Zeus by submitting to the curse of age.

The beard cascades to his chest in ringlets, oiled and perfumed and meticulously arranged. Zeus has softened with age, but the barrel chest remains strong above a small paunch.

Zeus perches absurdly high at the end of an absurdly vast throne room. Other men convene at the bottom of the throne's pedestal. Hades strides up the aisle.

A few steps below Zeus stand two guards who have approached the seat of Zeus in order to impart the urgent news—Hades of Erebus has returned!

"Brother!" Zeus bellows with cheer. "Welcome."

Hades stops at the bottom of the throne. He projects a monotone voice at half the volume of Zeus's thunderous bellow. "Come down from there so we can talk as equals."

To the guards, Zeus blurts gaily, "What did he say?"

One clears his throat, unhappy to be an elected mediator. "Majesty . . . Hades of Erebus requests you descend and speak with him as an equal."

"It is hard to hear you, brother, from up this high." Zeus grins down at Hades. The old brotherly ribbing, not entirely good-natured.

"Then come down and hear me."

Zeus laughs his jolly laugh. "Equals. I like that."

With theatrical slowness, Zeus rises—a bear of a man, thick in the chest and shoulders. Smiling, he descends the steps, removes the sapphire crown from his head, and thrusts it into the guard's plated stomach.

"Hold on to this for me, will you? The High King of Erebus wears no crown. Neither will I."

Several long moments tick by as Zeus makes his way down the massive stairs. There is a slight stiffness to his walk. The brilliance of pain radiates from one of his knees. Age catches up with Zeus in more ways than appearance. He aches from the rigidity of his muscles and joints after years of neglect, lazing up there on a throne and shrugging off his training.

"Brothers should be equals." At the base of the stairs, Zeus remarks, "Right, Hermes? Hades, you remember my son."

"I remember all your sons."

"I imagine you do." Face-to-face they stand, neither looking away. The little half-smile on the mouth of Zeus is a lie. His eyes are unsmiling and steeped in challenge.

Finally, Hades says, "I am not here to talk about sons."

"No?"

"I am here about your daughter."

"Which one?"

"The one called Kore."

"Never heard of her."

Inside the hues surrounding Hermes, Hades catches Kore's true name for the first time.

Persephone.

"To you, she is Persephone."

Hades considers pushing into the light surrounding Zeus. But as brothers, they swore not to harm one another, and so far, neither has broken the trust. If the eyes of Zeus bleed, war is certain.

Amicably, Zeus asks, "What about her?"

Hades is aware of the others inside the room. The guards. Two young men gather at the foot of the stairs, hanging around after Hades barged inside. Hermes, jangling that puerile cube inside one fist.

Never mind privacy or negotiation or politics. He opts for expedience and speaks without hesitation.

"I intend to take her as my wife."

The room silences. Heads turn.

The face of Zeus lights. His brother bursts with laughter that leaves his throat before he has a chance to rethink it. There is genuine pleasure in it, in fact.

Cheerful gold and white swirls all about the

body of Zeus. Still, Hades detects the spark of red, showing venom that Hades's words come in the form of a command, not a request.

"Sanction it," Hades says, anyway. "We are too old to start fighting now."

"We are not old." Zeus glances at Hermes. He scowls at his son's jiggling fist, and Hermes folds his arms behind his back to still them like a child reprimanded for horseplay. "How did you stumble across my daughter?"

"She nearly died on my land. I made sure she lived." Hades adds, "And lives still."

"What was she doing on your land? That child is Cretan."

"She was on her way to you."

Incredulous, Zeus glances again at Hermes. "I see."

"Did you send for her?"

Hermes shifts in place. Exchanged between the men, a small thread of indigo light. Hades cannot help himself. He presses into the colors of Hermes, a slight nuzzle, to make Hermes's eyes burn for an instant. It could easily be a fleck of sand to cause it.

"Zeus has his eye on a match for Persephone."

"Now that you mention it," Zeus says, "I did. The message went over like a wine goblet full of shit. Mother did *not* approve. Hermes?"

Hermes shifts in place. "You know mothers. Never wanting to loosen their grip."

"I am glad you convinced me to come down

from my perch," Zeus says, placing a hard-gripping hand on his shoulder. Hades winces. Zeus is not without sin. The corruption of his touch makes Hades lean back in an effort to dislodge his hand.

"I need to stretch my legs," Zeus continues, slinging a heavy arm around his shoulder. "Walk with me. Later, there will be a banquet to honor your visit. No fighting me. I know how you hate a crowd, but think of the feast, the music, the women! You are a little hollow-faced, brother. I believe a king should eat well and eat often."

Hades glances down at a soft midsection hiding under Zeus's royal finery. Zeus bellows a laugh and slaps him on the back. Hades clenches his fists but follows Zeus out of the room and away from the others.

If not for the relief of getting away from people, Hades would not budge. Behind them, a sluglike trail of energy. A team of guards, shadowing, jangling armor with each unified step. They exit the throne room from the back. A sumptuously curtained doorway leads them into a hall lined with carvings of naked bodies of women along the columns.

Outside, green hedges are carved in varying shapes of artistry. Gold and red leaves wave like flags—it is festive. Celebratory and bright. Olympus appears clean, thoroughly tended, and manicured to show a labyrinth of hedges at waist level. What is more innately confining than a maze? And yet, in Olympus, it is trimmed short enough to give the illusion of freedom. Walled in, but able to see plenty of sky.

They walk a straight line through the center of the labyrinth, along the foothills of Mount Olympus where the trees part into a well-kept clearing.

As they stroll along, Zeus's hands link behind his back. "Are we really going to pretend you are not here because of my son?"

"You know me to pretend?"

"Listen," Zeus levels, "once Heracles redeems himself—and he will redeem himself—he will be made new. New name, new life. Who told you about this? Creon? The aggrieved father. Bah. I suppose I would do the same."

"You refuse to surrender Heracles." It is not a question. Nor threat. Simply a statement of fact, as one might say the grass is green. Also as fact, Hades states:

"Your daughter will take his place."

Zeus's smile returns, broad and easy, as if there is no problem between the two of them. Zeus's cockiness is like a pinch. Hard to ignore.

"You sent for Persephone," Hades continues. "What for?"

"A sixteen-year-old virgin priestess with the good looks of her mother and me combined? Yes, I sent for her."

The smell of pine sails along with the wind. They walk north, where a small pocket of gray clouds wafts from the west to the eastern shore.

Although he knows exactly where Zeus is taking him, Hades is unconcerned. He goes along with it.

"I spread my seed with purpose," Zeus belts. "One Zeus begets another and so on and so forth. In time, my blood will run the length of the world."

A faint growl comes from within the clouds. Thunder. Zeus continues his boastful rant. Red in the face, he preaches, "Each child is a boon, and when it is time to reap the harvest, I reap the harvest. The girl you want is a bountiful harvest. And that reaping is upon me. I intend to make the most of it."

Through a clearing in the path, a stone bridge arcs over a ravine. The parapets are painted gold. The roadway, a rich-swirled marble. Together, they cross the bridge between the divide.

Hades says, "Our disagreement can end today."

Below them, the tops of trees rustle from the impending storm.

Behind them, footfalls of Olympian guards.

"You will make her an awfully young widow," Zeus says.

"A widow with many kingdoms."

Overhead, falcons circle. Distant squawks of birds warn of storm clouds. Not far off stands an oblong arena open to a sullen sky.

"Back at my throne," Zeus says, "there were two men. Notice them?"

"More seedlings?"

Zeus laughs. "Pirithous, King of Thessaly, and his *friend* Theseus. But his friend has a cock, and

Pirithous needs heirs. He is on a mission to get a wife, so I sent for one."

Cold droplets plunk from the sky. Hidden in the gloom, distant flashes of lightning.

"Now," Zeus practically sings, "as much as I like the idea of solidifying our friendship, what am I supposed to do about Pirithous? He did claim her first. You understand. You love fairness and all."

They enter the arena before the deluge arrives. On Mount Olympus, storms flash in and out of existence.

"Oh," his brother says abruptly, as if he just thought of it. "I am sorry about this. Did I mention I have an execution? I hate to juggle duties, but when the sky god beckons, I answer."

They pass through the colonnades. Guards part curtains the color of wine. They emerge into Zeus's box, with a view at the forefront of the arena. Standing before his massive cushioned chair, Zeus scans the arena. "The gods wait for no one."

In the center of the arena, the dirt floor contains a single object:

A silver rod, mounted upright in the ground and reaching to the heavens. This rod, a beacon for sky-given power. Hades grits his teeth.

At the base of it, a man bound in chains. He glows terror of the most primitive kind.

Closer, the crack of thunder.

"The time has come," Zeus calls to the man. "I draw the bolts near."

The prisoner babbles. Urine runs down his leg.

Zeus leans in. "When they piss themselves, they cook extra crisp."

In that instant, light pierces the sky. An earsplitting crack reverberates inside the arena. It is miraculous that Zeus is not deaf by now, subjecting his now-mortal ears to this sound. The metal rod comes alive with blue-white light. With a tormented cry, the man stiffens like a corpse, and his body sizzles against currents that spark and vibrate with the harnessed power of lightning.

The body smokes from the pole.

"What was I saying?" Zeus sticks a finger in his ear, wiggles it around as if his hearing will be restored faster this way. "Oh. Pirithous. It seems the fair thing to do, the *just* thing, is to honor tradition. A couple of suitors, fighting it out for my daughter. To the death."

Zeus's pride brings about a sense of false security.

"Do not play with me." Hades stares hard at the silver-bearded king.

To this, Zeus drops the smile for the first time and begins to take his leave. As he does, the shoulder of Zeus nudges his own—the bad shoulder, stiff from ten days of travel. His old brother-in-arms stops.

"I decide the fate of my children." Zeus seethes. "Not them. Not you. Me."

In this vein, the night concludes, and clouds

move from Olympus with their bolts undirected and free to dissolve back inside the haphazard whims of nature.

VANISHING POINT
9

Out of nowhere, a gruff voice arises. "We call this the vanishing point."

At first light, Kore set out, gathering dogs along the way, wandering beyond the palace, beyond the courtyard. From the slowness of her gait, an observer might mistake it for sleepwalking. Morning fog hangs low, veiling the path. With each step, the roar of Oceanus grows louder.

The dogs do not growl at the voice materializing from behind. Kore peers at their lurking shapes and wonders, irrationally, if it is one of the mastiffs speaking to her.

"I suggest," the voice continues, "you stop walking, young Kore."

From the murk, the crabby old judge materializes. Bundled in his robe, Judge Aeacus smiles with a tranquility Kore has never witnessed on his face. Whatever drives Aeacus today is without the usual hostility. The mastiffs, sensing his pleasantness, accept bits of meat from a lowered hand. Crooked fingers sprout with silver hairs.

"I hear the ocean," she says. "It reminds me of home."

Aeacus wipes his hands on his robe and comes to her side. She finds herself flinching involuntarily. Though Judge Aeacus approaches her in a gentle manner, Kore expects the worst. Perhaps she is wrong about him. Being stern does not necessarily mean he is bad—for why would Hades trust a man who is bad?

"Take my arm."

She does.

"Do not fall prey to the seductive call of Oceanus," he says.

Like pulled-apart cotton, the fog thins.

Head spinning with vertigo, she scrambles backward and sinks to the dirt. She plants her palms upon the earth for safety.

"No need to worry," Aeacus muses. "I am sure the mongrels would have stopped you as I stopped you."

The drop is dizzying. Far down, waves burst upon rocks, shattering foam and sea spray. Gulls fly below where they stand. The horizon glimmers with morning light.

"Come now." The judge helps her up. "You are perfectly safe."

Once her tears begin, they flow freely.

The judge turns to face the sea, his arms open in a lavish stretch. "A scare, was it not? There, there. Cry it out."

"I am sorry to cry so much." She stands up and sucks back the tears. "I a-am lonely, I guess."

"Lonely?" Aeacus gestures to the dogs. "With this many of us to look after you?"

"He may not return for another moon."

Kore swallows. As the mist thins, the judge's cloak becomes a brighter shade of blue. The blackness of the dogs contrasts sharply against yellow earth. Kore studies her canine protectors. When they walk, the pack maintains a wide circle around her. They exist to guard her. But what if they also exist to prevent her from escape?

In the clearing fog, the angular outline of the palace emerges, an impossibly straight erection of obsidian and jasper. Three towers shoot upward and jut at rigid angles, the center of which is tallest. A burst of sun reflects against the slick surface. Long windows blink down at her, watchful. This is where she has been hidden away for ages, and Kore has never been far away enough to get a good look.

"You have never fully seen it, have you?" Aeacus asks, reading her thoughts.

"Only the courtyards."

"Only the—?" he marvels. "How inhospitable of us. I thought Minos would have shown you around."

"No."

"With His Majesty gone, my days have been freed up." With a resolute nod, Judge Aeacus extends a hand. "Allow me to show you."

"With His Majesty gone . . ."

With no promise of running into Hades, there is nothing to look forward to anymore. The familiar plunge of the heart collides with the intrigue of doing something—anything—outside of the ordinary. It takes little time before they locate a simple cobblestone road with tufts of grass growing between the cracks. Aeacus leads her alongside the palace exterior. Once they turn their first corner, the path ramps downward at a steep angle, and steps replace the walkway.

Aeacus points overhead at a window two stories above where they stand. "Those are your quarters, if I am not mistaken. Do you recognize the view?"

She spots the northern mountain range covered by a thick pine forest. "Yes, Judge."

Down the steps they travel, until the palace seems to burrow into the ground. Obsidian towers disappear behind an overgrowth of vine and shrubs. Wincing, the judge negotiates the steps. The gradient slope taxes his legs and hips.

Ahead, an overlook of the entire valley. A jagged river glints in the sun. Wind siphons through the range and slams into them, pushing their bodies and flapping their cloaks. They come to a landing that veers right. A line of aspen trees fences them from another nasty drop down a sharp embankment.

White trunks, topped with leaves of brilliant yellow, remind her of pillars. To their right, vines grow over limestone swirled with orange-red.

Judge Aeacus surprises her by saying, "Minos tells me you inquired about the priesthood in Asphodel."

Kore fidgets, unsure how to respond.

"Specifically," he says, "you asked why no one holds ceremony on these grounds."

"He told you about that?"

"We confer on everything." After weighing his words, Aeacus corrects himself. "Confer, yes. Agree, no."

So engrossed in what he is saying, Kore hardly notices as the stone face of the mountain transforms beside her. Ahead, the path evolves into a broad portico where two horses drink from a trough. Chariots, too. One of these probably carried her to Asphodel the day the soldiers came and snatched her from Hecate's care.

"After dark, we light it up. A man can see it from the river bend. During the day, it blends like the sly chameleon. A wonder, is it not?"

The facade of Hades's palace is carved directly into the side of the mountain. It must have taken the slaves years to turn a mountain into a home fit for kings. Limestone columns flank the entryway, strangely gnarled and twisted. Columns. Yes, they are columns. But they are carved into naked bodies twisted together like woody vines. Strained hands

hold the entablature aloft, as if these entangled souls
bear the weight of the structure, much like Sisyphus
bears the weight of a boulder.

She cringes.

"Hades rules from within the earth, and the
caves of Tartarus run far below." Aeacus flashes a
confidential smile. "But you must know that, eh?
Having been there yourself."

Kore braces for a reprimand or tirade, but
instead he prattles on.

"Up," he says, pointing, "is the assembly room.
Imagine the towers as a crown for the earth itself.
Ah, and there in the highest tower—you see?—
those are the quarters of the High King. It is easy to
keep an eye on things from high."

Although a welcome change, the judge's
friendliness confuses her.

"Well?" With a lift of bushy eyebrows, Aeacus
grins. "How do you like it?"

"I-it is," she stammers, "overwhelming."

"Indeed, it is." He scratches his chin in
puzzlement. "Forgive me. What were we talking
about again?"

"Priests and priestesses." Kore studies the
carved embellishments of men and women in
torment and hesitates to say more. Minos was firm
in his stance. Aeacus will be firmer. "Judge, will my
theíos return soon? It has been a long time—"

"There is no certainty on when he will return."

Chewing her lip, Kore gazes at the steps leading

to the entrance, at the chiseled likenesses of mastiffs on each side.

"You miss him, do you?" Aeacus asks. "That is nice, I suppose."

Kore pushes a rock with her toe. "I want to ask him something."

"Perhaps I can answer."

He will think her stupid. She should not ask him—but today, Aeacus does not appear to judge her. In fact, quite the opposite.

"If the holy men and women will not come here, I thought I might . . ." She looks to the ground. "Well, I thought I might purge the grounds myself."

"Hmm." Aeacus taps a finger to his chest.

"I-I know how. Honestly!"

"Sweetness, I believe you. I told Minos to let you do it."

"Really?"

"The child of a High Priestess could easily rise to the task. If I had the authority, I would decree every citizen of Asphodel must attend by order of the court. The bigger the crowd, the happier the gods."

Kore gives a self-deprecating laugh. "Thank you, but I am n-not courageous enough for a crowd. My mother is, but not me. I am not as special."

"Of course you are special!"

Tears scald her sinuses. Inside, she curses this childish sensitivity.

"You are the daughter of Zeus, Loud Thunderer.

King of Kings, they call him . . . or he calls himself."
He winks. "Who can say?"

"Moreover," he continues, "you need not
wait for Minos to approve—or any of us, for that
matter. You hold nearly as much authority as Hades
himself."

Dropping her head, she flushes. "You make fun
of me."

"Never," he says with a crooked smile. "It
would be reckless of me to mock a future queen."

She furrows her brow. He teases her by saying
silly things.

"In theory," he encourages, "the absence of
Hades puts you in command. You see?"

Uncomfortable, Kore wrings her hands. "N-no
. . ."

With a sigh, Aeacus says, "I suppose there is no
harm in waiting for formal permission. Perhaps his
journey will be a quick one."

Affairs of kings are of no interest to her. It never
occurred to her to ask about them, for who is she to
pry?

"Judge," Kore says, reaching for the head of a
dog. She finds a furry skull waiting for her to pet,
and it makes her feel safe again. "Where did *Theíos*
go?"

"To Olympus, of course. To speak with your
father."

Her face blanches. In the silence that falls, a
raven pierces the air with its cry.

"M-my father. When can I go to him?"

"When you are better."

"B-but . . ."

"But?"

"I am still here."

"Yes, you are still here." Judge Aeacus chuckles.

For a long time, she has been patient. The matter of her health is no longer questionable. Kore is sure of it. She is more than well enough to make the journey safely.

"Why," she asks, "have I been left behind?"

"Negotiations are in place. It would not be approp—" Aeacus stops, brow cratered. "To what extent have you been told of your future, sweetness?"

Again, she tries to stifle the urge to cry. "Wh-what future do you mean?"

"I thought when you spoke with Minos, he was candid with you."

"Judge Minos said my *theíos* left for political things?"

"Very political. We are acquiring you."

Despite a warm sun, she shivers. "Acquiring?"

"Are you cold?" he says. "You are shaking, child. Let us go back inside where it is warm."

To mask the tremor, Kore folds her arms. "P-please, tell me."

"I should not have spoken freely. Forgive me. These things can be complicated."

Minos told her the same thing. Why must it be complicated? Frustration mounts, and when she opens her mouth, her mother's strength emboldens her. "I trust you can explain it simply."

Aeacus wheezes laughter, throwing back his head to reveal beige, pitted teeth. "Fair enough. Where to begin? With your brother, I suppose."

The word *brother* elicits a faint smile. Since she was small, Kore would often fantasize about having a robust family. By word of mouth, she knows her father sired many children. Her brothers and sisters. Delightful!

"Hades insists your brother answer for a number of wretched crimes," Aeacus says, "but your father refuses to allow it."

Kore startles. "C-crimes?"

"Oh yes." Aeacus sighs, throwing information at her with the casualness of a man throwing chicken feed. "Your brother is charged with murder, and Hades is staunch in matters of justice."

Face draining of color, Kore braces against the sturdy form of a mastiff.

"Whining, arrogant pest . . ."

"You consider no one but you . . ."

Panic shocks her heart like a spurred horse. Suddenly, his loathing makes sense. "Wh-why does Hades want to keep me here?"

"My dear," he consoles. "Surely, you must know the role of a daughter. Think of yourself as treasure! Men value their daughters as much as they value their livestock. I am merely a judge, but once I was king of a little island called Oenone. Heard of it?"

She shakes her head.

"No matter," he says. "My point is, I understand the dealings of kings. If I were your father, I would be eager to offer my daughter to spare the life of my son."

"Offer me to do what?"

"To become Hades's child bride, silly girl. Hades has reluctantly agreed to take you off your father's hands. He is an extremely wealthy king, and Zeus could not hope for a better arrangement. Peace between houses will be restored for now. That is all you need to know."

The sun blares, and her head aches. What is this strange scheme? In her head, the words jumble, and she struggles to place them in an order she can understand.

"In my house, you are nothing."

Nothing.

Every bid for affection, he denies her. Pushes her away. Handles her roughly. He thinks of her as a brat of Zeus, as he must think of this murderer whom they claim is her brother.

"You look pale," Aeacus says.

Unblinking, Kore mutters, "But he hates me."

"Poor child," he says, "of course he hates you. That is unavoidable but irrelevant. He has no interest in interacting with you. Simply stay out of his way, and enjoy your new title as High Queen. Other girls would kill for such an honor."

Kore reaches out and steadies herself on a furred body. She lowers herself to the ground.

Mother. She needs her mother.

Judge Aeacus continues as though she gazes up at him with a bright smile instead of panic. "The point is, seeing as how you will be queen, you can do whatever you please. Purge away, sweetness. Enjoy what few perks come with your fate."

Aeacus grins up at the palace facade. "Welcome to eternity."

THE LOUD THUNDERER
10

Hades does not attend the banquet held in his honor.

The evening carries on without the Erebusian High King, who hibernates somewhere in the palace, although Zeus feels no need to check on him. Earlier, he puffed up his chest and threatened his brother in the arena. The "victim" chained to the silver pole would have found himself there eventually. To make an example out of him, Zeus ordered the prisoner to be yanked from his cell, a criminal not expecting death tonight but facing it nonetheless.

Hades, stroll into a party after that? No. He must lick his wounds.

Anyway, Zeus meant no real harm. At the root of it, Zeus wants good things for his brother. Good, distracting things.

Now, the one known as the King of Kings reclines in the *andron* of his palace, sleepy and ready for bed and too tired to bother getting up. Lulling him with waggling hips, a small-breasted flautist plays for the room, showing off for Hermes. Hermes accompanies her with an instrument of his own invention.

It is easy to take pride in such a clever boy. Hermes invented the lyre when he was waist-high, fashioning the instrument from the shell of a tortoise he happened upon in the mountains. The lyre-playing of Hermes is as lovely as the flautist with her little lips pursed and blowing into the reedlike instrument. From the way she flirts with his son, it is not the only reedlike thing her lips will encounter tonight.

As for Zeus, his wife awaits upstairs. Clamped at the knees, though it makes no difference. Earlier, he had his appetites satisfied by a pretty twenty-year-old brunette princess named Semele. He may be in love with her, a problem that will bleed into his marriage and drive Hera to lunacy (again), which will put Semele—and any children they create—in danger. A jealous wife gets revenge one way or another.

It is a queen's right to be this way, he supposes. Zeus has loved more women than a normal man could love in a hundred lifetimes. He will, no doubt, love many more. In sex, power wins all. Power gets a man anything he wants, and it is a fun thing to play with, as long as a ruler keeps his sights on the overall good of the ones he governs.

This is why he and Hades get along. As different as they are as men, they are aligned as kings. Both rule fairly and are respected by the masses. Both kings take generous care of their people. Both kings detest tyranny. And both strike fear when crossed.

Surveying a room packed with diplomats, noblemen, whores, and slaves, Zeus considers the oddity who is Hades, High King of the southernmost land. His ability is no illusion conjured by a savvy king. It is bizarre, fearsome, and another reason why Zeus gives great importance to their brotherhood.

Zeus has seen Hades do abominable things. Men bleed from the eyes. The ears. Cough up stringy rivulets as the tacky stuff pours down their throats. Grisly deaths without a finger laid upon them.

Thus, Zeus made his uncanny brother promise him early on, "Never try that on me. Ever. You promise me that, you have a friend for life."

When Hermes finishes the duet with the flautist, he shoulders his way through guests and plops down at the foot of Zeus's couch.

"Well?" His son sighs, glancing around.

"Well, what?"

"Where is he?"

"Who?"

"Hades," Hermes says. "Is all this not for him?"

Zeus chuckles. "I gave him a hard time today."

"Right. Trying to prove your cock is bigger?" Hermes says. "Come on, Father. End this. It is what you want."

"Of course I do."

"Why push him?"

"He needed a reminder," says Zeus, swinging heavy legs from the couch and onto the floor. "You understand brotherly dynamics. You stole an entire herd of cattle from your brother for comeuppance. Do not talk to me about measuring cocks."

"I was ten! Are you ten?"

Zeus chuckles again. "Bah. Hades will be fine. I need to keep him in his place. Nobody comes in here bossing me around in my own kingdom. He should know better."

"Is there a gentler way to assert yourself," Hermes says, "besides summoning death from Father Sky?"

Lightning comes at his command. That is the impression he gives. This time around, it came with such perfect timing, Zeus could not have planned it better.

As a boy squatting inside the moss-covered cave of Mount Dikte, he had studied the ways of the sky. Counted the moments between flashes and booms. Predicted how long it might take for one cloud to migrate to another location based on the momentum of the wind and those mysterious noises rumbling from the heavens.

The golden discovery came when he was nine as he watched the dancing Kouretes, armed with shields clashing together in rhythmic percussion. Kouretes, leaping around a pyre as clouds raced in from the west. Bare-chested protectors, too entranced by the rhythm of shields and dance to let a little rain stop them.

Boy Zeus, groin covered with a wool flap, saw one of the Kouretes raise a spear to the sky. In that instant, a white current drew from the heavens and cooked the soldier in mid-dance.

Sizzled with a flash to his spear.

It was a fatal movement for the soldier, but a critical one for an intelligent boy being raised apart from his family, all so his kingly father would not kill him. Eat him, as he ate the other infants torn from the womb of Zeus's mother. The certainty of infanticide prompted his mother to give her son to a couple of goat-herders to be raised in secret and apart from promises of wealth and privilege. Cute goat-herders—a pert young widow and her two daughters—but goat-herders, nonetheless. The Kouretes became his model for manhood, these large-muscled tribal men who failed to heed the weather one night.

Terrible timing for the Kourete. Magical timing for the observant boy.

And tonight. Tonight, the timing was equally magical. Usually, a prisoner wiggles on the pole for a torturously long time, to the point where Zeus grows tired of teasing and taunting with words like:

"Here it comes."

And:

"I draw the bolts closer. Can you hear them?"

Tonight, it was as if nature waited for *him* to show up and got on with business so as not to waste the time of Zeus, Loud Thunderer.

Zeus knows the truth, however. Weather is controlled by no mortal. Man bends to nature, and so it will always be. The unpredictability of nature, Zeus surmises, is what makes man superstitious in the first place.

Everything that happens in life happens because of one of the gods.

Want something? Ask a god.

Things going well? Praise a god.

Have a problem? Blame a god.

That is the way it goes. Man loves his superstitions, and Zeus loves them too. It is easier to blame Gaia or Oceanus than to bother wondering what strange phenomenon makes the earth and sea do the things they do. Man will always create their gods. And the ones proclaimed as gods will always buy into it. It serves them to do so.

Just as it serves Zeus to let the world assume he controls thunderbolts. It served him, for sure, today when that aberration from Erebus showed up at his throne demanding to marry his daughter.

"Are you going to walk me to my room or squawk at me?"

"Squawk," says Hermes.

Zeus throws an arm around the shoulder of his son to prove Hermes's words are not totally lost on him. Well, actually, he throws his arm around people quite a bit, and it must look chummy, but the truth is his knee freezes up on him when he first stands up, and it is nice to have a sturdy shoulder to lean on.

"Do not make me zap you with a bolt or two, little boy." Zeus pokes his son in the rib cage.

"Sure you will, old man." Despite himself, Hermes snickers at his father. "Who else will escort prisoners to Erebus for you? I am the one son of yours Hades allows on his land."

"This is so." Zeus brightens. "*And* he has no desire to kill you!"

"Yet!" Hermes jokes back. With the pointy bone of his elbow, he nudges Zeus and carries on. "We can negotiate the dowry after we settle the contract."

"Can I not have some fun beforehand? Let him sweat a bit?"

Though a trickster himself, Hermes says, "You should take this a bit more seriously."

"I am, son. I am."

"Good. All is settled."

"Almost," says Zeus. "Although, I did suggest he and Pirithous battle it out for her. It is too fun a bluff to retract right away."

In a hallway bright with celestial mosaics, Hermes slows to a halt. His boyishly pretty face goes blank, humorless. "Why would you do that?"

Zeus shakes his head at his too-serious son. "According to law, it is within my right as the girl's father to ask for a competition among suitors."

"Yes, but there are no suitors. Persephone was

always intended for—"

"I know that!" Growing tired of the topic, Zeus turns and continues to walk the length of the corridor toward the staircase to his apartment. "Go to bed, Hermes. You are annoying me."

"Father," Hermes calls. "Hades was not the only absentee tonight."

As Zeus stops and turns to face his son, Hermes says, "Pirithous was not there, either."

They stare at each other.

Hermes says, "You want me to check on them, I suppose."

Zeus gives his head a nod. "Please, and thank you."

Uneasily, they go their separate ways—he and his son, both wary. To his surprise, there is no knock on his door that night. Zeus endures a fitful sleep.

The following morning, Hermes trots into the dining hall, finding a puffy-eyed Zeus seated next to his wife. The bovine, thick-lidded eyes of Hera shift to the young man as he crouches beside his father. The queen is as tall as Zeus and equally stately and handsome. Mahogany hair piles into a pyramid of curls, frosted with gray along the sides. Although Hera is not Hermes's mother, she tolerates Zeus's bastard for one reason. He kisses her feet.

When it comes to a vindictive queen, prostration works miracles. Heracles could learn a thing or two from Hermes, but the boys are too different to expect as much.

Hermes kneels to the right of his father. Zeus mutters, "Has Pirithous been slain?"

"No."

"Then what?"

"I will show you."

Without a word, Zeus takes his leave. Hermes leads Zeus out of the dining hall. Beneath the silence, a mountain of understanding.

When they enter the central courtyard, a small collection of young men loiters on the patio. For those who await their turn with the King of Kings, couches and chairs spread about. During the day, slaves bathe dirty feet and serve men whose day will be spent here, awaiting their turn with Zeus.

As he and Hermes approach the little crowd, heads turn. Men prostrate themselves as Zeus walks to the source of curiosity. They move aside.

There stands Theseus, clasping the jaw of his lover. Pirithous is seated in an angular stone chair. His hands are splayed and immobile on the slabbed armrests. His chin droops. Drool oozes from one corner of his mouth.

His eyes, while open, are blood red. One pupil is blown. The other is as small as a gnat.

Moving his face from side to side, spittle running between his fingers, Theseus urges, "Piri? Pir, you have to speak."

As if drowsy, Pirithous gives a slow blink and slurs, "Who . . . you?"

When he speaks, the left side of his mouth

moves. The right sags like the wax of a melted candle.

"I waited for him at the banquet," Theseus tells Zeus. "I thought he found entertainment elsewhere."

"Pirithous," Zeus instructs in a voice like thunder. "Your king commands you to answer."

The head of Pirithous lifts. With drooping lids, Pirithous struggles to focus on the one who commands.

Blood-ridden eyes leaking pink tracks down his cheeks, Pirithous gawks at Zeus, the most well-known of all rulers and mumbles, "Who . . . you?"

Zeus looks to Hermes. "What is wrong with him?"

Pirithous also looks to Hermes. "Who . . . you?"

One day before, King Pirithous of Thessaly was whip-sharp with a keen sense of humor that kept everyone entertained. This is painful to witness.

"Majesty, forgive him. He has said nothing else since we found him." Theseus bites the inside of his cheek to keep from breaking. A strong warrior, Theseus does not fret easily. It was the confident Theseus who caught up to King Minos years ago when the batty old king fled to Malta. Theseus, captor of Minos, is clammy and pale-faced.

Pirithous hears him. In protest, he opens his mouth to say something, but when he does, his face grows red, and his cheeks quiver. A single word labors from his mouth.

"M-m-m-move."

"Yes, that is right." Zeus frowns. "Move. Get up."

The arms of Pirithous affix to the chair. Large muscled legs, immobile as a mountain. Pirithous trembles from strain.

"He cannot move," says Theseus.

"Pick him up," Zeus mumbles. "Get him care. And something strong to calm his nerves."

Steady footfalls clomp toward the young king. Metallic jangling of armor. Guards trickle in. Theseus wrenches his lover's hands from the chair, but King Pirithous of Thessaly is frozen as a man freezes not long after dying, hands like claws and muscles death-rigid. At last, clutching fingers pull clean from the arm of the chair. When they lift him, the body of Pirithous remains frozen in a sitting position and unable to straighten.

"Where is my brother?" Zeus asks Hermes.

"I could not find him," Hermes admits. "Do you want me to issue another search?"

To hide a shiver, Zeus sniffs. "No, no. Do not concern yourself with this any longer. I will put it to rest."

"Truly?"

"Truly. Leave me to it."

There is no mystery of his brother's whereabouts. No mystery for Zeus. Flanked by guards, he makes his way out of the courtyard, through the palace, and out the other side where the labyrinth of hedges stretches far and wide. They cut a straight path through the maze and emerge into a thicket of trees, then to the bridge spanning the ravine and leading him to the arena.

At the bridge, he releases the guards.

"Equals. I like that."

As the blinding light of Helius beams above the horizon, Zeus crosses alone. Normally, when he does this, storms fill the air with leaves swishing and thunder resonant enough to rumble the earth. Today, the day is young and bright. Larks sing, and the distant creek water rushes on.

When Zeus enters the arena, it is without fear. Instead, he finds himself pulling war memories out of the dusty recesses of his mind, to remind him of the love a man can have for his brother. He is a man with much love—love for women, for his children, for his brothers in war. He loves them in specific ways. Women, with hunger. His children, without condition.

Brothers, with loyalty.

But . . .

Hades has serious dissension with his son. And he is blind to true justice in this case. Because of the arrow he took to the shoulder, he takes the whole thing personally. Gods help the man who enrages Hades the Unseen, for he is sure to pay a hefty price.

The curtains leading to his box are closed. Golden ropes hang idle at either side of the entry. With a beefy hand, adorned with rings and battle-scarred, Zeus parts the curtains.

Hades is where he had been last night. Has he moved at all? Bah. Yes, of course he has. To injure Pirithous the way he did? He could not exact that sort of harm from afar.

His ankles are crossed and propped up on a stool. When Zeus enters, making plenty of noise with the shuffle in his walk and the clearing of his throat, Hades does not turn around. Instead, he stares out at the circular floor, the center of which holds the mighty silver pole often touched by Father Sky.

"I have enough trouble from Poseidon," Zeus tells him. "One brother at odds with me is enough. I do not desire it from you too."

As he sits next to Hades, neither bristles. A decade of war has conditioned them. They are accustomed to being on the same side. At ease together. Their survival instincts fail to respond to such intellectual things as grudges. Historically, they trusted each other as they trusted themselves, and the tightly woven threads of that bond hold, despite the conflict rending them apart.

"Poseidon?"

Zeus shakes his head. "With him, it is always land. Coveting land rightfully belonging to my children, my wife. He challenges them for it. Loses. Sore loser, that one. And hotheaded."

He studies the austere king beside him, compact and taut, shorter than Zeus by half a head and nowhere as meaty. The glinting beard is short and unkempt, grown during travel and hardly that of a king. Despite Hades having a few years on Zeus, the hair on his brother's head remains black with traces of silver making themselves known. Age, it is coming. It is going to catch up to him as it caught up to Zeus—he will find out!

"By the way," Zeus tells him with a waggle of the finger, "I am not ignorant to the fact you sent a little boat of goodies to Crete. A humanitarian all of a sudden? You would not be trying to align yourself with Poseidon in case of a big falling out between us?"

"Say what you mean."

Zeus leans forward, elbows balanced on his silver-haired knees. "Understand, Heracles is my son. I will not turn my back on him. Since he was a babe, the queen has tormented him. She has fed him so much poison over the years, it is no wonder he is not stark raving mad by now. At heart, he is good. There is a narrow divide between justice and revenge. Do not seek revenge. A vengeful heart is Poseidon's shortcoming. You are wiser than that."

Hades stays consistent and short with his replies. "I am not here to negotiate on Heracles."

Zeus sits back and studies the hollow eyes across from him. Poor hermit king. Full of anger, all pent-up and about to burst. Maybe it will not solve *everything*, but a woman can cure pent-up aggression nine times out of ten. At least long enough to forget grudges for a little while, until he has no choice but to satisfy the aggression again.

"If I give you Persephone," Zeus says, shrewd in eye and voice, "our negotiation will address Heracles as part of the arrangement. He will remain under my ultimate authority. I am his father." The charming smirk returns. "And, in marriage, I will also be yours."

Hades gives a lift of the brows. His mouth spreads into a half-grimace. "Agreed."

"We will seal it in blood. A contract for Persephone."

Zeus struggles not to laugh. Hades is a man in love. Lost to it.

A man who never leaves his apartment has no feast of women to enjoy. Hades is used to isolation. It is what he knows. Aeacus told Zeus as much, warned him beforehand.

"Hades is different. His father is as mad as yours. Your mother protected you, but his could not."

That is how he learned of Hades, Prince of Asphodel, through *warning,* as if he was a sort of gifted monster.

Aeacus explained. As a boy, odd Hades spent too much time in the caves of Tartarus. The ground would swallow him up inside—gulp him down much like Cronus gulped the flesh of his own children. When the punishment was over, he was released into the hands of Aeacus, a skilled adviser to the king. The adviser, first honing Hades into a warrior, had introduced him to a young man from

Crete whose prized possession was a goat but who wanted much, much more.

This, Aeacus told Zeus, too:

"Expect him to disappear. You will see little of him, but he will be of tremendous value."

In war, Hades performed in isolation, doing stealth work and infiltrating camps from cave systems, making them vulnerable to attack. His strategy, always on point. Each battle, going out on his own, no one expected him to return alive.

But he always turned up. Carried through with quick and quiet attack, like a fleck of disease implanting in the body.

In the arena at Olympus, Zeus reaches for his belt and slides a blade from its sheath.

No one needs witness. It is Zeus and Hades. Brother to brother, forging a deeper union in blood.

The blade slides across palms. Stinging, burning. The blood of High Kings merges. The hand of Hades, hot and sticky.

Finally, mopping blood from his hand with the length of his chiton, Zeus asks, "And Pirithous? What is to become of him?"

"He fared better than he would have in a duel," Hades says, flicking blood over the side of the rail. "But he will never remember any promise of marriage. He will be lucky to remember his own name. Strange, though. I tore through his life and saw no mention of Persephone."

Zeus stands up and swats his way through the

part in the curtains, blood nearly invisible against the burgundy fabric. "Stay. A few days, at least. Relax and celebrate with me."

In the morning, Hades of Erebus is gone.

Zeus likes to think when they part, both received what they planned. Hades leaves smug, with a beautiful sixteen-year-old virgin priestess at his disposal. Heracles is safe from wrath and can follow a path to redemption. And Zeus, as proud as ever before, rests in the assurance his brother can still be trusted.

The old pact, unbroken.

"Never try that on me. You promise me that, you have a friend for life."

Had Hades pushed into the past of Zeus, he would have uncovered the schemes inside.

Of the time Zeus first sent for Persephone and was turned away by the mother.

"You know mothers. Never wanting to loosen their grip."

Ah, the mother would not dream of letting her child go. What Demeter forbade, the gods made happen regardless. To Zeus's delight, they took hold and guided Persephone to her intended path. A path to Erebus, where a pent-up king needed something good in his life.

After all, at the root of it, Zeus wants good things for his brother.

Good, distracting things.

PART FIVE
PERSEPHONE

But when the tenth bright dawn came upon
[Demeter], Hekatê came to her, holding a light
ablaze in her hands. She came with a message, and
she spoke up, saying to her:
"Lady Demeter . . . I quickly came to tell you
everything, without error."

—*Homeric Hymn to Demeter*

THE MESSENGER

1

There came the day when the messenger appeared. Hermes. Handsome, beardless—a genteel version of his father. Bronze-skinned like Kore. His half sister.

Once she brought him inside the house and away from onlookers, Demeter asked at once:

"What do you want?"

"Zeus has his eye on a match for Persephone."

"What?"

"One prospect he favors over others."

"You are telling me Zeus has arranged a marriage?"

"I am saying you should prepare for that day soon."

Oh, how it rocked her, this idea of Kore gone from her life, used for the benefit of a father who never bothered to meet her. Never calmed her during one of her terrors when she claimed to see the dead. Never held her on his knee or playfully searched for her inside the house, where the little ghost hid for sport.

Demeter had Kore to herself for sixteen years. For thirteen of them, Kore shared her bed, and they curled together to keep each other warm. As the friction grew, so did the space between them. Soon, Kore migrated to the floor next to her mother, and finally to a separate room altogether where the domesticated animals would often sleep during harsh weather.

Apart and apart and apart, they grew.

Then, this.

"I forbid it," she said. "My Kore is sworn to the gods."

"Sworn how?"

"At birth, Kore was dedicated. She will be like my sister, Hestia of Attica."

"You mean a virgin priestess?"

"Yes."

How Hermes laughed! "No child of Zeus will stay a virgin. I have been asked to bring her to Olympus."

She threw a clay pot at him. He dodged it, shocked at her belligerence. To say no to the King of Kings—audacious! Treason!

"Get out of my house. Using my daughter to his own advantage is an insult to the gods. Tell him. Or have him face me. I will tell him myself."

For as long as she could, Demeter would stave off the messenger, buy more time with her daughter, because as of late it seemed more and more like they were being torn apart. Who knew how long Demeter could maintain her grip?

Who knew how long she had with a daughter who no longer cleaved to her as she once did, as a timid little child?

Apart and apart and apart, they grew.

Who knew Demeter would lose her, regardless?

Before dying, the wizened old priest spoke of prophecy.

"I begin to sing of Demeter, the holy goddess with the beautiful hair. And her daughter, Persephone, too."

With the dead priest, she shares a small space. They are in a temple, but the hour is late, and when she rushes from the room and searches, she finds no one.

The drunkard on the steps, gone.

She searches the temple for oils, collects what she can. She gathers incense and water and cloth.

In these holy chambers, she leaves the door open to allow the steam and heat to roll out. Demeter prays. Blood flowing with kykeon, she performs rites for death. The potion runs strong, and she has not eaten, but she focuses on the task.

As she bathes the creped skin of the old priest, she hears him speaking.

"Where the girl was, Demeter knew not, but she reproached the whole wide world."

He is not free. He is a shade, one she cannot

see even with the powerful brew in her stomach provoking divine madness. Kore would see him without a single sip!

The shade roams about her. He remains in the room, awaiting blessing. And how he speaks, whispers, reminds her over and over, words spinning around the room in circles that make her dizzy. Why does he continue to speak to her in death?

"And her daughter Persephone, too . . ."

"The one with delicate ankles, whom Hades seized . . ."

Parched lips moving in feverish prayer, Demeter struggles to drown out the voice. At times, she cries.

The words of Hermes return, too.

"Zeus has his eye on a match for Persephone."

Cruel, unfair of the gods to bless a woman with child, then snatch her away and leave a mother empty and without direction.

Apart and apart and apart.

Time passes. She sleeps. Stomach empty of food, of child. Hollow, she sleeps on a pallet in the corner of the adyton while the priest stiffens, an empty shell. Throughout the night, the whispering ceases. The potion runs its course, and Demeter sleeps hard.

In the morning, she wakes to three priests entering the room. They cough, as if the smell of decay already offends. She cannot smell it. They inquire—who is she?—and she tells them enough. She is Demeter. She is High Priestess of Knossos. A mother in search of her child.

She imparts what she can about the priest. Excludes the prophecy. She does not want to rehash it. The holy men bring her food and remove the corpse. While guzzling warm goat's milk, thirsty and ravenous, she realizes she should be elsewhere.

She is to meet Iasion in the agora. She has not been outside yet today and has no sense of the time. Panic leaps.

That is when she spots him coming into the temple. At the door, he places an offering on the table and scans the room.

A man is with him. The sleeve of the man's arm is pinned shut, hiding the stub where a hand used to be.

The drunkard. Yellowed-eyed, he comes forward with Iasion by his side.

"Did someone die?" Iasion says, regarding the commotion.

Demeter stares at the drunkard. His sallow flesh hangs on long, strong bones. He is taller than she thought, as tall as Iasion, and missing two teeth at the bottom. From where she stands, she smells wine coming from his pores.

"Who is this?" she asks.

"Charon and I have sailed many seas together." He clasps the drunkard's shoulder.

Grinning, cheeks gaunt and chapped, Charon holds up the pinned sleeve in display. "I could use calmer seas."

Demeter shakes her head. Looks to Iasion. Back to Charon as if to say—*so*?

"Charon was captain of the *Narcissus*."

A jolt to the chest sends her to her knees. Hope, now dependent upon whatever the drunkard has to say. She expects him to toy with her, the man who last night was knocking water from her hand and asking her to be his whore.

But sobriety is his bridge to compassion, and Charon says, "I have no answers for you, Priestess. But I can take you to one who does."

DEATH OF THE GUARD
2

When the guard dies, Kore knows instantly.

She turns from her window one afternoon. Hands wringing, unable to sit. Too much on her mind and sick for her mother.

With a twirl, she runs smack into the dead man. Were he alive, Kore would have felt his breath on her temple. He towers, face hidden inside his helmet. Kore gasps.

Immediately, the dogs leap from the foot of her bed and growl with haunches raised.

As a shade, the guard is whole. In her short life, Kore has seen this phenomenon before. Death erases the physical missteps of life. Missing limbs grow back. Disemboweled athletes stand with innards safe inside.

In death, she witnesses this kindness. What happens once the shades move on, Kore cannot say. She hopes there is kindness in the afterworld, too.

He is clad in the helmet he wore when the dog mauled him. Through it, his small eyes fixate. At her? At anything at all? The thin line of his mouth opens, gawking.

He does not know where he is.

He is afraid! As much as she!

On her lips hangs an apology, but apology means nothing.

Kore runs. Bare feet slap against stone. Behind her, the dogs catch up. She pays them no mind. Kore zigs and zags down stairs and through corridors. Dogs gallop like horses with talons.

She locates the dankly familiar hallway made of rough stone. Torches throw monstrous canine shadows up the walls. At the end of the hall, double doors made of raw-knotted wood.

Kore pulls at the heavy bronze ring attached to the door. The door does not budge. Blowing hair from her eye, she grabs with both hands and uses her weight to pull it open. Hinges creak.

Inside the infirmary lingers the iron smell of blood. It smells of feces and urine and vomit. Her gut churns, and she places a hand to her stomach. Four beds hold injured soldiers. From what do they suffer? How did they come to be here?

She spots the husky figure of a man in the first bed. Motionless, he lies flat on his back. His left arm is wrapped much like it had been on the day she assisted with the amputation. Splotchy, bruised patches of skin creep from under the bandages to his armpit.

"Please, no."

She goes to him. His face is moon pale, waxy. Lips colorless. For the first time, his face is unmasked by a helmet. His nose is crooked from an old break. One brow scarred. His lower lip shows signs of a bad tear healed with a pucker.

Injuries. Many. His body is a ruin of battles fought. And yet he is dead, not because of any war but because of Kore.

She spins on the dogs. Over a dozen of them slink around, sniffing.

"L-look at him!" she accuses. Mastiffs switch from leg to leg, not understanding why their mistress is upset with them. Why is she yelling at them when all they do is protect her? Kore rakes at her hair. "Dogs, go. *Go*."

They yawn and whine.

"What are you doing here?" From one of the beds, a soldier with a patch over his eye sits up. Hair dirtied with sweat and oil, he squints around. "Gods help me, it is true. You have them under a spell."

Kore drops to her knees beside the dead man. She folds her arms over a swollen belly and weeps into them. His torso is granite bloat.

"I k-killed him."

How could she have left her mother? She was better off where her mother could make certain she could do no harm. Demeter kept her *good*. Without her, look what happens. Everything is wrong! An innocent guard is dead. Her life is sealed to a man who barely tolerates her, who will never regard her as anything more than a device to address a grudge with her father.

The physician shakes her. A snarl catches her attention. She is vaguely aware of the voices of guards struggling to gain control of the dogs.

The shade of the corpse stands on the other side of the bed. Blank staring. Kore gives a little cry. His lips part. Mouth a perfect open circle, a whisper emerges.

"I begin to sing of Demeter, the holy goddess with the beautiful hair."

"Want someone else to lose an arm, girl?" the physician brays. "Why would you bring a pack of dogs into a den stinking of blood?"

The gape-mouthed shade continues his strange song.

"And her daughter, Persephone, too."

She shivers.

Crazed dogs stand on hind legs. Howls and barks echo against the walls. With spears, the guards prod them into a little group where men round them up with chained collars. Inconsolable animals, reacting in chaos.

The hissing voice of the shade lulls her with poesy.

"The one with delicate ankles, whom Hades seized . . ."

One of the dogs snaps at a guard. Hornlike

teeth clash at the air in front of his nose, and the man recoils. In the fogginess comes the yelp of a dog poked by a spear. The four wounded men, previously lying in their beds, cower with knees clutched to their chests.

The voice coming from the shade is not that of a man. His mouth is open, lips unmoving, and from the depths comes the hiss voice of serpent.

"She was given away by Zeus, the Loud Thunderer, the one who sees far and wide."

A lilt of euphoria unhinges her arms from her sides. Her child's voice rings clear and flutelike.

"Be still."

The rearing beasts fall to all fours. All noise ceases. No snarls or howls. No lashing of jaws. Every dog in the infirmary rolls to the ground with bellies up. Whimpering in surrender.

Legs shoulder-width apart, the guards look to each other with white knuckles trembling around spears.

Kore sways, and the euphoria flies from her body as suddenly as it came.

The physician studies the dogs. He takes one step away from Kore, like one might step away from a poisonous spider. "Take them out," he says slowly.

The guards tug at chains attached to the collared dogs. Bellies exposed, they slide stubbornly across the ground.

"What is wrong with them?" The physician watches the guards lug the belly-up bodies of dogs toward the door. One of their massive, upside-down heads catches Kore's eye.

Kore nods at the dog. Eager, the pack springs to their feet and follow the guards out without resistance. In their beds, the other men relax.

The physician peers at her.

The ghost folds in on itself, like a blinking eye. Still, she can feel him lingering.

"He must be guided into the afterworld." Her skin buzzes from inside out. "I can do it. He remains with m-me because of my part in this."

She has only observed burial rituals. Never has she conducted one of her own. Nevertheless, an internal voice tells her this is right. She can do it.

"We cannot keep him here," the physician says. "He is starting to stink."

Kore feels oddly sleepy. Chills prickle along her neck and arms. Gooseflesh peppers her golden skin. As nausea might come in waves, so does the essence of the gods. "He lingers," she murmurs, eyelids heavy.

The physician shakes his head. He glances at the wounded—searches their faces for signs they will judge him if he gives in to the entitled brat of Zeus. Fear surfaces beneath incredulous expressions.

The dogs are gone. Of what are they afraid?

"Have it your way," he says. "You cannot kill him twice, can you?" And he laughs. Wounded men snicker.

Before the waxen corpse, Kore stands utterly

still. The pink-purple splotches of infection show brightly against bloodless skin.

A cold mist swirls around her. She is aware of the physician fetching water and cloth and oil. The three wounded men talk among themselves. The noise bounces off her ears without permeating her awareness. The strange prickly sensation returns once again. Invocation. The ecstasy of invocation, usually heightened by kykeon, although as a young priestess, she has not drunk of it. Yet this must be what her mother feels as she calls to the goddess.

What draws her close to the body now? Underfoot, clouds seem to float her forward.

From fingertips to crown to toe, the fibers of her body feel porous as a net drawn through the sea. Coldness moves through her. Pulse light and fast, she forms prayers with her lips, a calling to the divine.

Her fingers press into the forehead and chest of the dead guard. Her skin and his skin—equally cold.

She clutches him. A frigid burst of air rushes through her, humming like a rung bell.

The dead man bolts upright.

The physician yelps and drops a clay bowl of water. It bursts onto the hard floor. Water sprays and floods her ankles. In their beds, the wounded men exclaim. One leaps to his feet in spite of a splinted ankle.

The body inhales, long and sweeping.

Kore stretches her arms upward. Something has

her by the wrists—the gods!—and pulls her hands high. The head of the corpse falls back. His nose is to the sky. Chin craning up.

His eyes open in radiant brilliance.

The physician scrambles to take refuge beside the other men. His foot slides against slippery stone, and he falls flat on his back.

The mouth of the dead man opens heavenward. A voice fills the air.

"And while you are here, you shall rule all that lives and moves and shall have the greatest rights among the deathless gods."

With a great rush of air, the body exhales the shade caught inside of it. There comes a flash of white ascending.

Sudden silence. The guard falls back onto the bed.

Her ears ring. Weak-limbed, Kore rotates on the balls of her feet. Quivering, she uncurls her fists.

The men gape at her.

A tiny "thank you" is all she can muster. Kore makes her way across a wet floor strewn with debris and goes into the hallway where dogs await.

By day's end, every person in Asphodel knows the tale.

UNLIKE LEUCE
3

"Do you remember what you told me?"

She whispers it. Like a secret.

Judge Aeacus flushes despite himself. It has been a long time since a pretty young thing has whispered to him.

"Every word," he answers.

"Is it true?"

"Every word."

The girl sinks beside him onto the stone ledge bordering the fountain. Red leaves float on top. Aeacus plucks one out and twirls the stem between thumb and forefinger. He knew once the shock wore off, she would return.

The whole of her is golden bronze. Glossy hair streaming to a clutchable little waist. In all his decades, Aeacus has never seen a girl so heartbreakingly beautiful. More striking today than when she arrived.

The first one, Leuce, was not much to look at. The union of marriage served a function and scratched no lovers' itch. Men and women, forced together for the sake of procreation. It is a ruse for which all men fall. For what? Legacy?

Ha.

A man toils in battle, earning the title of king through merciless work and a skill for endurance. The son of a king comes into the world doomed by entitlement. A throne should be earned, not inherited.

Their entitlement breeds impatience. A son no longer wants to wait for his father to die so he can inherit the throne. A son schemes. Aeacus has seen it more often than he has not.

A just and pious ruler, King Aeacus of Oenone earned his title. And he did exactly as he was supposed to. Married. Had sons, three of them: Telamon, Peleus, and Phocus. Of the three, Phocus was his favorite. Aeacus made no secret of this. Phocus was patient, a diligent learner who would assume the throne when his father was gone. Oh, but the other boys did not like that, did they? Threatened, they murdered their own brother in a conspiracy to overthrow King Aeacus.

And overthrow him, they did.

Aeacus sought the help of his allies. One ally, Nonios of Asphodel, agreed to help him take back his throne.

On one condition. Aeacus must act as mentor to the strange boy often kept below ground. Aeacus kept his side of the bargain, but the tyrannical king of Asphodel did not.

Thus, the cycle continued. Sons overthrowing fathers.

Aeacus experiences no remorse over it. It was the only way. Orchestrating the uprising was the smartest thing he ever did. Why should he feel remorse in watching the titan kings fall victim to plots they had once participated in themselves?

After all, the one called Cronus castrated his own father, Uranus. Once Uranus bled out, the throne was up for the taking. Actions have a way of coming full circle. What Cronus did to his own father, he feared would one day happen to him. He recalled past actions and allowed them to feed the present and taint the future. Cronus made an enemy of time. Fixation eroded sanity. Such madness would not be tolerated by the spawn who escaped him.

Thus, sons continued to overthrow. The rebellion of Zeus, Hades, and Poseidon became self-fulfilling prophecies for Cronus.

The last thing Hades needs is an heir. A wife is a vehicle to the disaster of offspring, and Aeacus must protect Hades from this fate.

Unlike Leuce, Kore has the protection of bloodthirsty dogs; therefore, Aeacus must think creatively.

With the gentlest shove, Aeacus took care of the first bride and the half-formed spawn in her belly.

"We call this the vanishing point."

"You say I am to be queen," Kore muses. "If this is so, I have a duty to man as well as to the gods."

Her words are lazy snowflakes. Airy. Slow. Fluttery.

But without a stammer.

He wants to say, "Y*our duty is to your husband and master*." What applies to common men applies to kings one hundred times over. Failure to please a king can be fatal. Plenty of unhappy kings extinguish their wives. Hades's own father, to name one.

Aeacus stifles the words behind a benevolent smile. He finds it easy to do, to play the role of Minos or his magnanimous brother, Rhad.

Instead, he says, "Indeed, both things are true."

Dreamy-eyed, she strokes one of the dogs, and the beast writhes against her hand as if no greater pleasure has ever existed.

"Then, I will hold a ceremony."

Aeacus grins, teeth gritted behind closed lips. "I see no reason why not."

"Are you sure *Theíos* will not be mad at me? Judge Minos said—"

"Minos is not without his faults," he interjects. "A kingdom is always better with a woman's touch. Why would anyone be angry with you for making a place *better*?"

She purses her glorious, berry-round lips and adds mournfully, "The gods are not honored here."

"You should make it so," Aeacus says. "It is

your right."

The wick is set. Aeacus will tell one or two guards of the upcoming ceremony. One gossiper will light the fuse that burns from man to man, until the guards and soldiers of Asphodel will gather to watch the presumptuous girl brandishing self-importance under the guise of holiness.

Rumor swirls of Kore's recent impishness. The daughter of Zeus makes the dead sit upright and speak words of prophecy! When he heard the story, Aeacus laughed until his eyes and bladder leaked. This sniveling little mouse—chosen by the gods? Even more shocking: over half of Asphodel believes it!

Idiots. Bodies do all sorts of bizarre things in death. Gaseous noises, twitching, shitting: all part of the dying process.

"Would it be possible for the slaves to gather tools for the ceremony?" she asks, as a child would ask for toys or sweets.

"Whatever you require shall be yours, dear Kore." He pats her hand. "Tell old Aeacus what you need, and I will convey the order."

Hers is no small list. She rattles off items as Aeacus listens in agreement. Most of the items are familiar, although some must stem from Knossian traditions, especially the final request, which she issues with the reluctance of a child pushing her limits.

"Did you say *chains*?" He cranes his ear, unsure

if he heard correctly.

With a nibble of the lip, Kore says yes. Chains. A great deal of chains.

She gives no further explanation, and Aeacus asks for no clarification. After all, he has no right to question a queen's motives.

It is nearly a month before Hades returns. Boredom mixes well with Kore's new bitterness toward a loveless future. At such depths, a girl is left with nothing but her own devices.

Kore makes perfect use of her time.

CEREMONY

4

"Poor child, of course he hates you."

The day of the ceremony, Kore approaches a crude altar with torch in hand. To honor the gods, winter flowers decorate the ground. Balls of purple lavender tumble with the wind. The upraised petals of pink cyclamen flutter like the wings of a butterfly. She is pleased by these reminders of spring, when things blossom instead of die.

On purpose, Kore chose the courtyard where the monument to Sisyphus towers behind a vined archway. Mastiffs arrive in a procession befitting the occasion. Their presence is critical, and yet Kore knew they would come of their own accord, without force. They follow her anywhere.

She shivers with the early morning cold. Or perhaps it is her nerves. Nerves can do that, too.

Rocks the size of human heads are arranged in a circle on dead grass. In the center, tinder and logs form a cone of perfect kindling. She slides the torch into an opening at the base. Fire takes hold.

These days, Kore does not feel like herself. Anger and heartbreak compete over her mood. She swings from one extreme to the other, prone to crying jags prompted by nothing in particular.

"In my house, you are nothing."

Hades said this, and she had not believed him. She did not want to believe him—she loved him!

If Kore allows herself to think about it for long, love tries to wither into sadness. Anger is better than sorrow. Hurts less.

"We are acquiring you."

This is the wheel kings have set in motion. Using her. Dictating her future as her mother did. Rage bubbles up. She must channel these feelings into something productive: a justice long overdue.

As long as sage burns, Sisyphus leaves her in peace. But sage cannot burn forever, can it? Threads of twirling smoke may ease the poison within her own quarters, but those threads do not help the people of Asphodel who also dwell within this mountain range, high above the pit of Tartarus. How gloomy must their lives be to coexist with the doomed?

This, too, is a problem created by kings. Her uncle and her father, claiming to know what is best.

They do not know what is best.

If this place is her fate, she will make it as she wants it.

Kore surveys the tools the slaves brought. As Aeacus promised, they have provided her with what she needs:

Incense. A blade, bowl, wine. A lidded basket with two leopard snakes inside. Sleep-inducing herbs. The lamb. And chains. As many as they can find.

Kore pulls the chains from the ground and rallies the mastiffs.

Dogs do not like chains. No one wants to be enchained. Yet, out of love for her, they offer themselves in faith and trust. She would never harm them as she will the lamb. It takes a long time to affix them. When she is done, her forearms ache from lugging.

Along the perimeters of the yard, Kore spies movement. Guards. Coming in droves. Standing along the sidelines, whispering and solemn-faced. Slaves collect, necks craning for a better look.

Stupidly, she had not expected an audience. With a spectacle like this, she should have.

A slave brings the lamb, the innocent. Unaware and, therefore, unafraid of its fate.

The creature stirs in her arms. Its wool feels grimy yet soft between her fingers. Herbs cupped in hand, she whispers words of solace and offers the fragrant plants to a searching tongue.

She hates this part! Deceiving the poor creature. Suffering is why the offering appeases the gods in the first place. A painless task would not be called a sacrifice. As the lamb grows drowsy, its neck bobs.

She has never killed anything before. Her stomach churns, but it must be done. When the lamb sleeps, she binds the legs in case it stirs awake before she is ready.

The basket wobbles, and Kore removes the lid and peers inside. The two snakes are the color of dirt, with red blotches and a crescent-shaped band spanning between the eyes. Devoid of venom, they will still strike if threatened. Behind a smoking altar, Kore observes their writhing shapes. Her mother knows how to capture them so they cannot lash out.

Kore is calculating the best strategy when they slither up the sides of the basket and spill onto the ground. At first, she moves to catch them before they get away. Tongues flicking, their red eyes glint. Serpents glide with such grace—she has always admired them, and today of all days, she knew they would be important. They are messengers, creatures traveling from the upper world to the underworld with news of regeneration.

The serpents wriggle toward her toes. One snake encircling each ankle, Kore stands, transfixed. Up her legs, they glide. At her hips, their bodies cross, one spiraling up the right side of her, the other climbing the left.

The spirit of the goddess whispers, feeding her words that must be spoken.

"Divinities, we call for renewal. As the serpent sheds its skin, this land must shed the condemned."

Kore raises her arms to the sky.

The snakes wind up her arms and willingly rest their necks into cupped palms.

Guards and slaves murmur in the distance. Words of invocation tumble from her lips, words she has heard time and time again, so habitual she might recite them in her sleep. When the prayer is complete, she uncurls her fingers from the necks of the serpents. They slither down her body, their role complete, and disappear into the yard.

Altar flames dance, hypnotic. The edges of her vision blur.

She forgets the chill in the air. Flurries spit from the heavens, cooling a face heated by fire. The tremble in her body subsides.

She considers the bound lamb at her feet and takes the dagger. Focuses.

Kore clutches the blade and begins.

Rhadamanthus

5

Until now, Minos has been sitting before the hearth alone.

"There you are!"

At last—the relief of a familiar, chiding voice. Excited by the prospect of levity, he leaps to his feet.

"How does a man get fat with travel?" Minos grins. "Only you could do it."

Rhadamanthus saunters into the assembly room, rose-cheeked and perky. Around the ears, Rhad's hair sticks out in cotton fluffs, orange and gray and brown, uncommitted in which direction to grow or what color to be. His beard is cut short and round so his head appears as circular as the sun.

"I ate like a king." Rhad throws an arm around Minos's neck and squeezes. As a boy, Rhad would do this and hang on his taller brother's neck by the crook of the elbow as his feet dangled above the dirt. As an old man, he releases Minos's neck before he strains something in both of them. "Knossians are fine hosts, and appreciative of His Majesty's generosity. Poseidon sends heartfelt regards."

"And the polis?" Minos asks. "Was the damage as severe as reported?"

"Near ruin. But salvageable. Gods be praised."

Some wounds remain open after many years. Intentionally, his brother spares him a salted gash by not speaking of the family Minos left behind. Or mentioning Lycastus, the son who died the day Gaia raged.

His wife and children will pass through life without him, untainted by his crimes, and it should be this way. King Minos perished four years ago, and Judge Minos was resurrected in his place. He will not look back.

"Good to see you, brother." Rhad looks around. "And the rest of our quartet? Soon to join us, I assume?"

"Grab something to eat. I have much to tell."

"Let me guess." Rhad pulls the loaf apart between small hands. "We got another dog?"

Minos tries to smile.

"What? I am funny."

"You *think* you are funny."

Rhad swallows. "Where are they?"

"Aeacus is—"

"The dogs," says Rhad. "Where are the *dogs*?"

Now that he mentions it, Minos has not come across a dog in hours. "If I had to guess? With their mistress."

"Come again?"

Minos huffs a laugh. "As I said. Much to tell."

"My ears are ready." Rhad urges like a young boy, poking his rib, giddy to be home.

"We must locate the dogs in the meantime. They have given us trouble lately."

"What kind of trouble?"

With his brother at his side, Minos strolls from the room and into the corridor. As best he can, he regales the story—they took the daughter of Zeus with the intention of mending and bargaining, but from the moment Kore regained consciousness, things went awry. Dogs and men found themselves charmed, and schemes hatched unexpectedly.

"When you left," Minos continues, "Kore was a nameless girl near death in Matapan. Soon, she will be queen."

"It is a good step toward peace."

"I knew you would say so."

"Yes," Rhad says, "but how does our dear Kore feel about this?"

"She has not been told."

Rhad stops walking and lifts a brow. "Pleasant news is rarely withheld."

"Come now," Minos says. "Surprises can be good."

"Name one."

Minos says the first thing he can think of. "The white bull gifted to me by Poseidon."

Rhad puts on his best impression of Poseidon, puffing up his chest and cocking his head with fists planted on hips. "'Behold!'" he mimics. "'As a reward for your service, I gift to you this exquisite, rare animal. Now, kill it.'"

"I suppose that is a poor example."

"If you thought marriage would make Kore happy, you would have told her already." Rhad shakes his head. "Your silence speaks loudly."

"My silence?" Minos challenges. "It is not my news to share—nor has there been formal confirmation."

"Bah. You know Zeus will leap at this chance."

Halls and staircases span out around them. The palace is oddly vacant, silent. They have not passed a single guard, slave, or mastiff. Disquiet simmers in his gut, and Minos peers around each corner in search of another soul.

Rhad asks, "How old is this girl again?"

"Sixteen."

Rhad whistles.

Rhad stares blankly into midair, stubby fingers toying with the seam of his sleeve. The wheels of ethics turn inside his brother's head.

"A girl must marry," Minos reasons. "Objectively speaking, there is no better match than this."

"Girls often marry uncles to strengthen households," Rhad lists. "That is no issue. And girls of fertile age wed men who can protect and provide, not boys. Their ages, though significant, are no barrier. Kingdoms will unite. Objectively, all of this is true."

"What is your concern?"

"Our king is adept at many things, but affection is not one of them. Hers will not be an idealized life."

They come to the short, wide door leading to the terrace overlooking the central courtyard.

"Well . . ." Minos sighs. "I am sure they will both be very . . . interesting to observe."

From the courtyard, a funeral cry of crows. A cold draft blows inside the thick-stoned doorframe. Outside in the open air, flurries race from the heavens to dirt and melt on precision-squared banisters.

Aeacus braces his hands on the railing. He views the courtyard, mouth cocked in a half-smile as snow melts on a wiry beard.

"Aeacus," Rhad greets him.

When Aeacus turns, his face bears no surprise or enthusiasm for reunion. On it remains the same mischievous awe.

Crows circle overhead, a wide, squawking loop.

Minos opens his mouth to say something, but whatever it is, it flies from his mind as soon as he sees Kore. Rhad spots her, too. They walk to the railing beside Aeacus, who turns his attention back to the yard.

Around the perimeter, guards and slaves gather in rapt attention.

At the vined arch leading to the monument of Sisyphus, Kore stands behind a makeshift altar. Blood runs from her fingers to wrists to arms. An animal cooks blackly on fire that forks like a serpent's tongue.

"This place needs to be purged of those who are trapped."

Minos clutches his heart, as if he might catch it before it falls right out of his body. All along, Aeacus has called the girl defiant, a nuisance. All along, Minos has defended her. She is merely a girl, one accustomed to the prestige of her father's name. Yet when he spoke with her, Minos gave clear and gentle direction.

"The Unseen must determine if it is appropriate."

Yet here she is, defying such direction. Here she is, a nuisance.

"That is the girl?" Rhad asks. "What is she doing?"

Every dog in the palace convenes on yellowed grass below. At last count, Asphodel tallied eighty-seven bull mastiffs. Ninety when counting the three dogs of Hades.

Dozens are chained to the monument of Sisyphus.

The rest of the dogs spread throughout the courtyard, worshippers devoted to their priestess. Minos squints through sleet. Lengths of chain run from one dog to the next. He thinks of slaves linked together as they work in unison to hoist some heavy thing uphill.

The mastiffs of Hades, Cerberus, sit tall in front of the altar where Kore stands, ears stiff and straight, gazing ahead, unmoving.

Kore raises gory palms to the sky. Her mouth moves—inaudible from where they stand—but Minos knows her small, musical voice speaks words of invocation.

Perhaps she is trying to prove herself. Perhaps he should have been clearer as to why he forbade this. Not out of doubt of her abilities, but in case of them.

"I told her no," he murmurs to himself.

With an eerie calm, Aeacus murmurs, "How wonderful."

"Why are you allowing her to carry on?" Minos asks him.

Kore lifts a chalice and tips it. Wine pours into an already large fire. Smoke billows upward and hisses for the attention of the gods.

He should have been truthful with her. Evasiveness never appeases the curious. Kore is nothing if not curious. Unfortunately, Minos also mistook her for obedient.

Aeacus smiles contentedly, like a snake with a rat in its belly. "Our young priestess decided to assert her authority a bit prematurely, would you not agree?"

"What harm can she do?" Rhad asks. "In Crete,

the priesthood is largely matriarchal, and the land both prosperous and peaceful. Perhaps she acts for the highest good."

"Why are there no priests or priestesses at the palace of Asphodel?"

"Hades will be furious," Minos says. "Without the damned, Tartarus holds no special terror. It will be as ordinary as any other dungeon."

"Crow shit," Aeacus says. "She is capable of no priestly magic. This is a show of vanity and pride. She is just like her father."

"Aeacus, you are a fool," Minos says. "Even a dog knows she is capable."

The sweet, childlike song of Kore reverberates a haunting invocation. It may be the saddest, prettiest voice Minos has ever heard. In response, the crowd of slaves and guards close in, growing calmer as they watch the dogs lie, content. No doubt, they fear getting close, and yet the dogs have never looked less menacing, less inclined toward violence, despite the strong stench of lamb's blood. Despite the guards and soldiers and slaves drawing closer.

"The dogs," Rhad marvels, "seem entranced."

Aeacus says, "I have warned her before. They are not pets."

"Look how calm they are! They are not pulling at their restraints." Rhad considers. "I believe the chains are unnecessary."

Cold dread creeps up his throat like bile.

The music of Kore's voice soars. Flames burn

higher and higher still. No altar blazes this much. Why does it burn so fiercely? Kore is hardly visible from behind it.

From the fire emerges a brilliant flash of light, as blinding as any bolt of Zeus.

Wailing ricochets from wall to wall.

Screeching. Without source, omnipresent. Beneath it comes the heavy grinding of stone against stone.

Rhad jumps. The haggard face of Aeacus goes white. Below, men and women clutch their ears.

A shadow forms around the marble boulder. Around the body of Sisyphus. A soul cannot be trapped within an object like this, and yet Minos cannot understand what he observes now—how the spherical shadow appears to pull away from the boulder. The shadow of the boulder enlarges. Slaves scream and throw themselves to the ground in horror. Guards stumble backward, drawing spears against an entity that cannot be pierced.

This is no illusion. Behind Kore's firelit body, the thing inflates and solidifies.

The mastiffs rise like horses and snarl in battle cry. As if by command, those bound to the monuments leap forward and strain against their chains with all of their might. Their mighty bodies lurch, and beneath the monument, the foundation rips away from the earth. Chunks of dirt and root and grass pull with it.

The marble boulder breaks free, dragging the

sculpture of Sisyphus. Its arms break against the ground, torso fracturing.

With the monument toppled, the great shadow of the boulder rolls forward, intent on crushing, and vanishes.

A cry of supplication erupts from the crowd.

Kore is hidden by fire. Minos cannot see her body. He sees instead a brilliant white likeness of Kore rush upward from the fire and hover over the courtyard. The spirit must be that of a goddess invoked, the radiant outline of a woman ascending high above the fire. Her eyes are empty, mouth open.

On each side of the courtyard, shadowy silhouettes rip from the walls of the palace. Sucked out by the massive lungs of a hovering goddess. Souls, trapped inside the palace for years, inhaled and torn free from bondage.

High above, clouds the color of slate gather erratically. Wind would sweep them in unison, rushing them along in the same direction. Instead, a squall forms like a swarm of bees working together to form a face. The almond shapes of eyes open and cast yellow light onto the courtyard.

"AND WHILE YOU ARE HERE, YOU SHALL RULE ALL THAT LIVES AND MOVES AND SHALL HAVE THE GREATEST RIGHTS AMONG THE DEATHLESS GODS."

The voice permeates his bones. It is sexless and not of this world or form.

Below, people shout and fall to the ground,

throwing their arms over their heads. Ninety mastiffs howl.

Thick smoke rises from the altar. No longer do the flames burn. Coal hisses as if doused with water, and yet no water makes it so. The blaze extinguishes on its own.

Clouds part and lighten to feather gray.

Hovering above the courtyard, the white form of the goddess breaks apart into plumes blown away with the wind.

Minos clutches the railing. He and Rhad have both dropped to the floor. They hide, trembling, behind the rail like criminals clinging to dungeon bars.

"What madness is this?" Rhad whispers to him.

Below, the slaves stand. Together with the guards, they move to retrieve mallets scattered against the wall.

On quivery legs, Minos watches as guards and slaves work together. They smash the monument of Sisyphus until nothing remains but grit.

POMEGRANATE FEVER
6

When it is over, sleep comes like death.

In time, her lashes part. Agony thumps in her head. A void exists where a full day used to be.

She smells dog. On both sides of her, they sleep. One curls into a ball with his head nuzzled against her womb. The other snores hot and wet into her neck.

She smells dog. Not sage.

Her vision blurs and focuses on the bedside table. No rue.

Toes wiggling against fur, Kore feels a third dog at her feet.

His dogs.

A tongue the size of her forearm licks at her fingertips, under her nails, hunting for the faintest trace of lamb's blood.

In a sickened delirium, Kore wants to ask the dogs (as if they will answer!)—why have they come to her? She croaks the word *why*, barely audible. Over thick short-haired fur, her hand trails.

His dogs. What are their names? The guardians of Hades. She bets they have clever names.

Down to the bone, her body aches. Head pounds. Mouth dry as desert sand. A hot tear leaks from the corner of one eye.

Still, Kore smiles.

Because at her bedside—no sage, no rue. Such remedies are no longer needed. She knows the power that put her in this sickbed. The goddess came and saved them. The unholy no longer dwell in Asphodel.

A smile lingers on her lips. Her head rolls to the side. The window is open to twilight. A setting sun turns the room orange-rose and begins to dip behind the horizon.

The shape of the sun, strangely round and burning blood red.

One of the dogs slides from the bed. Cool air replaces the warmth of his body. Her teeth chatter. The dog slinks to the window, feline in movement and grace.

When he reaches the window, the mastiff tips his giant skull over the ledge. His tongue laps, reaching out to taste the air.

His tongue touches the setting sun, rolls it safely between his teeth. This animal—plucking the sun right out of the sky!

He trots to her. Drops the red sun beside her.

An offering.

Kore reaches out and touches the smooth object. It is not a sun. It is a pomegranate, sweetly delicious and mouth-watering.

The dog says, *"And while you are here—"*

No, but it is not a dog anymore. Why does the world keep shifting? Why can a dog not remain a dog? The sun remain a sun?

The dog is a man. Looming over her, the figure of a man. But it is not a man, not exactly. His body is twice as tall as a regular man, twice as wide. The shape of him, pure blackness. This entity, telling her:

"You shall rule all that lives . . ."

A dream. She is caught in a dream. Panicked, she tries to thrash, to kick, to scream. Wake up. She cannot move.

Wake up. Wake up.

Panting, Kore opens her eyes. The sage and rue are still gone. So are the dogs.

But the Unholy is still there, reaching down with a monstrous hand to touch her ankle.

SUPERFICIAL RESULTS

7

"*H*ades *will be furious.*"

Aeacus is counting on it. Something decent must come of this mess. What transpired in the yard, he witnessed with disbelief. Even now, days afterward, he doubts what he saw.

Save for the bare patch of soil where the monument once stood, nothing appears different. The ground is frozen, frosted with a pale dusting that will melt within the hour, once the sun comes out. It is early yet. The sky announces the upcoming arrival of Helius's fiery chariot in the east. Night is over. Day might be a stone's throw away.

Daylight comes, but already Aeacus can feel the light. He has felt the light since Kore did her magic. She spoiled precisely what Hades sought to create. Fear. Severity. Oppression. She might as well have planted a garden of pretty flowers and filled the air with butterflies and chirping birds. At least it would look like it feels.

Yet from behind, feet crunch against grass, and when he turns, he spots the girl rushing to him with her cheeks shining pink. Her hair, as light as the impending sun.

"It did not work," Kore huffs, desperate.

He masters a beatific grin.

"But why!" she moans. "Did you not see the dead depart?"

Of course, he did. Yes, yes.

Agreeing agitates her further. This willowy young thing bites at her lip and rends silken locks between two hands. Golden brown eyes fix on him, puffy and creased. She sits beside him.

He asks, "What causes you to believe your ritual failed, sweetness?"

Kore shakes her head, clutching her cloak like a blanket. "Because something lingers. It is with me always."

"You mean, some*one*?"

"Help me, Judge," she begs.

"Who am I to advise on matters of the spirit?"

"You advise my *theíos*," she cries. "He trusts you." She adds weakly, "So I trust you."

Oh, but how tortured she is.

How in need of counsel.

"Perhaps," he suggests, "the ceremony produced superficial results."

"What do you mean?"

"Be calmed, my Kore. You skimmed the

surface, and that alone is a marvelous feat. Truly, you are favored by the gods."

Her face registers a controlled effort not to burst into tears. Pity. He does enjoy those tears. Aeacus clears his throat and leans close enough to smell the floral oils on her skin. "The realm of the Unseen runs far below."

The gullible prize of Hades furrows a brow. "The caves?"

"Tartarus," Aeacus tells her, using reassurance as an excuse to touch her leg. "There is no peace as long as Tartarus poisons our roots."

THE CYCLE
8

Long after the abduction, the girl haunts the old woman.

"There is a narcissus. Beautiful—and I pick it."

The untarnished face of youth, regaling nightmares in a softly tremulous voice.

"But when I do, the ground cracks and smoke pours out and floods inside of me, and from deep inside the chasm, a chariot races, and I am taken."

Yet there was nothing to be done about it beyond protest. A crone, wise or not, has no voice among men, and surely, no voice among kings.

Her sex renders her voiceless. Her age renders her obsolete. Most people humor her. Or she is ignored as she was that day when soldiers came from Asphodel and snatched the girl right from under her nose.

For countless days, the sun rises and falls. The moon bares her face in cycles. Through them all,

Hecate wonders what became of the girl.

The day arrives when Hecate stoops over her little dogs, allowing them to enjoy the remains of her morning meal. The rabbit, she eats. The viscera from the rabbit, the dogs eat. They gobble it from her fingers before the slippery organs touch the ground.

Their ears perk, and they listen to a distant noise she cannot hear. Innards wet and warm in her hand, Hecate totters as the dogs dart from underfoot, headlong toward the dirt path down the side of the hill.

Today, the light of Helius has the sky to itself. With no clouds in sight, Hecate uses a thick-veined hand to shield an eye. She watches a robed woman hitch her skirt and climb the dirt path to her cave. Gleeful dogs jump and yap at the feet of the approaching stranger.

Ah, but this is no stranger.

Hecate wipes a bloody hand on a bib in need of a wash. The squatty, long-bodied dogs accompany the woman as she crests the hill and trudges to where Hecate stands with hands on hips.

That cornsilk hair—lovely! Hecate thanks the goddess she never suffered such loveliness. As a young woman, Hecate possessed the sharp rectangular face and beady features of someone not worried about fending off the opposite sex terribly often. For this, she is glad. Years of observation taught her: good looks come at a price. In youth, they afford a woman luxuries she might not get otherwise. Inevitably, though, when beauty departs, these women are crushed as if something vital was stolen from them. Oh, the horror of turning into a crone! Always, lovely aging mothers visit her for *pharmakia*. Herbs to make them remain young and fertile and, therefore, valuable. Tonics by Hecate's magic hands. It is akin to asking a leper for the cure to a skin rash. Hecate laughs at this.

The woman draws closer. The corners of her pretty mouth are lined from years of smiling. Now the smile is gone, and the woman is left with the opposition of those lines: an embedded crease of worry between the brows.

"Are you Hecate?"

"Mother of Kore," Hecate greets her. "You have traveled far."

With those words, the woman hiccups a cry and places her hand over her mouth to hide it. Legs buckling, she kneels and clutches Hecate's cloak, forehead pressed there as her tears soak wool. "Is my daughter here? Is she safe?"

Hecate lowers herself to the ground and covers the woman's thin shoulders with one arm. She lifts a flat face to the sky. Rays of sun brave the old crone who silently gives another word of thanks.

What became of the girl?

Often, she prays to the gods for answers. The woman crying into Hecate's cloak is the answer.

"I knew you when I saw you." She smiles through the last of her rotten teeth. "I knew you by the sorrow. Your Kore is alive, but she is gone from me. For some time."

"Where is she?"

"I saw her snatched up with my own eyes." She grins up at the sky. "No doubt the god Helius sees her still, or else he would not have sent you to my cave."

"She is alive?"

"Yes, lady mother." Hecate squeezes the woman against a bony breast and clumsily pats her shoulders. "Come with Hecate. Up, up."

Tears form tracks down the mother's dusty cheeks. Staggering a little, Hecate steers the woman into the coal-warmed cave. Demeter trembles. Her face is swollen from crying and exhaustion.

Inside, Hecate waters the wine and gives it to Demeter to drink. She sits the woman down on a thick pallet made of leaf-stuffed wool.

Hecate brings a bucket of water and a basin to wash the feet of her guest. "Your Kore nearly drowned. I bandaged her head. Coaxed water from her chest. When last I saw the child, she lived."

To this, Hecate expects many questions. Instead, Demeter gazes silent at the floor.

"The girl was seized," Hecate says. "Taken to her father, I imagine."

"Seized by Hades?"

Hecate raises her head from the basin. She sits back and props her elbows on her knees, hands dripping water. "If you knew she was not here, why did you come?"

Demeter shakes her head at the ceiling, as not to spill another tear. "At the temple, a priest told me of a prophecy."

"Old Vlasis?"

"You know him?"

"I hold keys to every temple in Matapan. I know them all. Vlasis confined himself to the adyton days ago. Imagine the old cat who senses death approaching. He sought a holy place to curl up and die."

"He died in invocation. I was there. And he told me things."

Hecate thinks back to the day before when she encountered Vlasis at the temple. Solemn face ready for the ultimate reckoning, he imparted recent visions to anyone who checked on him during his final days.

"I begin to sing of Demeter, the holy goddess with the beautiful hair . . . and her daughter, Persephone, too . . . the one with the delicate ankles, whom Hades seized . . ."

"By now, your child is surely in her father's custody."

"Kore ran from me," the mother says. "Did she tell you that?"

Hecate studies her.

Demeter continues, "Kore took off on a trade ship because she heard rumor her father requested her."

"Rumor? Truth? Which?"

"Truth." Demeter buries her face in her hands. "She spoke to me as if I conspired against her. And how we fought. This was not my Kore. She said she hated me. Accused me of destroying her chance at motherhood. Destroying her life, she said! And I was so angry, I could not stop myself. 'You and your father,' I said, 'fooling everyone with charm, but I know the truth.' I am her mother, and I know the darkness she holds inside of her. It was from *his* blood, I said—from Zeus, she got this darkness. From *him.* At the time of her birth, she was sworn to the gods. And—and—and I threatened her! I said the gods would have her one way or another, even if I had to sacrifice her to save her from her own fate. I was the one who made her get on that ship. I was the one who caused her to lie dying in your care. In this, I see the darkness in myself, and I am ashamed."

"You cling because you fear death."

Demeter laughs through tears. Against the heat of a clay oven, Demeter's cheeks flush. "I fear death?"

"Yes."

"I am High Priestess. My time is spent in communion with immortals. Death is not—"

To this, Hecate blows her tongue through tight lips. Spittle flies. "Save your reasoning. No grieving mother is reasonable. You crossed an ocean for a girl who ran from you and who might have been dead."

"I grew her inside of my belly. She is *of* me.

How can I let it end like this?"

Hecate's face is calm, half-smiling. "A woman's life is like the moon. When you stop clinging, Kore will be gone from your nest. She will be a mother like you. You will become like me. And what am I to become? What awaits me if not death? And you see, lady mother, you cling to your child because you want to stop the cycle. There is no stopping the cycle. It is the snake that bites its tail."

"What would you have me do?" the mother demands. "Leave her?"

"If I said yes?"

"I can never leave her. Never."

Hecate cackles softly. "Then you have already resolved."

"I will stand before Zeus if I have to."

"Ooh." She clucks. "Are you as brave as that?"

"I am not afraid of him."

With a smack of the knee, Hecate snorts a laugh. "He is not the one you must fear. Fear the high queen, Hera. She torments all lovers of Zeus and often his bastards, too. She might kill you on sight."

"How do you know this?"

"She is a dear friend," Hecate answers happily. She pats Demeter's leg in assurance and winks. "Let me make a pallet for you. You will eat. Sleep. In the morning, we will go together."

"Together?"

"Tut-tut, Priestess. I am old, but I will not slow

you down. Even in my decrepitude, I can be of service to you."

For this, the High Priestess of Knossos bows her head and clasps Hecate's gnarled hands. How lovely is the mother and with such a passionate heart. This sort of strength arouses powerful favors from gods. And if prophecy unfolds as old Vlasis predicted, Demeter's wrath may mean death to man and ox alike. If Hecate must traverse mountains to assuage this wrath, so it will be.

Once more, the day folds to night, and the moon waxes fuller than the previous night.

A FINE ARMY
9

No one questions her anymore. Since the day the guard died of infection from a severed arm, no one questions.

They look at her strangely now. Or perhaps it is not the looking that is strange—how their faces flush and corners of their mouths pull downward in a frown—but the *not looking*. Eyes previously glinting with mockery lower to the ground.

Lower, as they would for a queen.

"Let me pass, please." This is all Kore needs to say for the guard to step aside. Mastiffs behind her, these loyal friends lurch forward with ears flattening like slicked-back hair while wet slivers of fangs show through their jowls.

The wide entryway is a portal leading to freedom. The caves of Tartarus await.

She did not expect it to be easy, frightening the guard away. Kore's army of dogs is a fearsome sight that makes the guard press his back to the wall and carefully edge along the corridor with hands clinging to the spear. The spear might be enough to level one of the dogs. Though the guard might impale a single foe, dozens more wait to attack.

A safe length down the corridor, the guard rushes from sight. Perhaps he will return with reinforcements. How long will they allow the daughter of Zeus to do as she wishes?

Although . . .

Aeacus told her, *"You have nearly as much authority as Hades himself."*

What a funny idea. A funny idea the guard proves when he flees his post. Kore surveys the canine army. When they sit, the tops of their heads reach the height of Kore's shoulders. A fine army. Fierce.

When she steps through the doorway, the army whines thinly from their collective throats. Thirty throats or more, protesting. Resisting the depth.

"Stay," she relents. "Keep watch. Let no one interrupt the work of the gods."

To assure them of her safety, Kore ruffles the ears of the nearest mastiff and kisses the top of his furry crown before disappearing underground.

HADES'S RETURN
10

On purpose, he arrives in the dead of night. The air hangs sharp and cold under a cloudless sky. The moon, turning gibbous.

An unconscious citadel makes for a perfect arrival. Like this, Hades can slip in without arousing much interest.

Now is a time when men sleep, with slave and guard absent from their stations. By night, the mastiffs take over. They roam the corridors, brawny shapes made elephantine by the shadows they cast.

Perhaps he has been gone for too long. It feels different here. *Cleaner*.

He arrives tired, filthy, aching in the hips, back, and thighs. Travel is no easy thing. Hades resolves: in his lifetime, he will not make another trip of this distance. Apart from war, there is no reason for it. His exchange with Zeus felt like war in its own right, where two opposing sides clashed spears and one came out victorious. To his pleasure, Hades emerged the victor.

For too long, obsession has eaten away at him. Thoughts of swollen lips. The dramatic slope of Kore's lower back molding perfectly against his hand. The divot in her chin where he had trailed a thumb and marveled at pristine young flesh.

Yet what he thinks of most often is mawkish, and Hades finds himself embarrassed by the sweetness of it. A man like him, replaying the image of her smile—a smile that could turn winter into spring. Of this, he catches himself thinking and wills himself to pervert it.

Kore, breathing against his cheek.

Kore, wheezing through tears.

Kore, begging.

"P-please, Theíos . . ."

The longing equates to that of a drunkard going a month without his wine. Worse at the start. Tolerable thereafter. With promise of intoxication in the near future, the craving reignites hotter than before. A fiery excitement courses from groin to gut to heart.

It is done. She belongs to him, and decisively, they are—the both of them—home for good.

WITHOUT THINKING
11

Kore expects the dead and finds the living. Encased inside the shell of earth, she struggles to remember these surroundings. After all, she has been here before. Oddly, it is not the burrowing staircase she recalls or the open cast pit carved by crude hammers with iron heads. This void inside the earth, like the belly of Gaia herself, echoes a faint *drip-drip-drip*, and the air is damp-cold and steams with each exhale. Torches gleam green against calciferous rock. She smells sulfur and moss and stagnant water.

Kore remembers none of this.

She remembers one thing. Here was the last place she saw her *theíos* before he left. Here, he spat words of contempt and meant them—and she had been too stupid to know it.

Certainly, Kore does not remember human voices ringing from inside a narrow tunnel.

She takes a tentative step toward the stone mouth, barely wide and tall enough to walk through upright.

"Hello?"

From far inside, a voice responds:

"I repent."

A spark from her torch sizzles small on her wrist. Numb to the cold, the pads of her toes advance on water-smoothed rock and carry her into the tunnel.

She swings the torch to the left. Iron bolts a thick door.

A memory surfaces, of Minos explaining:

"They should be trapped and unsettled. They are prisoners."

Prisoners. She had not considered them. A cruel leader would take advantage of this torment. Of course. It is the perfect place for torment.

Right and left, Kore shines her light. Five doors bolted shut on each side.

Her heart breaks for the men behind these doors.

"H-hello?" she says again, not sure what else to say.

From a door farther down, a muffled voice emerges.

"Help me!"

Farther down, behind another door:

"Is someone there? Please, mercy . . ."

One by one, a macabre chorus joins in a song of pleading. It surprises her, how much worse the song of torment from living men. Pleas from the dead can be heard, but not with her ears. She has heard them through a veil separating this world from the other.

The voices of imprisoned men land upon her eardrums like scythes. Real, tangible humans, trapped by a king who has no capacity for mercy as far as she can tell.

No man deserves such torment. No girl.

Without thinking, Kore props the torch against the wall and seizes the metal latch keeping the prison door in place. It takes all of her weight to slide it free from the lock.

Without thinking, she unbolts door after door. She watches men, fat and thin, tall and short, stumble past her with no words of thanks, tripping over themselves to scramble up the winding stairs.

Without thinking.

As exhausted muscles strain to unhinge the last door, a terrible thought flashes in her mind.

"Keep watch."

Upward and upward, the prisoners race to freedom.

Upward and outward, an army of mastiffs obey her command.

The final prisoner bursts out in a blur of hair and flailing limbs.

"Wait!" she cries, but there is no stopping a man who yearns for freedom. They skitter away like roaches, not understanding prison was their source of protection.

HOMECOMING MASSACRE
12

W hen they see their master, the dogs stop what they are doing.

Homecoming. It almost makes him smile.

The three mastiffs called Cerberus trot to greet him. Between upraised ears, Hades touches them as a priest might touch the head of supplicants. He is glad to see them.

Where they had been sitting, two white objects. From inside the doorway of his quarters, he cannot discern what these objects are.

"What do you have?" Hades follows them to the center of the room.

They have been relishing a treat.

A femur. Stringy red gristle clings to one end. Proí nudges it with his nose and wraps his jaws around the thick, knobby end, tonguing and gnawing.

Mesméri and Nýchta fight over a larger bone,

two crescent shapes meeting in a thick center. The animals wrap their teeth around each side and tug and growl in battle for the whole thing.

It is not merely a pelvic bone. It is the pelvic bone of a man.

The dark floor masks the color of blood. A king never looks at the ground—he keeps his chin level with it. Of course, he would not notice the trail glistening out of his apartment and into the corridor.

Hades follows the trail into the hallway. At the staircase, a soft triangle of blood is topped with four ovals. Pocking the steps, taloned paw prints travel from bottom to top.

The prints confirm what he already suspects.

Instinctively, he knows where the trail will end. Knows, but does not want to believe.

At the entrance of Tartarus, more dogs than he has seen in one space. Except for that day, long ago, in the courtyard when a maiden frolicked and threw a stick and treated them as if they were pups.

The human bodies upon which they feast are mostly digested. The bones have been licked clean, snouts guilty with blood. Flies buzz in search for scraps, finding none.

Among the carnage, no bronze or spear. The victims were not guards. Hades struggles to find fabric. Zealous for the feast, the dogs devoured most of the clothes along with the men.

The fibers in his neck and shoulders quiver a vibration of fury. Red, glistening snouts rise from their feast.

Rarely is he astounded. It is nearly impossible for man to astound him. He gazes at a sea of shapes, fat and happy from an unexpected meal of escapees.

Though ungroomed, travel-worn, and common as a vagrant, Hades advances. The dogs allow it. Their recognition is not based upon features but his essence, smell, and carriage. He navigates through a sea of flat-muzzled faces and makes his way past the homecoming massacre.

DOMINION
13

She killed them all.

One by one, freed men return to their prisons. Death restores mangled bodies to immortal wholeness. Puzzled, the shades mope through the caverns, and Kore swats them away with prayers and blessings as one would swat away flies. Spirits depart readily, for this is no place to spend eternity. They do not belong here.

Kore does not belong here.

Stone walls hang low inside this cell, a pocket carved into the earth and fitted with a heavy wooden door. When Kore came inside, she left the door open. It remains open. Nothing disrupts the door. Nothing disrupts the torch dying of its own momentum, nor the two-wick candles scattered about the floor.

For hours, Kore sits upon a slab strewn with wool blankets, a bed where prisoners once slept. Exhaling clouds into the dank air. Hugging knees to breast. Rocking in place. Unblinking. She recites prayer and slurs songs of invocation in a childlike voice.

This must be the brink of madness, for she knows something is wrong here. *Please. Something must be wrong.* If not, she killed those men for nothing. She harmed the ones she sought to help, not considering what might happen if she tried to save them.

Please. There must be evil to purge.

Yet the cocoon of Tartarus rests in harmony. Nothing grabs her ankles. No ominous specter appears with his eyes shooting white. Beyond the melody of her voice, there is silence.

Did she dream of the hands that grabbed her ankles in the night? Was it as much a dream as the sun turning to fruit? Or the dog speaking in a human tongue:

"And while you are here you shall rule."

Now, a figure appears at the threshold, asking, "What have you done?"

He is a real man. A prisoner, perhaps, returning unscathed by dogs. His tunic is plain and dusty. His beard is scroungy with flecks of silver along the cheeks. Mussed curls sweep the tops of his ears. When she sees impossibly black eyes lined with impossibly black lashes, shadowed by a heavy brow, there comes a jolt to her heart. Coldness washes through her veins, followed by a wild infusion of heat.

"Ohh . . ." The sound comes out like wind from a punched stomach.

Hades steps inside. "What happened to the prisoners?"

Her chin rests low to her chest, as a child facing parental judgment.

". . . I let them go."

"You let them go."

She nods dumbly.

Hades squints. "On whose authority?"

Mine, she nearly answers out of spite. She selects a safer answer. "The authority of the gods."

He sweeps the room with dour eyes, eventually resting them on Kore. This man will soon be her husband. Odd how her perspective shifts, as if she sees him with new eyes. Menace flares around him. Has it always been so? Has there always been an undercurrent of fury in the way he stares at her? Always a fire surrounding him?

"A father holds dominion over you from birth. He holds dominion over you until the day your husband assumes dominion."

A lump constricts her throat. For the first time in her life, she feels pure danger. There is nothing to protect her anymore. This man, ruler of the southland, now rules over her. Dominion over her actions, over her future. Over her body.

Ca-thump goes her pulse, hard percussion in the veins.

That time he found her running from her room

in the middle of the night—to *calm* her, he hit her, and it hurt. How much worse is a fist flown in anger?

A tremble permeates down to her bones. Her muscles are as loose as water.

"Do you remember," he says with two deliberate steps, "what I told you?"

She knows what he means. His warning. But she will not satisfy him with the answer he seeks.

"I remember," Kore says. "You said, 'In my house, you are nothing.'"

He issues a mirthful laugh.

"Except," she swallows, "I do not think that is altogether true."

"No?"

"Are you tired, *Theíos*?" she pities softly. "You look tired. Olympus is very far."

He stops. The knots of an already sharp jaw tighten.

"Was it a secret, where you went?" asks Kore. "Oh, but I know where you went. You saw my father. Without me. You *left* me. You promised I would see him as soon as I was well enough."

Her gut urges her to stand. Get away. The door. Prey should make no sudden movements, lest she draw attention from predator. As she edges along the wall, Hades tips his head as a dog might do when curious.

"It is all I wanted." She swallows. "And you lied."

Yet Hades does nothing except stare with a

face set like stone—indifferent, perhaps, because he does not care enough to yell or beat her. Anger and contempt would be attentive.

"And I know *why* you saw him. I know everything."

"Then," he finally monotones, "you know your father had no problem giving you away. A brat he has never met? Had I wanted, he would have sold you to me as a slave."

These muttered words cut to the quick, as he knew they would. He knows her well enough to hurt her, and she lifts a stubborn chin in denial that he could know her in this way, that he would presume to know anything about her. Perhaps this is the price for what she did to her mother. Perhaps she deserves to suffer, but he deserves to suffer, too! Kore yearns to fling the curse: *Suffer!*

"So?" She pants. "He has never met me. He does not know me at all, and yet he sent for me as a father would. Zeus, *King of Kings*, sent a messenger to take me from my mother's house. She told me. My father had plans for me—but my mother sent him away. Did you know that? Do you know *why*?"

He grimaces, staring at this anomaly who dares speak to him in a way no human ever would.

"No, you would not know. My father would not know, either. Neither of you bothers to know me. What if my mother rebuked him for good reason?"

Is this the brink of madness?

Not caring what violence befalls her? Inciting

it? Hurling words in hopes one will pierce?

"Oh, *theíos*," she taunts, "did neither of you imagine I could already have a husband in Knossos?"

He thinks it is ridiculous. It *is* ridiculous—but she must wound him.

"I am sixteen, you know. I am old enough to have been claimed."

Hades closes his eyes. A surge of victory draws blood to her cheeks, and Kore folds her arms, surprised and proud of her own cleverness.

He does not speak, but this time it is because she has given him much to think about. Kore should let those wounds fester.

She has distracted him enough to storm past. This is what she believes.

With a flash of a quick-darting hand, he seizes her hair so hard, she thinks her neck will snap, and pulls until her chin points upward. She slaps at his clutch in an effort to dislodge it, rolling onto her toes to relieve the sting on her scalp, but he maintains a white-knuckled grip and yanks, prompting a high yelp. The long curve of her neck juts, vulnerable to a hand that folds around her throat and squeezes enough to make her lightheaded.

This is how she will die, throat crushed by a man who once deemed her worthy of marriage. For a moment, Kore knows beyond a doubt he intends to kill her so he can put an end to the havoc she creates out of a childish attempt for attention. He would sooner murder her than tolerate her within this house.

Hades looks at her open mouth with something hot like loathing. As the room grays from the lack of air in her throat, as sparks of light dance in her vision, his expression changes to one of curiosity. When he lowers his mouth to hers, he does it like a man dipping one toe into water to test the coldness. Kore shakes, hating how her body reacts however it wants, whether in fear or rage or this visceral sensation pleasantly similar to both. As the beard tickles her nose, she feels herself losing consciousness from where he chokes her, chokes her with his hand and lips and cuts off the breath of her nose with the force of what must be a kiss. This, this, unlike the exploration of sex play between little girls in a field, where she and Lyris once tried their skills at kissing like they saw men and women do sometimes. How grown-up, how scandalous it must be to kiss, and they used their tongues in circles because it felt like a silly act of playing adult. This is no silly act, for silly acts never feel truly scandalous—and the way he kisses her does feel scandalous.

Somehow, she is still breathing; she has not been strangled to death but is very much alive and offers a sweet, searching tongue as a call for peace. The heavy beat of her heart begs, a steady *ca-thump ca-thump* of *Love-me, Love-me.*

Surely, he accepts this plea for peace, as his hand is no longer in her hair and his other hand is no longer around her throat—both migrate to knead her hips. No, not kneading, for perhaps they had never been kneading, but fumbling. Pulling up the fabric of her gown, grasping the soft underparts of her buttocks, lifting her off the ground, and bullying her legs open with one of his.

Should love feel this way? Violent disappointment always wishing for kinder words, a gentler touch?

No, it cannot be like what it feels: pain.

Lay me down. A girl's wistful dreams cannot be spoken because the act alone is chaos. A rough-bearded mouth brutalizes her own and bites down on her shoulders and neck. Hades forces her back to the wall, tender flesh bludgeoned by the knots and spikes of jagged limestone, and she screams as the little fangs of the earth tear virgin skin. Screams as he lifts and plants his thing inside of her as a war-savage victor might plant a flag into the earth, earth that cracks open and breaks apart and shows the scorching, red cinders of the underworld, flashing embers of pain. There comes a ripping away, an invasion and merger with no kind arrival. The length of him burrows inside of her, as if he cannot go deeply enough, might shrink his entire body if he could and crawl right up into her womb and nestle there forever. Impaled by his body, by the wall, smashed—this is love, she fears with every plunge.

Blood tickles her spine and the backs of her arms and her bottom lip from where he bit it. The injury is bright hot, all over, and yet she wraps her arms around him and cries into his neck because all she can seem to do is surrender, accepting the punishment of love, tasting the salt of his skin and her tears.

With shot seed comes a primal growl she has never heard before from any human, and if nothing else, she finds shameful pleasure in eliciting such a growl, of causing an experience for him other than hatred. Her heart begs with the rhythm of:

Love-me. Love-me.

Afterward, he brushes Kore's adoring hands from his face. He clasps her bitten shoulders and pushes away, emptying her, leaving her shaking against a bloodied wall.

Kore finds herself reaching for him. He allows it.

"Th-theíos . . ."

His fingers slip between her legs, touching the point of invasion. She shudders, swollen, sensitive.

"Who claims you?" Evidenced on fingertips, blood intermixed with milky fluid.

"You."

"Good girl," he says, not touching her anymore, revoking attention—even the bad kind of attention—as a king might seize the meager food of peasants in an attempt to starve them.

Hades leaves her shivering against the wall. The door slams. The lock creaks and snaps into place.

She is cold. Woozy, sick in the stomach. For all the pain she felt before, now there is numbness and a pull-away sensation of her soul floating outside of flesh where things like skin and muscle and loins are irrelevant, temporal.

Hands quivering, hot liquid running down her thighs, Kore staggers to the slab where a prisoner would sleep. Her legs give way, palms catching the brunt of her fall, and she presses her cheek to the coldness of rock.

Is this the quickening of love, however brutal?

Is it indoctrination? A welcoming?

Is this a lesson? An act of teaching her even the queen of the underworld answers to someone?

Is this why her mother fought to protect her? From the destruction of maidenhood?

Is this the brink of madness?

Is this?

In the void, Kore swears she hears whisperings from the god realm.

"And while you are here, you shall rule . . ."

Rule.

Surely, the word cannot apply to Kore. She is no ruler; she is *ruled*. It has always been so. To hope it could ever change—delusion.

For now, she nestles inside the belly of Tartarus, stored away for later. A musical cascade of giggles ricochets among low-hanging stalactites. Someone laughs. Someone finds this terribly funny. It occurs to Kore it is her own laughter she hears, denying the trauma of what her child's body endures. She weeps at the shock of her own laughter and screams herself hoarse.

It is at that moment a cunning entity clutches her ankles.

At her feet, the man-shaped giant looms with a body made of sky and stars. The air buzzes from Its presence. The hairs inside her ears prick and rise. She lies motionless on torn flesh that burns and speckles the blankets red.

The great specter reaches out and opens a cosmic hand to show the ruby-skinned fruit inside of it.

Kore giggles again and, in the timelessness of the moment, submits to prayer—an end-of-day sigh.

When she sleeps, she sleeps like the dead and dreams nightlong of pomegranates.

Acknowledgements

This book series is the product of immaculate conception, and I'm not being entirely cheeky. I thank God, first and foremost, for giving me an idea I never would have come up with on my own. Cliché or not, I've said before that this book was divinely inspired, and I'll say it again here.

Prior to this novel, I wrote dark comedies. Several years ago, vowing that I could no longer continue to write novels with no payoff whatsoever, I swore off writing for good. Instead, I went back to school. A few years passed. Midway through my master's thesis on Jungian archetypes of the collective unconscious, the spark of an idea came down from above. God began to harass me into writing again, and *The Rape of Persephone* was born. And this showed me something important— that the payoff of writing books is simply the joy of writing them.

The last thing I expected was to find such joy in

spinning this ancient tale.

The first thing I thought was, "But this isn't the type of thing I write!"

To which my husband, Aaron, responded with, "But maybe you *do*."

So, I must thank Aaron, too. Not only did he encourage me to run with this idea and immerse myself into Bronze Age Greek history and mythology, he also put up with all of the wailing and gnashing of teeth while I proceeded to give birth to this idea. It wasn't the prettiest journey (and still isn't), and I'm thankful for a partner who has my back and pushes me to do important things even when they're hard. For that matter, I also owe a big thanks to my parents and my daughter, Rowan, for supporting me every step of the way.

My beta readers, I thank you. This isn't the easiest book to tackle, and I appreciate the discussions that arose afterward. So, thank you to Brooke Schroader, Carla Rowan, Pat Brillhart, Dava Esman, and Jackie Cornish. I owe you all lunch.

Thank you to Valerie Kalfrin and Lauren Bailey at Kirkus Editing. Huge props to the impeccable line editing skills of Ron Butler, my grammar guru, who gave me a finished product that I can be proud of. Speaking of finished products, I need to give a high-five to Eddie Diaz, the graphic designer who took my vision for the cover and map and made them better than my wildest dreams.

Much gratitude to Terry Wolverton, founder

of Writers at Work in Los Angeles, for turning me into a writer who gives a damn about plot. And to my fellow Fabbies, Eric, David, and Sage, for all of our post-workshop lunches, where we could discuss writing ad nauseam and not worry about boring anyone in the process.

Lastly, I'd like to thank a few folks who have no idea they helped me along the way. To the late Dr. Paul Leon Masters, whose mystical wisdom allowed me to explore such things as archetypes in the first place. And to Joseph Campbell, who helped me dig into the deeper meaning behind mythology. Mythology may seem like a thing of the past, but it's a fantastic teacher for those willing to remain open and aware of how these same archetypal patterns play out in our own lives. To quote Campbell, "All the gods, all the heavens, all the hells, are within you."

I couldn't agree more.

GLOSSARY OF CHARACTERS

KORE (PERSEPHONE): the maiden

DEMETER: the mother

HECATE: the crone

HADES (THE UNSEEN, *THEÍOS*): High King of Erebus

ZEUS (THE LOUD THUNDERER): High King of Olympus

POSEIDON: High King of the Cyclades

MINOS: exiled king of Knossos, one of three judges for Hades

AEACUS: former mentor of Hades, one of three judges for Hades

RHADAMANTHUS: brother of Minos, one of three judges for Hades

HERACLES (ALCIDES): bastard son of Zeus

HERMES: messenger son of Zeus

CHARON: captain of the *Narcissus*

CREON: regent of Thebes and father of Heracles's murdered wife

KING EURYSTHEUS: king of Tiryns who assigns the twelve feats to Heracles

HELIUS: titan turned god of the sun

OCEANUS: titan turned god of the earth-encircling river

GAIA: titan turned goddess of the earth

URANUS: titan turned god of the sky

CRONUS: titan turned god of destructive time and father of Zeus, Hades, and Poseidon

POTNIA: ancient Cretan goddess of nature

Discussion Questions

1) Why is Demeter protective of Kore? Is her protectiveness justified?

2) Is Kore right to escape her mother's clutches?

3) Why does Hades see white light surrounding Kore when he sees auric colors surrounding everyone else? Why does it injure him to scrutinize Kore when the opposite occurs with everyone else?

4) Sisyphus is described as a tyrant king. Hades condemns him to push a boulder up a mountain. What is the relevance of this particular punishment?

5) Both Minos and Heracles pursue redemption in this novel. What qualities make a person worthy of redemption?

6) In what ways are Hades and Zeus similar? How are they different?

7) What attracts Kore to Hades?

8) Kore believes the "unholy" apparition and the ghost of Sisyphus are the same being; however, we learn that they are not. What is the "unholy" apparition?

9) What is the significance of pomegranates in this tale?

10) With which character do you most identify? Why?

11) Is Hades a villain? Why or why not?

12) Is Kore raped? Why or why not?

13) Demeter has sexual encounters with both Zeus and Poseidon. Kore has her own encounter with Hades. How did your personal feelings differ with each of these sexual situations?

14) Although *The Rape of Persephone* is based off of the *Homeric Hymn to Demeter,* other myths appear throughout the story. What others could you identify?

Exclusive Preview of Book Two

A MOTHER'S NATURE

PROAULIA

1

Iron to iron, the latch screeches an awakening. If not for the cold, Kore might mistake the cell for the womb. Until now, there was no need to open her eyes. The world was just as black with them open.

Light falls upon the prison bed and fans wide. Body curled tight in sleep, she breathes damp air and stirs beneath woolen blankets.

He shut her away in this room beneath the ground. Hades, ruler of Erebus, beloved uncle and captor.

Kore has not been here long. Not long enough to grow hungry or thirsty. She wept her lungs into spasms, and now the cries have stopped, the spasms stilled.

A male voice punctuates the silence.

"Persephone?"

And never having heard it before, she knows. This name belongs to her.

Today, for the first time, she is called by her true

name. Far down inside the caves of Tartarus, a girl named Kore slips away. A death of sorts. *Kore* is a worn-out identity no longer befitting, and she replies to the man's question with a voice worn ragged from screaming.

"Who calls me this?"

The rumpled man in the doorway is older than her uncle, but younger than two of the judges who counsel him: Judges Minos and Aeacus, the elderly purveyors of wisdom. He holds a torch above the level of his eye. She has never seen him before, yet he knows her somehow.

A look of horror hangs on his crinkled, raised-brow face.

With an unexpectedly youthful voice, he answers, "Persephone is the name given to you by your father."

Until now, she has not known this name existed. Mother called her *Kore*.

Young lady. This is all her "name" has ever meant, and the name-lack spared her that vain identity belonging to humans. She would not be a girl with willpower and desire but a selfless gift for the gods, a virgin priestess. A *kore* is simply a girl of adolescent age, too young to know anything. Too trusting and innocent to run away.

A name brands her a Someone. A youth of sixteen with willpower and desire and purpose, qualities that make a person trouble for the gods.

Persephone likes it.

About the Author

MONICA BRILLHART grew up in Kentucky, relocated to Los Angeles where she worked as a healthcare administrator for 20 years, and now lives in Sedona, Arizona with her husband, daughter, and dog. She has a master's degree in metaphysical science and a doctorate in philosophy. *The Rape of Persephone* is her first novel.

CPSIA information can be obtained
at www.ICGtesting.com
Printed in the USA
LVHW110840090922
727941LV00002B/287

9 781737 799139